HER HEART WAS BEATING SO FAST, SAVANAH THOUGHT SHE MIGHT FAINT

She couldn't stifle a gasp when Rane's arm circled her waist and drew her close. She could feel the latent strength of him, knew that he could crush her with no effort at all. Never in her life had she felt so helpless, so vulnerable.

She looked up at him, hardly daring to breathe. The rest of the world faded away until all she saw, all she knew, was this man holding her close, his breath fanning her cheek as he bent his head toward hers. He was too near, his presence too overpowering. She started to say she had changed her mind, but it was too late. His mouth captured hers in a kiss that left no room for coherent thought, no room for anything beyond the wave of sensual heat that unleashed a familiar tingling in the pit of her stomach and threatened to turn her blood to liquid fire. For a moment, she stared into the depths of his eyes, and then, with a sigh, she closed her eyes and surrendered to his touch.

NIGHT'S PLEASURE

AMANDA ASHLEY

ZEBRA BOOKS
Kensington Publishing Corp.
http://www.kensingtonbooks.com

For Julie
She knows why

Prologue

The magician billed as the Remarkable Renaldo stood alone in the center of a large, well-lit stage. A pair of tight black trousers clung to his long, muscular legs. His feet were shod in a pair of supple black leather boots. A long black cloak hung from a pair of broad shoulders and swirled around his ankles when he moved. Posed against the bloodred curtains behind him, he was a formidable sight, one to make nine-year-old Savanah Gentry press closer to her father. Savanah didn't know what the devil looked like, but she had always imagined him as being ugly and wearing a long black cloak. The Remarkable Renaldo had the cloak, but he definitely wasn't ugly, and as far as she could see, he didn't have horns or a tail.

The magician looked out over the audience. "For my final illusion of the evening, I will need several volunteers."

Savanah Gentry nudged her father. "Raise your hand."

"What?"

"Raise your hand!" She was eager to know how the magician did his tricks. Perhaps, if her father got on stage, he could find out. "Hurry, Daddy!"

William Gentry looked at his only child. As always, he

could deny her nothing that was in his power to give, and so, with a shake of his head, he raised his hand.

"You, there in the fourth row," the magician said, gesturing for Savanah's father to come forward.

"Is it all right if my daughter comes with me?"

The Remarkable Renaldo turned his attention to Savanah. The touch of his gaze on her face sent a shiver down her spine. It wasn't fear; it was more like the feeling she had on Christmas morning when she knew the present she had hoped for all year was waiting for her under the tree. Hardly daring to breathe, she waited for the magician's decision.

"If you wish," Renaldo decided at last.

Savanah felt as if her heart were trying to jump out of her chest as she followed her father up the stairs and onto the stage, which was empty of props or scenery save for an ordinary-looking white door that was mounted on wheels and stood in the middle of the floorboards.

The magician quickly selected three other men. Then, with a flourish, he moved across the stage to stand beside the door. He opened it, stepped through, and then turned toward the men.

"Gentlemen. And little lady," he added, sketching a bow in Savanah's direction, "please examine the door and see that it is quite ordinary."

Savanah's father was the first to step forward. He ran his hands over both sides of the door, inspected the frame from top to bottom, and then stepped through the opening.

The other men did likewise.

Feeling self-conscious, Savanah stepped through the opening, then hurried to her father's side.

"And now, if you will examine the floor," the magician requested. "All of it. I wish you to assure the audience that there are no hidden trapdoors."

Amid some laughter from the audience, all the men got down on their hands and knees and crawled around the stage, running their hands over the floorboards. One by one, they gained their feet.

"Are you all quite satisfied?" Renaldo asked.

The men nodded in the affirmative.

"Very well." The magician turned to face the audience once more. "May I please have four more volunteers?"

Hands went up all around the room, along with shouts of "Over here" and "Pick me."

When the new volunteers had been chosen and were onstage, the magician pointed to one of the men and said, "I would like you to move the door to a place of your choosing. Anywhere at all. On the stage, of course," he added with a smile.

The man looked thoughtful a moment. After closing the door, he pushed it toward the middle of the stage, as close to the footlights as possible.

"Very good," the Remarkable Renaldo said. He turned to the other volunteers. "If you will all follow me, I would like you to form a circle around the door so that you will be able to see me clearly from every angle."

Savanah looked at the magician, wondering if he meant her, as well, but afraid to ask.

As though reading her mind, he turned toward her and smiled. "You, too, my little lady," he said with a courtly bow.

Everyone on the stage moved toward the door's new location, making a loose circle around it.

Savanah felt her cheeks flush with heat as she took a place in the circle, with her father on her right and another man on her left.

The eyes of everyone on the stage were focused on the magician as he stepped into their midst and instructed them to hold hands.

When they complied, the Remarkable Renaldo opened the door. He stuck his arm through the opening, waved to the crowd, and then closed the door.

"I hope you have enjoyed this evening's performance," he said, looking out at the audience, "but the time has come for me to bid you adieu."

And so saying, he opened the door and stepped across the threshold.

And disappeared from sight.

Chapter One

Savanah Gentry stared at the stage, her eyes narrowed as she studied the magician who strutted back and forth. This time, he was billed as Santoro the Magnificent. He wore his long black hair pulled away from his face and his attire was a little different, but she knew he was the same man she had seen on a number of other occasions under a variety of names. Clad in a pair of tight black trousers, a white muscle shirt that clung to his upper body like a second skin, and a pair of knee-high black leather boots, he was the most handsome man Savanah had ever seen. She had seen him at least a dozen times in the last sixteen years, thanks to her father's fascination with magicians.

She had to admit that she was also intrigued by the art of magic and by those who practiced it, even though she knew none of it was real, and that the amazing effects performed on stage were accomplished through collusion with a member of the audience, misdirection, deception, or sleight of hand. She knew David Copperfield hadn't really made the Statue of Liberty disappear, but she had been amazed by the video just the same.

Of course, magic was a two-way street, with the magician attempting to perform a trick that was so incredibly clever it would completely baffle the audience, while the audience let itself be entertained by an effect they knew was accomplished through deception.

William Gentry's passion for magic, illusion, and the Supernatural bordered on obsession, surpassing even his daughter's interest. He seemed especially obsessed with the man now calling himself Santoro the Magnificent, and had, in fact, compiled a notebook that spanned the magician's career over the last sixteen years. Of course, finding the magician through the years had been hit and miss, since he continually changed his name. And now Renaldo or Zander or Antoine or whoever he was, was in Kelton again, albeit under yet a different name.

Savanah had gone to the theater every night for the last week. Sitting in the front row, she couldn't decide if the "Magnificent" in Santoro's title referred to his remarkable abilities as a magician, his arrestingly handsome face, or his incredible physique. Most likely all three.

She had to admit that, aside from his astonishing good looks and his hard, lean body, he was far and away the best prestidigitator she had ever seen, and she had seen many. Santoro the Magnificent didn't do anything as ordinary as sawing a woman in half or making an elephant disappear, although Savanah was pretty sure he could manage both feats with ease. No, he stood on a bare, well-lit stage and performed the impossible. She had seen him step into an open box on the left side of the stage and, seconds later, step out of a similar box on the right side. He had caught a bullet, fired by the local chief of police, in his bare hand. He had levitated a full-grown horse into the air. He had levitated himself three feet off the floor, and while hanging suspended in midair, had invited everyone in the audience who was so inclined to come up and see for themselves that there were no invisible wires holding him up. Savanah had accepted that invitation and left the stage more convinced than ever that he was the real deal, a true magician. A recent article in a neighboring newspaper suggested that Santoro the Magnificent had sold his soul to the devil in order to obtain his remarkable powers. She couldn't help wondering if that also accounted for his devilish good looks.

One of the highlights of the magician's act occurred when he stood in the spotlight at the front of the stage and vanished from sight, only to reappear moments later in the rear balcony of the theater. She had seen similar gags performed before, but always there had been a trick involved—some sort of sleight of hand or a stunt double, because it was virtually impossible for a man to teleport himself from one place to another in a matter of seconds.

Savanah would have traded her brand new Jimmy Choo suede boots—boots that she had scrimped and saved for— to know Santoro's secret. If it was a trick—and what else could it be?—it was the best one she had ever seen. She remembered standing on the very stage he was on now, close enough to touch him, when she was nine years old. Remembered watching him open an ordinary-looking door, step through the opening, and disappear. To this day, she was convinced he had dropped into a cleverly hidden trapdoor. After all, people didn't just vanish into thin air.

Santoro's most astonishing feat occurred when he transformed into a wolf in full view of the audience. Smoke and mirrors, some said, but Savanah was sure it was more than that. Mere illusion, others said, and she might have agreed if she hadn't seen him perform, up close and personal,

on several occasions. There were rumors that he was a
Werewolf, but she had dismissed the idea, since she had
seen him change on nights when the moon wasn't full.

Savanah recalled seeing him perform on her four-
teenth birthday. He had been billing himself as The Marvelous Marvello at the time. Once again, he had called
her out of the audience. Was it mere chance that he had
picked her, or did he remember her as she remembered
him? He had bid her watch closely as two men tied his
hands and feet with thick rope and then bound him with
golden chains. Once again, he had disappeared before
her eyes, leaving the ropes and chains behind.

The last time she had seen him, he had been calling
himself the Great Zander, but she had known it was him
the minute he'd walked onto the stage. Hardly daring to
blink, she had watched his every move closely, hoping
to catch him using sleight of hand or a device of some
kind as he performed one amazing trick after another,
convinced once again that he was either the greatest magician since Harry Houdini, or a wizard gifted with Supernatural powers. That had been two years ago.

Last night, Santoro had again called her out of the audience. He had taken her hand in his and kissed her palm,
sending little frissons of electricity shooting up her arm.
He had felt it, too, she was sure of it, though he had given
no sign of it. Even-voiced, he had asked her if she was
afraid of heights and then explained that he was going to
levitate her. She had expected him to put her into some
kind of trance or hook her up to an invisible wire while he
distracted the audience; instead, he had looked into her
eyes and then, to her utter astonishment, he had lifted his
hand and she had risen vertically into the air. She had hung
there for what seemed like an eternity, with his gaze locked
on hers, before he slowly lowered his hand until her feet

again touched the floor. Before she'd left the stage, his gaze had caught and held hers. In that brief moment, she had found herself wondering again if he remembered her from times past and then, to her amazement, she realized that he hadn't changed at all. He looked exactly the way he had when she had first seen him sixteen years ago. Why hadn't she ever noticed that before?

Now, as he finished his act, she applauded as wildly as the rest of the audience. Perhaps he really was a wizard. Perhaps he was a magician in league with the devil, but whatever he was, he was the most amazing showman she had ever seen.

In his dressing room, Rane Cordova removed the trappings of Santoro the Magnificent and slipped into a pair of well-worn jeans and a bulky black sweater. The crowd had been with him tonight, eager to suspend belief and be entertained. Another two weeks, and he'd move on to another theater in another town. It was an easy life, and one that suited him perfectly. In the winter, he did an eight o'clock show during the week, shows at six and nine on Saturday nights, and one show at eight on Sundays. In the summer, he cut the six o'clock shows. Matinees were out of the question at any time of the year.

He ran a comb through his hair, thinking, as he did so, of the woman he had called on stage that evening. He wondered if it was coincidence that she had been in the audience again, not only in this city, but in others. He had seen the recognition in her eyes when she'd stepped onto the stage, knew she remembered him from times past. The hell of it was, he remembered her, too. She had been a cute kid sixteen years ago.

She wasn't a kid any longer, but a beautiful young

woman with hair the color of moonlight. Long and thick, it fell in waves down her back and over her shoulders. Her eyes were a soft shade of blue, reminding him of the noonday sky he hadn't seen in over ninety years. Her skin was smooth and clear, what used to be called a peaches-and-cream complexion. And her mouth . . . He swore under his breath. Her lips were full and pink, the kind of mouth that made a man think about cool sheets, long nights, and hot skin.

Rane frowned as he turned out the lights. There was something about her that was vaguely familiar. He shook his head. She reminded him of someone he had met long ago.

Grabbing his keys, he left the theater by the back door, quickly blending into the shadows. He sensed the woman waiting for him in the alley, but he passed her by without her ever being the wiser.

In the old days, he had looked forward to talking with his fans. He had answered their questions, signed autographs, and posed for pictures that, when developed, would show only a white haze where his likeness should have been. Oddly enough, in this age of digital cameras and cell phones, his image appeared on the screen, but once the camera or cell phone was turned off, his photo disappeared. He had found a way to turn that peculiarity to his advantage by letting it be known that he was superstitious about having his picture taken. At the beginning of each show, he asked that no photographs be taken, adding that any pictures captured without his permission would vanish from cell phones and cameras. People had been skeptical at first, but when they discovered it was true, the fact that he apparently made his photographs disappear only added to his mystique.

He couldn't explain his inability to be photographed any more than he could explain why he cast no reflection in a mirror. It was just a fact of life, one he had learned to accept long ago, as he had learned to accept so many things that were part of his bizarre lifestyle, not the least of which was his eternal thirst for blood. He had tried to ignore the craving, tried to satisfy it with the blood of beasts, or with blood stolen from hospitals and blood banks, but to no avail. The blood of beasts could sustain his existence but, like blood in bags, offered no satisfaction. Sooner or later, the need for fresh blood drawn from human prey became overwhelming.

It had always been so easy for his brother, Rafe. Rane remembered their first hunt, remembered the woman their father had chosen, the way she had felt in his arms, the enticing beat of her heart, the intoxicating scent of her blood. He had wanted to drink and drink until there was nothing left.

"We're not going to kill her," their father had said, and Rafe had dutifully obeyed. Rane had complied, as well. What other choice had he had with his father standing there, watching?

But later, when Rafe and his parents were occupied elsewhere, Rane had left the house. He had found a young woman plying her trade on a dark street where nice people didn't go, and he had taken her. Oh, he had given her pleasure first—she had deserved that much—but in the end, he had taken what he so desperately craved. He had taken her blood, her memories, her life.

Taken it all, and reveled in the taking.

And in so doing, had damned himself for all eternity.

Savanah huddled deeper into her jacket, wondering if Santoro the Magnificent had somehow managed to slip past her in the dark. Of course, being a master magician, she supposed he could have just turned into a bird and flown away. She had lost track of the number of times she had seen his act. Each time, his tricks had been more amazing, more spectacular, than the last. Each time, her curiosity about his prowess had grown. He was no ordinary magician. Of that she was certain. But if his tricks weren't tricks, what were they, and how on Earth did he do them? She didn't believe for a minute that he had sold his soul to Satan, and yet . . . it made for interesting speculation. She had read countless stories of men and women who had made deals with the devil, trading their souls for youth or longevity, for power or wealth. But they were just fables. At least, she had always thought so, until now.

She waited another half an hour before giving up. He wouldn't elude her tomorrow night. One way or another, she was determined to talk to him. Not only was she eager to satisfy her own curiosity about the man, but she was slated to write an article about him for the local paper. In addition to that, she hoped to include him in a book she was thinking of writing about famous magicians, past and present, magicians like Houdini, David Copperfield, and Criss Angel.

Turning up the collar of her coat, she returned to the parking lot for her car and drove home.

When she entered the living room, she found her father sitting in his favorite easy chair watching a high-stakes poker game on the satellite screen.

"Hi, sweetie," he said. "How was the show?"

"Amazing, as always." Taking off her coat, she hung it in the hall closet, then kissed her dad on the cheek before dropping down on the sofa and kicking off her shoes.

"Did you get to interview him?" William Gentry asked.

"No, I didn't see him." She hated to admit defeat, especially since her father was the one who had given her the assignment. If necessary, she would just write the article without the interview.

Her father chuckled softly. "Seems like he's a hard one to catch. Are you going to try again?"

"Sure, if you want me to, but honestly, Dad, I don't know why you're so determined about this. The man is a great magician, but it's not like he's a rock star or anything. I mean, how many people even know who he is?"

"If it's too hard for you, just let it go."

Savanah's eyes narrowed. "Did I say that?"

"So, you'll try again?"

"Of course, and I'll get him. You just wait and see."

"I don't doubt it for a minute. It'll make a good story."

"I hope so."

For the last five years, her father had been the editor-in-chief of the local newspaper. Before that, he had been an investigative reporter, one of the best in the country. He had blown the whistle on high-level government officials and small-town gangsters alike. He had brought down drug lords and pimps and put an end to a group of scumbags who had been selling crystal meth to high school kids. Once, he had spent several months in jail because he had refused to give up a snitch. He had been honest and fearless, never turning away from a story, no matter how gritty it might be, never backing down when the going got tough.

Although he was now the editor-in-chief and no longer a field reporter, she knew he was working on a story, and she knew it was something big because he refused to talk to her about it.

Savanah wanted to be just like him; however, being just a rookie, she hadn't yet been assigned to any big stories. Of course, in a small town like Kelton, there weren't too many big stories to begin with, but once she had gained some experience, she hoped to move to New York, Chicago, or Los Angeles.

Savanah smiled at her father. Though he was still a relatively young man, his hair was tinged with gray. Lines of pain were deeply etched around his mouth and eyes. He rarely smiled. Savanah couldn't blame him. Eighteen years ago, her mother had passed away from a mysterious illness. Savanah had been seven at the time. She remembered very little about her mother except that she'd had an infectious laugh, made the world's best chocolate chip cookies, and loved to dance.

Seventeen months ago, Savanah's father had been the victim of a hit-and-run accident that had cost him the use of both legs and left him confined to a wheelchair. He had spent several months in the hospital. The driver had never been found. For a time, Savanah had feared that her father would never recover, and then, one night, on the spur of the moment, she had bundled him into the car and headed for the next town to see a new magician. To her surprise, it had been the man now billing himself as Santoro the Magnificent. Miraculously, her father had regained his old zest for living. He had gone back to work, and bought a special van to get around in.

Savanah chatted with her father for another few minutes, then excused herself to go upstairs and take a bath. Her father hadn't slept in the master bedroom since her mother died. It was a nice, big room, and while her father couldn't bear to sleep there, it made Savanah feel closer to the mother she scarcely remembered. Her father slept in one of the bedrooms downstairs, and used the downstairs' guestroom as his office. When Savanah had turned fifteen, her father had given her carte blanche to redecorate the master bedroom. She had spent weeks looking at paint and wallpaper and new furniture.

Savanah's old bedroom now served as her office. It was her favorite room in the house. An antique oak desk held her computer, a state-of-the-art printer, a small gumball machine, and a photograph of her parents on their wedding day. Her first newspaper story published under her byline hung in a silver frame on the wall across from her desk. A large bookcase filled with paperback novels, a couple of dictionaries, a thesaurus, a world atlas, and several encyclopedias took up most of one wall.

After filling the tub and adding a generous amount of jasmine-scented bubbles, Savanah sank into the water and closed her eyes. Tomorrow night, she vowed, tomorrow night she would get that interview with Santoro the Magnificent, or know the reason why.

Chapter Two

The dark-haired woman was there again, front row center. For the first time in his life, Rane found it difficult to keep his mind on what he was doing while on stage. He was aware of the intensity of her gaze as she followed his every move. She wasn't there to be entertained, he thought. She was there to discover how he did what he did. Rane grunted softly. If he told her his secrets, she would undoubtedly run screaming into the night. Not that he would blame her. He was a predator, a killer, and she looked good enough to eat.

Showing off a little, Rane left the stage and strolled up the wide center aisle. Stopping at one row after another, he asked men and women chosen at random to think of something that no one else could possibly know, and then he told them what it was. No doubt most of the people in the audience thought those he spoke to were shills, but he had no need of such. He had only to open his mind to hear the thoughts of those around him.

From time to time, he glanced back at the dark-haired woman sitting in the front row, annoyed by the blatant skepticism in her eyes. Backtracking, he stopped in front of her.

"Good evening, Miss Gentry."

Her eyes widened in surprise when he called her by name.

"Your expression tells me you think that maybe the people I've talked to are shills, planted in the audience to make me look good."

She blushed under his regard. "No . . . that is, well . . ." Her chin came up defiantly. "Maybe I do."

He took a step closer, heard her heartbeat increase as he deliberately moved into her space. "Shall I tell you what you're thinking now?"

The pink in her cheeks turned brighter, darker. She shook her head vigorously. "No!"

He laughed, amused, because she had been thinking he was the handsomest man she had ever seen, and that she would like to run her fingertips over his bare chest.

Savanah pressed her hands to her burning cheeks. There were several people in the audience that she knew, including one of the reporters she worked with. How would she ever face any of them again if Santoro the Magnificent blurted out what she had been thinking?

Sensing her mortification and unwilling to humiliate her in public, Rane asked, "Would you care to think of something else?"

She nodded, wishing she was anywhere but there. His nearness sparked an odd tingling in the pit of her stomach. Nerves, she thought, and who could blame her, when he was standing so close, when his gaze rested on her face like a physical caress?

"In high school," he said, "you had a crush on your journalism teacher, Mr. Tabor."

Savanah's cheeks grew hotter. She had never told

anyone about that, not her dad, not even Liz, who had been her best friend at the time. It had been a well-guarded secret, until now.

"Is that true?" Rane asked, already knowing the answer.

Savanah nodded. It didn't really matter if her secret was out now. Mr. Tabor had married one of his students and left town years ago.

Rane bowed in her direction and then returned to the stage. In what had become his signature farewell, he walked to the front of the boards and took a bow, then crossed his arms over his chest, and vanished from sight.

As soon as the curtains were drawn, Savanah ran out the side door and headed for the alley behind the theater. Hiding in the shadows, she settled down to wait for Santoro to leave the building, determined to catch him this time.

Rane quickly changed into a pair of jeans and a T-shirt, ran a hand through his hair, and then, as was his habit, he left the theater by the back door. Being close to the Gentry woman, smelling the warmth of her body, hearing the siren call of her blood, had aroused his hunger. He needed to feed, he thought, and soon. If he waited much longer, his prey would pay the ultimate price.

As soon as he stepped into the alley, he knew she was there. Lifting his head, he sniffed the air, felt his fangs lengthen as he honed in on her hiding place. There, in the shadows beside the Dumpster. Foolish woman, to wait for him in the dark where there was no one to see her, no one to save her.

From her hiding place, Savanah watched the magician lift his head, his nostrils flaring as if he was sniffing her out. Her heart raced as he headed straight toward her hiding place. Did he know she was there? But that was impossible. There was no light where she stood, no way he could see her in the dark. She could scarcely see her hand in front of her face. And yet, like a jungle cat on the scent of prey, he moved unerringly toward her, his footsteps eerily silent on the damp pavement.

She had him now, she thought triumphantly. He wouldn't escape her this time. But as she watched him stride purposefully toward her, she forgot that she had been trying for days to see him. Her only thought was to run, to hide, before he found her. But there was nowhere to hide, and it was too late to run.

"You waiting for me?"

Savanah practically jumped out of her skin. How had he crossed the distance between them so quickly?

"Are you waiting for me?" he asked again.

She had always found honesty to be the best policy, so she said, "Yes," dismayed by the quiver in her voice. She had never been a coward, but there was something about being alone in a dark alley with this man that frightened her almost as much as he intrigued her.

"Well, here I am. If you want an autograph, I hope you brought a pen and paper."

Savanah cleared her throat. "I want an interview."

"I don't give interviews."

"I know. You don't pose for pictures, either."

He arched one dark brow. "If you know all that, why are you wasting your time, and mine?"

"I want to know what you're hiding."

He uttered a soft sound of derision. "What makes you think I'm hiding anything?"

"Because you don't do interviews."

Rane chuckled softly. She was more than a pretty face

and a shapely figure, he thought, charmed in spite of himself.

"So," she said, smiling, "how about that interview?"

Rane shrugged. "I'm on my way to have a drink. Bring your poison pen and come along."

Without waiting for her reply, he set off down the alley toward the street.

Now that she had almost achieved her goal, Savanah felt a sudden sense of trepidation as she stared after him. She only knew two things about Santoro the Magnificent—he was an amazing performer, and he could read her mind.

He had almost reached the mouth of the alley. It was obvious he wasn't going to wait for her. Gathering her courage, she hurried after him. It wasn't easy, trying to match her shorter strides to his long ones.

She almost changed her mind when he stopped in front of a dreary-looking nightclub. The name HELL'S HOLLOW flickered in bloodred neon lights above the door.

For the first time, he looked back to see if she was behind him. "Coming?" he asked, a challenge in his dark eyes.

Praying that she wasn't making a fatal mistake, Savanah took a deep breath and followed him through the doorway.

Inside, Savanah glanced around in amazement. Judging from the outward appearance of the place, she had expected to find some crummy nightclub populated by drunks and winos, so the interior of Hell's Hollow came as quite a surprise. The walls were papered in a decadent red-and-gold stripe, the floor was gold-veined marble. Rich red velvet draperies hung at the windows; dozens of candles set in beautiful black wrought-iron wall sconces provided the light, adding to the club's ambience. A three-piece band occupied a raised platform in one corner of the room. The musicians, all women, wore tight black sweaters, skintight stretch pants, and black boots. Their music was soft and seductive, with a dangerous sensual edge that did funny things in the pit of Savanah's stomach.

A man elegantly attired in a black tux and crisp white shirt bowed them through the door. A tall woman with a mass of sleek red hair escorted them to a secluded table for two in the back of the room. She took their drink order and glided away.

Savanah glanced around, thinking that black seemed to be the color of choice, as nearly everyone in the place was wearing it. She felt conspicuous in her white skirt and red sweater.

"So," Rane said, "what do you want to know?"

"The secrets to all your tricks, of course." She laughed self-consciously. "I'm just kidding. I know magicians are sworn to secrecy, but you really are the most amazing performer I've ever seen. I had an uncle who was a pretty good magician, but he was nowhere as slick as you are."

Rane shrugged. "I've practiced for a long time."

Savanah pulled a small tape recorder from her pocket and laid it on the table. "Do you mind?"

He shook his head.

"Is Santoro your real name?"

"No."

"You've had several names, haven't you?" She recounted the ones she remembered. "The Remarkable Renaldo. The Marvelous Marvello. The Great Zander. The Amazing Antoine. Are they all stage names?"

"Of course."

"What's your real name?"

"Rane."

"Is that your first name, or your last?"

"It's the only one you need to know."

She regarded him a moment, her brows drawn together

in a vee. "I don't suppose you want to tell me who or what you're hiding from?"

"No."

"I didn't think so. How long have you been a magician?"

"About twenty-five years."

She stared at him in disbelief. He couldn't be much older than twenty-five, thirty at the most. "I don't believe you! What were you, five when you started?"

He smiled faintly. "I'm older than I look."

"Really?" Her gaze moved over his face; there were no telltale signs indicating he'd had any work done. "He must have been a very skilled doctor."

Rane laughed. "Trust me, I've never gone under the knife."

"Are you married?"

"No. Are you?"

"No. So, where's home?"

"Here."

"You live in Kelton?"

"I don't *live* anywhere."

"You're making this extremely difficult," Savanah remarked, wondering at his emphasis on the word *live*.

"Sorry," he said with a sly grin. "I said I'd grant you an interview. I didn't say it would be easy."

Savanah hit Pause on the tape recorder when the waitress arrived with their drinks.

Rane smiled at the waitress, then dropped a twenty-dollar bill on the tray. "Thanks, Sylvie."

The waitress winked at him, then sashayed away, hips swaying provocatively beneath her tight black skirt.

Savanah had ordered a strawberry daiquiri. She sipped it slowly. Rane was extremely closemouthed. She would have given a year's pay to know what he was hiding.

Setting her glass aside, she started the tape recorder again. "Do you have relatives here in town?"

"No."

"Any family anywhere?"

"Sure. I wasn't hatched under a rock."

"I'd ask for their names, but I'm pretty sure you wouldn't tell me."

His smile confirmed her suspicions. "Anything else you want to know?"

"You haven't told me anything yet," she said irritably. She glanced around the club while she gathered her thoughts. "You know, I must have passed this place a hundred times and never noticed it."

Rane shrugged. That wasn't surprising. She wouldn't be able to find it again if she looked for it. "Enough about me," he said. "Tell me about you."

"Why don't you just read my mind?"

"I could do that, but conversation is more stimulating, don't you think?"

"How did you know about Mr. Tabor? No one, and I mean no one, knew I had a crush on him."

"I saw it in your mind, just like I said."

"That's impossible."

"Is it?"

"What am I thinking about now?"

"You're wondering if coming here with me was a smart thing to do."

Savanah blinked at him, unnerved to realize that he really could read her mind. "Who taught you all those amazing tricks?"

"No one."

"But . . ."

"I just do what comes naturally."

She frowned. "Are you telling me that they aren't illusions, that they're real?"

He nodded.

"Aside from reading my mind, can you do any of those other magical feats offstage?"

"Sure."

"Which ones?"

"All of them." He cocked his head to one side. "You don't believe me, do you? What would you like me to do? Transform into a wolf, or just disappear?"

"I should imagine doing either one in here would cause quite a stir, don't you think?" Savanah said dryly.

He smiled. It was the first genuine smile she had seen from him and it hit her like a bolt of electricity. For a moment, she forgot everything else, thinking only that she would be willing to do anything he asked if he would just smile at her like that again. His physical presence was almost overpowering, but that smile . . . it was a deadly weapon.

The waitress appeared a moment later, giving Savanah a chance to regain her composure.

Rane ordered another glass of red wine. Savanah declined a refill. Rane's smile was intoxicating enough.

"Have you run out of questions?" he asked after the waitress moved away.

"No, but what's the point? You haven't answered any of them."

"No?" He arched one black brow. "I thought I was being very cooperative."

Savanah shook her head, then took a deep breath. She hadn't expected this to be easy, but she hadn't expected it to be this difficult, either. He was hiding something, she thought again. But what?

He lifted his glass, his gaze intent upon her face as he sipped the wine.

The heat of his gaze brought a quick flush to her cheeks and made her stomach quiver with pleasure. Lordy, he had the most mesmerizing eyes she had ever seen.

"Well," she said, dragging her gaze from his, "since you're not going to answer my questions, I might as well go home."

Rising, she turned off the tape recorder and dropped it into her handbag. "Thanks for the drink."

"Don't go." His voice was little more than a whisper, but she heard it clearly enough.

"Give me a reason to stay."

"The night is long," he said, his voice soft and somehow vulnerable, "and I don't want to be alone."

Chapter Three

It wasn't Rane's words so much as the look of desolation in his fathomless black eyes and the tone of his voice that made Savanah decide to stay. Resuming her seat, she studied the man sitting across from her. It was hard to imagine that he was ever lonely. He was devastatingly handsome, he could be charming. She doubted he ever lacked for female companionship when he wanted it. His voice, his smile—how could any female possibly resist? And yet there was a deep sadness in his eyes that she hadn't really noticed before. Was he mourning for someone? Was that why he seemed so melancholy?

"So," she said, "what now?"

"I still want to know about you."

"There's not much to tell. I'm a reporter for the *Kelton Chronicle*. I live at home with my father. And I'm not very good at getting interviews with magicians."

A slow smile spread over his face. "If I was going to tell anyone my secrets, Savanah Gentry, it would be you."

There was that smile again. She could almost forgive him for being so taciturn. Almost. "That's very flattering, but I still don't have a story."

"Maybe there isn't one."

"I don't believe that."

She ran the tip of her finger around the rim of her glass. "What do you do when you aren't mesmerizing audiences and ignoring reporters?"

He shrugged. "Nothing very exciting. Watch the sports channel. Go to the movies. Take long walks . . ."

"Walks? Really?"

"Why do you sound so surprised?"

"I don't know. I guess I pictured you more as the zero-to-sixty type."

"Can't I enjoy both?"

"I knew it! So, what do you drive? Something incredibly fast, I'll bet."

"Fast enough." He had tried his hand at racing for a while, until he got into a monumental wreck that no mere mortal would have survived. They had pronounced him dead at the scene. He hadn't raced under his real name, of course. There had been quite a stir the following day when his body turned up missing at the morgue. The newspapers had had a field day speculating on what had become of his corpse.

He leaned forward, his gaze intent upon her face. "How about it, Savanah Gentry? Are you brave enough to go zero to sixty with me?"

He wasn't talking about cars and they both knew it. For one impulsive moment, Savanah was tempted to go with him, to indulge in one crazy, wild, once-in-a-lifetime night of unbridled passion, to do something totally outrageous and out of character. But only for a moment before her good sense kicked in. "I don't think so."

"Afraid of me?" he asked, a challenge lurking in his dark eyes.

"Not exactly."

"Then what, exactly?"

"I don't make a habit of hot-rodding with men I hardly know."

"Afraid I'll make you disappear?" he asked with wry amusement.

Savanah nodded. That was exactly what she was afraid of. She had covered too many stories where women got involved with seemingly nice, wholesome guys and were never heard from again. Sometimes their bodies turned up in a ditch, sometimes they were discovered by joggers in remote areas of the mountains, and sometimes their bodies were never found. When Savanah got her name in the paper, she wanted it to be in the byline of a great story, or as the recipient of the Nobel Prize for literature, not as the hapless victim of a violent crime.

Sitting back, he muttered, "Smart girl," then gestured at her glass. "Can I buy you another?"

"I don't think so. I'd really like to know how you transform into the wolf."

"You and a couple hundred other people."

"Would you tell me if I promise to keep it a secret?"

"I'll show you," he said, "but it will cost you."

"How much?"

"No money involved."

She canted her head to the side. "What do you want?" she asked suspiciously.

His gaze slid across her lips. "A kiss."

She blinked at him. "A kiss? That's all? Just a kiss?"

"Along with your promise that this is completely off the record."

Her expression betrayed the battle between her hunger for a good story, her ethics, and her curiosity.

He leaned back in his chair, his elbows resting on the arms, his chin resting on his folded hands as he waited for her to make up her mind. Even if she wrote the story, most people wouldn't believe her. The war between the Vampires and the Werewolves had ended eighteen years ago. Mortals being what they were, they had quickly brushed aside what they couldn't explain once the conflict was over. Since that time, the Supernatural creatures had been keeping a low profile. But it would only take one sensational story to bring the hunters out again.

"So," he said, "do we have a deal?"

"Yes." Savanah glanced around the club. Did he mean to kiss her here, in front of all these people?

"We'll have to go outside," he said. "For the kiss, and for the transformation."

"Where outside?" she asked suspiciously.

He shrugged. "The parking lot out back?"

She thought about it a moment. It was against her better judgment to be alone in the dark with this man, but she was a woman and a reporter and her curiosity would not be denied. "All right."

She told herself she had nothing to worry about as she followed him out of the club. There were people on the street, and she had a healthy set of lungs if he tried anything funny, not to mention a can of pepper spray in her handbag.

The parking lot wasn't as dark as she expected, thanks to a full moon and the floodlight affixed to one corner of the club's roof.

Rane stopped between two cars, which would afford them a degree of privacy from anyone driving by on the street or walking down the sidewalk.

Savanah looked up at him, her heart pounding like a drum. Why had she agreed to this? If she screamed, would anyone hear her?

Rane lifted one brow. "Have you changed your mind?"

She had, but she didn't want to admit it, didn't want him to think she was a coward, so she shook her head. "No, have you?"

"Not a chance." He moved toward her, his heated gaze fixed on hers.

She wanted to back up, to run away, but she seemed rooted to the spot, unable to move, unable to tear her gaze from his.

"Savanah." Murmuring her name, he reached for her.

Her heart was beating so fast, Savanah thought she might faint. She couldn't stifle a gasp when his arm circled her waist and drew her close. She could feel the latent strength of him, knew that he could crush her with no effort at all. Never in her life had she felt so helpless, so vulnerable.

She looked up at him, hardly daring to breathe. The rest of the world faded away until all she saw, all she knew, was this man holding her close, his breath fanning her cheek as he bent his head toward hers. He was too near, his presence too overpowering. She started to say she had changed her mind, but it was too late. His mouth captured hers in a kiss that left no room for coherent thought, no room for anything beyond the wave of sensual heat that unleashed a familiar tingling in the pit of her stomach and threatened to turn her blood to liquid fire. For a moment, she stared into the depths of his eyes, and then, with a sigh, she closed her eyes and surrendered to his touch.

Lost, she thought, she was lost in a churning sea of ecstasy. A dim part of her mind set off warning bells. If his kiss was this arousing, she would be wise to avoid anything more intimate.

It took her several moments to realize the kiss had ended.

As sanity returned, she glared at him, annoyed by the smug look in his eyes.

His arm tightened around her waist. "Are you ready?" he asked.

She blinked. "Ready for what?"

He laughed softly. "I thought you wanted to see me perform."

"What? Oh, yes, of course. Are you going to do it now?"

He grinned at her.

She slammed her fist against his shoulder. It was like hitting a block wall. "Get your mind out of the gutter," she said irritably, "and do your trick."

His grin widened. His teeth were very white.

"Stop that! You know what I mean."

Releasing his hold on her, he took a step back. There was a tremor in the air, a rush of Supernatural power as Rane's body shimmered, and suddenly he was gone and a large black wolf stood in his place, staring up at her out of Rane's deep black eyes.

Savanah shook her head. She glanced around the parking lot, looking for Rane, looking for something, anything, that would explain what she had seen. But there was no one else there, no accomplice lurking in the shadows.

She looked back at the wolf. It was sitting on its haunches now, grinning a wolfish grin.

Feeling foolish, she whispered his name. "Rane?"

And the wolf wagged its tail.

She took several steps backward. "It can't be."

Yet even as Savanah told herself that what she was seeing was impossible, bits and pieces of ancient folklore and mythology surfaced in her mind. In her senior year in high school, she had done a paper on shape-shifters for her English class. She had found the subject so fascinating, she had researched it far more than was necessary for one paper. In British folklore, fairies, witches and wizards were all known to have the ability to change shape.

In Norse mythology, both Loki and Odin had been shape-shifters. Buddhist folklore featured stories of the *naga,* snakes which could take on human form. There were numerous tales of Werewolves, humans compelled to turn into wolves when the moon was full. One of the most highly debated themes in shape-shifting was whether it was voluntary or induced by outside influences. Circe had transformed those who intruded on her island into swine. Some Indian shamans were believed to be able to take on the form of animals. Then there was Savanah's favorite fairy tale, *Beauty and the Beast,* in which the prince had been cursed by an enchantress and turned into a beast, only to be saved by Beauty's love.

Savanah shook her head. Werewolves and curses and old Norse gods were all just stories and legends, but the wolf looking up at her through Rane's eyes was real.

She tensed as the wolf stood and padded toward her, insinuating its head under her hand, pressing its body against her legs.

Oh, yes, it was very real.

And then the wolf's body shimmered and Rane stood before her.

A memory from her childhood rose from the misty corners of her mind. She had been six or seven at the time, feigning sleep on the sofa, when she overheard her parents talking about the Werewolves that were terrorizing the countryside.

Feeling light-headed, Savanah stared at Rane. Werewolf, she thought. She had kissed a Werewolf, and liked it. It was her last thought before everything went black.

Muttering an oath, Rane caught her before she hit the blacktop. He supposed he really couldn't blame her for fainting. She had thought his transformation on stage was a trick, an illusion. Sometimes the truth was more than the mortal mind could handle.

Cradling her to his chest, he debated what to do with her. He could wait until she regained consciousness and take her back into the club, he could drop her off at her place, or he could take her home with him.

If he was smart, he would bid the lovely Miss Gentry farewell and never see her again. But he was tired of being smart, and tired of being alone. He would be in Kelton for another two weeks. What better way to spend his free time than getting better acquainted with the beautiful woman in his arms?

With his mind made up, he picked up her evening bag and shoved it into his back pocket, and then, using his preternatural powers, he took her home.

Of course, it wasn't really his home, just a small, non-descript house he had rented during his stay in Kelton. Truth be told, he didn't have a place to call his own. No strings, no roots, nothing to tie him down. Like the wind, he was footloose and fancy-free.

And damned tired of it.

He reached the house in a matter of moments. A thought opened the front door, another lit the candles on the mantel and brought the banked fire in the hearth to life.

Rane glanced around the room, wondering what Savanah would think of it when she woke. It wasn't much to look at—just a square room with beige walls, brown tweed carpeting, and mismatched furniture. There were no pictures on the walls, no mementos, nothing of a personal nature save for a program from the Kelton Performing Arts Center. Call it vanity, but he had a collection of programs from the various venues where he had performed.

He lowered Savanah onto the fake leather couch,

tossed her handbag on the mantel, then stood there, gazing down at her. Why had he brought her here? She would be repulsed if she knew what he was.

He swore softly as a decidedly jealous inner voice reminded him that Kathy hadn't been repulsed by his brother, Raphael. His mother hadn't been disgusted by his father's true nature, nor had Grandmother Brenna been repulsed by Grandfather Roshan. True, the females in the family might have had some problems in the beginnings of their various relationships, but sexual attraction hadn't been one of them.

Attraction. Rane grunted softly. He was definitely captivated by Savanah Gentry. And she was equally fascinated by him. If she was agreeable, they could spend a pleasurable two weeks together before he moved on. If not . . . his gaze lingered on the hollow of her throat. If not, bringing her here would not be a total loss.

He brushed the hair away from her neck, his nostrils flaring at the scent of her blood. His fangs lengthened as he bent over her. He would treat himself to a taste of her life's blood now. Later, if things went awry between them, he would wipe his memory from her mind and send her on her way, none the wiser.

Savanah woke with a start. Sensing something amiss, she didn't open her eyes immediately. Where was she? The last thing she remembered . . . Oh, Lord, the last thing she remembered was watching Santoro the Magnificent transform into a large black wolf.

Was she in the wolf's den? Opening her eyes just a crack, she found herself staring up at an unfamiliar ceiling. Fear made her heart race as she sat up, her gaze darting from left to right. She frowned as she took in the unfamiliar surroundings.

Where was she?

Where was he?

"Feeling better?"

Startled, she glanced over her shoulder. He was standing behind the sofa, a glass of water in his hand.

"What happened?" she asked. "Where are we?"

"My place." Taking a step forward, he offered her the glass. "You fainted in the parking lot."

"I did?" She had never fainted in her life.

"Are you all right?"

"I guess so." Stalling for time, she sipped the water, her mind reeling. She had to get out of there before it was too late, before he ripped her throat out. He didn't look like a Werewolf, but then, she had no idea what a Werewolf looked like. Had she imagined the whole thing?

Eyes narrowed, she studied Rane, but, aside from the fact that he was probably the handsomest man on the planet with his thick black hair and heavily lashed black eyes, she didn't see anything out of the ordinary. But looks could be deceiving. He had proved that in the parking lot.

He lifted one brow. "Something wrong?"

"Other than the fact that you're a Werewolf, everything's fine."

"I'm not a Werewolf. I don't howl at the moon. I don't turn furry once a month. I just change shape."

She didn't believe him, but she nodded anyway. One should always humor Werewolves and crazy people. Setting the glass on the end table, Savanah glanced at her watch, surprised to see it was almost midnight. How long had she been unconscious? Her father would be wondering what happened to her.

Struggling to keep the panic from her voice, she said, "I think I'd better go." Rising, she looked around for her handbag, wondering if he would let her leave, or if someone would find her mutilated body in a ditch come morning.

"Not yet."

"What do you mean?" She didn't need her handbag, she decided as she glanced anxiously at the door. She just wanted to go home.

"I'd like to get to know you better."

Oh, Lord. A Werewolf and a lech! She stared at him, unable to think of anything to say while her mind scrambled to find a way out.

Rane dragged a hand through his hair, thinking he sounded like some tongue-tied high school kid. "What I mean is, I'm gonna be in town for another couple of weeks and I'd like to spend some of that time with you."

"Oh." His words, obviously sincere, took her by surprise.

"What do you say?"

"I don't know."

"You're bothered by what you saw tonight."

"Can you blame me?"

"No, I guess not."

"How long have you been a Werewolf?"

"I told you before, I'm not a Werewolf." He couldn't tell her the truth, not all of it, so he told her a part of the truth. "I'm a shape-shifter."

"But . . ." She dropped down on the sofa again, thinking that a shape-shifter seemed a lot less scary than a Werewolf. "How did it happen? I mean, is it hereditary?"

"You could say that."

"So, your parents are shape-shifters, too?"

Skirting the truth yet again, he nodded.

Savanah shook her head. "Amazing," she muttered, and then frowned. "Can you change into other animals?"

"Yes." Rane smiled inwardly, remembering how he and Rafe had often passed the quiet hours of the night by changing into lions and tigers and wolves. They seemed to have an affinity for predatory creatures, though he supposed, given their nature, that wasn't surprising.

"Cats? Dogs? Elephants?"

He could see the wheels turning, knew she was thinking about what a great story it would make. He could see the headlines now: MAGICIAN'S SECRETS REVEALED. STORY ON PAGE TWO. "Remember your promise," he said. "Everything that happened here tonight is off the record. You can't write it up."

"Who would believe me?" she muttered, and then frowned. Years ago, Werewolves and Vampires and shape-shifters had made the news. She had read about the war between the Supernatural creatures in the morgue files. No one really knew what had started the war, or why it had abruptly ended, but once it was over, the Supernatural creatures seemed to have disappeared. And now Rane was here. If the Supernatural creatures were surfacing again, it could be the story of a lifetime. But a promise was a promise.

Rane scooped her handbag from off the mantel and handed it to her. "Come on," he said, "I'll take you back to the club so you can get your car."

With a nod, Savanah followed him outside to where a sleek silver Porsche waited in the driveway. He opened the passenger door for her and she slid into the seat. The leather, as soft as melted butter, seemed to enfold her.

"I knew it," she said. "Zero to sixty in nothing flat."

Chapter Four

Savanah's father was in the living room, reading the newspaper, when she got home.

"Dad, what are you doing up so late?"

Folding the paper in half, he tucked it between his thigh and the side of his wheelchair. "Waiting for you, of course."

"You don't have to do that." Shrugging out of her coat and kicking off her shoes, she padded across the floor and dropped a kiss on his forehead. "I'm a big girl now."

"Maybe so, but . . ." He shrugged.

"I know, you don't have to say it. I'll always be your little girl." Plopping down in the chair across from his, she curled her legs beneath her. "What did you do this evening?"

"Oh, the usual. How about you?"

"I had sort of a date."

Her father arched one inquisitive brow. "Sort of a date? Is that something new?"

"Actually, it wasn't a date at all. I went to the theater to see Santoro the Magnificent again. After the show, I waited for him in the alley, hoping to get that interview."

Her father nodded his approval. "Any luck?"

"Not really, although we did go out for drinks."

"I see."

Savanah drummed her fingertips on the arm of the chair. She had promised she wouldn't write anything about Rane's shape-shifting ability, not that she could blame him for wanting to keep it a secret. If people knew he was a shape-shifter, it would not only ruin his image as an amazing magician, but it would garner a lot of unwelcome attention from other reporters and curiosity seekers that he would probably rather not have. On the other hand, if he wanted to stay out of the limelight, he had certainly chosen the wrong profession.

Still, a promise was a promise and she wouldn't divulge what she had learned, but she hadn't promised not to tell her father. She was splitting hairs, and she knew it, but she had to tell someone.

"So, you didn't get an interview," her father remarked. "What did you get?"

"More than I bargained for."

"I'm listening."

"This is just between you and me," she said. "And totally off the record."

He nodded. "All right."

"He's a shape-shifter."

William Gentry leaned forward in his chair. "Did he tell you that?"

"He showed me."

Leaning back, her father swore softly. "So," he drawled thoughtfully, "that's how he does it."

"Well, it explains how he turns into a wolf. I still don't know how he just disappears into thin air," Savanah said, and then frowned. "Unless becoming invisible is part of shape-shifting."

Her father frowned thoughtfully. "Could be," he murmured. "Could be. There might be a moment between one form and the other when he's invisible long enough for him to vanish."

"Maybe. He said he'd like to see me again."

"I don't think that's a good idea, Savanah. In fact, I think it's a terrible idea."

"Why?"

"In the first place, we don't know anything about him, and in the second place, he's a shape-shifter, which means he's not entirely human." Her father shook his head. "I don't like the idea of the two of you spending time together."

Savanah shrugged. "He seems nice enough."

"Yeah, well, they said Bundy was a nice guy, too."

"Rane's a magician, Dad, not a serial killer." Savanah frowned inwardly. Not an hour ago, she had been scared half out of her mind, and now she was defending the very man who had frightened her out of ten years of her life.

"Rane? Is that his real name?"

She nodded. "Maybe he'll give me that interview when we get to know each other better."

"Maybe, but I still don't like it."

"You know, Dad, he's not any more closemouthed than you are," Savanah muttered. "You still haven't told me about the story you're working on."

"That's right, and I'm not going to, not yet, anyway."

"It must be something really hush-hush," Savanah remarked. Her father had worked on big stories before, but he had always shared them with her. This was the first time he had refused to discuss any part of it with her. So far, he hadn't given her so much as a hint. It was maddening and frustrating. Being a journalist and naturally nosy, it had her curiosity ramped up as high as it would go. "Is it dangerous?"

"No more than any of the others," he said with a shrug. "Don't worry."

"Worry?" she asked with exaggerated nonchalance. "Who, me?"

Gentry snorted softly. "I'm off to bed, honey. See you in the morning."

"All right. Good night, Dad."

Closing her eyes, Savanah leaned back in her chair and replayed everything that had happened that evening, from the time she'd stepped into the theater until she'd woken up in Rane's house with no recollection of how she had gotten there.

He was a world-class magician.

He was gorgeous.

He was a shape-shifter.

She wondered what he was doing now. Was he perhaps thinking of her? Had it been foolish of her to agree to see him again? Her father certainly thought so. Did he know something she didn't? But that was silly. If her father thought it was really dangerous for her to see Rane again, he would have said so and told her why.

In her mind, Savanah envisioned Rane transforming into the wolf. It had been a scary thing to see. Scary and beautiful, she thought, the way his body had taken on a sort of shimmery glow as his muscles and ligaments shifted, stretching, realigning themselves, until the man was gone and a big black wolf had stood in his place. Did it hurt when he changed? Where did his clothing go? Questions, questions. Would he answer them when she saw him again?

Rising, she went upstairs to get ready for bed.

Later, snuggled under the covers, her eyelids heavy,

she stared out the open window, her thoughts turning once again toward Rane. Was he home in bed, thinking about her, or was he in his wolf form, running beneath the light of the moon?

Ignoring a sudden, inexplicable urge to go out into the night and look for him, she flopped over onto her stomach and closed her eyes.

Later, hovering on the brink of sleep, she thought she heard a wolf howl beneath her bedroom window.

Rane prowled the shadowed streets of the city, the lust for blood thrumming through his veins. The hunger was always worse when the moon was full, which he found oddly amusing. He had never known Vampires to be influenced by the cycles of the moon; it was a Supernatural law that applied only to Werewolves.

Hoping to subdue his hunger, Rane turned his thoughts to Savanah Gentry. She reminded him of someone, but again, he couldn't make the connection. Pushing the troubling notion aside, he let his thoughts linger on Savanah. The next two weeks should be interesting indeed, he mused, thinking it was almost like he was a mortal man and she was his girlfriend. He laughed at the idea. He hadn't had a girlfriend since he'd had a crush on Wendy Simpson when he was twelve.

Rane's whole life had changed when he turned thirteen. Until then, he and his identical twin brother had been like any other boys on the brink of puberty. They had gone to school, played a harmless prank now and then, switched places with each other from time to time to see if anyone could tell the difference. But the world as they had known it had changed the night after he and Raphael turned thirteen. For one thing, they didn't wake up the next morning.

Rane had learned later that his mother had tried to rouse him and his brother, but to no avail. They were sleeping the sleep of the Undead and there had been no waking either of them until the sun went down. He had risen with an unrelenting thirst he didn't understand. His parents hadn't known what to do. His father, Vince, had taken Rane and his brother outside and told them what he thought was happening, although there was no way to be sure, since as far as anyone knew, no other Vampire had ever sired children.

Vince Cordova's explanation had been simple. He had been a Vampire only a year or so when he had married Rane's mother. It was Vince's opinion that he had retained enough of his humanity to sire Rane and his brother. After that brief explanation, Vince had taken his sons hunting. He had mesmerized a young woman and taken a small amount of her blood. As soon as Rane caught the scent, he had known it was what he had been hungering for, what he wanted. Needed. He and his brother had both fed from the woman. The little they had taken had satisfied Rafe, but not Rane. He had wanted more. He had wanted it all. He had made his first kill later that night, a secret he had kept to this day, a secret that gnawed at him even now.

He and Rafe had been full-fledged Vampires from that night on. Of course, going to school had been out of the question after that, so his parents had hired a tutor who had been willing to teach them at night. Later, after Rane and his brother reached adulthood, their father had brought their mother across.

"Just one big happy Vampire family," Rane muttered, unable to keep the bitterness out of his voice.

Rane had left home shortly after his mother was turned. He had never gone back.

He had kept up with his family's whereabouts as best

he could since then. He knew that his brother, his parents, and his grandparents had all been involved in the recent war between the Vampires and the Werewolves, a war that might have gone on forever if Mara and the head Werewolf, Clive, hadn't come to their senses and realized that the war between the Supernatural creatures was a big mistake. A good many Vampires, Werewolves, and hunters had been killed before peace had been achieved.

Rane had been surprised to learn that Rafe had fallen in love, married a mortal woman, and settled down in Oak Hollow, a town Rane had never heard of and couldn't find on a map. He grunted softly. Falling in love with mortal women seemed to run in his family.

The thought brought Savanah Gentry's image quickly to mind. He had known many women in the course of his existence, some more intimately than others, but he had never let himself fall in love with any of them. Every time he started to care too deeply, the memory of the first woman he had killed burst through the mists of time, reminding him, in vivid detail, that he was a monster.

Chapter Five

William Gentry sat in the backyard, a blanket spread over his useless legs, a glass of strong whiskey cradled in his hands. There were times, like now, when sleep eluded him. When that happened, he came out here to try to forget.

He drained the glass and then refilled it from the bottle on the table beside him. He drank to forget old hurts, old wounds, and usually it worked, but tonight not even whiskey could drive away the ghosts of the past.

He remembered the day he had met Barbara. He had taken one look at her and known she was the woman he would marry. They had been dating only a few months when he proposed. He had been surprised when she not only refused to marry him, but refused to tell him why. Not one to give up easily, he had sent her flowers and candy every day, called her every night, until she admitted that she loved him, too, but that marriage was out of the question. It had taken another month before she'd told him why.

"I'm a Vampire hunter, Will," she'd said. "I can't marry anyone."

He had looked at her in disbelief. "You're a what?"

"You heard me."

"But how . . . why?"

"It's in my blood, Will. It's what I was born to do."

He had listened as she explained what she did and how she did it, his stomach churning as she explained, in vivid detail, how one went about staking a Vampire and taking its head. It was a brutal business. She had showed him the kit she carried in the trunk of her car, explained why she always wore a silver cross and carried a small bottle of holy water in her pocket, why she could never have children. He had assured her that none of it mattered. He loved her.

They were married two months later. In his mind's eye, he saw her as she had been on the day they wed—a beautiful, vivacious woman filled with the joy of life. They had been happy together, happier than any other couple he knew. He had hated what she did, but it was a part of her, a part she felt strongly about. They never talked about it. He never questioned her on those nights when she went hunting, never let her know how he worried, always afraid that she wouldn't come home.

A year passed and then another and another, and their joy in each other grew, spilling over into every aspect of their lives together. Sometimes, in the quiet of the night, Barbara lamented the fact that as much as she wanted a child, she would never have one. She had explained to him that few hunters ever married. Spouses and children could all too easily become pawns in the deadly game of cat and mouse that hunter and hunted played. At those times, William had held her and consoled her, but secretly, he had been glad they remained childless. He didn't want to share her life with anyone, not even his own child. And then, after five years of wedded bliss,

Barbara had announced that, despite all their precautions, she was pregnant. In spite of her determination not to have a child, she had been overjoyed with the news.

William had pretended to be as happy as she, pretended until the doctor placed a tiny, squirming bundle in his arms and announced that he had a daughter. William had feared that a baby would ruin their lives, but Savanah had drawn them even closer together. Barb had quit the hunt when she learned she was pregnant. Will had never said anything about it—it was her decision, but he had been relieved. He had been busy with his career, but always, in the back of his mind, had lingered the fear that one night Barb wouldn't come home. But Savanah had changed all that. He recalled how happy he and Barb had been at each new milestone in Savanah's life—her first smile, her first tooth, her first step, her first word.

He had been content, certain that the future would hold the same joy as the present. And then the unthinkable had happened. The Vampires and the Werewolves came out of the shadows and went to war. He had prayed that Barb wouldn't become involved, but he should have known better.

"I can't just sit at home, Will," she'd said. "I can't just do nothing while people are being killed. I couldn't live with myself if someone died because I wasn't there to save them."

He had been at the newspaper office, working late on a story for the morning edition, when he got a frantic phone call from the baby-sitter telling him to get to the hospital as fast as he could; Barbara had been in an accident. It was the call he had been dreading their whole married life.

He didn't remember leaving the office, didn't remember getting into his car and driving to the hospital, didn't remember anything until he reached Barb's bedside. At first, he had been afraid he was too late, that she was already gone. Her skin had been fish-belly white, her lips blue; she didn't appear to be breathing.

"Barb?" He had taken her hand in his, felt the icy coldness of her skin seep into his own. "Barbara!"

Her eyelids had fluttered open and she had stared up at him out of the eyes of a stranger. "Will?"

"Barb! Thank God!"

"Kill me."

"What?" He had stared at her, certain he had misunderstood her.

"I want you . . . to kill me."

"What are you saying?"

"My neck . . ."

He frowned. "There's nothing wrong with your neck."

"Look . . ." A single tear trickled down her cheek as she turned her head to the side. "Look."

Somehow, he had known what he would see. Two small red puncture wounds, hardly noticeable.

She was looking at him again, her eyes haunted. "Do it, Will. You have to do it."

"I can't."

"If you don't do it, the sun will do it in the morning."

"No! We can handle this somehow."

She squeezed his hand. He had been surprised by the strength of her grip. "I don't want to burn, Will. I don't want to become what I've spent a lifetime hunting. . . ."

"Dammit, Barb, I can't . . . I don't care what you are." He swallowed hard. "You can feed off me."

"No, Will. I won't live like that. And what about Savanah? I can't take a chance of hurting her. Don't let me burn, Will. Please. In the morning, I'll succumb to the

Dark Sleep and when I wake again, I'll be a Vampire. You must destroy me before the sun sets. Promise me."

"I can't," he said miserably.

"Will, I don't know if I'll be able to control the hunger when I rise. New Vampires sometimes go mad with the lust for blood. I don't want to be a monster. I won't put your life, or Savanah's, in danger. I won't live half a life. I don't ever want Savanah to know. . . ."

In the end, he had agreed to do as she asked. Against the advice and wishes of the hospital staff, he had taken her home that evening. He had covered the bedroom window with a heavy quilt to ensure no light could find her. Holding back his tears, he had washed her, dressed her in her favorite lavender-and-white dress, brushed her hair until it gleamed, and then he had sat beside their bed, holding her hand.

As the sun came up, she had whispered that she loved him, and then she had fallen into the deep, deathlike sleep of the Undead.

Early the next morning, a doctor had pronounced her dead and signed the necessary papers. William had called in a few favors and arranged to have her buried that afternoon.

He had sat at her graveside the rest of the day, slowly consuming a bottle of Irish whiskey. Just before sunset, with tears streaming down his cheeks, he had dug up the coffin and looked on the face of his beloved one last time. And then, using Barb's stake and mallet, he had taken the grisly steps required to assure that when the sun set, she would not rise as a newly made Vampire.

William swallowed the hot bitter bile that rose in his throat as he remembered that horrible night, a night forever imprinted on his heart and soul as he had destroyed the woman who had been his wife. If he lived to be a hundred, he would never understand how the gentle woman who had shared his bed and borne their daughter could have spent her adult life doing what he had done that night—not just once, but dozens of times in her career as a hunter.

In spite of his revulsion, he had become a Vampire hunter that night, though his kills had been few. The war between the Vampires and the Werewolves had ended soon after Barbara's death and his life had returned to normal until a hit-and-run driver put him in a wheelchair. The police had never found the man who hit him, but Will was pretty sure he knew who had been behind the wheel, or at least who had ordered the hit. He had been working on a story about government corruption in the city, and had taken the accident as a sign that he was getting too close to the man behind the money. He knew he was supposed to die that night. By the time he recovered enough to get back to work, the money trail had dried up. All things considered, he supposed someone in the Vampire community might have been behind the attempt on his life, but hit-and-runs really weren't their style.

Will had never been able to prove who had been driving the car that hit him, nor had he ever learned who had attacked Barbara, but he hadn't given up. Hopefully, he would live long enough to solve both mysteries.

Sipping his drink, Will stared up at the stars wheeling across the midnight sky. "I'll find him, Barb," he murmured. "I'll find him, and I'll make him pay if it's the last thing I do, I promise."

Chapter Six

Rane stopped by to pick up Savanah on his way to the theater the following night, and thoughtfully arranged for her to have the best seat in the house—front row center.

She was mesmerized, as always, while she watched Santoro the Magnificent do his act. Even though she had seen his show several times, she was just as fascinated as she had been the first time. Now and then, she wondered what her friends at the newspaper would think if they knew she had a date with him after the show. She had dressed with care that evening, choosing a pair of black slacks and a deep blue sweater that made her eyes seem darker than they were.

Savanah felt a strange sense of satisfaction every time the audience applauded, a kind of proprietary pride in Rane's performance. She didn't understand why she felt that way. It would have been understandable if they were married or engaged, but he was little more than a stranger to her, someone who would soon be gone from her life. Maybe it was just because she had seen his act so many times through the years. Maybe it was because they had spent a few hours together the night before. Whatever the reason, it pleased her when the audience responded to his act.

When he received a standing ovation, she rose with the rest of the crowd, then ducked out the side entrance that led to the dressing rooms. Her heart was pounding with anticipation when she reached his door.

He opened it before she knocked. "Come on in."

"How did you know I was out here?"

He smiled, a slow sexy smile that made her heart beat even faster. Shirtless and barefooted, he was a feast for feminine eyes. She couldn't help staring at him. He was so beautiful, it was all she could do to keep from reaching for him. Even now, her fingers itched to explore the broad expanse of his chest, to slide up his arms, to measure the width of his biceps, to tangle in his hair . . .

"There's a bed behind the curtain," he remarked. His voice was deep and sinfully rich, edged with wry amusement.

She looked up at him, her cheeks burning with embarrassment. "I'm sorry. I . . ."

"It's all right, honey. I like the way you look, too."

She didn't know what to say, so she wisely said nothing.

"I thought we might go dancing," he said, reaching for a dark gray shirt. "That okay with you?"

Savanah nodded, thinking it was a shame to cover up that beautiful chest, those broad shoulders, those gorgeous arms.

"Or we could go to my place," he said with a knowing grin, "and I could take it all off."

She would have said it was impossible, but her cheeks grew even hotter. What was the matter with her? She had never felt such . . . such lust, for a man. But then, she had never known a man who exuded such raw masculinity. His voice, his smile, the roguish look in his eyes . . .

Shape-shifter or not, she defied any woman past puberty to resist him.

"Dancing sounds like fun," she remarked.

He pulled on a pair of soft leather boots, then grabbed a black jacket from the back of a chair. "Let's go."

She couldn't think of anything to say on the way to the club. She was acutely aware of the man sitting in the car beside her. His scent filled her nostrils, his nearness made her edgy in a way she had never experienced before. Every nerve ending seemed to be on alert, just waiting for the touch of his hand. The fact that he didn't speak made her wonder if he was as nervous as she, though she doubted it. Besides being the sexiest man she had ever seen, he was also the most confident, self-assured man she had ever met.

Rane slid a glance at the woman beside him. He didn't have to rely on his preternatural powers to know she found him attractive, or that she was as nervous as a week-old kitten confronting a hungry tom. He couldn't blame her. She was right to be on edge. He didn't think she was aware of it on a conscious level, but he knew her instinct for self-preservation was warning her that she was in danger. He wondered if she sensed that he wanted more from her than a few nights of passion, that he wanted her life's blood, and perhaps her life, as well.

He pulled into the parking lot a few minutes later. Killing the engine, he turned toward Savanah. Under his gaze, her heart beat a little faster. The sound stirred his hunger. For a moment, he thought of surrendering to the need within him. It would be so easy to take her, here, now, to take it all.

The scent of her fear filled his nostrils, arousing him still further.

Muttering an oath, he got out of the car. After taking

a couple of deep, calming breaths, he opened her door and helped her out. He felt the tremor in her hand and cursed himself for putting it there. He smiled, hoping to put her at ease, when he wanted nothing more than to drag her into the shadows and inhale her very essence.

The Midnight Sun was a hangout for the under-thirty crowd. A typical pick-up place, it had a live band, a large dance floor, and a lot of dark, intimate corners.

Rane found a table for two near the back, and after seating Savanah, he went to the bar to order their drinks—a strawberry daiquiri for her, a dry red wine for himself.

A willowy brunette clad in skintight jeans and a low-cut T-shirt sidled up to him while he was waiting.

"Hello," she said in a breathy voice. "I don't think I've seen you in here before." Her smile, the tone of her voice, the come-hither look in her eyes, all proclaimed that she was his for the taking.

Rane glanced over her head to the table in the back. Had he been alone, he would have taken what the brunette was so blatantly offering, but Savanah was waiting for him.

"Maybe some other night, darlin'," he murmured.

"Why not now?" she asked with a pout.

"'Cause I'm not alone."

She raked a dark red fingernail down his cheek. "I'll be here until closing if you change your mind."

"I just might," he replied. "You look good enough to eat."

He wondered if she would have smiled so smugly if she had known he meant it literally. Picking up the drinks the bartender set before him, Rane returned to Savanah.

"Is she a friend of yours?" Savanah asked, glancing at the brunette sitting at the bar.

With a shake of his head, Rane dropped into the chair across from hers. "Never saw her before."

"Really? She certainly seemed to like what *she* saw."

He shrugged. "Can I help it if women like me?"

"I don't know. Can you?"

In truth, he could, if he put his mind to it, but for the most part, he didn't bother. All Vampires possessed an aura that was almost irresistible to mortals. He could subdue it if he chose to, but why bother when it made hunting so much easier?

Savanah was watching him, waiting for an answer.

Rane shrugged again. "I like women. They like me."

"Could you try liking them a little less when you're with me?"

He grinned, amused by the spark in her eye and the jealousy in her voice. "Yes, ma'am, I'll do my best." He jerked his head toward the dance floor. "Wanna give it a whirl?"

Savanah took a sip of her drink, wondering if being in the arms of a man she found so attractive was really a good idea, and then shrugged. What was there to worry about? They were in a public place, after all, and she very much wanted to be in his arms.

Rising, she put her hand in his, felt a familiar tingle as his skin touched hers, and then he was leading her onto the dance floor.

He drew her into his arms with the ease and assurance of a man who knew how to please a woman. The music was like the man—dark, sultry, and sensual. Her body reacted immediately, to both the music and the sheer masculinity of the hard male body pressed intimately against her own. He held her close, so close she knew which way he was going to move before it happened. Butterflies fluttered in her stomach; her heart pounded like thunder in her breast. When she risked a glance at his face, his heavy-lidded gaze captured hers, making her think of sweat-sheened limbs tangled in cool silk sheets.

Time seemed to slow as he guided her around the floor. Caught in the seductive web of his gaze, surrounded by the music, it seemed as if her feet never touched the floor. She wasn't aware of anything else, anyone else, only Rane, his strong arms holding her close, his breath fanning her cheek, his voice whispering in her ear. As the music ended, she glanced up at him. What had he said to her? She recalled the husky timbre of his voice, the way it had made her insides melt like ice cream on a hot summer day, but for the life of her, she couldn't remember a single word he had said other than her name.

He held her chair for her when they returned to their table. Resuming his seat across from hers, he sipped his wine.

Savanah shook her head to clear it. Feeling as though she had just awakened from some kind of enchanted sleep, she picked up her own glass and took a long drink.

"So," he remarked, setting his glass aside, "aren't you getting tired of watching my act?"

"No, never." Being a shape-shifter explained how he transformed so easily into a wolf, but it didn't explain how he disappeared from sight, or levitated people and objects off the ground, or did a dozen other seemingly impossible things. "Besides, I'm still hoping to get that story."

"There is no story. I'm just a magician who's good at what he does."

"Well, that's not quite all there is to it."

"True, but you can't print that part."

"I know." She couldn't help thinking it was a shame, though. A story about a shape-shifting magician didn't come along every day. In spite of his assurances to the contrary, her instincts told her he was hiding something else, though she had no idea what it might be.

Later, they danced again, but there was nothing out of the ordinary this time. She was thrilled to be in Rane's arms, but she was aware of the other couples around them, of the waiters moving on the fringes of the dance floor, of the jealous gaze of the brunette at the bar.

Returning to their table Rane ordered another round of drinks. They danced a few more times, and then Rane drove her home.

He walked her to her door, then drew her into his arms. "I had a good time tonight."

"Me, too," Savanah said with a smile. She was tempted to ask him if anything unusual had happened during their first dance, but she was too embarrassed to mention her temporary lapse, or the fact that she couldn't remember a thing he had said to her.

He caressed her cheek, his fingertips trailing fire as they slid over her skin, and down the curve of her throat. She shivered with pleasure when he bent down to kiss the sensitive place behind her ear, felt her eyes widen as an image of Rane bending over her neck, his lips pulled back to reveal his teeth, burst into her mind.

Startled, she drew back.

"Something wrong?" he asked.

"Yes . . . no . . . I mean . . ." She shook her head, confused.

"It bothers you, my being a shape-shifter?"

"Isn't that just another word for Werewolf? I mean, you change into a wolf. Doesn't that make you a Werewolf?"

"Would it bother you if I was?"

"Well, a little." There had been a time when everyone believed that Vampires and Werewolves were just creatures of myth and legend, but then the Werewolves and the Vampires had gone to war, leaving no doubt of their existence, or their danger to the human race. For the most part, the shape-shifters had remained neutral.

"Does that mean I won't be seeing you again?" he asked.

"I didn't say that."

"I'm not a Werewolf, Savanah. I swear it on the life of my mother. Does that make you feel better?"

"I guess so." As far as she knew, the shape-shifters were peaceful creatures, preferring to live in small communities of their own kind.

"So, does that mean you'll go out with me tomorrow night?" he asked. "We could take in a late movie after my last show."

She hesitated a moment, then said, "I'd like that."

But later, in bed, with the covers pulled up to her chin, the image of Rane bending over her crept into her mind again. She saw him clearly. His dark eyes. His sensuous mouth. His very sharp teeth. If he was the wolf, did that make her Little Red Riding Hood?

Rane stood in the shadows outside Savanah's house, his gaze fixed on a second-story window. He guessed it was her bedroom, since it was the only room showing a light.

Standing there, he closed his eyes, his mind expanding until he felt her thoughts brush his. She was troubled by what had happened on the dance floor, as well she should be. Unable to resist her, he had woven a preternatural spell around her, and then taken a small taste of her life's blood. She was as sweet as he remembered. Her blood had intoxicated him, burning through him like gentle fire. Like an addict, he craved one more fix even though he knew one would never be enough. Even now, it was all he could think of.

He licked his lips as he recalled the taste of her blood, warm and salty, on his tongue. Did he dare take more tonight? A single thought could carry him quickly to her side. He could take what he wanted, what he craved, and wipe the memory from her mind, as he had done earlier that night. . . .

Muttering an oath, he drew in a deep breath. Patience, he chided. He must have patience. He would drink a little each night, nothing more. He would relish each taste, savor it like rare, vintage wine, until he took it all.

In the clear light of morning, Savanah told herself she had imagined the whole incident. Nothing out of the ordinary had happened on the dance floor. She had been caught up in the thrill of being in Rane's arms. After all, she had never been with a man who radiated such raw sensuality. All that potent masculinity was bound to have an intoxicating effect on a girl's senses.

She could hardly wait to see him again. Tonight, she would keep her wits about her. She would ask the questions she had intended to ask last night. And she would try again to get that interview. She grinned inwardly, remembering how Yoda had informed Luke that there was no try. Either she would get that interview or she wouldn't. And she would.

After taking a quick shower, she dressed in a pair of tan slacks and a white sweater, brushed her hair, and then went downstairs to have breakfast with her father.

He was waiting for her in the kitchen. She smiled as the smell of freshly brewed coffee tickled her nostrils.

She had always loved sharing this part of the day with her dad.

"So," he asked, looking up from the morning paper, "how was your date?"

"Wonderful!"

Her father lifted one brow.

"We went dancing."

"He must be some dancer, to put that glow in your eyes," her father remarked dryly.

"Oh, he is." She smiled at the memory. "He is."

"I don't like it," her father said. "If I thought it would do any good, I'd tell you not to see him again."

Savanah frowned at her father. "Are you having one of your mysterious premonitions?"

"Not exactly. There's just something about him . . . and I don't just mean the obvious. I mean, why does he keep changing his name every few years?"

"I'd think *that* would be obvious, but I'll ask him." She patted his shoulder as she moved toward the fridge. "I can't get a story if I don't see him."

"Your life is more important to me than any news story."

"I know, Dad. I love you, too," Savanah said, then paused. "Do you think I'm in danger?"

"No, not really. The shape-shifters have never been a threat to us. I was just being an old worrywart, I guess."

"I'll be fine." Going to the fridge, she pulled out a carton of eggs for French toast, a package of bacon, and a bottle of orange juice, and proceeded to fix breakfast.

When it was done, she dished it up, got the butter and syrup, then sat at the table across from her father.

"So, what's up for today?" he asked as he tucked into his breakfast.

"I'm going over to the high school and see what I can

dig up on that car accident, and then I'm going to the morgue to see if they turned up anything new on that John Doe those kids found in the vacant lot last week. Nothing really exciting. How about you?"

Her father shook his head. "End-of-the-month paperwork. Interview with some kid who wants to be a reporter. Like you said, nothing really exciting." He pushed his plate away and reached for his coffee cup. "Ask Chang if there was an unusual amount of blood loss in the John Doe."

"All right." Savanah quickly cleared the table. "I've got to run. See you tonight."

"All right, honey. Be careful."

Frowning, Savanah left the house. It wasn't unusual for her father to tell her to be careful, but there had been something in his tone this morning, something that bothered her, almost like he was expecting trouble.

Shaking it off, she got into her car and headed downtown.

William Gentry sat at his computer, his fingers flying over the keys. He had asked Savanah to do a story on Santoro the Magnificent, or whatever the hell his name was, on the off chance that she might turn up something on the man that he couldn't. She was a pretty woman, after all, and men had been known to betray confidences and countries for less.

Leaving the Web, he pulled up the story he was working on. A story in which the magician was the lead suspect. There had been suspicious deaths and disappearances in every town where the man had performed, far too many to be mere coincidence. There was no rhyme or reason to tie the deaths together, other than the fact that all of the victims had been drained of blood.

In truth, the story he was working on would never see the light of day. It wasn't an assignment for the paper, just more research in an effort to find out who had turned Barbara. In his mind, the Vampire who had done so was also responsible for her death.

Gentry muttered an oath as another Web site turned out to be a dead end. Whoever said you could find anything you were looking for on the Web obviously hadn't been trying to track a Vampire. For the last few years, he'd had a niggling suspicion that Santoro the Magnificent was more than a magician, that the reason the man could do such amazing tricks was because he possessed Supernatural abilities. He had suspected that Santoro might be a Vampire, but according to Savanah, the magician claimed to be a shape-shifter, creatures that had little in common with Vampires other than their ability to change shape.

Gentry shook his head. It had been a Vampire who had turned Barbara; there was no doubt about that. Even as the thought crossed his mind, he was reminded that Vampires could take on many shapes. Perhaps Santoro the Magician was a Vampire masquerading as a shape-shifter.

He swore softly. Maybe there was no story. Maybe Santoro was nothing more than a talented magician with the ability to change shape. Maybe the fact that people died wherever he performed was just a bizarre coincidence.

Gentry blew out a sigh. But what if Santoro was indeed a Vampire, the very Vampire that had turned Barbara? Was he willing to risk his daughter's life to find out? He knew Barbara would never have done anything that would put Savanah's life in danger, not for a few columns of newspaper space, not even to avenge her own death.

And yet, what if Santoro had killed Barbara? The thought repeated itself over and over again. Savanah was his best chance to get close to the magician, a chance that might never come again. Vampire or not, Santoro was hiding something, and Gentry was determined to find out what it was.

Chapter Seven

Savanah sat back in her chair. A glance at the clock on the wall behind her desk told her it was almost quitting time. She'd had a busy day and the time had passed quickly. She had gone to the morgue and talked to Bobby Chang, the mortician, who had informed her that there had been about a teaspoonful of blood left in the John Doe's body. The mortician had no explanation for the blood loss, other than two small puncture wounds located on the inside of the corpse's left arm.

Returning to her office, Savanah had read and answered her mail, gone to lunch with one of her coworkers, done a little writing on the story she was working on, and spent every minute she wasn't busy thinking about Rane.

She had Googled his name on the Web. Lots of links came up for various products and services. There was even an old movie titled *Rane,* but none of the links applied to her magician. She felt her cheeks heat at the thought of Rane being hers. When she Googled the stage names he had used in the past, she found numerous rave reviews of his shows posted by fans all across the country, as well as dozens of online videos, and at least fifty fan sites. But nothing she didn't already know.

Feeling as though she were banging her head against the proverbial stone wall, she shut down her computer, grabbed her bag, and headed for home, figuring she had just enough time to get out of her work clothes, take a quick shower, and get ready for her date with Rane. Just thinking about seeing him again put a smile on her face.

"And a song in my heart," she said, and giggled like a teenager with her first crush.

It was near dark when she pulled into the driveway. Switching off the ignition, she grabbed her handbag and her briefcase and hurried into the house.

No lights were on, but out of habit, she called, "Hey, Dad, are you here?"

When there was no answer, she went into the kitchen to see if he had left her a note. Finding none, she hurried upstairs. In her room, she undressed and headed for the shower. She stood there a minute, letting the hot water ease the tensions of the day. She wondered where her dad had gone. It was unusual for him to take off without letting her know he was going out.

Stepping out of the shower, she pulled on her robe, quickly did her hair and makeup, and then spent ten minutes going through her closet trying to decide what to wear. She settled on a pair of camel-colored pants and a white silk shirt.

She had just posted a note for her dad on the fridge when the doorbell rang.

Her date had arrived, right on time.

Taking a deep breath, Savanah stepped into her sandals, her heart pounding a mile a minute.

Rane whistled softly when she opened the door.

"Thank you," she said, smiling.

"You look good enough to eat."

"You always say that."

"It's always true." He couldn't wait to taste her again, to savor the sweetness of her life's blood, to feel the warmth of it on his tongue.

"Come on in. I just need to grab my coat."

Rane followed her into the living room. He glanced around, noting the room looked comfortable, clean, and lived in. A home, he thought, something he hadn't had in more years than he cared to remember. Looking at the photograph on the mantel, he felt a sharp stab of recognition. He had seen the woman before, he was sure of it, though he couldn't recall her name, if he had ever known it.

"Ready?" Savanah asked, coming up behind him.

"Always ready."

He gestured at the photograph on the mantel. Savanah bore a striking resemblance to the woman in the picture. "You look a lot like her."

"Thank you."

"Your mother?"

"Yes. She was beautiful, wasn't she?"

"So are you."

"She died when I was a little girl."

Rane glanced at the photo again. He remembered the woman now. She had been a Vampire hunter, and a good one. But for her, he would have been dead years ago. Did Savanah know her mother had been a hunter? Was it something that ran in the family? It wasn't the kind of question he could ask without arousing her curiosity, but he needed to know the answer.

Murmuring Savanah's name, he trapped her gaze with his. "Listen to me," he said. "I'm going to ask you a question, one you will forget as soon as you tell me the answer. Do you understand?"

She stared at him, unblinking. "Yes."

"Did your mother ever hunt Vampires?"

"No."

"Are you certain?"

"Yes."

Releasing his hold on her mind, he said, "You must miss her very much."

Savanah blinked at him a moment, then nodded. "Every day," she replied wistfully.

Rane felt a sharp stab of guilt. His mother was alive—he could visit her any time he wished—but he hadn't seen her, or anyone else in his family, in decades.

Pushing the thought aside, he followed Savanah outside, waited while she locked the front door, then walked her to his car. He held the door open for her, then went around to the driver's side. Sliding behind the wheel, he turned the key in the ignition and the engine purred to life.

The car reminded Savanah of the man—sleek and sexy and way out of her league.

"Does it hurt?" she asked abruptly.

Rane glanced at her, one brow lifted. "Does what hurt?" he asked as he pulled away from the curb.

"When you shift into the wolf. Does it hurt?"

"No."

"Where does your clothing go?"

He looked at her a moment, and then he laughed. "Beats the heck out of me." It was a good question. Werewolves had to disrobe before they changed or risk shredding their shoes and clothing. He had never before wondered what happened to his own attire when he shifted.

"Why do you change names so often?"

He shrugged. "Boredom?"

"And how do you just . . ." She lifted one hand and let it fall. "Just disappear?"

"Ah, now, that's a secret," he said with a wink.

"Does it have to do with shape-shifting?"

"Hey, we're on a date," he reminded her. "No more questions unless they're of a personal nature."

"Personal, huh? Like, do you wear plain old white cotton boxers or sexy briefs?" Savanah clapped her hand over her mouth, unable to believe she had uttered the words out loud.

Rane waggled his eyebrows at her. "Or maybe nothing at all," he said with a wicked grin.

"I didn't mean . . . Just forget I said that!"

"Oh, I don't think so," Rane said, chuckling.

He pulled into the parking lot a few moments later, sparing her the necessity of coming up with a retort.

Rane bought their tickets and they went into the theater. He wrinkled his nose at the smell of buttered popcorn, nachos, and hot dogs.

Being a gentleman, he asked Savanah if she wanted anything to eat or drink, relieved when all she asked for was a small Coke.

There were only a dozen or so people in the theater when they took their seats.

"Hardly seems worth running the film," Savanah remarked, looking around.

Rane grunted softly. "I hope the small crowd is due to the late hour and not because the movie stinks."

"Well, I heard it was good," Savanah said, and then shrugged. "Of course, you never know about critics."

"Yeah, I rarely agree with the reviews."

"I know what you mean," Savanah said, then sat back as the lights dimmed and the previews started.

Rane tried to concentrate on the trailers but it was difficult. He was all too aware of the people in the theater, and particularly aware of the woman beside him. Her scent filled his nostrils. Her nearness stirred his desire and his hunger. He could hear the steady beat of her heart, as well as the heartbeats of other people sitting nearby. It took a great deal of effort to shut out the siren call of all those beating hearts, to close his mind to the scent of prey. It was easier when he was performing on stage. His mind wasn't on the hunt then, but now . . . he had an almost overpowering urge to unleash the beast within him. It would be so easy. He could take them all before they realized what was happening. . . .

Taking a deep breath, he glanced at Savanah. Her scent wrapped around him—the fragrance of her skin, the soap she had bathed with, a hint of perfume. And overall, the heady, musky scent of the woman herself. Oblivious to his inner turmoil, she appeared lost in the love story unfolding on the screen. His gaze moved over her face, admiring the delicate curve of her cheek, the fine line of her jaw, the way her nose tilted up at the end just a tiny bit. Her hair fell over her shoulders in a sheen of pale silk.

Muttering an oath, he glanced at the screen, and swore again as the hero swept the heroine into his arms and carried her up a long, winding staircase. At the top of the stairs, he kicked open the first door he came to. Striding inside, he dropped the heroine on an enormous bed. Ignoring her outraged cry and her struggles, he sank down on the mattress beside her. With his hands holding hers captive over her head, he covered her body with his and kissed her, a long, passionate kiss that put an end to the heroine's struggles and soon had her purring like a kitten.

The rapid beat of Savanah's pulse and the quickening of her breath reached his ears. Was she imagining, as he was, that he was the hero and she was the heroine?

She looked at him and smiled when the movie ended and the lights went on. "Well, the critics were wrong that time," she declared. "I loved it! What did you think?"

"Chick flick," he said with a grin.

She stuck her tongue out at him. "Chauvinist."

"Who, me?"

"I don't see anybody else sitting there."

"Okay, okay, I give up," Rane said as they left the theater. "Where do you want to go now? That is, if you don't mind being seen with a chauvinist pig."

"I don't mind, but I should probably go home. It's late, and I have an early interview in the morning."

With a nod, Rane took her hand and they walked toward the parking lot.

"So," he asked, "who are you interviewing, or can't you talk about it?"

"I have an appointment at the morgue."

"Yeah, you wouldn't want to be late for that," Rane said dryly.

"Very funny."

They were passing an alley when Rane's senses went on alert. Before he had time to react, someone shoved a gun against his spine.

"Don't turn around," the assailant warned, his voice gruff. "Don't even blink. Just give me your money. You, too, lady."

Murmuring, "This can't be real," Savanah pulled her wallet from her handbag. She wouldn't miss the money, but she hated to lose her driver's license. The thought of waiting in line at the DMV was almost more frightening than being robbed at gunpoint.

Not daring to so much as look at Rane, who stood a little behind her, she thrust her hand behind her back, her wallet extended, and prayed the robber would be content to take their money and spare their lives.

A muffled thump, like a body hitting the pavement, sent her heart leaping into her throat. Had the robber killed Rane? Wouldn't she have heard a gunshot? Unless, oh, Lord, unless the robber had a knife, too.

She almost jumped out of her skin when she felt a hand on her shoulder.

"Relax," Rane said. "It's over."

Slowly, Savanah turned around, relieved to see that Rane was apparently unhurt. She started to ask where the robber had gone when she saw him lying facedown on the pavement. Was he breathing? In the dark, she couldn't be sure. "Is he . . . did you . . . ?"

"He's still alive," Rane said curtly. The man would never know it, but if it hadn't been for Savanah's presence, he would have been dead.

"How did you overpower him?" she asked, stuffing her wallet back into her handbag. "I mean, you're unarmed, and he had a gun."

"This is hardly the time to discuss it." And so saying, Rane grabbed the man by the ankles and dragged him into the alley.

"Shouldn't we call the police?" Savanah asked when Rane returned.

"Probably, but we're not going to."

A dozen thoughts flitted through Savanah's mind. She was a reporter. This was news. How could she let it go? A man had tried to rob them on a public street near the theater. He should be arrested and locked up.

As if he were reading her mind, Rane said, "I don't need the publicity, if it's all the same to you." He also didn't need to be interrogated by the law, or summoned to appear in court if the man went to trial.

Rane rocked back on his heels, prepared to erase the incident from Savanah's mind if she insisted on doing the right thing.

"I can't ignore it," she said, reaching into her handbag for her cell phone. "Not just because it's news, but because he might try something like this again and the next victim might not have you to protect her. You understand, don't you?"

He nodded. "Savanah."

She looked up at him; when her gaze met his, the phone in her hand was forgotten.

"You will not report this to anyone," Rane said, his gaze holding hers. "You will forget that it happened. You will remember only that we went to the movies and then I drove you home. Do you understand?"

"Yes."

Taking the phone from her hand, he dropped it into her purse, then took her arm and began walking. "It was a good movie, wasn't it?"

She looked up at him, her eyes slightly unfocused, and then she blinked. "Very good. I'll have to tell Jolie."

"Who's Jolie?" he asked.

"One of the secretaries at work. We go to lunch together sometimes. I can't wait to tell her about it."

Smiling, Rane unlocked the car door. He waited for Savanah to get inside, then gently closed the door behind her. He hated to play tricks with her mind, but she really hadn't given him any other choice.

Chapter Eight

The next two weeks seemed to fly by. Rane gave Savanah a pass to the theater and she went to see his act every chance she got. She never tired of watching him. Each time she saw him perform, she became more convinced that he really was a wizard beyond compare. Not every trick could be ascribed to the fact that he was a shape-shifter. On those nights when, for one reason or another, Savanah couldn't make a performance, she met him in his dressing room after the show. She lost a lot of sleep, but she didn't care.

Rane made her life fun, exciting. They went to the movies again. They took long walks in the moonlight, holding hands and talking about their favorite books and plays and movies. One night he took her sailing on the lake and there, under the stars, they kissed and cuddled like a couple of teenagers.

He filled her every waking thought and her dreams at night. In spite of all her doubts about having a relationship with a man who was not only a shape-shifter but who would be leaving town in a few days, Savanah knew she was falling for him, and falling hard.

She thought it odd that he didn't take any nights off from the theater, but when she asked him about it, he just shrugged and said that, until he'd met her, he didn't have anything else to do with his time, so why not work?

Tonight, they had gone to the mall so Savanah could find a present for her father. His birthday was only a few days away and, as always, she had no idea what to buy him, but then, he had always been a hard man to shop for. He didn't have any hobbies, he rarely took the time to read for pleasure, and he wasn't particularly handy around the house. So she usually bought him clothes. And he either returned them, or they sat on his shelf, untouched, for years. But maybe this year would be different. This year, she had let Rane decide what she should buy in hopes that her father would approve of something another man had picked out.

After they finished shopping for her father, Rane tried on a long black leather duster reminiscent of the coats cowboys had worn in the Old West. It was very flattering, and she told him so.

"If you like it, I'll buy it," he said, and headed for the customer service desk to pay for it.

"Don't you want to see how it looks?" she asked, thinking it odd that he didn't want to catch a glimpse of himself in a mirror before he shelled out four hundred and fifty dollars.

"It fits," he said with a shrug. "You like it. I like it. That's all I need to know."

Rane had paid for the coat and they were about to leave the store when a young woman hurried by calling, "McKayla! McKayla!"

Moments later, the woman rushed past them a second time, her voice rising in panic as she called "McKayla!" again and again. Shortly after that, a Code Yellow came over the loudspeakers, alerting others in the store that there was a lost child. A description of the little girl quickly followed. She was two years old, with curly blond hair and blue eyes, and was wearing a pink-and-white skirt and a hot pink Winnie-the-Pooh T-shirt.

Savanah's heart went out to the mother. Losing a child had to be the scariest feeling in the world, especially these days, when so many children disappeared and were never seen again.

"Stay here," Rane said, and before Savanah could ask where he was going, he had dropped his shopping bag at her feet and was gone.

Savanah tapped her foot on the floor. She could hear the mother frantically calling for her child as she ran through the store. The fear and desperation in the woman's voice tore at Savanah's heart. Had someone kidnapped the little girl?

Savanah glanced at the time and jotted it down in the small notebook she always carried with her, along with the child's name and description, the headline already forming in her mind.

And then Rane was back, with a pretty little blond-haired girl in his arms. The child's pudgy cheeks were wet with tears. Rane spoke to the salesclerk, who announced that the child had been found and advised the mother to come to the counter in the men's department.

The harried woman showed up, tears streaming down her cheeks as she took her little girl from Rane's arms and crushed her close. "Thank you! Oh, thank you so much. I don't know how she got away from me so fast. One minute she was right beside me, and the next . . ." She shook her head. "How can I ever repay you?"

"No need," Rane said. "I'm just glad she's okay."

The woman put her arm around Rane's shoulders and gave him a hug. "Thank you again. God bless you."

Rane nodded, his throat suddenly tight. People had damned him more times than he could count, but he couldn't remember anyone ever asking God to bless him.

Savanah dropped her notebook and pen into her handbag. "How did you find her?" she asked.

He shrugged. "Just luck."

"I don't believe that."

"I didn't think you would. If you must know, I smelled her fear and went after her."

Savanah stared at him. She had heard that animals could smell fear. She didn't know people could. Then again, Rane was a shape-shifter, which gave him powers ordinary mortals didn't possess.

He tucked their packages under his arm. "Ready to go?"

"I guess so."

As had become his habit, Rane took her hand and they left the mall. On the drive home, Savanah stared out the window, her thoughts on Rane. He wasn't a normal man, and while that added a bit of mystery to their relationship, did she really want to get involved with a man who was different? And just how different was he? Was he like any other man, except for his ability to change into a wolf? If their relationship continued and they married, would their children be shape-shifters, too? She had a sudden image of herself giving birth to a litter of wolf pups.

Grinning inwardly, she shook the bizarre image from her mind. They had only been dating for a few weeks. It was way too soon to be thinking about a relationship, serious or otherwise. Besides, his last show was tomorrow night. In a day or two, he would be leaving town for his next engagement, wherever that might be, and she would probably never see him again.

"Anything wrong?"

His voice drew her back to the present. Looking around, she realized they were parked in front of her house. "No, I was just thinking . . ."

He switched off the ignition and turned toward her. "Thinking about us?"

She nodded.

"Thinking that you'll miss me when I'm gone?" he asked, one brow arched. "Or thinking you'll be glad to see the last of me?"

She would miss him, she thought, more than she wanted to admit. How could she feel so strongly about him so soon?

"Savanah?"

"I don't want to miss you," she said quietly.

"But you will."

"Yes."

Rane looked at her a moment, then got out of the car. He opened her door and offered her his hand, pulling her up and into his arms.

"I'll miss you, too," he said, "so much that I think I'm going to have to cancel my next engagement and get to know you better."

Her heart skipped a beat. "You're going to stay?"

He nodded slowly. "I can't leave you. Not now, not yet."

"Won't you get in trouble, canceling on such short notice?" she asked, but she didn't really care. All that mattered was that he was staying.

He shrugged. "Maybe, but it doesn't matter," he said, and then he smiled. "I'll just take a new name and start over."

She smiled because she couldn't help it, because he wasn't leaving town, because she knew he was going to kiss her. And even then, he was pulling her closer, his dark eyes intense as he brushed a kiss across her cheek, then claimed her mouth with his own.

He leaned back against the side of the car, drawing her with him, so that her body was flush with his from shoulders to thighs. He deepened the kiss and she felt the stir of his arousal, felt her own body grow warm and moist as his tongue plundered her mouth, then laved the sensitive skin behind her earlobe. His teeth nipped her flesh and she pressed herself against him, driven by a need she had never known before. Someone moaned softly. Was it her? She didn't think she had ever made a sound like that in her life, a hungry, lusty purr that was almost a growl.

He lifted his head and looked at her. His eyes were deep and dark, burning with a hunger of their own. "Tell me what you want."

What did she want? She gazed into his eyes as she weighed her answer. Was it the moon's bright light that made his eyes burn with such fire? Or was it just the reflected glow of her own desire?

Whispering, "I don't know," she buried her face against his shoulder.

"Don't you?"

She did know. Why was she being such a coward? Lifting her head, she looked deep into Rane's eyes. "I want you," she said, "but it's too soon, and . . ."

"And I'm a shape-shifter."

If they were to have any kind of lasting relationship, she had to be honest with him. "Yes."

"Okay." He tucked a lock of hair behind her ear, then slid his knuckles down her cheek. "We'll take it slow and easy."

And so saying, he wrapped his arms around her and claimed her lips a second time.

It was more than just a kiss, she thought, swaying against him. It was a promise of more and better things to come.

Chapter Nine

Savanah was still thinking about Rane's parting kiss when she slid her key into the lock on the front door, only to find the door already unlocked. That was odd, she thought. She knew she had locked it when she left. Even though they lived in a small town, her father always insisted on locking the doors, undoubtedly a holdover from the days when he had investigated high-profile cases involving drug lords, hookers, and politicians on the take.

Shrugging it off, she stepped into the living room, Rane still uppermost in her thoughts. One thing was for certain: whether he was a man or a magician, Santoro the Magnificent knew how to kiss. She could still taste him on her lips and her tongue, feel the heat of his body pressed close to hers. The man had enough sex appeal to light up a city, she thought. Look at the way he turned her on!

She dropped her purse and her shopping bags on the sofa, called, "Dad? Hey, Dad, I'm home," on her way into the kitchen to get a bottle of water.

"The better to cool off with, my dear," she murmured, though she wasn't sure she wanted to cool off. What she wanted was to be in Rane's arms again, to revel in his kisses, to hear his voice whispering in her ear, though she couldn't now recall what he had said. But it didn't matter. He wanted her. There was no doubt about that. And she wanted him.

Returning to the living room, she paused in the doorway. The lights were off, but the satellite screen was on, so where was her father? It wasn't like him to go to bed without turning off the screen. Saving energy had always been one of his quirks.

She glanced around, a sudden feeling of unease skating down her spine. Murmuring, "I don't like this," she switched on the lights.

Something was different. . . . She moved through the room. The books on the bookshelf had been moved, the drawers in the small desk that had been her mother's were open. The trio of candles on the coffee table had been knocked over. Her father's favorite coffee cup lay on the floor surrounded by a dark stain.

She stood in the middle of the room. Should she leave? What if the intruder was still on the premises? Goose bumps prickled along her skin. "Dad?"

When there was still no answer, she picked up one of the heavy candlesticks. She couldn't leave. Her dad might still be in the house, hurt, unable to answer.

Tension coiled deep within her as she walked down the hall to her father's bedroom. The door was open. The lights were off. In the light from the hallway, she could see that his bed was empty.

Chilled, she stepped into the room. "Dad?"

Looking closer, she saw his wheelchair lying on its side by the bathroom door. Fear's icy hand clamped Savanah's insides. Where was her father? Why didn't he answer? Her fingertips tightened on the candlestick as she hurried around the foot of the bed, her eyes focused on the bathroom door.

She looked down when her foot hit something soft, felt her heart go cold when she saw her father sprawled face-down on the floor.

"Dad!" Tossing the candlestick on the bed, she switched on the bedside lamp. "Dad?"

Kneeling, she turned him over, gasped in horror at what she saw. His face was as pale as paper, his lips were blue, his eyes sunken. Had he had a heart attack? She placed her hand on his heart. Was he breathing? She couldn't feel a heartbeat.

She had to call 9-1-1, had to get help. He couldn't be dead. She was reaching for the phone when his fingers curled around her arm.

"Sa . . . vanah . . ."

"I'm here, Dad. Hang on."

"Listen . . . things you need to know . . ."

"Later, Dad, I need to call . . ."

"Listen! Things about me . . . your mother . . ."

Savanah stared down at her father as he struggled for breath. What was he trying to say? Whatever it was, it would have to wait. He needed help and he needed it now. "You can tell me later."

"No time." His hand tightened on her arm in a viselike grip. "My desk . . . envelope . . ." He took a deep, shuddering breath. "Envelope . . . behind . . . bottom drawer . . . for you."

"Yes, whatever . . ." It wasn't important, not now, when he was growing paler, weaker, by the moment. A prayer rose in her mind. Only one word, *Please, please, please* repeated over and over again. She grabbed his cell phone from the bedside table. "I need to call . . ."

"Too late . . ." His fingers dug into her flesh. "Be . . . careful."

"Dad, please, just hang on. . . . I can't lose you, too."

"Love . . . you . . ." He looked up at her, a faint smile on his lips, and then, with a sigh, his hand fell away from her arm, the light went out of his eyes, and he was gone.

"Dad? Dad! No, please, no." Gathering him into her arms, she rocked back and forth, her tears dripping onto his face.

Guilt speared her heart. She had hardly spent any time with him in the last few weeks, what with spending her days at work and her nights with Rane.

If only she had come home earlier, or called to see how he was. Time lost all meaning as she sat there cradling her father's body.

She held him until her legs cramped. Rising, she went into the bathroom and washed her hands and face. Returning to the bedroom, she pulled a blanket from the bed and covered him, only then noticing that someone had gone through his dresser and the drawer on his nightstand.

Someone had broken into the house. Who? And why? Had her father surprised the culprit in the act? Choking back her tears, she went into the living room and called the police. While waiting for their arrival, she went through the rest of the house. Every drawer had been ransacked, every bookshelf had been searched, but as far as she could tell, nothing had been taken. What had the robber hoped to find? There was no sign of forced entry, no broken windows. Had her father been acquainted with the robber? Knowing someone had gone through her personal belongings left her feeling violated.

The police arrived a short time later. Savanah answered their questions, a growing sense of numbness enveloping her as a crime team arrived to dust for fingerprints. A policewoman escorted her out onto the front porch and informed her that she would have to stay outside until the police finished their investigation.

Savanah glanced toward the front door. Her father was still in there; she needed to be with him. "How long will that take?"

"We could be finished here in a few hours, or a few days. I really couldn't say. Do you have somewhere you can go? Is there anyone you can call?"

"Yes."

"Don't leave town," the policewoman said. "And I'll need a number where we can reach you."

Savanah gave the woman her cell phone number.

"I'm sorry for your loss," the policewoman said before going back into the house.

Savanah stood there a moment, and then she dialed Rane's number.

He answered on the first ring, almost as if he had been waiting for her call, and promised he would be right over. He arrived less than two minutes later. In a distant part of her mind, Savanah wondered how he had gotten clear across town so fast.

Rane caught the mingled odors of blood and death the minute he approached the house, and beneath it, the scent of Vampire. He drew in a deep breath. The Vampire's scent was unfamiliar, but one he wouldn't forget.

Rane took one look at Savanah's tear-streaked face and drew her into his arms. "What happened?"

He stroked her back lightly as she explained, her voice a dull monotone. When she fell silent, he said, "You can't stay here."

"That's what the police said."

Taking her by the hand, he led her into the house and

spoke to the policewoman, who allowed Savanah to go upstairs and pack an overnight bag.

"Ready?" Rane asked when Savanah came down the stairs, a small suitcase in one hand, her handbag in the other.

She stared at him out of grief-stricken eyes.

"Where are your keys?"

She pulled them from her purse and handed them to him, then followed him out of the house. He unlocked her car door and tossed her suitcase into the backseat.

She didn't ask him where his car was, and for that, Rane was grateful, since he hadn't driven to her house.

"Savanah, do you want to go to my place or a hotel?"

"I don't care."

He dragged a hand over his jaw. As tempted as he was to take her home with him, a hotel seemed the wiser choice. Having her in his room, in his bed . . . He shook his head. Definitely not a good idea.

The Kelton Inn was located at the end of town. If it wasn't for the adjoining restaurant, the place would probably have gone bankrupt years ago. Rane asked for the best room the hotel had to offer. He signed the register with an old alias; then, lifting Savanah into his arms, he carried her and her overnight case up the stairs, all too aware of the hotel clerk's curious gaze on his back.

The room was spacious and well-appointed, although the furnishings were sorely out-of-date. Dropping Savanah's bag on the floor beside the sofa, Rane sat down, cradling Savanah in his arms.

For a time she just sat there, stiff and unmoving, and then the tears came, slowly at first, then building in intensity as the full impact of her father's death washed over her. Knowing the healing power of human tears, Rane said little. He simply held her, one hand lightly stroking her back, wondering all the while if the Vampire he had scented had killed her father and if so, why, and if it had anything to do with Savanah's mother being a hunter. Savanah had said the house had been ransacked. What had the Vampire been searching for, and had it been found?

After a time, Savanah's tears subsided and she rested in his arms, her body limp.

Blinking back her tears, she looked up at Rane. "I'll miss him so," she murmured, her voice little more than a whisper.

"Of course you will."

"I can't imagine my life without him. He was always so good to me, so patient." She sniffed. "He tried to be both father and mother to me. It wasn't easy for him, but he did it. He helped me with my homework, he went with me to buy my first prom dress, he held me in his arms after I broke up with my first boyfriend." She sniffed again. "When I got older, we took care of each other. And now he's gone. . . . Oh, Rane, what am I going to do?"

"You'll grieve a while," he said, brushing a lock of hair from her cheek, "and you'll miss him, but, with time, the pain will get a little easier to bear. You'll get on with your life, and eventually the hurt will go away and you'll be able to remember the good times without crying."

"You sound like you're speaking from experience?"

"In a way." He hadn't buried anyone he loved, but he had grieved when he cut himself off from all contact with his family.

"Thank you for coming over."

"I'll always be here if you need me."

She blinked at him. That sounded like a commitment, which was odd, since they had only known each other a few weeks. Still, there were times, like now, when it seemed as if she had known him her whole life.

Rane brushed a kiss across her cheek, and tasted the salt of her tears. "I should go so you can get some sleep," he said, though he didn't intend to go far. Until he discovered otherwise, he would assume that one of the Undead had killed her father. It would be an easy thing for him to find out. A quick trip to the morgue after Savanah was asleep would tell him everything he needed to know. But whether the killer was mortal or Vampire, Rane intended to stay with Savanah tonight and every night until he was certain that whoever had killed her father hadn't also marked her for death.

"I don't want to be alone tonight," Savanah said, her voice little more than a whisper. "Will you stay with me?"

"Sure, darlin', if that's what you want. Go brush your teeth and put on your nightgown and call me when you're done." He winked at her. "And I'll come and tuck you in."

Blinking back a fresh wave of tears, she slid off his lap. Retrieving her overnight case and her handbag, she went into the bedroom and closed the door. She unpacked her nightie, her robe and her toothbrush, and then went into the bathroom.

Were the police still at her house, searching for clues? Would they be able to gather enough evidence to find and arrest whoever had killed her father? The culprit had ransacked the house from top to bottom, but as near as she could tell, nothing was missing. What had the intruder been looking for?

With a shake of her head, she splashed cold water on her face, then brushed her teeth. She had packed the most modest nightie she owned, a plain white cotton gown that fell to midcalf. She slipped it on and then brushed out her hair. Going into the bedroom, she crawled under the covers, and then she called Rane.

He appeared in the doorway as if by magic. She knew it was only her imagination, but his presence seemed to fill the room.

"They were looking for something," Savanah said. "Whoever killed him was looking for something."

"Any idea what it was?"

"No. We don't keep anything valuable in the house." She smiled faintly. "Not that we have anything of value to anyone else. Oh, Rane, they killed him for nothing."

"Try not to think about it now." Sitting on the edge of the bed, he bent down and kissed her cheek. "Get some rest. I'll be nearby."

She grabbed his hand when he started to rise. "Don't go."

He gazed at her for stretched seconds, then nodded. "All right." He took off his shoes and socks, removed his shirt, and slid under the covers.

Savanah scooted closer. "Hold me."

Muttering an oath, Rane put his arm around her and drew her against his side. Did she know what she was asking? Did she expect him to lie there beside her, to breathe in the warm, womanly scent of her body, listen to the siren call of her blood, and do nothing? Of course she did. She had no idea what kind of monster she had invited into her bed. He fought for control as the predator within him stirred, sharpening his senses, urging him to take her. His tongue brushed his fangs as his innate lust for blood sprang to life. Each indrawn breath only added to his desire. Drinking from her would satisfy him on so many levels; he would revel in the sounds of her sighs as he seduced her, in the heat of her flesh warming his own, the enticing smell of her surrender, the rich taste of her life's essence pouring sweetly over his tongue . . .

He swore again as she rested her head on his shoulder and closed her eyes. A moment later, he felt the dampness of her tears on his skin.

Her trust routed the beast within him as effectively as if she had splashed holy water in his face.

Drawing her closer, he kissed her cheek. "Go to sleep, darlin'," he whispered. "There won't be any bad dreams tonight."

"Make love to me, Rane."

"Savanah . . ."

"Please make love to me, Rane. Make me forget . . . everything."

He wasn't surprised or shocked by her request. It was common enough in times of grief or stress for mortals to seek forgetfulness, either by drinking themselves into oblivion, or indulging in the primal urge to mate, not as an act of love but of renewal.

Drawing Savanah into his embrace, he kissed her gently, but she didn't want gentle. She wrapped her arms and legs around him, slid one hand behind his neck, and kissed him as if her life and her sanity depended on it. And maybe they did, he mused, as he deepened the kiss.

He trailed his hands over her body, his own absorbing her heat. She was young, her skin smooth and firm, supple as she writhed against him. He slid his hand under her nightgown, his fingertips sliding up her calf, lightly massaging the smooth skin of her thigh, her belly, the underside of one breast. Her moan was one of pleasure and invitation.

He rose over her, his nostrils flaring. She smelled of toothpaste and soap, of woman and musk. It was a powerful combination, but stronger still was the steady beat of her heart, the constant lure of her life's blood flowing just beneath the surface of her heated flesh.

He closed his eyes against the temptation to lower his head to her neck; instead he brushed a kiss across her cheek and tasted the salt of her tears.

Rane swore softly. He had done a lot of despicable things in his life, but he had never violated a woman who was grieving for the loss of a loved one. She might want him tonight, but she would hate him tomorrow, just as she would surely hate him when she knew the truth about his existence.

"Savanah, you should get some rest."

"Don't you want me?" She ran her hands over his chest, lightly, provocatively.

"Of course, but . . ." He groaned as her hand dropped lower, covering his arousal.

"Then take me," she whispered.

And because it was what she wanted, because he wasn't made of stone, he caressed her until she was on the brink and then he sheathed himself deep inside her.

There was a moment of resistance. A telling moment that had Rane cursing himself as he realized he was the first man Savanah had taken to her bed. It touched something deep within him, something he had thought forever dead.

And then she murmured his name, her voice whisper-soft, filled with love and need, and in that instant, he knew he would willingly sacrifice his life and everything he possessed to protect the woman in his arms.

Chapter Ten

He stood looking out the window, a glass of expensive whiskey in one hand, his eyes narrowed as he watched her cross the room. "Well, is it done?"

"Just like all the others," she replied with a toss of her head.

"Did you have any trouble getting into the house?"

She crossed her arms over her breasts and then, shoulders slumped, she looked up at him out of eyes swimming with tears. "What do you think?" she asked, sniffling.

He chuckled softly. He defied any man, human or otherwise, to resist her when she looked so pathetic, so helpless. "Ah, Tasha, I was a fool to doubt you."

She basked in his praise. "I don't understand you. What do you hope to gain by this?"

"I intend to accomplish what we failed to achieve in the war."

She closed the distance between them. "What do you mean?"

"Why, the destruction of all the Vampires, of course."

"Then why kill the hunters?" she asked, frowning.

"Because they don't just hunt Vampires."

"I see," she murmured, though she didn't see at all. But then, it wasn't important. She was in love with him. She would do anything he asked.

"Did you find the books?"

"No. What made you think Gentry had them?"

"Just a hunch."

"Why do you want them?"

"Because they're valuable. One of them contains an updated list of hunters. It would be a handy thing to have, don't you think?"

"I suppose so."

"The other one contains a list of Vampires, both the quick and the dead."

She hadn't known that, and she didn't like it. She had managed to stay under the radar for the last fifteen years and she liked it that way.

"There aren't as many hunters today as there were twenty years ago," he went on, his expression thoughtful. "With peace between the Vampires and the Werewolves, there hasn't been any need for them. The schools have shut down. The old hunters are dying off. If my information is correct, there are only a hundred or so left in the world. When they're gone, most of their knowledge will die with them."

"What of Mara? She won't like it when she hears what you're doing. It was her idea to call off the war."

"Ah, yes, Mara. We've nothing to fear from her. She's gone to Egypt, most likely for a good long time."

"And when all the hunters are gone, what then?"

"We'll kill a few important politicians, a few famous celebrities, an innocent or two. It will arouse the populace against the Vampires, and there will be hunts to rival those of the last century." He smiled, his teeth gleaming in the moonlight. "It will be glorious!"

She nodded, even though none of it made a lick of sense to her. Sometimes she thought Clive was a little crazy, but then, weren't they all?

Moving closer, she ran her hands through his hair. It was thick and brown and curled over her fingers. He was a handsome man, his body tall and compact, his eyes brown with a hint of yellow. She loved being with him, loved it when they both changed into wolves and hunted the night.

His arm snaked around her waist, his eyes burning with lust when he drew her body against his. She didn't care what happened to the Vampires or the Werewolves or the humans or anyone else, as long as he wanted her.

Chapter Eleven

Savanah woke abruptly, her initial alarm at waking in a strange bed with a man quickly fading when she realized it was only Rane, and that he was asleep, one long leg draped over both of hers.

She stared at him, shaken anew by the events of the past night.

Someone had killed her father.

In the middle of the night, she had begged Rane to make love to her.

What had she been thinking? Of course, the real problem was that she hadn't been thinking at all. She had been feeling lost and alone. Caught up in the reality of death, she had reached out to Rane and surrendered her virtue in the most life-affirming act known to mankind. And it had been wonderful, she thought with a guilty sigh. Wonderful, and all wrong.

Sitting up, with the sheet tucked under her arms, she cradled her head in her hands. Lord, what if she was pregnant? Would her child be a shape-shifter? She groaned softly. What had she been thinking, to indulge in unprotected sex with a man she hardly knew? And yet, right or wrong, she had found comfort in Rane's arms.

On some deep, primal level, she had been aware of his presence beside her even while she slept, had taken comfort in having another human being nearby.

Except that he wasn't human, at least not entirely.

Holding the sheet over her breasts with one hand, she studied the man lying beside her, his face barely visible in the faint glow of the night-light he had thoughtfully left burning. He was truly the most amazing-looking man she had ever seen, his features strong and remarkably handsome. Lying there, with one arm folded behind his head, he looked like some pagan warrior prince awaiting the arrival of his favorite courtesan.

The thought brought a rush of heat to her cheeks. Last night, she had played the courtesan. Shame made her cheeks burn hotter. What kind of woman was she, to make love to a man she hardly knew, on the same night her father had been killed and her house had been ransacked? How could she be in bed with a man she hardly knew?

A man who was awake and watching her through dark, heavy-lidded eyes.

He sat up, exposing a pair of broad shoulders and a chest Savanah knew all too well.

Savanah searched her mind for something witty and urbane to say and came up blank, so she waited, hoping he would break the awkward silence between them.

"Why didn't you tell me you were a virgin?" he asked, unable to completely disguise the accusation in his voice.

She stared at him, thinking the silence hadn't been so bad, after all. And then she shrugged. "You didn't ask."

He grunted softly, his gaze searching hers. "Regrets?"

"No. Yes. I don't know."

"There's no need for you to feel guilty about what happened."

"Isn't there?" Tears scalded her eyes.

"No. It was a normal reaction. You were hurting and in need of comfort." What they had shared last night had been more than sexual intimacy. How could he make her understand that?

"Is that what we shared? Comfort?"

"No, it was more than that, and we both know it." He brushed her cheek with his knuckles, then wiped the tears from her eyes. "Go on," he said, drawing her into his arms. "Let it out."

With a sob, she buried her face against his chest and let the tears flow.

Rane stroked her back, unmindful of the flood of tears dripping down his chest. Gradually, her sobs subsided. She dried her face with a corner of the sheet, then rested in his embrace, her eyes closed.

Rane took a deep breath as he fought the urge to do what came naturally, what he had intended to do since the beginning. He had seduced women before, seduced them and taken their life's blood, and sometimes, when they had been lost and unhappy and tired of living, he had taken their lives, as well. But he couldn't steal Savanah's life. He cared for her too much, feared that if he tasted her again, he would never be able to let her go.

It surprised him to realize he had grown truly fond of her, that he cared more for her future and her well-being than he did about satisfying his craving for her life's blood.

He grunted softly, wondering when he had grown a conscience. Heaven knew it hadn't made itself known in decades.

He was pondering this odd turn of events when his

skin began to tingle. Muttering softly, he glanced at the window. The sun was rising. It was time to go.

He stirred restlessly. He hated to leave her, but he had to go now or be trapped in the hotel until nightfall. He glanced down at Savanah's face. Even with her cheeks stained with tears and her hair sleep-tousled, she was the most beautiful, delectable creature he had ever known.

"Rane?"

He was sorely tempted to stay, to take her in his arms and bend her will to his, to bury himself in her sweetness before he surrendered to the Dark Sleep. He swore under his breath. He had to go, now, before he did something they would both regret.

He kissed her, hard and quick. "I'll see you tonight."

"Where are you going?"

"I don't have time to talk now." He kissed her again, then pulled on his shirt and trousers and fled the hotel with the sun's light nipping at his heels.

Savanah sat up, frowning as she tried to make sense of what had just happened. One minute they were cuddling and the next he was gone, with no explanation.

With a sigh, she buried herself under the covers and went back to sleep.

The ringing of Savanah's cell phone roused her several hours later. She flipped open the phone and heard the cigarette-roughened voice of Mr. Van Black, owner of the *Chronicle.* Savanah accepted his condolences, answered his questions about what had happened to her father as best she could, and thanked him for his offer to take as much time off as she needed.

Breakfast was a cup of hot black coffee, and then, with a heavy heart, she sat down and called the cemetery. She was relieved to learn that her father had made arrangements for his own demise shortly after her mother had passed away, thereby sparing Savanah the stress of picking out a plot and a casket. Next, she called the church and set the date for the funeral.

With that taken care of, she made the necessary phone calls to her father's brother, Arthur, in New York and his cousin, Frank, in South America. Arthur said he would have to rearrange several meetings, but he would be there; a message on Frank's answering machine advised her that he was somewhere in the jungles of Brazil and would be without any means of communication for several weeks. She left him a brief message.

She sat there a moment, blinking back her tears, and then she called the police department, relieved when the officer at the desk informed her that she was free to return home. Home, she thought. It would never be the same without her father. After what had happened, she wondered if she would ever feel safe there again.

With a sigh, she dropped the phone on the bed, only to pick it up moments later to call Rane. She was disappointed when his answering machine picked up.

"Sorry, I can't get to the phone right now. Leave your name and number and I'll get back to you as soon as I can."

"Rane, hello? Please pick up if you're there."

When there was no answer, she hung up, only to call back a second time just to hear the sound of his voice on the machine, and then she went back to bed and cried herself to sleep.

It was early afternoon when she woke again. She took a quick shower, dressed, checked out of the hotel, and drove home.

She sat in her car a moment, staring at a strip of yellow

police tape fluttering from a bush. She could only wonder what her neighbors must think about the goings-on last night. She still couldn't believe it hadn't been some horrible nightmare. If only she could wake up and find her father waiting for her in the kitchen, the morning paper spread out on the table in front of him. If only she could turn back time. . . .

She shook the thought away. Wishing she could change the past served no purpose.

Getting out of the car, she stooped to pick up the newspaper, then unlocked the door and went inside. The house was as she had left it, except that now every surface appeared to be covered with black fingerprint powder.

After tossing her keys, the paper, her suitcase, and her handbag on the sofa, she went into the kitchen and filled a pail with hot soapy water. She pulled an apron from one of the drawers and slipped it over her head, then pulled on a pair of rubber gloves and began to wash the black powder from the doorknob, glad to have something to do to occupy her mind.

She was cleaning the top of her mother's desk when she suddenly recalled her father's last words, something about his desk and an envelope.

Dropping the gloves into the pail, Savanah dried her hands on her apron, then walked down the hall to her father's office.

She paused outside the door. She had never entered his work space uninvited; her father had respected her privacy, as well.

Blinking back a rush of tears, she stepped across the threshold. The furniture in here had also been dusted with fingerprint powder, leaving a fine black residue on the oak file cabinet, her father's old-fashioned rolltop desk, the bookshelves, and his keyboard.

Savanah blew out a sigh as she looked around. Whoever had invaded their home last night had gone through her father's office with a vengeance. Books had been pulled from the shelves and tossed on the floor. A photo of her parents, taken on their wedding day, had been knocked off its customary place on top of the file cabinet. Fighting the urge to cry, she picked it up and put it back where it belonged. The top two drawers in the file cabinet, always locked, had been forced open. Her father's desk had practically been turned inside out. All the drawers had been opened, the middle one had been removed, its contents strewn on the floor. Had the intruder been searching for the envelope her father mentioned? Had they found it?

Taking a deep breath, she removed the bottom drawer from the desk. Setting it on the floor, she peered into the opening, wondering if the envelope was still there. Reaching inside, she ran her fingertips over the wood. A muffled sound of success rose in her throat as her fingers encountered something taped to the back panel of the desk. Tearing it free, she stared at the long white envelope. Her name was scrawled across the front.

Savanah stared at it for several moments before opening it. Inside, she found a folded sheet of flowered stationery that had belonged to her mother. She recognized it immediately. She had given it to her mother on the last Mother's Day they had spent together.

With trembling fingers, Savanah unfolded the letter. It was dated a month after her father's car accident, and written in his own bold hand.

My darling Savanah,
  I had hoped never to have to tell you these things, but after what happened last month, I feel

the need to write them down, that you may know the truth.

There are many things about your mother that I never told you—things she could have explained so much better than I.

Your mother's maiden name was not Johnston, but Van Helsing. Yes, she is a direct descendent of the well-known Vampire hunter, Abraham Van Helsing. And like her predecessors, she, too, was a Vampire hunter.

Savanah stared at the words. Vampire hunter. It wasn't possible. Her mother had cringed at the thought of killing a spider.

Her passing was not from some mysterious disease, as I told you. It was a Vampire who was responsible for her death.

You may remember that I left you with your aunt Ramona shortly after your mother passed away. I spent the time hunting for information, trying to track down the monster responsible for your mother's demise, but to no avail. I'm sorry to say that I'm not the hunter your mother was. As my grief ebbed, I realized that my daughter needed a father more than I needed to avenge your mother's death, and so I came home.

Your mother told me that Vampire hunting is in your blood, that the day may come when you will feel the need to take up where she left off. Whether you choose to accept the call will, of course, be up to you. I hope you do not follow in your mother's footsteps. It is a nasty business, but the decision, of course, must be yours.

Under the tree to the right of where we buried your bunny, you will find a box. Inside, is a silver crucifix on a silver chain. It belonged to your mother. Wear it always. You will also find several wooden stakes and a number of other implements used for destroying the Undead, together with two books. One contains a list of known Vampires; the other is a book of instructions written by your mother.

The house and everything in it is yours. All the legalities have already been taken care of. Always remember that I love you and, according to my faith in the Almighty, I know that I will see you again, just as I know that I am now in paradise with your mother.

God bless you, my darling daughter.

> *Always,*
> *Your loving father,*
> *Will*

Blinking back her tears, Savanah read the letter a second time, then replaced it in the envelope. Her mother had been killed by a Vampire. Hatred was a new emotion for Savanah. She had been taught to believe that there was good in everyone. But Vampires weren't people. They were Undead creatures who existed on the life's blood of others, monsters who killed without mercy or compassion. One of them had killed her mother.

Had one of them also killed her father?

Last night, she wouldn't have believed it, but now it looked like a very real possibility.

She sat there for a time, unable to come to terms with the fact that her sweet, lovable mother had been a Vampire hunter. It seemed ludicrous to think that a woman who had taught Sunday school, loved to play hide-and-seek, and made the best chocolate-chip cookies on the planet had spent her days hunting the Undead. And yet, as impossible as it was to believe, Savanah knew in her heart that it was true.

"Savanah Gentry, Vampire hunter," she muttered, then shook her head. Other than bothersome flies and an occasional insect, she had never killed anything in her life. She couldn't begin to imagine driving a stake into anybody's heart, dead or Undead. But then she thought of her mother being drained of blood to extend the existence of some creature of the night, and she knew there was one Vampire, at least, that she could kill without a qualm.

Curiosity drove her outside. She found a shovel in the shed out back, then walked down the red brick path that divided the yard. There were fruit trees and tomato plants on one side, grass, a covered swing and a pretty gazebo on the other. As a child, she had pretended the gazebo was a castle and she was a princess. Her dog had been a fire-breathing dragon, and her dad . . . She blinked back her tears. Her dad had been the white knight who vanquished the dragon, then carried her away to the land of Mile High Cones for ice cream and cookies. Savanah had stopped believing in fairy tales when her mother passed away.

She found the tree she was looking for and started digging. The ground was soft and it wasn't long before the shovel hit something hard. Kneeling, she reached into the hole and pulled out a large, square metal box inscribed with her mother's initials *BG*. Barbara Gentry.

Savanah set it aside, filled in the hole, brushed the dirt from her knees, and then carried the box into the kitchen. Putting it on the counter, she lifted the lid. Her stomach churned as she looked at the contents: several sharp wooden stakes, a mallet, a long, heavy-bladed knife in a leather sheath, several bottles filled with what she suspected was holy water. A wooden box, its lid carved with runes and symbols, held two leather-bound books, one black, one brown. There was also a small gray velvet box that held a beautiful silver crucifix on a sturdy silver chain.

Savanah slipped the chain over her head, then picked up the books and went into the living room. Curling up in a corner of the sofa, she opened the brown book. She ran her fingertips over the words, words written by a mother she scarcely remembered, and then began to read the precise script that told how to identify a Vampire, listed the Supernatural powers they possessed, detailed how to find them, and how to destroy them.

Vampires were remarkable creatures. They could change shape or cross great distances in the blink of an eye. They could turn into mist, scale the side of a building like a spider, hypnotize a person with a look. Vampires had the ability to confuse or control a person's thoughts, and to shield their presence so as to become invisible to mortals. They had the power to control the weather; they could call animals and people to them. Their wounds, if not fatal, healed almost overnight. Silver burned their skin, as did holy water. The touch of the sun's light turned all but the very oldest to dust. They couldn't enter a home without an invitation and had to leave if that invitation was rescinded. A handy thing to know, she mused, should a Vampire ever come calling.

In reading the next few pages, Savanah learned more about destroying Vampires than she had ever wanted to know. In addition to driving a stake through their hearts, Vampires could be dispatched by severing the head from the body and burying the parts of the creature in separate graves. Fire was another sure way to destroy the Undead. Her mother recommended both staking and beheading in order to ensure that the Vampire did not rise again. A note written in one of the margins noted that the best stakes were made of ash, juniper, buckthorn, whitethorn, or hawthorn, with hawthorn being the wood of choice for most hunters.

Toward the back of the book was a list of Vampire hunters. She skimmed over the names—Abraham Van Helsing, Pearl Jackson, Travis Jackson, Rick McGee, Edna Mae Turner, Edward Ramsey, Tommy Li, Barbara Van Helsing Gentry.

Savanah swallowed the bile that rose in her throat as she tried to imagine her sweet, gentle, cookie-baking mother indulging in such a grisly business not once, but many times.

A small section in the back of the book was devoted to Werewolves. They were harder to find than Vampires since they were able to move about in the daytime, and able to mingle with society with no one being the wiser until the full moon turned them fanged and furry. A single silver bullet to the head or the heart was the best way to kill a Werewolf. Depriving them of oxygen by strangling or suffocation was also effective, though harder to accomplish. Unlike Vampires, once dead, Werewolves did not rise again.

Putting the first book aside, Savanah picked up the second volume. It was far older than the other book. The ink was faded, the pages yellow with age. The flyleaf read: *I take pen in hand that my heirs might finish the work I have begun* and was signed *Abraham Van Helsing*.

Thumbing carefully through the yellowed pages, she saw that the book contained a record of known Vampires up to the time of her father's death. Columns listed the date the Vampire had been turned and, if applicable, the date it had been destroyed. There was also a place to note who had sired the Vampire, if known, as well as a place to include the name of the hunter who had destroyed it.

The first name on the list of Vampires was Mara. Beside her name was a notation declaring that she was the oldest-known Vampire in existence, and that it was believed that, due to her longevity, she had become impervious to the effect of the sun's light.

Savanah skimmed over the names of the Vampires: Gabriel, Kitana, Petrina. A Vampire named Cristophe had been killed by a Werewolf during the war. Dominic St. John was a Vampire who had killed quite a few of his own kind, then turned the woman he loved. There was a note beside the name Rayven, claiming that he had been restored to humanity. Further down, she read the name Jason Blackthorne, with the same notation. Odd, she thought. Once a Vampire, always a Vampire. Everyone knew there was no cure.

The list went on: Navarre, Alexi Kristov, Grigori Chiavari, Alessandro deAvallone, Rodrigo, Elisabeth Thorndyke, Khira, Zarabeth, Laslo, Joaquin Santiago, Roshan DeLongpre and his wife, Brenna. Jason Rourke, Antonio Battista, Ramon Vega. Edward Ramsey, Edna Mae Turner, Travis Jackson, and his grandmother, Pearl Jackson.

A grandmother, Savanah thought. *Good grief.*

She stared at the notes written beside the last four names. It stated that Ramsey, Turner, Travis and Pearl Jackson had all been dedicated hunters before they were turned. Ramsey had been considered one of the best. His family had been in the business for over a hundred years. It gave her a funny feeling to see his name and the other three hunters added to the list of Vampires. She wondered if it happened often, that the hunter became one of the hunted.

How did those who had devoted their lives to destroying Vampires reconcile with becoming one? How did anyone accept such a drastic change in his or her life?

Savanah tried to imagine herself as a Vampire, sleeping by day, hunting for prey at night, never to see the sun again, never to enjoy a turkey dinner at Christmas or a glass of eggnog on New Year's Eve, never to have children and grandchildren, or do any of the other ordinary things she took for granted.

With a sigh, she turned the page and felt her blood turn to ice. There, in neat black handwriting, she read the names Vincent Cordova, Cara DeLongpre Cordova, Raphael Cordova, Kathy Cordova.

And Rane Cordova.

She stared at the name. It couldn't be. Not her Rane. It was just a horrible coincidence that he had the same first name as a known Vampire. Sure, he was a shape-shifter, but not a Vampire. He couldn't be a Vampire. It had to be someone else. But what if it wasn't? What if he was one of them, a blood drinker, the same kind of despicable creature of the night that had killed her mother?

Even as she tried to deny it, she knew on some deep inner level that it was true. Rane was a Vampire.

It answered so many questions.

It explained so many things.

It explained everything.

Like a splash of cold water came the memory that she had let him make love to her. Let him? She had begged him! Feeling sick to her stomach, she wrapped her arms around her middle and rocked back and forth, and as she did so, she felt something stir within the very depths of her being, something that bubbled up from deep inside her soul like a purifying fountain.

And its name was vengeance.

Chapter Twelve

Rane gazed at the young woman standing pliant in his arms. She was a pretty thing, in her late twenties, with blue-tipped blond hair and green eyes lined with black mascara. Her name was Brandi, and she had been on her way to meet some friends when he waylaid her. He took a deep breath, the scent of her blood arousing his hunger. He savored the anticipation for a moment, then lowered his head and drank, savoring the thick coppery taste on his tongue.

He took only enough to satisfy his hunger, then licked the wounds in the girl's throat to seal them. By tomorrow, they would be gone. He caressed her cheek, and then he released his hold on her mind and sent her on her way, none the wiser.

He was about to get into his car and head over to Savanah's place when he was overwhelmed by a rush of Supernatural power. Pivoting on his heel, he came face-to-face with the most beautiful woman he had ever known.

"Mara."

She stood before him like an enchanted goddess come to life. A white dress clung to her shapely form; her only adornment was a heart-shaped ruby pendant on a fine gold chain. Thick black hair fell over her slender shoulders. Her eyes were a deep, dark green and slightly slanted, like those of a cat. She had been born in Egypt, had known its most famous queen, Cleopatra. Some believed that the blood of pharaohs ran in Mara's veins, but Rane knew that was only a rumor, perhaps started by Mara herself. According to Vampire lore, she was truly immortal now, impervious to stake or silver, though a well-placed blade could still take her head. Even the sun no longer had any power over her and she walked freely in its light. It was said that whenever she grew weary of her existence, she traveled to Egypt where she rested in the earth of her homeland.

Rising on her tiptoes, she kissed his cheek. "Good evening, my handsome one."

"What brings you here?" he asked.

She linked her arm with his. "Do I need a reason to visit my godson?"

"No, I guess not." Mara was a law unto herself. Like Cleopatra of old, she was queen of all she surveyed.

"It's been too long since I saw you last," she remarked, urging him to walk with her. "Too long since you've seen those you love, those who love you."

"Did my parents ask you to check up on me?"

"No, though they are naturally worried about you."

He took a deep breath and blew it out in a wistful sigh. "Are my parents well?"

"Yes, of course, but they miss you. Your mother worries. Your father blames himself for your absence."

"And Rafe?"

"It pains him that you've severed the blood link between you."

"I doubt if he spends much time thinking about me."

"Is that bitterness I hear in your voice? If you're unhappy, you've no one to blame but yourself. Go home, Rane. Go home where you belong."

"I'm not ready."

"What keeps you here?" Mara asked, and then, with a soft laugh, she answered her own question. "Ah, a woman, of course, The Cordova men are like wild stallions, overflowing with the juices of life."

"Very funny," he muttered.

"A woman," Mara said, and it was no longer a question. She regarded him for several moments, and then shook her head. "You still have not made peace with what you are, have you? The lives you've taken still prey on your conscience after all this time."

He didn't answer, but there was no need. She knew the truth as well as he did. He didn't kill often these days, but when he did, the guilt stayed with him, one more stain on his already-black soul. In time, the guilt faded, like everything else, but it never really went away. He remembered each of their faces, the taste of their blood, hot and sweet on his tongue, the faint sigh that always sounded like regret as they breathed their last.

"If it bothers you to take the lives of the young and vibrant, then take those who are sick and eager to go." She smiled at him; it was a hungry, predatory smile. "Think of it as culling the herd."

"It doesn't bother you to take a life? You never regret it?"

She stopped walking and turned to face him. "I am Vampire. It was not something I sought, nor was it bequeathed to me of my own choosing. I could have spent my existence bewailing my fate. Instead, I choose to embrace what I am. I am Nosferatu. It is my nature to hunt, to kill, just as it is yours. If peace is what you are searching for, you will never find it until you fully accept who and what you are. There is no going back, Rane. There is no magic cure. You are what you were born to be."

"Why do you hide in the night when you can walk in the sun?" he asked, hoping to steer the conversation away from himself.

"The night was my day for many centuries," she said with a shrug. "After all these years, there is little difference between the night and the day, save the hunting is better in the dark." She smiled at him again, her eyes aglow. "Come now, let us go and cull the herd."

He shook his head.

"Ah, Rane, what am I to do with you?" she asked, pouting prettily.

He looked at her and laughed. She was thousands of years old, yet she looked like a young woman trying to wheedle her father into letting her take the car. Her eyes were alight with a lust for life as she tugged on his arm.

"Come, Rane. I'm your godmother. You must do as I wish."

He snorted softly. "Do I look like Cinderella to you?"

Her laughter spilled over him, as warm as the sun he hadn't seen in almost a hundred years.

"More like the handsome prince. You must introduce me to the princess sometime soon. Come," she coaxed, tugging on his arm. "I'm going to Egypt on the morrow. Who knows when we shall have the chance to hunt together again?"

"Why are you going to Egypt?"

"The land calls to me. Every hundred years or so, I get homesick for the valley of the Nile. I want to bury myself in my native earth and rest a while."

He grunted softly. Very old Vampires often went to ground to rest, sometimes for a year, sometimes for a century or more.

Resigned to doing as she wished, he allowed Mara to lead the way as she searched for prey.

After a time, they came upon a middle-aged man and woman emerging from a nightclub. Hanging on to each other, the couple staggered down the street to where they had left their car.

Mara followed them on silent feet.

Rane followed Mara. Even though he had fed earlier, his excitement escalated as the two of them closed in on the unsuspecting couple. He was a Vampire and as such, he was a predator without equal. There was no denying the thrill of the hunt, the anticipation of holding his prey captive in his embrace, the primal excitement that came with knowing that he held the power of life and death in his hands, the first taste of life's elixir sliding over his tongue.

Mara took the man as he was fumbling in his pocket for his keys.

Rane swept the woman into his arms. He silenced her startled cry with a look and a touch. Speaking to her mind, he wiped away her fear, and then he stood there a moment, gazing down at her, wishing he held another woman in his arms, a woman with hair the color of summer moonlight and eyes as blue as the sky.

Muttering an oath, he summoned Savanah's image to the forefront of his mind.

And then he lowered his head and drank.

Chapter Thirteen

Savanah woke with a start. She glanced at her watch, noting that it was after ten. Sitting up, she stretched her arms and legs, a little surprised that she had fallen asleep, and then she shrugged. At least she'd had a few minutes of blessed forgetfulness, but now, all too soon, everything she had learned earlier that evening came rushing back.

Rane was a Vampire.

She didn't want to believe it was true, couldn't abide the thought that he was one of them, a blood drinker, like the hideous creature that had killed her mother and very likely murdered her father, as well. Nor did she want to believe that Rane drank blood. She didn't want to believe that he had lied to her about what he was. A shape-shifter, indeed! Not that she could blame him for lying. Who would admit to being a godforsaken, blood-sucking, creature of the night? She didn't want to remember that she had made love to him only hours ago. At least she didn't have to worry about getting pregnant, she thought with relief.

She picked up the book that had slipped from her fingers when she dozed off. Thumbing through it, she

frowned when she looked at the list of Cordova names
again. How could Rane's parents be Vampires? Everyone
knew the Undead couldn't create life. She glanced at his
mother's name. A notation in the margin indicated that
Cara Aideen DeLongpre Cordova had been adopted by
Roshan DeLongpre and Brenna Flanagan. There was no
such notation alongside the names of Rane or his brother,
Raphael. Had it been an oversight on her mother's part?
Or had Rane's parents found a way to reproduce?

Savanah shook her head. Such a thing was unthinkable. There were enough Vampires in the world already
without their being able to mate and produce dozens,
maybe hundreds, of Vampire offspring. And since male
Vampires didn't age and females didn't go through
menopause, they could probably reproduce indefinitely.
Lordy, that was a scary thought, a world overrun by
Vampires. Not to mention Werewolves and who knew
what else.

She wrapped her arms around her midsection as she
imagined giving birth to a Vampire child. Would it sleep
all day and need blood to survive? She was letting her
imagination run wild. Rane and his brother had to have
been adopted. Vampires didn't age. If they had been born
Vampires, they would have remained infants forever.
Wouldn't they?

Shaking off her disconcerting thoughts, she closed the
book and set it aside, then glanced at her watch again.
Rane had said he would see her tonight. What would she
do when he showed up? Alarm skittered down her spine.
Vampire.

She jumped when the doorbell rang. Was it Rane? Gaining her feet, she ran into the kitchen. Opening the metal
box on the table, she grabbed one of the wooden stakes and
slid it into the waistband of her slacks. It felt reassuring

against the small of her back. Deciding it was better to be safe than sorry, she dropped a bottle of holy water into her pants' pocket.

She took a deep breath when the doorbell rang again; then, shoulders back, she went into the living room and peered through the peephole. Rane stood on the porch. She didn't have to let him in, she thought, her mind racing, but then, he no longer needed an invitation. If she didn't let him in, would he huff and puff and break down the door?

"Calm down," she muttered. "He's never hurt you before. He doesn't know that you know what he is. Just open the door and revoke your invitation. He can't come in without it. And don't look in his eyes!"

She waited a moment more, and then opened the door just a crack.

Rane sensed the change in Savanah the minute he saw her, knew that, somehow, she had discovered the truth about him. The knowledge was in her eyes, though she avoided meeting his gaze directly, and in the way she held herself, as if poised for fight or flight. He could hear it in the rapid beat of her heart, smell the fear on her skin. See it in the heavy silver filigreed cross that nestled in the hollow of her throat.

"You can't come in," she said quickly.

"Yes," he said dryly, "I guessed that."

She blinked at him, surprised that he could find humor in the situation.

"Who told you?" he asked, curious in spite of himself.

"My mother."

"Indeed?"

"Well, not directly, of course. I found your name in a book."

He didn't like the sound of that. "What book?" he asked sharply.

"Does it matter?"

It mattered a hell of a lot. For years, it had been rumored that Van Helsing, the most famous hunter of them all, had compiled a list of all the known Vampires in the world, and that it had been handed down from generation to generation. Rane, like most of his kind, had scoffed at the idea. Now it looked like such a book did, indeed, exist, and that Savanah had it. Did she have any idea that just possessing such a book put her life in danger? That it was, in all probability, the reason her father had been killed.

"Savanah . . ."

"You lied to me."

"Did I?"

"You know you did! Withholding the truth is the same as lying."

"Is it?"

"Stop that! I want you to go. Now. And never come back." She blinked back her tears, her hand closing over the crucifix at her throat. It was unfair to lose her father and Rane within days of each other.

She stared up at him, hurt and anger warring within her. "Why did you pretend you cared for me? How could you let me care for you and not tell me the truth?"

"I wasn't pretending," he said quietly. "Don't ever think that."

"Right! As if Vampires were capable of . . . of . . ." She made a dismissive gesture with her hand, unable to say the word aloud.

"Love?" He grunted softly. "My parents have been together for well over a hundred years. Are you going to tell me that they aren't in love?"

Savanah shook her head in disbelief. A hundred years was longer than most people lived. But it didn't change anything. He was still a Vampire. He had still lied to her. For all she knew, he could be the one who had killed her father . . . and maybe her mother, as well.

She took a step backward, intending to slam the door in his face, but he forestalled her by putting his foot in the way.

"What do you think you're doing?" she demanded. "Move your foot!"

"No. I'm not leaving until we settle this."

"There's nothing to settle. You're a Vampire, and I hate you!"

"Why? I've done nothing to you."

Savanah stared at him. "Why? You dare to ask me why?" Her voice rose with her anger. "You stole my virginity!"

He lifted one brow.

Savanah's cheeks grew hot under his gaze. He hadn't stolen anything. She had practically begged him to take it.

"And . . . and that's not all. A Vampire killed my mother."

"It wasn't me." It occurred to him that Mara might very well know who had killed Savanah's parents.

"My mother was a Vampire hunter," Savanah said. "Did you know that?"

"Yes."

Savanah blinked at him. "You did?"

He nodded. "I saved her life one night, and she returned the favor by letting me live."

"I don't believe you."

He shrugged. "It's true nonetheless."

She lifted her chin defiantly, her hands clenched at her sides. "Did you know that I'm a Vampire hunter, too?"

Rane's laughter cut across the stillness of the night.

The sound of it stiffened Savanah's spine and spiked her anger. How dare he laugh at her! Her mother was dead, killed by one of his kind. She would soon be burying her father who, for all she knew, had also been the victim of a Vampire attack. And Rane dared to laugh at her! It was too much.

Slipping her hand into her pocket, Savanah flipped the top from the bottle of holy water and threw the contents in his face. "Laugh at that!"

With an oath, Rane darted to the side. He avoided most of the bottle's contents, but not all. Drops of holy water sprayed across his left cheek and down the side of his neck, leaving pinpricks of fire in their wake.

Savanah stared at him, horrified by what she had done. She had never raised a hand in violence against anyone or anything in her life. A strange state of affairs for a future Vampire hunter, she thought with wry amusement. But there was no time to think about that now, not when she was face-to-face with an angry Vampire.

"Dammit!" He hissed the word through clenched teeth. "Why the hell'd you do that?"

His anger frightened her, but she refused to let him know it, refused to back down. Barbara Gentry had killed Vampires, and when she died, William Gentry had taken his wife's place. Now it was up to Savanah to carry on in their stead.

"You're lucky I didn't drive a stake into your heart," she said, her words underscored by a bravado she was far from feeling.

Rane drew in a deep breath. It had been years since anyone had tried to destroy him. He had forgotten how painful even a few drops of holy water on preternatural flesh could be. Never taking his eyes from Savanah, he drew another breath, and then another.

Guilt warred with the anger in Savanah's heart as she watched Rane's skin redden and blister. "Are you all right?"

Rane regarded her warily for a moment. He could tell by the tone of her voice that it hadn't been an easy question for her to ask. "I will be, but if it makes you feel any better, it hurts like hell."

She didn't say she was sorry, and he didn't expect it.

Savanah Gentry was a pretty woman, and he would miss her, but there was little chance that they could have a future together now, not when her mother had been killed by one of his kind, not when she was deluding herself into thinking she could become a hunter. It wasn't an occupation a man or a woman decided to pursue on a whim. It took years of training, a strong heart, and a stronger stomach.

And yet, looking at her now, at the fire in her eyes and the determined tilt of her chin, he thought she might become the most dangerous hunter of them all.

Savanah kept her hands tightly clenched to hide their trembling. In his Vampire form, Rane couldn't cross the threshold, so she was safe. But what if he transformed into the wolf? Was he still bound by the same rules?

"I'm sorry it's come to this," Rane said quietly, "but it's probably for the best for both of us. Good-bye, Savanah."

He didn't give her a chance to respond. By the time she realized what he was saying, he was gone and she was alone, more alone than she had ever been in her life.

Savanah stood there a moment, unsure of how to feel, or what to think. Rane was a monster, inhuman, a killer, and she had wanted him gone from her life, so why did she suddenly feel so bereft? She told herself that the heaviness in her heart had nothing to do with Rane's departure, that it was grief over her father's death, shock from learning that her mother hadn't died from an illness, as she had long believed. But she couldn't shake the fear that she had just lost a part of herself, a vital part she could never get back.

Closing the door, she went into the living room and curled up in a corner of the sofa. She glanced at the two books lying on the table. The volumes listed the known Vampires and Vampire hunters, and obligingly listed the ways to find and destroy the creatures of the night. The only thing the books didn't explain was how one gained the courage to take stake and mallet in hand and get started.

Rane stood in the shadows outside Savanah's house, his fists shoved deep into his pants' pockets as he stared at her silhouette in the window. So, she thought she was a Vampire hunter, did she? The very idea was ludicrous and yet he couldn't forget the stubborn set of her jaw or the determined look in her eyes. Did she actually mean to take up stake and mallet and go hunting the Undead? To do so would be suicide. Surely she knew that? She had no training, no one to teach her, no one to guide her. If she was foolish enough to go up against a Vampire who had been turned for more than a year or so, she would be way out of her league. Vampires might not be able to abide the sun, but once they had a few years under their belt, many of the stronger ones were able to defend themselves even if they were attacked while at rest. With her inexperience, Savanah would be no match for any but the weakest fledgling.

He frowned as another thought occurred to him. Even though he had stayed out of the war between the Vampires and the Werewolves, there were secret, out-of-the way places in every big city where the Undead gathered.

He had kept up-to-date with the war news, listened to the rumors, heard the names of those who had been killed on both sides. When the war ended, there had been a period of relative peace as the Supernatural community withdrew to lick their wounds. After six months or so, the Vampire hunters had gone into retirement. For a time, all had been quiet but then, after a few years, Rane began to hear rumors that another war was being waged. If what he heard was right, this war was being carried out by an unknown assailant who was quietly and methodically killing Vampire hunters. Was it a Vampire? The same one who had killed Savanah's father? Did that make Savanah the next victim? And was it hunters the killer was after, or the book Savanah had mentioned?

Rane told himself it wasn't his problem. Savanah was over twenty-one, old enough to know her own mind and make her own decisions. He swore softly. Maybe that was true, in mortal matters, but in Supernatural affairs, Savanah was in way over her head. One way or another, he needed to get his hands on that book before it was too late.

He told himself again it wasn't his problem, but to no avail. He wasn't sure how or when it had happened, but he had fallen into the same trap as his grandfather, his father, and his brother. He was in love with a mortal woman, one whose life might be in danger even now.

So, what was he going to do about it? Protect her, or just turn his back on her and walk away as he had on so many things in his life?

Protecting Savanah could be dangerous, he mused, lifting a hand to his face. His cheek and neck still hurt like hell, ample proof that she wasn't afraid to strike out, given enough provocation. Considering the way she felt right now, she was just as likely to drive a stake into his heart as not. In spite of what he'd said earlier, letting her go was out of the question. He wanted her, and not just her blood. He wanted all of her—her laughter, her smiles, and yes, even her hatred. He wanted her, and he meant to have her.

If he was a mortal man, he could go back and kick in the door, if necessary. However, since he was Nosferatu, breaking down the door would be little more than an empty gesture since he couldn't go inside unless she invited him, and she wasn't likely to do that in her present state of mind. He had no explanation for the odd effect thresholds had on the Undead, but he knew from experience that they effectively repelled his kind. Logical or not, thresholds possessed a Supernatural power of their own.

Of course, even though he couldn't force his way into her house, he could always hypnotize her and call her to him. With his preternatural power, he could compel her to do anything he wished, but there was damned little pleasure in that, he thought irritably. Might as well make love to a robot.

Muttering an oath, he began to pace back and forth in front of her house. He was a Vampire, the most powerful creature on the face of the earth, kept from what he wanted by a stubborn woman and a slab of wood.

But not for long.

Chapter Fourteen

Savanah couldn't sleep. She had taken a long, hot bath, hoping it would relax her, slipped into her favorite comfy PJs and a fluffy white robe, then drank a cup of herbal tea laced with honey and a touch of brandy, but sleep wouldn't come.

Rising, she went into her father's bedroom and curled up in the easy chair next to the window. Sitting there, with her legs folded beneath her and one hand clasped around her mother's silver crucifix, she made a mental list of everyone her father had known. It was possible that a complete stranger had killed him, but highly unlikely. Murders were usually committed by a family member or a friend of the victim. Since Savanah hadn't done it, the only family left was her father's brother, Arthur, who lived in New York City, and his cousin, Frank, who was somewhere in the jungles of Brazil. As for acquaintances, there were too many to name.

Who would have wanted her father dead? And why? If only she knew what her father had been working on, it might have given her a clue, but she had no idea what story he had been pursuing, no way of knowing if there was any connection between his job and his death.

She reread the letter he had left for her. Maybe it hadn't been an acquaintance or anyone connected with the story he had been working on. Maybe he had been killed by a Vampire. But there hadn't been any telltale bites on his neck. . . .

Savanah frowned. One of the books had mentioned that Vampires didn't always bite their victims in the neck.

Suddenly wide-awake, she ran into her office and turned on the light. Being a reporter, she had friends in some strange places, and one of them worked nights in the morgue.

Vance Rutherford answered on the first ring. "Rutherford, County Morgue."

"Hi, Vance, it's me, Savanah."

"Hey, girl, you're up late. I've been meaning to call you, but, well . . ."

"Thanks, Vance. Listen, I need a favor." Savanah took a deep breath. "Do you have my . . . my father's records there?"

"Sure. Listen, I'm really sorry about what happened. . . ."

"I know. Could you see if there's any mention in the report about bite marks?"

"Bite marks?" She heard the frown in his voice. "What kind of bite marks?"

"Like from a Vampire."

There was a long silence on the other end of the line before Vance said, "Sure. Hang on."

Savanah prayed she was wrong, but it was the only answer that made any sense. There had been no signs of a struggle, no bloodstains on the floor, no knife wound, no gunshot wound. Thus far, the coroner hadn't determined the cause of death.

"You there?"

"Yes." She took a deep breath. "Is there . . . ?"

"The coroner's report said there was very little blood left in the body. The only injuries he found were a shallow cut on the back of the deceased's . . ." Vance cleared his throat. "On the back of your father's head, and two small puncture wounds on the inside of his left arm, just below his elbow." Vance muttered an oath. "You don't think the Supernaturals are at it again, do you?"

"I don't know. I hope not."

"Me, too. I was just a teenager back then, but I remember those days. My old lady wouldn't let me out of the house after dark. Sure put a cramp in my love life." He cleared his throat, as though realizing that levity was out of line at the moment. "Anything else I can do for you?"

"No. Thanks, Vance, you've been a big help."

"Don't mention it."

She paused a moment before asking, "Have there been any other suspicious deaths in the last month or so?"

"I don't know. I've been on vacation. I just got back to work a couple of days ago. Hang on and I'll check."

Savanah heard the faint tap of computer keys, then a low whistle.

"Damn! We've had five deaths similar to your father's in the last three weeks, and two cases where the victims were mutilated."

Savanah frowned. Seven suspicious deaths in the last three weeks and she hadn't heard about them? Why had their deaths been kept from the public?

"Can you hang on a minute, Vance?"

"Sure, quiet as a tomb here. Oh, sorry."

Savanah carried the phone to her computer. It took only a few minutes to call up the newspaper's files. "Vance, there were only three deaths listed in the obits during that time—Cecilia Roger's husband, who died of old age, Bart Matthews, who died in a car accident, and Marlynn Steffner, who passed away after a heart attack. There's no mention of any suspicious deaths."

"Maybe because they were all strangers in town."

"All of them?"

"Yeah." She heard Vance typing furiously. "Four of them were college kids from back East. Their bodies were sent home after a preliminary investigation. Two were vagrants with no ID. One was an antique dealer from River's Edge."

"Thanks, Vance."

Savanah hung up, then sat there, feeling numb. Her father had been killed by a Vampire. Why? The war between the Vampires and the Werewolves had ended years ago. She had been a child then, hardly aware of what was going on in the world beyond her home and school. She knew now that her parents had shielded her from the worst of it. They hadn't watched the news when she was in the room, they had stopped taking the daily paper, thereby sparing her from seeing any pictures or headlines that might have upset her, or prompted questions they didn't want to answer. When the war ended, the Supernatural creatures had all just sort of faded into the woodwork. Savanah had no idea which side, if any, had won the battle for supremacy, or why the war had abruptly ended. Life had returned to normal and now, eighteen years later, it had been mostly forgotten.

She blew out a sigh. Even if a Vampire had killed her father, why now, after all this time? According to the information in the books, the last time a Vampire had been destroyed in Kelton had been shortly before the war between the Vampires and the Werewolves ended. The hunter credited with the kill was Barbara Gentry. Her mother had been killed by an unknown Vampire six months later. Since then, hunters had destroyed a few Vampires and Werewolves in other parts of the country, mostly in big cities, but there hadn't been any paranormal activity to speak of in Kelton.

Until Rane came to town.

And now her father was dead.

"No." She refused to believe that Rane had had anything to do with her father's death. Rane might be a Vampire, a killer, but surely he wouldn't have murdered her father. But what about the other seven deaths? Was he responsible for those?

Shutting down her computer, she went into the kitchen and made another cup of tea, then went into the living room and turned on the satellite screen. She surfed through the channels until she found an old movie, but she couldn't concentrate on the images in front of her, couldn't forget that her father was dead and that Rane might have killed him.

She was dozing when the doorbell rang. Startled, she jerked upright and glanced at the clock. It was after midnight. Who would be coming to call at such an hour?

Thinking it was probably just some of the local high school kids playing ding-dong ditch, she gathered her robe around her and went to the door where she peered through the peephole.

"Rane." His name whispered past her lips. What on earth was he doing here?

"Open up, Savanah, I know you're in there."

How could he possibly know that? Folding her arms under her breasts, she backed away from the door, her heart pounding loudly in her ears.

"Dammit, Savanah, open the door."

She stood there, determined not to answer. There was

no way he could know she was home. Even with a light on and her car in the driveway, that didn't mean she was home. She could have left a lamp burning and gone out on a date . . . even she didn't believe that, but it was still possible.

"Savanah, I know you're there. I can hear you breathing."

"Go away, Rane. Please, just go away."

"You're in danger."

"I wouldn't be if you would just go away!"

"Not from me," he said, his voice edged with impatience. "Dammit, I'm not going to hurt you."

"Right," Savanah muttered. "Everyone who believes that, raise your hand."

"Have I ever hurt you?"

"No, but I didn't know what you were before." Even though she was pretty sure he couldn't enter the house, she wished suddenly that she had a wooden stake close at hand.

"I haven't changed." He didn't raise his voice, but she heard him clearly. For a moment, she was tempted to open the door, but only for a moment. Her mother and father had both met violent ends. She didn't intend to join them, not until she had destroyed the Vampire who had killed her father. And if that Vampire was Rane Cordova . . . then so be it.

She just wished that the sound of his voice didn't warm her soul, or spark memories of his long, lean body melding with hers. She recalled all too clearly the touch of his hands on her skin, the way his body had quivered when he rose over her, the rock-hard feel of his biceps beneath her questing fingertips.

She shook the memories away. Vampire. Vampire.

Vampire! He was a monster, a creature of the night. Undead. She had to remember that and nothing else.

The Vampire has the ability to take on a pleasing shape . . . She had read that in one of the books. For all she knew, Rane Cordova's appearance was a sham. In reality, he could be ugly, hairy, and misshapen, like the pitiful creature in the movie *Nosferatu.*

"Savanah, I'm not leaving until you open the door."

His stubbornness made her mad, and then she smiled. "It'll be daylight soon," she said smugly, "and you'll have to leave."

She jumped as something—his fist, no doubt—slammed against the door frame. "Nothing to be afraid of, huh?"

"What can I say to convince you that I'm not going to hurt you?"

"I can't think of a thing."

"Fine, have it your way, but I'm not leaving here until the sun comes up. Your life's in danger, Savanah, but not from me. Someone is killing hunters. They killed your father." Having checked the morgue, he knew that for a fact. "They might have killed your mother, as well. What makes you think you won't be next?"

"I don't believe you. If someone was hunting the hunters, it would be in one of the books."

"Books?" Rane said sharply. "You mean there's more than one?"

"Yes," she replied absently. She hadn't finished reading the black book yet. Did it hold the key to the mystery of who was killing the hunters?

Pivoting on her heel, she hurried into the living room, plucked the black book off the end table and turned to the last few pages. And there, in her father's bold handwriting, she found a list of deceased Vampire hunters.

There was a period of fifteen years or so after the war ended where there were no violent deaths recorded. A few hunters had passed away from natural causes, one had been killed in a car accident, one had drowned. And then, starting about three years ago, there were reports of hunters being killed. At first, there had been only a couple deaths a year, not enough to cause alarm or suspicion. Then three or four. In the last year, eight hunters had been killed. Five were confirmed dead from Vampire attacks, three had died under suspicious circumstances, although there was no hard evidence linking their deaths to the Vampire community.

Was Rane right? Was she next on the list? Had he come to help her? Or was he the executioner? And how was she to know?

Stunned by what she had read, Savanah dropped the book on the sofa, then glanced at the front door, wondering again if Rane was to be her savior or her executioner. She couldn't avoid him forever unless she locked herself in the house every evening before the sun went down. Did she want to live as a prisoner in her own home for the rest of her life?

Did she want to die tonight? Or worse, become what he was?

She stood there a moment, wondering what she should do, and then she heard Rane's voice in her mind. Unable to resist his command, compelled by an irresistible power she didn't understand, she picked up both of the books, opened the front door, and crossed the threshold.

Chapter Fifteen

Rane experienced a sharp twinge of guilt as he compelled Savanah to do his bidding, but he quickly swept it aside. If she hadn't been so stubborn, he wouldn't have had to resort to using his preternatural powers. But it was the only way he could think of to get her out of the house, to prove that he meant her no harm. She could hate him if she wished. He could live with that. What he couldn't live with was the thought of her being prey for one of his kind, or worse, being turned by anyone but himself.

Taking her into his arms, he willed the two of them to his rented bungalow. Inside, he turned on the lights; he was at home in the dark, but he didn't want to frighten her if he could help it. A flicker of Supernatural power secured the door and the windows, assuring him that she couldn't leave until he was ready for her to do so. When that was done, he took both of the books from her hands and quickly thumbed through first one and then the other. No wonder her father had been murdered. Rane could think of any number of Vampires who would kill to keep those books out of human hands.

Muttering an oath, he slid the books under the sofa,

and then he freed Savanah's mind from his compulsion and waited for the explosion.

It wasn't long in coming.

Savanah turned on him with a vengeance. "What did you do to me?" she demanded, her hands fisted on her hips. "Why did you bring me here?" She glanced around. "Where are my books?"

For all her bravado, he heard the underlying edge of fear in her voice. Not that he could blame her. Here, in his lair, she was alone and defenseless. He waited a moment before answering, letting that fact sink in.

"Damn you!" she exclaimed. "Answer me!"

"I brought you here to prove that you have nothing to fear from me."

"Fine, I'm going home." She held out her hand. "I want my mother's books."

"All in good time."

Shoulders back, Savanah marched to the front door and turned the handle. When nothing happened, she grabbed hold of the knob and gave it a hard yank, and then she twisted it back and forth.

When the door refused to open, she glared at him over her shoulder. "Let me out of here!"

"Not until you calm down."

"I am calm!"

"Yeah," he muttered dryly. "I can see that."

Arms crossed over her breasts, she turned to face him, her expression mutinous, her eyes blazing with fury. "All right, convince me and let me go. My father's funeral is in the morning."

Rane swore softly. "Savanah, listen to me. I'm a Vampire. I admit it, but I had nothing to do with the deaths of your parents, but I know who killed your father. . . ."

"What? Why didn't you tell me this before?" She

began to pace the floor. "Where is he? How do I find him? We need to call the police. . . ."

"Slow down, darlin'. I guess I said that wrong. I don't know who it is, but I caught her scent. I'll know it if I find it again. . . ."

"Her scent? You mean a woman killed my dad?"

"I think so."

"But why?" Savanah frowned. The possibility that the killer was a woman put a whole new spin on things. Had her father been having an affair she didn't know about? Had the two of them had a quarrel that turned violent? She dismissed the thought out of hand. She was grabbing at straws, hoping to explain away what she knew was the truth. In her heart, she knew a Vampire had killed her father, just as Rane had said. "Why?" It was a question she couldn't seem to stop asking.

"I don't know," Rane said, "but I've got a pretty good idea."

She stared up at him, her eyes welling with tears. "I don't understand any of this," she said, sniffling. "Why would anyone want to kill him? He was old and crippled and . . ."

"Shh." Rane moved toward her, wondering if she would accept comfort from him.

She didn't move when he wrapped his arms around her. Ramrod stiff, she stood in his embrace while tears ran down her cheeks and then, with a sob, she collapsed against him, warm and soft and vulnerable.

He held her a moment, then lifted her into his arms and carried her to the sofa. Taking a seat, he cradled her to his chest.

"I should be trying to kill you," she said, sniffling.

"I give you leave to try later."

She laughed through her tears. He took that for a good sign.

"I'm not going to hurt you, Savanah, I swear it."

"I don't think I care."

He chuckled softly. "Hey, talk like that's going to give Vampire hunters a bad name."

"I don't care," she said, wiping her eyes with the back of her hand. "I just want my dad back."

"I know." He stroked her hair, gentling her to his touch. She was vulnerable now, ripe for the taking, but as he held her, he came to the grim realization that he had been caught in his own trap, and that in the midst of seducing her, he had lost his own heart instead. Anyone who tried to harm Savanah would have to go through him first.

Rane swore softly. Since the night of his first kill, he had punished himself for what he was, for the lives he had taken. He had adhered to the mores of traditional Vampires. For years, he had spent the daylight hours resting inside a coffin, refusing to stir until sundown, even though there was no need. Like his brother, he could function during the day, undoubtedly a benefit of having a mortal woman for a mother, and a father who had been turned by the world's oldest Vampire. But even though he could be awake and active, he didn't have the power to walk in the sun's light. Years ago, Mara had offered to share her blood with him. Had he taken it, power straight from the source, so to speak, he would now be able to withstand the sun's light, at least for short periods of time, but he had refused her.

"Why?" she had asked. "Why would you deny yourself so great a gift?"

"Because," he had replied succinctly. "I don't deserve it."

"What foolishness is that?"

"I'm a Vampire, a creature of the night. I belong in the darkness, and that's where I'll stay."

Mara hadn't tried to change his mind. He was sorry now that she hadn't persuaded him, and even sorrier that she was currently somewhere in Egypt, no doubt resting in the earth of her homeland, leaving him no way to get in touch with her. Damn.

With a last sniff, Savanah sat up, putting some space between herself and Rane. Her gaze rested on the shriveled skin on the side of his face and neck. She had done that to him in a moment of anger and frustration.

"Does it still hurt?" she asked, surprised that his cheek wasn't still raw and red.

"Oh, yeah."

"I'm sorry, really I am. Will it leave a scar?" It would be a shame to mar that handsome profile.

"No." He lifted a hand to his cheek. "I'm a fast healer. By tomorrow night, the worst of the pain will have subsided. In a few days, the burns will be gone."

Remarkable, she thought. If her skin had been burned like that, it would have taken weeks to heal. "How long have you been a Vampire?"

"Almost ninety years."

He didn't look that old, of course, but then Vampires didn't age once they were turned.

"How is it possible for both of your parents to be Vampires?" The brown book had stated quite clearly that Vampires couldn't reproduce, but Rane's existence seemed to contradict that. She placed one hand over her stomach. She had been certain she couldn't be pregnant, but what if she was wrong?

"How do you know about my parents?" he asked.

"It's in one of the books."

Ah, yes, the books, Rane thought. Aloud, he said, "My father turned my mother after I was grown."

"Is Raphael Cordova your brother?"

Rane nodded, more certain than ever that the Vampire who had killed William Gentry had been looking for those accursed volumes.

"Did your father turn you, too?"

"No, being a Vampire was in my blood, and Rafe's, from the day we were born."

"How can that be?"

"My father had only been a Vampire a short time when he married my mother. It was his opinion that he had somehow retained enough of his humanity to father a child. Two, actually. Rafe and I are twins."

"Oh." Since Rane had been a Vampire for ninety years, it was doubtful he could have gotten her pregnant. "Why would a Vampire kill my father?"

"I should think that would be obvious," Rane said dryly. "Your father was a hunter." Even as he said the words, he wondered if that was the reason, or if Gentry had been killed because he refused to disclose the whereabouts of the books now resting under the sofa.

"But the war ended eighteen years ago. Why would anyone want to kill him now?"

"Eighteen years isn't long to a Vampire," Rane said.

Of course it wasn't, Savanah thought. She didn't know how long Vampires lived, but according to the black book, the Vampire, Mara, had lived for thousands of years with no end in sight.

Savanah tried to imagine what it would be like to live that long, but it was beyond her comprehension. These days, humans in good health could expect to live a hundred years or more, but to live for thousands of years . . . She wondered if Vampires ever got tired of living, of forever staying the same while the rest of the world evolved and grew older.

Curious, she put the question to Rane.

He frowned a moment before replying. "It depends on the Vampire. Like mortals, we're all different, colored by the lives we led before we were turned. Some of us pursue education to keep our minds active. Some give up entirely to the lust for blood. Others never fully accept the change. Yearning for their old lifestyle, feeling alienated by the Dark Trick, they usually destroy themselves."

"Do you have a lust for blood?"

Rane's gaze moved to the pulse beating strongly in her throat. "Always." He could see by her expression that the idea repulsed her on many levels.

"How can you do it? How can you prey on innocent people and drink their blood?"

"Once a Vampire is turned, it's normal. Only those who don't fully accept what they've become, or who try to cling to their humanity, are bothered by it."

Savanah lifted a hand to her throat. "Have you ever wanted to drink my blood?"

"Every night." He met her gaze, wondering what her reaction would be if she knew he had already tasted her—tasted her and yearned for more. He smiled inwardly. There was no need to wonder what her reaction would be. She would doubtless grab a stake and plunge it into his heart.

"Are there other Vampires in Kelton?"

"Would you expect me to tell you if there were?"

"No, I guess not." She rubbed her hands over her arms. "Have you fully accepted being a Vampire?"

"I had little choice in the matter."

"Oh, right, I forgot. Do you like it, being a Vampire?"

Rane shrugged. "I scarcely remember any other way of

life." He had forgotten what the sun felt like on his skin, what mortal food tasted like, what it was like to sleep at night. He had never had a regular job, and although he had a first-rate education, there weren't many nighttime jobs that appealed to him. He had started pretending to be a magician because he could pick and choose where and when he wished to perform, and because he could work nights. Unlike his grandfather, he didn't have a great deal of wealth. He didn't own property or a home, didn't own much more than his car and his clothing, but then, he didn't need much, and his meals were free.

"Do you sleep in a coffin?"

"Not anymore." Once he had decided to become a traveling magician, taking his rest in a casket became impractical.

"What do you sleep in now?"

"My underwear," he replied, purposefully mistaking her meaning. He grinned when she scowled at him. "A bed, like most of my kind." These days, most of the Undead had forsaken coffins for the comfort and roominess of king-size beds.

"Well, this has been very educational," Savanah remarked.

"Are you convinced that I'm not going to hurt you?"

"I guess so." She bit down on the inside corner of her lip, hesitant to ask the next question, but needing to be sure. "I couldn't be pregnant, could I?"

"No, you don't have to worry about that."

To her chagrin, she felt more regret than relief.

"I suppose you're hating yourself now for sleeping with a monster, and grateful that you don't have to worry about carrying my child."

She looked up, surprised by the undercurrent of hurt in his voice. "Rane . . ."

"I know what I am, Savanah. I know what you're feeling. I know what you're thinking, probably a hell of a lot better than you do."

"You think so?" She stabbed a finger against his chest. "Do you really think so?"

"You're repulsed by what I am and what I do to survive. You're disgusted because you took me to your bed, you're wondering if I drank your blood . . ." He swore softly. He hadn't meant to mention that again.

Savanah blinked at him, and then her eyes narrowed. "Did you? Drink my blood?"

He went still, debating whether to tell her the truth or a lie. "I wouldn't call it a drink, exactly," he replied slowly. "More of a small taste."

She stared at him. "When? How many times? Why don't I remember it?"

"Several times, and you don't remember it because I didn't want you to, because I didn't want to see the look in your eyes that I see now."

"And you don't call stealing my blood hurting me?"

"No."

"I want to go home now."

"And I want you to stay here."

"You said I could go home when I was convinced you weren't going to hurt me. And since you don't consider stealing my blood hurting me, then I believe you. So give me my books and let me go."

"It's dangerous for you to be there alone, at night. And even more dangerous for you to have those damn books."

Savanah stared at Rane a moment. *The books,* she thought. *Of course.* Her father's murderer must have been looking for them. Why hadn't she realized that sooner?

"You can sleep here tonight," Rane said, "and go home in the morning."

She would have argued, but she could tell by the obdurate expression on his face that it wouldn't do her the least bit of good. "Fine, I'll sleep on the sofa."

"As you wish. I'll get you a pillow and a blanket."

"Fine."

"I never should have laughed at you, Savanah Gentry," he said, rising. "You have the heart of a warrior. I think you'll put every other hunter that ever lived to shame." He bowed in her direction, and then left the room.

Savanah stared after him. So, he thought she had the heart of a warrior, did he? Whether it was true or not remained to be seen. Still, she thought it might be the nicest compliment she had ever received.

She just hoped he was right.

Chapter Sixteen

Unable to sleep, Savanah flopped over onto her back and stared up at the ceiling. So much had happened in the last few weeks. She had met Rane. She had lost her father. She had discovered that her parents were Vampire hunters, and that the man she was falling in love with, the man she had slept with all too soon, was a Vampire.

And tomorrow morning, her father would be laid to rest. She couldn't believe he was gone, that the one constant in her life had been taken from her. Tears burned the backs of her eyes. William Gentry had been a good provider, a loving husband and father. He had taught her right from wrong, told her what he expected, and let her make her own mistakes. He had trusted her judgment, and on those occasions when she had made the wrong decision, he had wiped her tears and put her on her feet again, admonishing her to remember what she had learned so she didn't make the same mistake twice. He had praised her talents and encouraged her in everything she put her mind to, and now he was gone.

Tomorrow, she would pay her last respects and then, for the first time in her life, she would be truly alone.

Turning onto her side, she buried her face in the pillow and let the tears flow.

Savanah awoke late after a long and restless night. Her dreams had been dark and unsettling. At first, she had wandered through gray mists and ever-changing shadows, searching for something that was just out of reach, and then she had started running, hurrying through the darkness as if her life depended on it, fleeing from a faceless wraith clad in long black robes. Death, she thought, she had been running from Death.

Sitting up, she clutched the pillow to her chest. Was it Death who had pursued her so relentlessly, she wondered, or Rane?

A glance at her watch told her she didn't have time to worry about it; her father's funeral was only two hours away.

Tossing the pillow aside, she wasted several minutes looking for her mother's books. She wasn't surprised when she couldn't find them. For all she knew, Rane had put some sort of Supernatural hex on the volumes. Drat the man's Supernatural abilities. She could be looking right at the books and not know it.

With a sigh of exasperation, she headed for the door, only to stop short as two thoughts crossed her mind, the first coming hard on the heels of the second. She was wearing her PJs and a robe, and her car was at home. Tapping her foot, she glanced around the room. Spying Rane's cell phone, she picked it up to call a cab, only then noticing the note beneath the phone.

Savanah, take my car. It's parked in the garage off the kitchen. The key is in the ignition. I'll pick it up tonight. R.

Barefooted, she padded into the kitchen. In passing, she noted that the room was empty save for an electric stove and a refrigerator. She wondered why a Vampire would have need of either one, and then remembered he was renting the house, so the appliances had most likely come with the place.

It wasn't until she was driving home that she realized she had missed a pair of golden opportunities—a rare opportunity to see a Vampire at rest, and the chance to make her first kill.

The sky was gray and there was a hint of rain in the air as Savanah picked her way around the tombstones to her father's final resting place. Her uncle Arthur trailed at her heels. He had called earlier, asking if he could drive her to the funeral.

The service at the church had been well-attended by those she and her father worked with at the newspaper. Uncle Arthur had given the eulogy.

Savanah blinked back her tears as she stared at the bronze casket covered by a blanket of red and white roses.

She scarcely heard the words that were spoken over the grave, felt numb as she shook hands and received condolences from her friends and coworkers.

She stood at the graveside long after the mourners had left, unable to tear herself away.

"Savanah? Are you ready to go?"

At the sound of her uncle's voice, Savanah glanced over her shoulder. Arthur Gentry was ten years older than her father and had a net worth of several million dollars. He lived in a swanky penthouse in New York, leased a new car every year, and had a summer home at Hyannisport. From time to time, she had seen his picture online or in the New York papers, always with a beautiful woman on his arm, but rarely the same woman. Savanah had often wondered why her uncle had never married; it seemed he could have his pick of the ladies.

The last time Savanah had seen her uncle had been at her mother's funeral. When she called to tell him of her father's passing, she had been surprised when her uncle said he was flying in for the service. Arthur and her father had had a bitter quarrel over thirty years ago, and as far as Savanah knew, they had barely spoken a word to each other since. Her father had never told her what the fight was about, but it hardly mattered now.

"He was a good man," Arthur remarked quietly. "An honorable man. I'm sorry for the years we spent apart."

"What did you fight about?"

He hesitated, as though debating whether or not he should tell her, and then said, "Your mother. Come on, let's go get a drink."

Savanah followed him to where his rental car, a new Lincoln convertible, was parked, waited while he opened the door for her, then ducked inside. The interior was luxurious, outfitted with every extra imaginable.

"Any place in particular you'd care to go?" Arthur asked.

Savanah gave him directions to the club where Rane had taken her, but when they reached the place where it should have been, it wasn't there.

"That's odd," she remarked. "I was sure this was the address."

"No matter," Arthur said, "we'll find a place."

A short time later, he pulled into the parking lot of Sid's Tap Room, handed her out of the car, and followed her inside. Savanah had only been to Sid's once before.

It was a hangout for the older crowd, mostly retired men who wanted to get out of the house for a few hours. There was a pool table in one corner. Pictures of prominent sports figures lined the walls. Arthur ordered a shot and a beer. Savanah asked for a white wine spritzer.

"Why did you and Dad fight over my mother?" Savanah asked.

"Because I was in love with her, too."

"You were?"

He nodded.

"Is that why you never married?"

"Yeah. I'd been in love with the most wonderful woman in the world. I never found anyone who could take her place, and I wasn't willing to settle for anything less." He shook his head. "I begged her to marry me. I could have given her the world, but she didn't want the world. She wanted Will."

"But after so long . . ." Savanah shook her head. "Surely there have been other women you cared for."

"Two or three, but they couldn't hold a candle to your mother, and after a while . . ." He shrugged. "After a while I was too set in my ways to change, and too stubborn to settle for second best."

Their drinks arrived then. Arthur tossed back the whiskey as if he couldn't go another minute without it, then stared into the empty shot glass. "I miss her every damn day. My only consolation, and it's damned little, is that Will made her happy." He picked up his beer and took a long drink. "At least they're together now."

It was late afternoon when Arthur drove Savanah home.

"Would you like to come in?" she asked. "We could order some takeout for dinner."

"No, thanks, I've got a plane to catch."

"So soon?"

"Too many memories here," Arthur said, glancing past her to the house. "If you ever need anything, call me." Taking her hand, he gave it a squeeze. "I mean it, Savanah. Anything at all, day or night. Whatever I have is yours."

"Thank you. And thank you for coming. It meant a lot to me to have you here."

Arthur Gentry blew out a heavy sigh, then patted her arm. "I just wish I hadn't let my pride keep me away from you and your father for so long. Keep in touch with your old uncle now, hear?"

"I will." Leaning toward him, she kissed him on the cheek, murmured "Good-bye, Uncle," and got out of the car.

Standing on the sidewalk, she watched him drive away, thinking that a new car every year and millions of dollars in the bank didn't guarantee happiness.

Feeling more alone than she ever had in her life, she walked up the stairs to the porch, unlocked the front door, and stepped inside.

The silence of the house engulfed her; the emptiness screamed in her ears. Never again would she hear her father's voice welcoming her home or asking how her day had gone. Never again would she share a quiet evening with him, or engage in a lively discussion about the day's events. Should she marry, he wouldn't be there to walk her down the aisle. He would never see his grandchildren, never hold a granddaughter on his lap, or take a grandson fishing. Her father was gone, stolen from her by some blood-thirsty creature of the night.

After closing and locking the door behind her, she retrieved her mother's Vampire hunting kit from under the bed and went through it piece by gruesome piece, familiarizing herself with each item. The stakes were long, smooth, and sturdy, the points very sharp. The mallet was heavier than it looked. Was it only her imagination, or did the vials of holy water feel warm to the touch? A wave of revulsion swept through her as she picked up a small hand-saw. She told herself she could do whatever was necessary to avenge her father, but inwardly she was assailed by doubts. Too bad she wasn't hunting Werewolves, she thought with a morbid grin. You could kill them from a distance with a silver bullet. So much easier and less messy than driving a wooden stake into a creature's heart, or cutting off its head.

It wasn't until later that evening, as she relaxed in the bathtub, that she remembered being unable to find the nightclub where Rane had taken her. After getting out of the tub, she slipped on her robe, went downstairs, and pulled the phone book from the desk drawer.

"Hell's Hollow," she murmured, thumbing through the pages. "Where are you?"

It was nowhere to be found. She went through the *H*'s twice, but to no avail. There was no listing for Hell's Hollow. Picking up her cell phone, she dialed Information. They had no listing.

Frowning, Savanah tapped her fingers on the desktop. The nightclub existed. She had been there. Why was there no listing? And why hadn't she been able to find the place this afternoon?

The answer popped into her mind. Because Rane didn't want her to. And why wouldn't he want her to find it again? Because it was a Vampire hangout, of course. How could she have been so blind? No doubt everyone in the club had been a Vampire or dating one.

The thought had no sooner crossed her mind than the doorbell rang. She knew it was Rane before she answered the door.

"Speak of the devil, and he appears," she murmured as she went to let him in.

Rane's gaze moved over Savanah, noting the sadness in her eyes. He had never lost anyone he loved. Save for the pain of separating himself from his family, he had never experienced grief.

Savanah frowned when he continued to stand on the porch. "Are you coming in?"

"Are you inviting me?"

"What?" She frowned at him a moment; then, remembering that she had rescinded her invitation, she said, "I forgot. Come on in."

He followed her into the living room, sat beside her on the sofa. Her sorrow was a palpable presence in the room. Wordlessly, he opened his arms.

Savanah took refuge in his embrace, finding solace in the strength of his arms around her, in the presence of another soul. She frowned, wondering if Vampires even had a soul, but at the moment, it didn't matter. She didn't want to be alone with her grief.

They sat in silence for a time. Finally, unable to hold back her tears, Savanah buried her face in the hollow of his shoulder and wept.

Rane blew out a sigh. At a loss for words, he stroked her back, brushed a kiss across the top of her head. Her hair was soft and smelled of strawberries.

"I'm sorry," Savanah murmured as she sat up. "I didn't mean to cry all over you."

"I don't mind."

"I just can't believe he's gone," she said, sniffling. "Have you ever lost anyone?"

"No."

"Have you ever loved anyone?"

"Just my family."

Savanah reached for a tissue from the box on the end table. She wiped her eyes and blew her nose. "Haven't you ever been in love?"

"You mean besides now?"

She looked up at him, startled by his words. "What do you mean?"

"I mean I'm in love with you." It was wrong, and he knew it. He had no right to love her, or any woman. He had done despicable things, horrible things, for which he would find no forgiveness in this life or the next. But the fact remained that he had fallen in love with her. He shrugged. "I thought you should know."

"Rane . . ."

"You must have known, or at least suspected."

"I guess so, but . . ."

"The idea displeases you."

"No, but . . ."

"But I'm a Vampire and you're a hunter," he finished for her. "And you're thinking it's going to make it difficult to take my head."

"Rane, what a terrible thing to say!"

"Maybe, but it's what you're thinking, isn't it?"

"It crossed my mind," she admitted.

"I give you leave to try."

He had told her that once before, she thought, and not so long ago.

"I need to find the Vampire who killed my father," she said, determination replacing her tears. "She's not going to get away with it."

"How are you going to find her?"

"I don't know. I don't suppose you'd help me."

"I might."

"Would you? Really?" She looked at him, her eyes

filled with hope. "I mean . . . really? You'd help me hunt one of your own?"

He grunted softly. "She's not 'one of my own.'"

"But she's a Vampire?"

"So it seems."

"Where are my mother's books?"

"In a safe place."

"Where?"

"It's better if you don't know."

Her brows drew together in a frown. "They're my books now," she said, her words slow and deliberate. "I want them back." She had very little that had belonged to her mother. The books weren't the kind of thing a mother usually passed down to her daughter, but one of them had been written by her mom and that, more than any other reason, made it important to her.

"I'll give them back to you when I'm convinced you're out of danger."

"You promise?"

He nodded.

"Say it."

"I promise," he said with a wry grin.

She wasn't sure she believed him, but what other choice did she have?

"It isn't safe for you to stay here." He ran his fingertips up and down her arm. "I want you to come with me."

"I can't just leave. I've got to settle my father's affairs. I've got a job, and—"

"None of that matters now. You won't be safe here as long as that Vampire knows where you live."

"But she can't come in unless I invite her."

"She's already had an invitation."

Savanah frowned, and then murmured, "Oh," with the

realization that her father had unknowingly invited his murderer into the house. "Well, I'll just rescind it."

Rane shook his head. "She's not working alone."

"How do you know?"

"I picked up the scent of a Werewolf on your property. I don't know if they were working together or not, but I'd rather be safe now than sorry later."

"A Werewolf wouldn't need an invitation, would he? Or she?"

"No."

She thought it over for a moment, then asked, "Where do you want to go?"

He shrugged. "It doesn't matter. We can go anywhere you want, so long as you don't tell anyone where you'll be."

"I can't hide forever," she said, and sighed. "I'll call Mr. Van Black and ask him if I can have more time off. Tomorrow's Thursday. We can leave Friday night, if you want. Or Saturday." The more she thought about leaving town, the better it sounded. It might be good to get away for a while.

"Friday night," Rane decided. "We'll leave at sundown."

Savanah nodded.

"All you have to do now is decide where you want to go."

"I'll think about it."

"In the meantime, I think you should get something to eat."

"I'm not hungry."

"You need to eat."

She didn't feel like arguing and she didn't feel like cooking. With a huff of annoyance, she went in search of her cell phone, thinking that pizza didn't sound too bad.

Life was never what you expected, she thought as she waited for the pizza place to answer. Here she was, planning to go away with a man for the first time in her life, but not for any of the reasons she would have thought.

No, she was going off with a man who wasn't really a man at all, and not for some romantic rendezvous in an exotic locale. No, not Savanah Gentry. She was running away from a murderer, and not just any old murderer, but one that was a Vampire, or perhaps a Werewolf.

Oh, yes, she thought again. Life was strange, indeed.

Chapter Seventeen

"Why isn't she dead?"

"He's always there with her."

Clive slammed his fist on the table, muttered an oath as the wood cracked beneath his hand. Damn the Cordova men. They protected their women like knights of old. An admirable quality, to be sure, but damned annoying at the moment.

"I don't know, Clive," Tasha said. "Maybe you'll have to do this one yourself."

He grunted softly. "Perhaps." But there was no hurry. He knew where the woman lived. It was doubtful she would be leaving home anytime soon. After all, she had just buried her father. Being mortal, she would need time to grieve, time to go through her father's belongings and decide what to keep and what to part with.

Or perhaps he would wait and see if Cordova's ardor for Savanah Gentry cooled.

In the meantime, there were other hunters out there, hunters with years of experience to their credit, which made them far more dangerous than William Gentry's un-learned daughter.

Chapter Eighteen

Savanah hadn't planned to go to work the day after the funeral, intending to use the time to clean the house and pack for her trip with Rane, but when she got up that morning, the idea of spending the day at home alone held no appeal. Not only that, but going into the office would give her a chance to clear up a few matters still pending, matters that couldn't be handled over the phone.

Yesterday, at the graveside, Mr. Van Black had told her to take as much time off as she needed. She had thanked him and said a week would be fine. But that was before Rane had convinced her that her life was in danger. When she got to work, she would tell Mr. Van Black that she had decided to take an extended leave of absence.

In the shower, she found herself wondering where Rane had gone. He had stayed the night with her last night. After she had eaten dinner, they had spent what was left of the evening watching a late movie, and then she had gone to bed. He had stretched out on the bed beside her, on top of the covers. The fact that they weren't going to make love filled her with relief and regret. On one hand, it would have been nice to lose herself in his embrace, to forget, if only for a short time, the horrors of the last few days. On the other hand, she wasn't quite ready to make love to Rane again now that she knew what he was. To be honest, she wasn't sure if she would ever be ready.

Savanah dressed quickly, then went downstairs, her heart skipping a beat when she saw Rane sitting on the sofa watching an early-morning news program.

She stared at him a moment, then glanced out the window. Yes, the sun was up. And so was he. How was that possible? Everything she had ever read about Vampires said they were compelled to seek their coffins at sunrise, and the sun had been up for hours.

Maybe he wasn't really a Vampire. The thought made her hopeful heart skip a beat. "Rane . . . ?"

He glanced at her over his shoulder. "Good morning."

"I thought . . . How can you be awake?" Hardly daring to breathe, she waited for his answer, hoping he would tell her he had been playing some horrible joke, that he wasn't really a Vampire at all, just a shape-shifter, as he had said.

He shrugged. "The sun doesn't affect me the way it does most Vampires. I don't know why. Probably because my mother was mortal."

She frowned at him. "So, you can go out during the day?"

"No, but I don't have to take my rest until I'm ready."

She pondered that a moment, and then frowned. "If you can't leave the house, where are you going to . . . ah . . . you know?"

He lifted one brow, amused by her rising concern for where he intended to succumb to the Dark Sleep. "Will it bother you if I rest here?"

"I don't know. I've never had a Vampire for a house-guest."

"I'm not particularly crazy about the idea of sleeping in a hunter's house, either," he remarked dryly.

"Talk about strange bedfellows," Savanah muttered.

"I promise not to bite you if you promise not to take my head."

Savanah grimaced at the grisly image. "It's a deal."

Rane took notice of her attire for the first time and frowned. "Where do you think you're going?"

"To work, of course."

"Oh, no, I don't think so."

"Why not?"

"I don't want you going anywhere alone."

"I went to my father's funeral."

He shrugged. "You couldn't very well avoid that. And you weren't alone. Your uncle was with you."

"I can call a cab. I should be safe enough at the *Chronicle* if I stay inside. Jolie can bring me home."

"No."

"Do you really think a Werewolf will attack me in broad daylight? There haven't been any reports of attacks during the day."

"There's a first time for everything. Besides, I'm sure no one expects you to go to the office today."

He was right, of course. Even though she was certain it would be perfectly safe for her to go to work, there was no point in taking chances when she didn't have to. Still . . .

As if sensing her indecision, Rane said, "I went outside late last night, after you had gone to bed. The Vampire who killed your father has been snooping around again, and the Werewolf, too."

His words sent a cold chill down her spine. "How do you know?"

"Their scent was fresh. One of them left a footprint in the dirt alongside the house. It can't be a coincidence that they're showing up at the same time. They've got to be working together."

Filled with a sudden sense of urgency, she said, "Let's leave tonight."

Savanah went through the items in her suitcase a second time, wondering if she had packed more than she needed, then decided it was better to take too much rather than too little. For one thing, Rane hadn't said how long they would be gone, and she still wasn't sure where she wanted to go. Exotic locales flitted through her mind: Hawaii, Rome, Bora Bora, Cabo, Portugal. They all appealed to her, yet on some deep level she didn't quite understand, she was reluctant to leave the country. Frowning, she tried to think of someplace a little closer to home, some vacation spot where she had always wanted to go. Graceland? The giant redwood forest in Northern California? Yellowstone? Disneyland?

Savanah shook her head. She couldn't imagine Rane wanting to visit any of those places; the thought of a Vampire touring Disneyland struck her as ludicrous, somehow. She had to grin when she pictured him in the Haunted Mansion. It was one ride where he would fit right in!

She slipped her mother's Vampire kit under the layers of her clothing before closing the suitcase, then checked her overnight bag. She had packed everything she needed, save for her comb, brush, make-up, and toothbrush; she would add those later.

With nothing else to do, she decided to change the sheets on her bed. While carrying them to the laundry room, she paused outside her father's bedroom. Rane slept inside. Feeling like Pandora, she put her hand on the knob, then hesitated. Did she really want to see him when he was caught in the sleep of the Undead? Did Vampires dream? Would he know if she opened the door and peeked inside? Would he look like he was sleeping, or would he look like a corpse, pale and unmoving? An image of her father as she had last seen him flashed through her mind, and with it a knifelike stab of grief.

She closed her eyes for a moment, then moved on down the hallway to the laundry room, which was located adjacent to the garage at the back of the house.

Blinking back her tears, she dumped the sheets into the washing machine, added soap, and turned the dial to Wash. How had her life turned into such a nightmare? Her mother and father had both been killed by Vampires. How could she be in love with such an odious creature?

Leaving the laundry room, she paused again outside her father's door. Overcome by her curiosity, she took a deep breath and pushed the door open just enough to peek inside.

The first thing she noticed was that Rane had covered the room's single window with the bedspread so that no light entered the room.

He lay on the top of the blankets, his eyes closed, one arm curled behind his head, the other resting at his side. He had removed his shirt, shoes and socks. From where she stood, she couldn't tell if he was breathing. If she called his name, would he hear her? Her gaze moved over him, her fingers yearning to delve into his thick black hair, to trace the outline of his broad shoulders, to run her palms over his muscular chest and six-pack abs. How did he stay in such good shape? Did Vampires work out? Somehow, she didn't think so, yet she knew from experience that he was firm and fit. If only things were different. If she wasn't mourning her father, if Rane was

an ordinary man, she would have crawled into bed
beside him and awakened him with a kiss.

With her curiosity satisfied, she quietly closed the door
and went upstairs to her own room.

At least he didn't look dead. She was grateful for that.
And grateful that the burns on his cheek and neck had
disappeared, just as he had said they would.

But he was still a Vampire, and Vampires killed to stay
alive. How many lives had he taken in the last week? In the
last ninety years? The possibilities were staggering. Even
if he had to feed only once a month, he would have killed
over a thousand people. And if he fed every night . . .

Until this moment, she hadn't really let herself think
about his feeding habits. He had said he'd "tasted" her.
She wasn't exactly sure what that meant, but obviously
he hadn't had to kill her to do so. Maybe he had never
killed anyone. Maybe all he needed to survive was a
"taste" now and then. But even as she tried to convince
herself of that fact, she knew it wasn't true. One of her
mother's books had described, in lurid detail, how Vampires fed off their victims.

Savanah stared at her reflection in the mirror above her
dresser, imagining Rane bending over her neck, his eyes
glowing red, his arms imprisoning her as he sank his
fangs into her throat. . . . Of course, he would cast no reflection. She wondered how female Vampires applied
their make-up without looking in a mirror. How did they
try out a new hairstyle, or decide on new clothes if they
couldn't see how they looked? She remembered the night
she and Rane had gone to the mall and he had bought that
long black duster that looked so good on him. She now
knew why he hadn't wanted to check it out in the mirror.

How could she be in love with one of the very creatures she was supposed to destroy?

* * *

With a sigh, Rane rolled onto his side. He had known that, sooner or later, Savanah's curiosity would get the best of her. She was a newspaper reporter and she was a woman. Add the fact that she was also thinking of becoming a hunter into the mix and her snooping was inevitable. He knew he was taking a chance, resting in her home, but at the moment it wasn't his life he was concerned about, but hers. And if she decided to drive a stake into his heart, well, so be it. Better to be sent to hell by the hand of a beautiful woman than by some heartless, no-account hunter.

He swore softly. Why were a Werewolf and a Vampire working together? Or were they? He could understand why a Vampire wanted the books now hidden under the spare tire in the trunk of his car, but of what interest would the volumes be to a Werewolf? Was he wrong to assume the only reason Savanah was in danger was because the books now belonged to her? What other reason could there be? Since she hadn't yet made a kill, he was reasonably certain that he was the only one who knew that Savanah intended to follow in her father's footsteps. Not that it mattered. So long as she was in danger, he intended to do everything in his power to keep her safe.

Since Savanah couldn't decide where she wanted to go, Rane made the decision for her.

"The mountains," Savanah exclaimed. "You have a place in the mountains?" She couldn't have been more surprised if he had sprouted horns and a tail.

Rane grinned at her. "It's not mine. It belongs to an old friend of the family." In point of fact, it was Mara's place. Through the years, she had acquired property in a number of towns and cities, not only in the States, but in a good many foreign countries, as well.

"The mountains," Savanah muttered, and went back upstairs to pack some warmer clothing.

An hour after sundown, they were ready to go. Rane had packed earlier that evening. It didn't take long to throw his clothes into a suitcase. Since he had no permanent home, he carried everything he owned in the trunk of his car. He had canceled his remaining tour dates and settled up with the owner of the house he had been renting.

He carried Savanah's bags outside, waited on the porch while Savanah locked the front door.

"My car or yours?" he asked.

"Yours," she answered without hesitation. Her car was nice and relatively new, but nothing like his.

Rane stowed their suitcases in the trunk, made sure her mother's books were where he had left them, and then slid behind the wheel. "Ready?"

Savanah bit down on her lower lip, then nodded. "Ready." She had canceled the newspaper, put a hold on her mail, informed Mr. Van Black that she had decided to take him up on his offer of an extended leave of absence.

Settling back in the seat, she sent a sideways glance at Rane, wondering what in the world had possessed her to think that going off to the mountains with a Vampire she hardly knew would be safer than staying home. But it was too late to worry about it now. For better or worse, she had put her life in his hands.

It was a beautiful drive, even in the dark. As the road wound ever higher, more and more stars were visible in the night sky. A full moon cast her light over the earth, bathing the tips of the mountains in silver splendor, while the car's headlights cut a wide swath through the darkness, occasionally startling a deer grazing in the meadow that stretched for miles along the side of the road.

Soft music came from the car stereo, lulling Savanah to sleep.

Rane took a deep breath, filling his nostrils with the scent of the woman beside him. He saw her clearly in the darkness. Her eyelashes lay like golden fans against her cheeks. Her hair fell over one shoulder in a fall of moon-shadowed silk, leaving the other side of her slender neck exposed to his view. The whisper of her life's blood flowing through her veins was like sweet music to his ears, the smell of it more enticing than the sight of her smooth, unblemished flesh. His gaze lingered in the hollow of her throat.

His hands clenched on the steering wheel. What madness had tempted him to bring her to this lonely place in the mountains? No one had come here in years. If he lost control of his hunger, there would be no one to save her, no one to hear her scream.

Chapter Nineteen

Savanah woke when the car came to a stop. "Are we here?"

"No. I thought you might want to buy a few things before we reach the cabin."

Glancing out the window, she saw that they were parked in front of a small market.

Rane followed her inside, then trailed behind her as she walked up and down the aisles, filling her cart with the basic necessities.

She shopped quickly and in less than half an hour, they were back on the road.

She was dozing when the car stopped a short time later.

Sitting up, she glanced out the window. To her left, surrounded by tall pines, sat a large white, two-story house with a slate-blue roof and a covered veranda. Beyond that was only darkness.

She looked at Rane. The word *Vampire* whispered through the back of her mind, sending a shiver of unease skittering down her spine. What was she doing here, with a man—a Vampire—she had known for only a few weeks? She told herself there was nothing to be afraid of.

He'd had numerous opportunities to drain her dry if he was so inclined. She told herself she was just being silly. She was tired from the drive. She had been under a lot of stress, what with her father's death and learning that Rane was a Vampire. But no matter how many excuses she made, she couldn't stifle that little innate twinge of fear that was experienced when creatures of prey were in the presence of a predator. And then she stiffened her spine as she remembered that she was a hunter, too! She had a sharpened stake in her handbag and a bottle of holy water in her coat pocket to prove it.

She forced a smile when Rane shut off the ignition and turned to face her.

"Second thoughts?" he asked.

"No," she said quickly. Too quickly. "Why?"

He smiled, a slow, sexy smile. "I hope you don't play poker."

"What does that mean?" she asked, frowning.

"It means your thoughts are as easy to read as print on a page."

She had forgotten he could read her mind. "That's not fair, you know."

"Honey, I don't have to read your mind to know what you're thinking. You don't trust me."

She started to deny it, but what was the point? He would know she was lying. So she went on the defensive instead. "Can you blame me? Vampires killed my parents, and—"

"Dammit, Savanah," he said quietly. "I didn't do it."

"I know that, but . . ."

"Forget it. I don't blame you for the way you feel. It's normal. Do you want to go home?"

"No."

He studied her face a moment, then got out of the car.

She watched him walk around the front of the car. Ever the gentleman, he opened the door for her. She didn't hesitate when he offered her his hand. For better or worse, her fate was now tied to his.

In spite of her brave façade, she followed him somewhat warily into the house. A wave of his hand and a fire sprang to life in the stone hearth. She figured she must be getting used to the Supernatural, since she hardly jumped at all.

He turned on the lights, revealing a large, rectangular room with plush beige carpeting and dark red velvet draperies. Twin white sofas were placed on either side of an enormous marble fireplace. In one corner, a round black table polished to a high sheen sat between a pair of overstuffed red velvet chairs. Several paintings decorated the walls. A sword in a silver sheath hung over the mantel. There were no mirrors in evidence.

"What do you think?" Rane asked, coming up beside her.

"It's very nice." When he'd mentioned a place in the mountains, she had pictured a little log cabin decorated with deer heads and secondhand furniture. "Who did you say this belonged to?"

"I told you, an old friend of the family."

"How old?"

"No one really knows," Rane said, grinning, "but it's rumored she knew Cleopatra."

"I don't believe you! Nobody, nothing, lives that long."

"Maybe not," Rane said with a shrug, "but that's the rumor. Come on, I'll show you the rest of the place."

In addition to the living room, the main floor housed a roomy kitchen with black appliances, a high, round oak table and four chairs, and shuttered windows. There were two good-sized bedrooms, both with fireplaces and private baths. Again, there were no mirrors to be seen. The décor was sparse, but what there was, was quality. She glanced at the Monets hanging in the bedrooms and the Picasso in the hallway. She wasn't an expert, but they looked like the real deal. She thought the frames alone probably cost more than her car.

"And this is the playroom," Rane said, leading the way downstairs.

The basement had been converted into a rec room dominated by a large satellite screen. Savanah shook her head. No expense had been spared in decorating this room. A couple of comfy-looking leather sofas sat on either side of an enormous glass-topped coffee table. Matching armchairs were arranged in a cozy grouping. A regulation-sized pool table occupied the far end of the room.

Savanah quickly perused a floor-to-ceiling shelf filled with books, puzzles, and a score of electronic games. She saw a desk with a state-of-the-art computer and a twenty-one-inch monitor at the other end of the room. A doorway led to a roomy bathroom, and beyond that, a laundry room.

"There's a pool out back," Rane said. He opened the curtains, then flipped a switch, illuminating a covered patio, a round table and a number of chairs.

"Your friend must be very rich," Savanah exclaimed.

"So they say."

"Are you sure she won't mind our staying here?"

"I'm sure. Besides being a friend of the family, she's also my godmother."

"I've heard of fairy godmothers," Savanah mused, "but a Vampire godmother? That's a new one on me."

Rane laughed softly as he drew Savanah into his arms. "You never fail to delight me," he murmured, brushing a kiss across her lips.

She blinked up at him, momentarily distracted by his kiss and his nearness.

A roguish smile lifted the corners of his mouth. Drat the man. He knew exactly what effect his kisses had on her, whether they were long and slow, or short and sweet.

Determined not to stroke his already inflated ego, she gestured at a narrow doorway beside the bookshelf. "Where does that go?"

"To the subbasement."

"What's down there?"

"Mara's private quarters."

"Really? I don't suppose . . . ?"

"No, you can't go down there. Come on, there's more to see."

Taking her hand, he led her back upstairs to the main floor, and then up a short flight of steps that opened into a master suite that held a king-size bed, a matching dresser and nightstands, a satellite screen, and a corner fireplace. The adjoining sitting area was furnished with two rocking chairs, a low table, and a bookshelf filled with a number of books and DVDs.

"It's lovely," Savanah said. And indeed it was. The walls were off-white, the quilt on the bed was burgundy, as were the matching drapes that covered the room's single window. The thick white carpet beneath her feet made her want to take off her shoes and wiggle her toes. "If she sleeps downstairs . . . ?"

"This is the, uh, guestroom, I guess you'd call it."

He didn't have to spell it out for her. Being a Vampire, Mara wouldn't let anyone else into her lair, so this was where she "entertained" her male companions.

Rane grinned wryly as comprehension dawned in Savanah's eyes and pinked her cheeks. "This will be your room."

"Are you going to share it with me?" She hadn't intended to ask that. Only hours ago, she had wondered if she would ever be able to share a bed with him again.

"Is that an invitation?"

She hesitated a moment, then said, "Only if you want it to be."

"What do you think?"

She pretended to consider it a moment, then smiled. "I think the bed is big enough for two." In point of fact, it was big enough for three or four. The thought made her cheeks burn hotter.

"Maybe we'll find out later," Rane said, winking at her. "Do you want to help me carry in our bags?"

"Sure."

Savanah followed Rane outside. Since they had stopped at the store earlier, there were several sacks of groceries in addition to their luggage. It took only a few minutes to collect everything. Rane dropped their luggage on the floor inside the front door, then took two of the grocery bags from Savanah's arms and followed her into the kitchen.

Savanah opened the nearest cupboard. She didn't know why she was surprised to find it empty. However, a second cupboard was filled with a set of beautiful crystal wineglasses.

She looked at Rane askance.

He shrugged. "My family likes a glass of wine now and then.

Savanah nodded, wondering if wine was the only thing his family drank out of the delicate stemware.

"What about the stove and refrigerator? Don't tell me your family likes to cook, too?"

He chuckled. "No, but occasionally Mara brings a mortal to visit."

Savanah looked at him, a question in her eyes.

"She takes mortal lovers from time to time," he explained with a shrug. "They need food and drink."

She couldn't help wondering if Mara's mortal visitors *became* food and drink, but she didn't ask. Shaking off the morbid thought, she opened the refrigerator to put the milk, butter, vegetables, fruit, and cheese away. "Does she keep the electricity on all the time?"

"No. I called ahead."

With a nod, Savanah closed the door. It took only moments to put away the rest of the groceries. With nothing else to do, she felt suddenly awkward and uncertain.

"Come on," Rane said, "let's go sit in front of the fire and relax."

"All right."

Savanah sat on one of the sofas, her legs curled beneath her. Rane sat at the other end, one arm draped along the back of the couch. Silence stretched between them.

Savanah watched the flames dancing in the stone hearth, her thoughts filled with memories of her father. It was hard to believe she would never see him again, never hear him crack his silly jokes, or read his funny e-mails. Never again would they argue politics, or stay up late working out the details of a newspaper article. Tears burned the backs of her eyes and the next thing she knew, she was sobbing.

She hadn't seen him move, but in the space of a heartbeat, Rane was sitting beside her, his strong arm around her shoulders. She collapsed against him, needing his strength, grateful for his hand lightly stroking her hair, his voice assuring her that, in time, she would be able to remember the good times she had spent with her father without feeling the pain of his loss.

"How long?" she asked. "How long will it take for the pain to go away?"

"It varies," he said, brushing a kiss across the top of her head. "Usually a year or two, but it will get a little easier to bear every day."

A year or two. It sounded like forever.

With a sigh, she snuggled against his side. Never, in all her life, had she been so confused. She was supposed to be a Vampire hunter, yet here she was, cuddling on the sofa with one of the Nosferatu when she should be thinking of ways to take his head. She was grieving for her father, wondering what to do with the rest of her life, yet she had invited Rane to share her bed. Did she really want to hunt Vampires? Did she want to continue working for the *Chronicle?* Would she be happier if she sold the house and moved to a new city? Someplace she had never been before, where there were no memories to remind her of all she had lost? She wished she had a crystal ball she could gaze into and see her future.

She wished . . . that Rane would kiss her.

Slowly, he drew her into his arms, his dark eyes searching hers, giving her plenty of time to change her mind.

For once, she was glad he could read her mind. It made everything so much easier. His kiss was long and slow and tender, masterful without being demanding, asking nothing, giving her only pleasure and forgetfulness.

Rane gazed down at Savanah. Her even breathing told him she had fallen asleep, her head pillowed on his chest, one arm draped across his waist. It amazed him that she trusted him enough to rest in his embrace. Of course, she had no idea how her blood called to him, whispering to his hunger. He could almost taste her on his tongue, feel the warmth of her life's essence sliding down his throat.

What was he to do with her?

He eased the hair away from her neck. Such a lovely neck, smooth and slender. His gaze was drawn to the pulse beating slow and steady in the hollow of her throat, echoing the rhythm of her heart's beat, calling to him, tempting him.

A taste, he thought. Just one taste, to ease his hunger, to satisfy his unholy craving. Just one taste . . .

He scraped his fangs along her throat. She stirred but didn't wake.

It took all the self-control he possessed to pull away. Cursing himself, he carried her up the stairs and put her to bed before his hunger overcame his willpower, and then he left the house.

A thought took him into the town. Although it was little more than a stop-off place for tourists, it boasted several nightclubs, all of which were open.

He picked the one closest to the edge of town. Going inside, he took a place at the bar, ordered a glass of dry red wine, and waited.

It didn't take long. A woman who had been sitting by herself moved toward him, her hips swaying provocatively, her lips parted in a smile that told him all too clearly what she wanted. He watched her saunter toward him, her black leather skirt so tight, he wondered how she could walk at all. A low-cut, off-the-shoulder, pink sweater revealed an expanse of creamy white skin.

Rane smiled back. Though she didn't know it, only one of them would get what they wanted that night.

"I'm Diane," she said, sliding onto the bar stool next to his. "Can I buy you a drink?"

He lifted his glass. "I have one, thank you."

"Anything else I could get you?"

"I don't know," he said, willing to play the game. "What do you have in mind?"

Her fingers trailed down his chest, then settled on his thigh. "Don't you know?"

"I've got a pretty good idea," Rane replied, thinking there were all kinds of predators.

She slid her hand up and down his thigh, moving a little higher each time, until Rane caught her hand in his. "Let's take it slow, shall we?"

She shrugged. "Slow or fast, honey, whatever you want. My place is just around the corner."

With a nod, Rane put his glass on the bar. "Let's go."

She lived in a modest cabin at the end of a long driveway. A single light burned in the window.

He waited on the porch while she opened the door. She was a few steps inside before she realized he hadn't followed.

"What are you waiting for?" she asked, glancing over her shoulder.

"An invitation."

"Well, come on in, sugar," she purred, tossing her handbag and keys on a shabby green-and-gold sofa. "I've got something to show you."

Rane grinned as his tongue brushed his fangs. "I've got something to show you, too."

Chapter Twenty

He was coming for her. She could see his eyes glowing red in the darkness, feel his presence looming over her like the angel of death. He smiled. His fangs were long and very white in the darkness. She opened her mouth to scream, but the only sound that emerged was a pitiful whimper. He had been deceiving her all along, making her think she could trust him, comforting her the night her father died. Lies, all lies. He had waited only for this moment, when she was far from home, alone and at his mercy. Only, he wasn't going to be merciful. His breath was like fire against her neck as he bent toward her, his red eyes blazing with an unholy light. Fear held her motionless. He was going to kill her, the way her mother had been killed, the way her father had been killed . . .

She had to scream. If she could only scream, he would go away.

"No! No!"

Savanah awoke to the sound of her own frantic cries ringing in her ears. Jackknifing to a sitting position, she glanced around the unfamiliar room, then placed a hand over her heart, hoping to calm the panic that roiled up inside her. Where was she? Where was *he?*

The thought had no sooner crossed her mind than Rane burst into the room. "Savanah? What's wrong?"

Momentarily speechless, she stared up at the man outlined in the doorway. The frightening creature from her nightmare. She blinked and it was just Rane standing there, his brow furrowed with worry as he moved through the dark room toward her.

"Are you all right?" he asked.

She nodded, her heart still pounding in her ears as her gaze moved over him. He was shirtless and barefooted, his hair sleep-tousled. "I'm sorry. I had a bad dream."

He sat on the edge of the bed and switched on the table lamp. "Better?"

She nodded, the last vestiges of her nightmare vanishing as welcome light filled the room. "What time is it?"

"A little after four."

"I'm sorry, I didn't mean to wake you up. . . ."

"You didn't." Brushing a lock of hair from her forehead, he smiled reassuringly as his fingers caressed her cheek. "Everything's all right. Go back to sleep. I won't let the bogeyman get you."

With a nod, she slid under the covers and closed her eyes. But what if he was the bogeyman?

Her nightmare seemed foolish in the morning. Sitting up in bed, Savanah stretched her arms over her head. A glance out the window showed the sun was up and shining brightly.

She wondered where Rane had gone. She had invited

him to share the room with her, but maybe he preferred to take his rest alone.

Going into the bathroom, she washed her face and brushed her teeth and then, because she hadn't done it the night before, she unpacked her suitcase. Even with all she had brought, her clothes took up very little room in the enormous closet. She considered unpacking Rane's suitcase, and then decided against it, thinking he might not like her going through his things.

After slipping her mother's Vampire-hunting kit under the bed, Savanah went downstairs. Coffee. She needed coffee—lots of it. And something to eat.

She peeked into the other bedrooms on her way to the kitchen. Both beds were empty. He wasn't in the rec room, either.

Frowning, she wondered where Rane had gone. Not outside, surely. He had to be in Mara's lair, she thought, since it was the only place she hadn't looked.

After breakfast, Savanah showered and dressed. Being in a strange house, a Vampire's house, made her feel decidedly uncomfortable. Without Rane to vouch for her, she had no idea how she'd explain her presence if the owner showed up.

With a shake of her head, she went out by the pool. It was a beautiful day, mild and clear. The patio was shaded by a white latticed cover that made pretty patterns on the cement. Birds sang in the trees, sunlight sparkled on the surface of the pool. She wished she had packed a bathing suit and then, looking around, decided she didn't need one, since a high wooden fence surrounded the backyard. There was no other house for miles.

Feeling daring, she undressed and dove into the pool, yelping as her sun-warmed flesh hit the cool water.

After a few laps, the water didn't feel so cold anymore. She swam for twenty minutes, enjoying the beauty around her, the feel of the water moving over her bare skin, the warmth of the sun's light on her face. Poor Rane, to forever be denied such simple pleasures.

She floated for a few minutes, her eyes closed, her thoughts drifting toward Rane, as they did so often. Abruptly, she opened her eyes, unable to shake the feeling that someone was watching her. She glanced around, but there was no one in sight. The only other living thing in the vicinity was a bushy-tailed squirrel watching her from the branch of a tree that hung over the fence.

With a shiver of unease, Savanah climbed out of the pool, grabbed her clothes, and hurried into the house to dry off.

Later, feeling somewhat bored, she found Rane's car keys and drove into town. The car was like the man, she thought. Smooth and sleek and a little bit dangerous.

Savanah eased off the gas as she turned onto the main street. She hadn't been able to see much of the town when they stopped at the store last night; this afternoon, she noticed how quaint the buildings were. The streets were clean, lined with tall pines. A pretty park made a splash of green at the end of the town; several young women and children were frolicking in a pool located near the center of the park. A number of people were standing in line at the corner Cineplex. On the spur of the moment, Savanah decided to take in a movie. It was one she had been wanting to see, a remake of an old John Wayne flick, and she couldn't think of a better way to forget her troubles than to lose herself in a good, old-fashioned, shoot-'em-up.

As it turned out, the movie wasn't as good as she'd hoped, but then she wasn't surprised. Remakes were rarely as good as the original. After leaving the theater, she stopped at a small café for a tuna salad sandwich and a chocolate shake, then browsed a couple of gift shops. At the Bon Ton Ladies Shoppe, she bought a green polka-dot sundress, a pair of white sandals, a bathing suit, and a beach towel. She added a hot pink T-shirt and a pair of jeans for good measure, and headed for home.

Only, the cabin in the woods wasn't home. Sadness fell over her like a dark cloud. Her father was gone and home would never be the same again. Perhaps she would sell the house. . . .

Shaking off her maudlin thoughts, she focused on the scenery. Tall trees and lacy ferns grew on both sides of the winding road. Wildflowers in rainbow hues grew intermittently, adding splashes of color to the edge of the roadway. She hit the brake when a doe bounded across the road. Slowing down, Savanah took a deep breath, thinking the winding mountain road was just as dangerous, in its own way, as the five o'clock traffic back home. . . .

Home. Tears burned her eyes and she let them fall, hoping they would help to wash away the grief that welled up from deep inside.

It was just after sunset when Savanah pulled up in front of Mara's house. She sat in the car for a few minutes; then, shaking off her melancholy, she grabbed her purse and shopping bags and went inside.

Rane was waiting for her just inside the front door. "Where have you been?"

"I went into town."

"Do you think that was wise?" A muscle throbbed in his jaw as he fought to control his temper. "Have you forgotten why I brought you here?"

"I thought it would be all right during the day. The Vampire . . ."

"Isn't working alone," he reminded her. "Werewolves have no aversion to the sun."

"I guess I just wasn't thinking."

"Well, you'd damn well better start! These people are playing for keeps, Savanah, remember that." He muttered an oath as her eyes filled with tears. Drawing her into his arms, he said, "I'm sorry, I didn't mean to upset you, but you've got to be more careful. I can't protect you if you're not here."

She dashed the tears from her eyes. She wouldn't cry. Rane was right. She had to keep her wits about her.

"So, what did you buy?" he asked.

"Nothing much. A sundress and some shoes, a bathing suit . . ."

He looked down at her, a roguish grin playing over his lips. "You didn't wear one this afternoon."

"How do you know?"

"I watched you swimming in the pool."

She blinked at him. "I knew someone was watching me."

"Did you?"

"Where were you? I didn't see you?"

"Up in the attic."

"Is that where you . . . ah, slept?"

"No. I slept in Mara's lair."

"What were you doing in the attic, then?"

"Watching you." He ran his fingertips over her cheek. "It would be a shame to hide that beautiful body under a bathing suit."

Knowing he had been watching her swim and that he found her beautiful unleashed a flurry of butterflies in her stomach.

"Maybe we could go skinny-dipping together sometime," she suggested.

"I'm game if you are."

Heat pooled low in her belly as she visualized the two of them swimming naked in the moonlight. What would it be like, to feel the length of his body pressed against her own, wet skin sliding intimately over wet skin?

His grin told her he was thinking along the same lines. "Perhaps in an hour or so," he said, "after we've both had time to dine."

His words were like a splash of cold water in her face, reminding her anew that although they sometimes thought alike, they were worlds apart.

He kissed the tip of her nose. "Keep the doors and windows closed and locked. I won't be gone long."

She nodded, her mind shying away from the image of Rane bending over some poor unsuspecting woman, his fangs piercing the tender flesh of her throat, stealing her life's essence, and perhaps her life, as well. What was she doing, spending time with a Vampire, when she was supposed to be hunting them, killing them? It was a question she had asked herself before, a question with only one answer, foolish as it was: she was in love with him. It gave new meaning to the phrase "dying for love." And yet, even if she didn't have deep feelings for Rane, she knew she would never be able to destroy him. He had comforted her when she needed comfort most, looked after her, brought her here to protect her. She laughed softly. Maybe love really was blind.

For Savanah, dinner was a chicken Caesar salad, a thick slice of cantaloupe, and a glass of iced tea. For some reason, swallowing the tea made her think of Rane, out prowling the shadows looking for prey. What was it like, to exist on a warm liquid diet? Did he ever miss real food, or think about sinking his teeth into a tart apple or a juicy orange instead of living flesh?

Repulsed by her thoughts, she put the glass aside,

washed up her few dishes, and went downstairs to watch a movie. If she had thought to forget about Vampires, she had picked the wrong night to watch the tube. It seemed every movie channel was featuring films about the Undead, from the old black-and-white Spanish version of *Dracula* to the latest remake of *Dark Shadows*.

She was flipping through the stations when Rane materialized on the sofa beside her.

"Sheesh!" she exclaimed, startled by his sudden appearance. "Give a girl a little warning, will ya?"

"Sorry."

She looked at him, wondering who he had fed on and if he had left his prey alive.

He cocked his head to one side under her perusal. "Want to tell me what that look is for?" he asked, then grunted softly. "Never mind, I'll bet I can guess."

"I'll bet you can, too, since you read my mind so well, so often."

"I don't have to read your mind, Savanah. It's written all over your face. You're wondering who I fed on, and how I picked her, or him, and if they're dead or alive."

"You can see all that in my expression?"

"Am I wrong?"

"No," she admitted.

Rane blew out a sigh. "She was a middle-aged woman with sad blue eyes and pretty brown hair and I left her where I found her, none the worse for wear. Happy?"

"I'm sorry," she said, her voice tinged with frost. "It's none of my business."

"Savanah, I can't change what I am. I wouldn't if I could. I love you. I think you love me. Do you want to try and work through our differences? If not, I'll protect you as best I can, but you won't see me anymore."

She stared up at him, her mind running in a dozen

directions at once. What did she want? How could she be a hunter and have a Vampire lover? Did she want to face the future without him in it? He might be a Vampire and loving him might be dangerous, but her life had definitely been more exciting since they met. Could she live with the differences between them? Would those differences bring them closer together, or eventually drive them apart? He would never look any older than he did now. How would she feel when she was wrinkled and gray and he still looked the same? Would their relationship even last that long? Would it be better to end it now?

"Savanah?"

"I don't know what I want." Her gaze slid away from his. "This is all so new. . . . Sometimes I want to grab a stake and a bottle of holy water and conquer the world, and other times I just want to crawl into a hole and hide. I don't know what I'm supposed to do! How could my parents keep such a secret from me?"

Rane swore softly. She was so young, so damn young. And remarkably innocent for this day and age. She worked at a newspaper, she had covered stories of rape and murder and incest, and yet she seemed strangely untouched by the ugliness in the world around her. Or she had been, until he came along.

Beside him, Savanah squared her shoulders, lifted her head, and met his gaze. "Yes, I want to try and work things out between us."

"You're sure?"

"Yes."

He cocked his head to the side. "What changed your mind?"

"My mom and dad were nothing alike, and yet they were happy together. If they could get along, why can't we?"

"Your father wasn't a Vampire."

"Well, everyone has a quirk of some kind. . . ."

"A quirk?" He almost choked on the word. A quirk was a funny habit, an odd trait. There was nothing remotely funny about being a Vampire.

"We'll just have to work around it," Savanah said. "There's just one thing. You have to stop reading my mind. It isn't fair, since I can't read yours. And you can't take my blood without telling me."

"That's two things," he mused, stifling the urge to laugh.

She stuck her tongue out at him. "Don't quibble. Do we have a deal or not?"

Rane grunted thoughtfully. She hadn't said he couldn't take her blood, just that he had to tell her. Before or after, he wondered. "We have a deal. Shall we seal it with a kiss?"

"Yes," she said, a slow smile spreading over her face. "I think we should."

Rane drew Savanah into his arms and kissed her. She was sweet, so sweet. There was no doubt that they were well-suited in at least one area of their lives; still, as much as he wanted her in his life, he couldn't shake off his doubts. How long would Savanah be content to stay with him now that she knew what he was? He was certain that the only reason Rafe's marriage had survived so long, as well as those of his parents and grandparents, was due to the fact that the women in his family had all chosen to cross the gulf between mortal and Vampire. Would Savanah eventually agree to accept the Dark Gift? If not, he doubted their relationship would last. And if she wanted children . . . He felt a sharp stab of regret that he could not give her a child. He wondered if Rafe's wife ever regretted marrying a Vampire. Did she secretly long for children her husband could not give her?

He grunted softly as Savanah poked him in the ribs.

"You're awfully quiet all of a sudden," she said. "Is something wrong?"

"No." His gaze moved over her. What would he do if she decided to leave him? Even before the thought was fully formed, he knew he would not want to go on existing without her. He had known many women in his lifetime. He had cared deeply for one or two but had loved none of them.

"So, do you want to go for a swim?" she asked.

His gaze moved over her, hot and slow. "Anxious to try on that new bathing suit, are you?"

"Maybe." She had been thinking of him when she bought it.

Rising from the sofa, Rane took both of her hands in his and pulled her to her feet. "Show it to me some other time," he said.

"You don't want to swim?"

"I don't want you to feel overdressed," he said with a roguish grin, "since I'll be swimming sans trunks."

She felt a blush warm her cheeks as Rane tugged off his shirt.

Head canted to one side, he winked at her, his eyes glinting with merriment. "What are you waiting for?"

With laughter bubbling up inside her, she kicked off her sandals. The walls rang with their shared laughter as they raced to see who could undress and make it into the pool first.

Rane won.

"You cheated!" Savanah accused, diving into the pool a few moments later.

"What do you mean?"

"You used your Supernatural hocus-pocus. That's not fair."

"I just wanted to warm the pool up for you."

She frowned as she realized that the water was, indeed, deliciously warm. "How did you do that?"

He shrugged. "I don't really know."

"Well, since you're Superman," she remarked, smiling, "it must be X-ray vision."

Grinning, he swam toward her with long, even strokes that barely made a ripple on the surface of the water.

"You're beautiful," he murmured. "More beautiful than any woman I've ever known."

"I guess there have been quite a few." She tried not to let her jealousy show, but she couldn't hide it completely. He had been a Vampire for over ninety years. The number of women he had known, intimately and otherwise, was probably staggering.

He drew her into his arms and held her close. "But none quite like you."

His words wrapped around her heart. Pressing herself against him, she lifted her face for his kiss. His skin sliding wetly over her own was remarkably erotic. She twined her arms around his neck, her eyelids fluttering down as his mouth closed over hers. The heat of his kiss, the stroke of his tongue, warmed her from the inside out. She smiled inwardly, thinking she wouldn't have been surprised if the water around her began to boil.

His hands slid up and down her back, pressing her closer. "Have you ever made love in the water?" he asked, licking a stray drop from the tip of her nose.

She looked up at him, a hint of a smile on her lips. "No, have you?"

"Not yet."

She felt a thrill of anticipation as he backed her up against the edge of the pool, foolishly pleased that they were doing something he had never done before. Wrapping her legs around his waist, she closed her eyes, and surrendered to his touch, every fiber of her being consumed with need as he kissed her again and yet again, his hands caressing her, arousing her past all thought or reason.

When his body joined hers, she thought that, water or no water, she might go up in flames. One thrust, two, and she shuddered in his arms as pleasure and release swept through her.

She was still trembling when he whispered, "A taste, love. Will you grant me one taste?"

Looking up at him through heavy-lidded eyes, she saw the need shining in his own, a need she would never understand, felt his body tense as he waited for her answer. "Rane . . ."

"Please, love."

"Just a taste," she said. "Promise?"

"Just a taste," he said, and bent his head to her neck.

She waited for the pain of his bite, but there was no pain, only an odd little tingling sensation that was followed by a wave of sensual pleasure that brought her to climax yet again.

Murmuring, "Thank you," she rested her head on his shoulder and closed her eyes, certain that she understood, at least in part, why his mortal mother had married his father.

Chapter Twenty-One

"What are you doing here?" Clive asked. "Shouldn't you be checking on the Gentry woman?"

"That's why I'm here," Tasha said with a shrug. "She's gone."

"Gone? What do you mean, gone? Gone where?"

"I don't know. Her car is there, but the house is empty."

"Has Cordova been there?"

"Yes, recently. They may have left together, but it's hard to tell. There's been a lot of people coming and going, what with the police hanging around and all."

A muscle ticked in Clive's jaw. He wanted results, not supposition. Suddenly sick of the sight of her, he jerked his head toward the door. "Go on, get out of here."

"I'm doing the best I can," Tasha said, unable to keep the whine out of her voice.

"Just get out!"

She knew better than to argue.

Clive slammed the door behind her. Dammit! He never should have trusted Tasha. She was a relatively new Vampire, and not too bright, but she had the heart-shaped face of a Madonna and the body of a temptress.

Frowning, he paced the floor. Where would Cordova have taken the woman? The Vampire hadn't seen his family in decades, so it was doubtful he would show up there with a mortal female in tow. As far as Clive knew, Rane Cordova had no home of his own. Of course, there was always the chance, however slim, that the Vampire had drained the woman and disposed of her body.

He swore again. Only the most trusted of his wolves knew what he was doing; a handful of them were working with him, moving quietly from town to town, sniffing out whatever Vampires and hunters they could find, destroying them when possible. So far, the Vampire community appeared to be oblivious to what was happening. As for the hunters, he had yet to penetrate whatever network they had. But he would. Slow and steady won the race. In time, the Werewolves would not only dominate mankind, but the Vampires, as well.

He was about to call his lieutenant when his cell phone rang.

He flipped it open, his hello more of a growl than a greeting.

"She's here."

At the sound of Roc's voice, Clive went still. "Where are you?"

"The mountains. The Gentry woman and one of the Cordova twins are staying at Mara's place."

Clive grunted softly. It was well-known that Mara had strong ties to the Cordova family.

"What do you want me to do?"

"Find those books." Dispatching the hunters would be like shooting ducks in a barrel if he had a list of names.

"What about the woman?"

"Don't worry about her. She's no danger to anyone."

"And Cordova?"

"Kill him."

"And if the woman gets in the way?"

"Then kill her, too. But whatever you do, find those books."

"Will do."

Clive shoved the phone into his pocket, a howl of excitement rising in his throat.

Soon, he thought. Soon the books and their knowledge would be his.

Chapter Twenty-Two

Mara sat atop the head of the Great Sphinx, her presence cloaked from the tourists who scurried around the base of the monument like ants with cameras. For a moment, she considered what it would be like if she suddenly landed in their midst, a wolf among sheep, so to speak. She felt her fangs extend as she contemplated the slaughter, the harsh cries of panic, the rich coppery scent of blood rising in the air and teasing her tongue. It would be easy, she thought, so easy to take them all, to fill herself with their life's essence until she couldn't hold any more. Oddly, the notion held little appeal, perhaps because she no longer needed to feed as often as she had in decades past. It was with some surprise that she realized she hadn't fed in months.

Sitting there, enjoying the warmth of the sun on her back, she thought how good it was to be home again. She had walked in the Valley of the Kings, made her way through the chambers of Nefertari's tomb in the Valley of the Queens, strolled through what was left of the Karnak Temple with its enormous stone columns. She had wandered along the Avenue of Sphinxes at the Luxor

Temple in what had been ancient Thebes, every step resurrecting a memory of days gone by. So much of what she saw and heard was familiar, and yet so much had changed. Little remained of the Egypt she had known so many centuries ago.

Feeling suddenly melancholy, she gazed at the people below, wondering what their last thoughts would be if they knew they were but a heartbeat away from death should she decide to feed.

And then she saw him, a tall man standing at the foot of the Sphinx, a sketch pad in his hand. He was hatless in the sun; his shaggy brown hair was highlighted with streaks of gold. He was tall, with the body of an athlete. His hand was quick and confident as it moved over the paper.

Curious, she floated down to the ground, jarring his shoulder ever so slightly as she materialized beside him with a murmured, "Sorry."

Kyle Bowden turned toward the woman who had jostled his arm, whatever words he had been about to say forgotten as he gazed into the greenest eyes he had ever seen. Feeling like a fool, he could only stare at the vision before him, his hand itching to get her image on canvas. Would she sit for him if he asked? Did he dare?

He needed to say something, he thought frantically, something witty to make her smile, something mysterious to pique her curiosity, something cool and worldly wise to impress her—but what? He had no gift for small talk. His talent was in his art.

"Good Lord, but you're beautiful." The words spilled out of his mouth. Mortified, he bit down on his tongue, but she only laughed, the sound deep and rich like ancient temple bells on a summer day. It reached into his very depths, filling a void he hadn't known existed.

"I'm Mara," she said, offering him her hand.

"Kyle." In spite of the heat of the day, her skin was cool against his.

She glanced at the sketch pad in his hand. "May I?"

"What? Oh, of course."

Accepting the tablet, she thumbed through the pages, admiring the sketches he had done of the Pyramids of Menkaure, Khafre, and Khufe, otherwise known as the Great Pyramid of Giza. There were several drawings of the solar barge of King Khufu, which had been sealed into a pit at the foot of the Great Pyramid sometime in 2500 BC, and drawings of the Great Sphinx, as well.

She returned to his sketches of the solar barge. She hadn't seen the ship in years, but the boat in his drawings looked exactly as she remembered. "These are wonderful," she said enthusiastically.

"Thank you. I intend to paint it when I get back home." He shook his head. "It's amazing to think that something so old and so exquisite has survived so long."

"Yes," Mara murmured. "Amazing." No one living knew why the ship had been buried. Even Mara didn't know. Some historians postulated that it might have been used as a funeral barge to carry the embalmed body of King Khufu from Memphis to Giza. Others speculated that it had been buried with the king in case he had need of it in the afterlife. Whatever the reason, it had been a remarkable find.

She turned her attention to the other sketches in the book—a child playing with a puppy, an old woman selling spices, the El-Azhar Mosque in Cairo, an old man nodding in the shade of a tree, the statue outside the Temple of Karnak in Luxor.

His work was exquisite. A few strokes of his pen and

he had captured the elegance of the Colossi of Ramses II that stood in front of the Sun Temple, the lumbering gait of a camel crossing the desert sand, the whimsical sight of a hot-air balloon hovering over the Nile, the sparkle in the eyes of a little girl as she chased a ball, the hopelessness on the face of a street beggar.

She handed him the sketchbook. When her fingertips brushed his, she was startled by the little current of electricity that arced between them. Odd, she had never felt anything like that before. She took a deep breath. He was neither Vampire nor Werewolf nor shape-shifter, so what had caused that peculiar preternatural spark?

She knew, by the sudden widening of his eyes, that he had felt it, too.

"Do you also paint portraits?" she asked.

"Yes," he said, his gaze probing hers. "I do."

"Would you consider doing mine?"

"I'd be honored."

She smiled, charmed by his eagerness and his obvious adoration. He was a handsome man, tall and slender, his skin bronzed by the sun. But it was his eyes that beguiled her. Clear gray eyes, open and honest, with nothing to hide. *A good man,* she thought with some amusement. *A truly good man in an increasingly wicked world.* That, in itself, intrigued her.

"So," she said, lifting a hand to the heart-shaped ruby pendant nestled in the hollow of her throat, "when can we begin?"

"Whenever you wish," he said. "Now, if you wish."

With the setting of the sun, she had intended to find a place to rest, to bury herself in the Valley of the Nile for a year or two, perhaps ten, but the idea no longer held any appeal. Suddenly, the world didn't seem like such a dreary place; the lethargy that had plagued her had disappeared. She wanted to see the world anew through his eyes, to discover what had caused that odd sensation when they touched.

"Come," she said, linking her arm with his, "let us begin."

Chapter Twenty-Three

For Savanah, the next few days passed like something out of a fairy tale. She was the princess, and Rane was the wizard, the big bad wolf, and the handsome prince, all rolled into one.

They spent their nights cuddling on the sofa, swimming in the pool, or stretched out under the stars, sharing bits and pieces of their pasts. They went to bed just before dawn. Some nights they made love, some nights, overcome by severe bouts of grief, Savanah cried herself to sleep in Rane's arms, only to wake late in the afternoon, alone. Several times, she had been tempted to peek into Mara's lair, but so far she had restrained her curiosity.

While Rane rested, she passed the time reading, working crossword puzzles, or playing computer games. It was a strange life. Sometimes it seemed as if they were the only two people on Earth; sometimes she felt like she was in limbo, caught between two worlds; sometimes it all seemed like some sort of fever dream from which she would eventually awake, and she would find her father waiting for her at home, a cup of coffee in his hand, a smile of welcome on his face as he asked about her day.

She thought of him often. At those times, the need to avenge his death burned hot and bright within her, along with a knife-edged sense of guilt for spending her days and nights with Rane when she should be out hunting for her father's killer.

After ten days and nights in the cabin, Savanah thought she might go stir-crazy if she had to spend one more day cooped up.

She confronted Rane when he appeared the following evening. "I have to get out of here. I need to go out to dinner or a movie, something. I need to see other people. I'm beginning to feel like we're the last two living souls on the planet."

Watching her pace the floor, Rane couldn't help muttering, "Only one of us is living."

She whirled around to face him. "You had to say that, didn't you? As if I could forget."

He regarded her thoughtfully for a moment. "I thought you had come to terms with that."

"I have."

"You just don't like to be reminded?"

"Well, if you must know, it doesn't thrill me."

"You'd rather I was mortal?"

"Well, of course."

"I guess I can't blame you," he replied, "since I'd rather you were Nosferatu."

Savanah stared at him, somewhat taken aback by what he had said. It had never occurred to her that he wished she was anything but what she was. Thinking about it now, it seemed perfectly logical. She recalled telling Rane that her parents had been happy together even though they were nothing alike. But the differences between herself and Rane were more than differing points of view on religion or politics or where to spend their vacation. She was a mortal female, subject to sickness and death; he was a Vampire, ageless and virtually immortal. She lived by day, he lived by night. She existed on food and water; he survived on the blood of others. Could they ever really find any common ground, other than the fierce physical attraction they shared? Could that be enough?

"Would you like to go into town?" he asked.

"What?"

"I asked if you'd like to go into town."

"Oh, yes! Yes, I would." She had a sudden, desperate need to be around other people. Normal people who didn't drink blood, sleep in coffins, or read minds. "Just let me change my clothes."

They left the house fifteen minutes later. Rane was unusually quiet as they drove down the narrow, winding road. Savanah glanced at him from time to time, thinking he was a feast for feminine eyes. As the silence stretched between them, she wondered what he was thinking. If only she could read his mind as easily as he read hers.

"Are you having second thoughts?" he asked.

"About what?"

"About us."

She met his gaze, her eyes filled with accusation. "You promised not to read my mind!"

"I didn't."

"Then why . . . ?"

"You looked surprised when I said I wished you were a Vampire. And you obviously don't like being reminded that that's what I am."

"I just . . ." She shook her head. "I guess it takes more getting used to than I thought, that's all. I mean, I never expected to meet a Vampire, let alone fall in love with one. In the last few weeks, my whole world has turned upside-down. Can't you understand that? I mean, my life will never be the same again."

"Who better to understand something like that than I? You think your life has changed?" He snorted softly. "One night I went to bed a perfectly normal teenager and when I woke the next night, I was a Vampire. That's life-changing."

"I suppose so." Savanah blew out a sigh. There was always someone worse off than you were.

Life-changing, Rane thought as he negotiated a sharp curve in the road. One taste of mortal blood and the world as he had known it had ceased to exist. He saw colors with crystal clarity, even in the darkness that had become his day. Each stitch in clothing, hairline cracks in buildings, individual brush strokes in a painting—no detail was too small to go unnoticed. It had been disconcerting at first. Supernatural hearing had taken some getting used to, as well. Without trying, he could hear voices across the room or across the street. He had listened to music as if hearing it for the first time, each note separate and distinct from the other. His sense of taste and touch and smell had been amplified; his physical strength was nothing short of phenomenal, and he had reveled in it, pitying the mere mortals who had become his prey. In the beginning, drunk with power, he had done things for which he was now ashamed. Oh, yeah, he knew about life-changing events.

Ten minutes later, the lights of the town cut through the darkness.

"So," Rane asked, "where do you want to go?"

"To the Lobster Pot for dinner, and then for a walk through the town. And maybe a late movie?"

Rane parked on the street in front of the seafood restaurant and followed Savanah inside. Because it was during the week, the crowd was small and they were seated right away.

Savanah ordered a fried shrimp dinner. Rane ordered a glass of red wine.

"Does it bother you," she asked, "to be in here?"

"No." It wasn't entirely true. The smells coming from the kitchen were unpleasant but not unbearable.

"When do you think I'll be able to go home?"

"I don't know. I should probably go back and see if anyone's been there."

"How would you know?"

"I'd know."

"How?"

"My senses are much keener than yours. I can see things, smell things, that you'd never notice."

"The way you smelled the Vampire who killed my father?"

"Exactly. I'll know if she's been there again."

"I can't stay here, hiding out, indefinitely. I have a life of my own." She took a deep breath. "And I need to pursue the family business."

"Killing Vampires?"

"Exactly."

"So, you intend to take up where Daddy left off?"

"If I do nothing else, I intend to find and destroy the Vampire who killed him. And any other Vampires who get in my way."

Rane suppressed a grin. It was big talk for an untried hunter whose head barely reached his shoulder, but he had to admire her grit.

"Does it bother you, my eating in front of you?" Savanah asked when the waitress arrived with her order.

"No." He watched her take a bite. "Shrimp used to be one of my favorites. That and lobster."

She speared one of the plump shrimp on her plate and dipped it in cocktail sauce. "Do you want to try one?"

He shook his head. He had tried solid food once, years ago. It was a mistake he remembered all too clearly— the salty taste of the meat, the vague smell of the wood it had been cooked over, the odd sensation of chewing, the revulsion when it had all come up again. It had been a harsh reminder that he was no longer human, and thus his body could no longer tolerate solid food. Nevertheless, his gaze lingered on the sauce. It was bright and red, like fresh blood.

Leaning back, Rane sipped his wine, ever aware of his surroundings, of the people coming and going. If he opened his senses, he could hear the conversations and thoughts emanating from everyone in the place, as well as what was going on in the kitchen, and in the alley beyond. As a new Vampire, he had often eavesdropped on the mortals around him, but the novelty had soon worn off. These days, he blocked all extraneous background noise and dialogue except when he was onstage, performing.

"Oh, my, that was good," Savanah said, pushing her plate away. "I couldn't eat another bite."

Rane signaled the waitress for their check and they left the restaurant. Outside, he took Savanah's hand in his and they walked down the street. She stopped to peer inside every shop window. It surprised her to notice that glass reflected his image, but mirrors backed by silver didn't.

They walked to the end of the business district, then turned and started back up the other side of the street.

Savanah had stepped into some fancy boutique to try on a skirt she had seen in the window when Rane sensed the presence of another Vampire. It took only moments to locate her, a tall, slender female clad in cutoff jeans and a bright purple tank top. Curly brown hair fell in riotous waves down her back. She had recognized Rane, as well. Standing on the opposite side of the shop, she was staring back at him, her blue eyes narrowed, her body poised for flight.

A moment later, another female stepped out of one of the dressing rooms, her expression wary as her gaze zeroed in on Rane. She was younger than the first; her hair was blond and spiked. A tiger tattoo adorned her left shoulder.

They were both young, little more than fledglings.

He crossed the distance between them before they realized he had moved. "Who are you?" he asked. "Who made you?"

"Who are you?" the curly haired female retorted.

"Rane Cordova."

The two females looked at each other, their eyes wide.

"I take it you've heard of me?" Rane asked dryly.

"Of course," the brunette said. "The Cordova family is well-known."

Rane didn't deny it. His family was unique among Vampires, not only because their mother had been mortal or because Mara was godmother to himself and Rafe, but because her blood ran in their veins, inherited from their father. In Mara's long life, she had bequeathed a taste of her blood to only a few. There were some in the Vampire community who were willing to go to any lengths to procure a little of her ancient blood for themselves. It was most effective when taken directly from the source, but there were some who wouldn't be adverse to getting it second-hand. Mara's blood had made Rane unusually strong, but not equal to Rafe or their father, both of whom had drunk from her and were therefore able to walk in the sun's light.

As he had before, Rane wished fleetingly that he had taken Mara up on her offer before she left for Egypt.

"I'm waiting," he said tersely.

"I'm Nona," the curly haired female said. "I was made by Richard Sachs two years ago."

"I'm Teri," the other female said. "Nona made me five months ago."

"Do you have leave from Mara to dwell here?"

The two females exchanged looks that told Rane everything he needed to know.

"What about you?" Nona asked, going on the defensive. "Do you have Mara's permission?"

"Damn right. And I want both of you out of here before sunrise."

"This isn't your territory," Nona exclaimed. "You can't make us leave."

"You think not?" Rane summoned his power, felt it roll off him like heat lightning.

The young Vampires felt it, too. With a shriek, Nona grabbed her friend's hand and bolted out the door.

"Well," Savanah remarked, coming up behind him. "What was that all about?"

"That skirt looks good on you," he said, turning to face her.

"Thank you, but that doesn't answer my question."

He shrugged. "Just a little Vampire business."

"Oh?" She glanced out the door, but the two women were already out of sight. "Did you know them? Was one of them the one who killed my father?"

"No."

"Why did they leave in such a hurry?"

"They've got no business here."

"In the store? Why not?"

"In the town. This is Mara's territory. She doesn't allow any other Vampires except those she invites."

"How do you know she didn't invite them?"

"I would have known. Mara would have marked them."

"Marked them how?"

Rane shrugged. "I don't know how to explain it to you. When cats want to mark something as theirs, they rub against it. It's the same idea."

"So, you're saying those Vampires would have smelled like Mara?" Savanah asked, looking skeptical.

"Something like that."

"Do you know where they're staying?"

"Why? Are you planning to take their heads?"

"It crossed my mind," Savanah replied flippantly. "I'm supposed to be a hunter, after all."

But they were empty words, and they both knew it. She lacked the knowledge, the expertise, and the desire to hunt down those two young women and destroy them. Except for their pale skin, they had looked just like the other women in the shop.

"I need to pay for this," she said. "It won't take more than a few minutes."

With a nod, Rane watched Savanah retreat into the dressing room. She talked a good fight, he thought, but only time would tell whether she had the fortitude to plunge a stake into a Vampire's heart.

Savanah pressed her forehead against the dressing room door. Vampires, here, in the town. Were they everywhere? she wondered as she pulled on her jeans and straightened her sweater. After stepping into her sandals, she collected her handbag and the skirt she had tried on and left the dressing room. She glanced around, searching for Rane. He was standing by the door with his back toward her.

She paid for the skirt, grabbed the bag with a mumbled thank-you, and hurried toward him.

He turned at her approach.

Savanah skidded to a stop, alarmed by the peculiar glow in his eyes. "Are you all right?"

He looked away for a moment; when he looked at her again, the glow was gone.

Had she imagined it?

He held out his hand. "Are you ready to go?"

With a nod, she put her hand in his, and felt the same little tingle she had experienced when she saw the two female Vampires in the store.

"What's wrong?" Rane asked.

"I don't know." She stared at their clasped hands. She had felt the sensation before, with Rane, but had always thought it was just her hormones jumping into overdrive whenever he was near.

"Savanah?"

"I felt something . . ."

"What do you mean?"

"Just now . . . and in the store . . . I felt . . . I don't know how to describe it. A kind of tingling."

"Go on."

"I've always thought it was just my reaction to you, but I felt it in the store when I passed those women. . . ."

Rane swore softly.

"What's wrong?"

"Nothing. I'd venture to say what you're feeling is a legacy from your mother."

"What do you mean? What kind of legacy?"

"Vampires and Werewolves can sense their prey. It's a handy trait."

"So?"

"What you sensed in the air was the preternatural

power common to all the Supernatural creatures. It's a trait shared by some hunters. No doubt your mother had it and passed it on to you."

"Why did I feel it when I looked at those two Vampires, but with you, I only feel it when we touch?"

"I've been a Vampire a long time. I've learned how to shield my power from those around me. I've done it for so long, it's second nature now. Perhaps when you get stronger . . ."

"But I sensed those women."

"They're both young Vampires, still learning to adjust to their new way of life. Sort of like you," he said with a grin.

No doubt Savanah and the two fledglings would get stronger in time, he thought. If they lived long enough.

Chapter Twenty-Four

"You mentioned my mother," Savanah remarked as Rane pulled away from the curb. "Did you really save her life?"

"Yeah."

"And she saved yours? How?"

"I was out hunting late one night and I came across your mother in an alley. She was a new hunter back then, trying to make her first kill."

"How do you know that?"

"She told me."

Savanah turned in her seat so she was facing Rane, eager to hear more about the mother she scarcely remembered. "Go on."

"Well, it was kind of like that old story about the hunter who tracked a cougar until he caught him and discovered the cougar wouldn't let him go. The Vampire was about to sink his fangs into your mother's throat when I came along."

"Why did you help her and not him?"

Rane shrugged. "I've always been a sucker for the underdog, and she was outmatched in every way. I stepped in and pulled the Vampire off her, and he turned on me. He was one of the old ones." Rane shook his head at the memory. "Strong as an ox. He grabbed me and buried his fangs in my throat, then held me down and let me bleed. I might have bled out, but your mother came up behind him and drove a stake into his back. It pierced his heart and he turned to dust right there in front of us."

Savanah shuddered at the grisly image.

"Anyway, there I was, lying on the ground, bleeding, with your mother standing over me. I figured I'd bought the farm for sure. Instead, she told me we were even, but that if she ever saw me again, she'd take my head." Rane grinned. "She was a tough broad, that one."

Savanah smiled faintly. Maybe things really did happen for a reason, she thought. Rane had saved her mother's life and now, years later, he was here, protecting hers, because her mother had let him live.

"Do you know who killed her?"

He shook his head. "No, but we can ask Mara when she gets back from Egypt. She might know." Of course, there was no telling when that might be.

"Thank you for telling me about my mom," Savanah said as Rane pulled into the driveway. "And for taking me into town. It was good to get out of the house for a while."

He nodded. "Anytime." Switching off the engine, he exited the car and opened her door for her. Savanah grabbed her package from the back seat, then took Rane's outstretched hand. They had only taken a few steps when he came to an abrupt halt. Lifting his head, he sniffed the wind.

"What is it, a skunk?" Savanah asked, although she couldn't smell anything other than the scent of pine trees and the honeysuckles that grew near the front porch.

"A little more dangerous than that."

Alarmed, she glanced around. Anyone, anything, could be hiding in the shadows. The night that had once seemed so lovely now seemed fraught with danger. Fear of the unknown sent a shiver down her spine.

"Stay close," Rane warned as he continued up the path.

"Like glue," she muttered.

Rane paused at the front door, his senses reaching beyond the barrier. There was no one inside. The house was empty.

"Rane?" Savanah tugged on his arm. "You're scaring me."

"Someone's been here." He removed the Supernatural barriers he had placed around the door, then opened it and stepped inside.

"Are you sure?" Savanah looked behind her, her gaze probing the shadows. Was the prowler still there, lurking in the darkness even now?

"Don't worry, they're gone."

"How do you know?"

Rane glanced at her over his shoulder as he crossed the threshold, his expression clearly reminding her that he was no ordinary man.

"Oh, right," she muttered. "Superman lives."

"I guess that makes you Lois Lane," he said as he switched on the lights. He locked and bolted the door; then, summoning his powers, he replaced the protective barriers around the house.

Savanah dropped her purse and shopping bag on the sofa. "Do you know who it was?"

"No, but I've got a pretty good idea what they were hoping to find."

"The books!" Savanah exclaimed, her eyes wide. "My mother's books."

"Right the first time."

"What if whoever tried to get in is still here?"

"They're gone."

"How can you be sure? What if they're hiding some-where in the house?"

"They didn't get in."

Breathing a sigh of relief, Savanah sank down on the sofa. "You're sure they didn't get in? That the books are still here?"

"I'm sure." He sat beside her, his arm slipping around her shoulders to draw her closer. "Why don't you destroy those books? You'll never be safe as long as you've got them."

"I can't. I have so little that belonged to my mother. . . ."

"Would she think they're worth your life?"

"I don't know. So," she said, changing the subject, "did your supernose tell you who was here?"

Rane shook his head in exasperation. She was a stub-born creature, but somehow, it only endeared her to him more. "It wasn't a scent I recognized," he said, answering her question.

"Was it a Vampire?"

"I'm not sure."

"Well, that's a first."

He grunted softly. "Whoever it was, they were wearing something to mask their scent. I'm not sure what they used, but it was common enough during the war."

"Were you involved in that?"

"Not as involved as Mara and the rest of my family." He had kept to the sidelines, getting his licks in when he got a chance.

"Tell me about her, about Mara."

"What do you want to know?"

"Is she really as old as they say?"

He nodded.

"And she's your godmother?"

"Yeah. She's the one who named me. And Rafe. She came to see us every now and then while we were growing up, checking on us, bringing us presents at Christmas and on our birthday. We didn't even know she was a Vampire until after we were turned." He laughed softly. "Rafe and I look older than she does."

"Is she pretty?"

"More beautiful than you can imagine."

"Oh."

"You're not jealous, are you?"

She was, but she didn't want to admit it.

Rane stroked her cheek. "Don't be. She might be beautiful on the outside, but you're more beautiful on the inside, where it counts."

She slipped her arms around his waist. "I love you."

"I know."

She grinned at him, thinking they sounded just like Princess Leia and Han Solo.

Rising, she took him by the hand and tugged him to his feet.

"Where are we going?" he asked.

"You'll see."

He let her lead him up the stairs and into the bedroom. "Now what?" he asked.

"I want to show you something."

"Oh?" His gaze moved over her from head to foot. He could hear the rapid beat of her heart, smell the musk on her skin. "And what might that be?"

With a smile, she slipped her sweater over her head and tossed it on a chair. "Me, of course."

Rane sat on the foot of the bed. "Show me more."

She kicked off her sandals, slithered out of her jeans and tossed them aside.

Rane's gaze moved over her, his eyes hot. "More."

The look in his eyes sent frissons of heat coursing through her. With hands that trembled, she removed her bra and stepped out of her panties. Even though they had made love before, even though he had seen her naked before, she was tempted to cover herself with her hands. After all, it was one thing to be naked together, and quite another to be naked alone.

"One more thing," Rane said.

Savanah frowned. What else did he want her to take off? She was naked. And then she realized she was still wearing her mother's crucifix. Reaching up, she slipped the chain over her head and dropped it on the dresser, and then she looked at Rane and said, "Now you."

"You want me to do a striptease?" he asked with a wicked grin.

"Yes." She tugged on his hand, then took his place at the foot of the bed when he stood.

With a wry grin, Rane removed his shirt and dropped it on the floor. He wasn't wearing an undershirt.

"More," she said, waggling her eyebrows suggestively.

Rane heeled off his shoes, removed his socks with a flourish, then unfastened his belt and drew it slowly out of the loops. After dropping his belt on top of his shirt, he removed his trousers, revealing a pair of black briefs.

"More," she said, her voice a hoarse whisper. He was gorgeous, all broad shoulders and rippling muscles.

Any doubts she might have had that he wanted her vanished when he removed his briefs.

She went eagerly into his arms, a soft moan rising in her throat as their bodies melded together. He moved deep within her, pleasuring her, completing her. Closing her eyes, she lost herself in the magic that was Rane.

Chapter Twenty-Five

The full moon cast long silver shadows across the countryside. Clive lifted his head, basking in the glow of the moon's light, feeling it swell within him, growing, expanding, calling forth the wolf that lurked just under the surface. It was a glorious sensation. Usually, he enjoyed running with the pack, but not tonight. Tonight, he didn't want to share the hunt with anyone else, didn't want to share his kill. As the alpha male, it was his right to hunt alone.

Eager to shift, he kicked off his shoes, excitement rising within him as he caught the scent of prey on the wind.

He was unbuckling his belt when his cell phone rang. He considered letting it ring; then, with a growl of annoyance, he reached for the phone. "What?"

"Clive? It's Roc."

"Did you find the books?"

"No, I couldn't get into the house. There's some kind of protective barrier around the doors and the windows."

Clive swore. "Is the woman still there?"

"Yeah."

"And Cordova?"

"He's with her. What do you want me to do?"

"Keep an eye on the house, follow them if they leave."

"And if I get a chance to grab her?"

"Take it, but don't kill her unless you have to. I'll get up there as soon as I take care of a few things here."

"Anything wrong?"

"Some pack trouble."

Roc grunted. That usually meant one or more of the wolves needed disciplining, or worse.

"Keep in touch," Clive said, and ended the call.

After dropping the phone inside one of his shoes, Clive removed his shirt and his trousers. He would take care of his business here, and then he'd call his lieutenant and they would pay a visit to the Gentry woman. He was pretty sure she wouldn't willingly give him the books, but that was all right.

Clive grinned inwardly as he threw back his head and surrendered to the beast within. He was sure he could persuade her.

Chapter Twenty-Six

She was dreaming, and she knew she was dreaming.

Lost and alone, she wandered through an unfamiliar landscape, searching, always searching—for her father's killer, for her mother's books, for a sense of peace and security. For Rane.

A dark mist surrounded her on every side. The air was thick, so thick she could scarcely breathe, barely see where she was going. A light shone in the distance, but she couldn't tell what it was. Sunlight? Candlelight? A will-o'-the-wisp?

She slogged on through the mist, her feet moving as if through heavy quicksand. Bottles of holy water clinked together in the pocket of her jacket; she carried a sharp wooden stake in one hand, a heavy wooden mallet in the other.

She felt a prickle of unease as she moved deeper into the gray haze. Someone was following her, she was sure of it. She spun around, her gaze trying to penetrate the thick vapor, but she couldn't see anything through the mist. Moving on, she walked faster

*and faster, until she was running blindly through the
haze. Heart pounding, side aching, she ran on and
on, her gaze fixed on the light, but it never seemed
to grow any closer.*

*Her terror multiplied when she heard footsteps
behind her, footsteps that grew ever louder, ever
nearer.*

*And then, to her horror, she felt a hand grip her
shoulder. With a cry, she flung herself around,
raised the stake in her hand, and plunged it into her
pursuer's chest, only to realize, too late, that it was
Rane.*

*She cried his name as dark red blood fountained
from his chest and then, to her horror, his body
turned to ash. She screamed in anguish as a gust of
wind stirred the ashes until nothing remained to
show that he had ever existed. . . .*

Savanah bolted upright, her cheeks wet with tears, her
last agonized cry ringing in her ears.

Frantic, she glanced around the room, blew out a sigh
of relief when she saw Rane lying beside her.

"Bad dreams?" Sitting up, he drew her into the shelter of his arms.

"Yes. It was awful. I dreamed I . . . that I . . ." She couldn't
say the words.

"Let me guess. You killed your first Vampire?"
She nodded.

"Was it the Vampire who killed your father?"

"No." She looked up at him, her eyes haunted. "It was
you."

He tucked a lock of hair behind her ear. "It was just a
dream."

"What if it was a—a premonition?"

"Is that what you think?"

"I don't know. I knew I was dreaming, but it seemed so real." She shuddered at the memory. "I don't think I'm cut out to be a Vampire hunter."

"I guess only time will tell. Do you want a light on?"

She did, but she didn't want him to think her a coward, so she shook her head. "I'll be all right."

Scooting under the blankets again, she turned onto her side. Rane slid his arm around her waist, pulling her close, so that her backside was nestled against his front. Spooning, she thought with a faint grin. Wasn't that what they called it?

With a sigh, she closed her eyes. Rane was holding her. There was nothing to be afraid of.

It was late afternoon when she awoke. In the light of day, her nightmare didn't seem as frightening or as real. She told herself it was only natural to dream about killing Vampires; she was supposed to be a hunter, after all. *A hunter without a kill,* she thought glumly.

Rising, she slipped on a robe and padded into the kitchen, surprised to find Rane sitting at the kitchen table.

His arm snagged her waist as she headed for the coffee-maker. "Good afternoon, sleepyhead."

"Hi."

He drew her down and kissed her, driving every other thought from her mind but the heat of his mouth on hers. How could there be such magic in one kiss? she thought, and then grinned. He was a magician, after all.

She sat on his lap, her arms twining around his neck, her tongue mating with his. She shuddered with pleasure as one of his hands cupped her breast while the other slid up her neck into her hair, holding her head in place as he deepened the kiss, his hungry mouth devouring hers.

She moaned softly, her hands clutching his shoulders. "Let's go back to bed," she murmured breathlessly.

"A wonderful idea," he said, his mouth trailing fire along the side of her neck. "But we have company."

"Company?" she asked, frowning. How could they have company? No one was supposed to know where they were. "Who can it be?" And where were they? No one had knocked at the door.

"Mr. Leon Webb. He's on the porch."

The words had scarcely left Rane's mouth when the doorbell rang.

"Who's Mr. Webb?"

"An acquaintance," Rane said. Lifting Savanah from his lap, he took her by the hand and went to admit their visitor.

Webb was tall and muscular, with short-cropped iron-gray hair and eyes so pale a blue they were almost colorless. Clad in a pair of well-worn camouflage pants, a dark green T-shirt, and scuffed combat boots, Savanah thought he looked like a walking ad for Gangs-R-Us. He carried a leather-bound case in one hand.

Rane invited Webb inside, then closed and locked the door behind their guest. "Savanah, this is Leon Webb. Webb, this is Savanah."

Savanah drew her robe more tightly around her. "Pleased to meet you," she said, though she wasn't sure she was pleased at all.

Webb gave her a perfunctory nod, then placed the leather case on the coffee table. He opened it with a flourish, revealing half a dozen handguns.

Savanah looked at Rane askance. What use did he have for a gun?

"I wasn't sure exactly what you wanted," Webb said, "so I brought the best of what I have."

"And ammunition?"

"Of course. The gun's no good without it." Webb lifted a nasty looking weapon from the case and handed it to Rane. "I think that's the best choice. It's lightweight, good for close-up work. It should take down anything she comes across."

She? Savanah sat on the sofa, a cold knot of suspicion forming in the back of her mind. "What does he mean, 'she'?"

"It's for you," Rane said.

"Me? Why do I need a gun?" As far as she knew, Vampires were impervious to bullets. She looked at Rane, willing him to read her mind since she couldn't ask him outright, not with Mr. Webb standing there, listening.

"I want you to have some protection against Werewolves."

Savanah frowned at Rane. What was he thinking, to mention such a thing in front of this man?

"That should do the trick," Webb said, apparently not bothered or shocked by Rane's mention of Werewolves.

After checking to make certain the weapon wasn't loaded, Rane offered it to Savanah.

She stared up at him. She had never held a gun in her life, much less fired one.

"Go on," Rane said. "Take it."

Reluctantly, she did as he asked. The gun nestled in her palm as if it had been made for her. From the look of it, she had expected it to be heavier than it was.

"We'll take it," Rane said. "And all the ammunition you've got with you."

Webb nodded. "Anything else I can get you?"

"No, that should do it."

"I've got a couple of paper targets out in the trunk."

"All right, we'll take those, too."

"What about gloves?"

Rane shrugged. "All right. Black. Leather."

Webb nodded again. "I think I've got just what you want." With a curt nod at Savanah, Webb headed for the door.

Rane followed him, but didn't go outside.

Savanah stared at the gun still clutched in her hand. Could she actually pull the trigger on a living creature? Would she be willing to take a life to save her own?

Rane returned, alone, a few minutes later.

"Where's Mr. Webb?"

"Gone." Rane dropped a large brown paper sack on the coffee table. "There's ammo inside, a couple of paper targets, and a pair of gloves. We'll see what kind of marksman you are after the sun sets."

"Who is he, Webb? What does he do? How do you know him?"

"I met him during the war. He's a handy man to know if you want a gun that can't be traced."

"He's a criminal?"

"Not exactly."

"What exactly?"

"I guess you could say he walks a fine line. No one who ever crossed him lived to brag about it."

"Oh."

"Any more questions?" Rane asked, a hint of a smile in his eyes.

"No."

Bending down, Rane kissed her on the forehead. "I'm going to rest for a few hours."

"All right." She placed the gun on the table, then watched him leave the room. He was going to sleep in

Mara's lair. Like a dragon. No doubt about it, Savanah mused. Her life just kept getting more and more bizarre.

Rane woke shortly after sunset. He remained where he was for a time, his arms folded under his head as his gaze roamed Mara's lair. The room was a reflection of the woman—ancient and beautiful. The king-size bed was hung with white gauze curtains. Wrought-iron sconces held fat beeswax candles. A thick white carpet covered the floor, expensive paintings adorned the walls, several pieces of rare Egyptian art were scattered around the room. A golden tiara set with precious stones lay in a careless pile amid dozens of other pieces of jewelry on the top of an antique dresser. Each one was likely worth a small fortune. An arched doorway opened onto a large bathroom done in black and gold. The sunken tub and oval sink had gold faucets.

Mara. She had the grace and bearing of a queen. Looking at her, no one would guess she had existed for thousands of years. What was it like for her to see nations rise and fall while she stayed forever the same? He had been a Vampire for almost a hundred years. Did he have the staying power to endure for centuries? Not many Vampires did. Mortals dreamed of living forever, but he wondered how many would accept it if they knew how long forever could be. It wasn't easy being a Vampire, watching the world change, watching those you loved age and die. Some Vampires kept to themselves, refusing to mingle with the mortal world, refusing to form attachments, preferring to endure in solitude rather than face the pain of losing those they loved over and over again.

Muttering an oath, he left Mara's lair and headed for the upstairs bathroom.

Savanah looked up from the book she was reading when she heard the shower come on. Rane was awake. Naked. In the shower upstairs. The thought sent a shaft of heat spiraling through her.

Setting the book on the table, she hurried up the stairs to see if Rane needed someone to wash his back.

She paused in the doorway a moment, admiring his broad back, the spread of his shoulders, his tight buns and long, long legs. He really was a beautiful creature, she thought, and felt herself blush when said beautiful creature turned around.

His brows went up when he saw her standing on the other side of the shower door, staring.

"Hi," Savanah said. "I just came to see if you, ah, needed someone to wash your back."

"Someone as in . . . you?"

"I don't see anyone else standing here, do you?"

"Not a soul," he said with a roguish grin, and opened the door.

Nerves thrumming with anticipation, she undressed quickly.

"I was hoping for another striptease," Rane remarked.

"Maybe next time." She was about to step into the shower when he shook his head.

"Get rid of that first."

Looking down, Savanah saw the silver cross resting between her breasts. Wearing it had become such a habit, she hardly thought about it anymore.

"Oh, sorry." Removing the crucifix, she placed it on the sink top before stepping into the shower, and into Rane's waiting arms.

"You can shower with me anytime," Rane murmured as he drew her closer.

Warm water sluiced over the two of them. Savanah

rubbed her breasts against his chest, wanting to be closer, loving the slick wetness of his skin against her own.

"We seem to spend a lot of time in water," Savanah remarked.

He licked a drop from the tip of her nose. "Are you complaining?"

"Oh, no, just making an observation."

Lowering his head, he dropped kisses along the length of her neck, along the edge of her collarbone, in the hollow of her throat where her pulse beat hot and quick.

"A taste?" he asked, his voice low and husky.

"You haven't fed yet, have you?"

"No." His voice was almost a growl now.

"I don't think so."

He swore under his breath, but didn't argue. Putting her away from him, he picked up the soap, worked up a lather in his hands, and starting at her shoulders, worked his way down.

By the time he reached her belly, she was having trouble breathing.

By the time he reached her thighs, she was a quivering mass of need.

"A taste, Savanah?"

"That's blackmail," she accused, but at the moment, she didn't really care. She wanted him, wanted all of him, now, inside her.

He ran his fingertips over her belly. "I know."

"Just one taste?" she asked. "You promise?"

He nodded.

She looked up at him, wondering if she could trust him when he was looking at her like that, when his eyes were glowing with hunger.

His fingertips caressed the outer curve of her breasts. "Just do it," she said, and turned her head to the side.

His mouth was incredibly hot against her skin, the pleasure beyond words. He backed her up against the glass, then lifted her so that she was straddling his waist, his mouth still at her throat as his body melded with hers, and she didn't care if he took one taste or twenty.

Didn't care if he took it all . . .

Chapter Twenty-Seven

"Savanah? Dammit, Savanah, can you hear me?"

At the sound of his voice, she opened her eyes and smiled. "I hear you."

His breath was warm against her cheek as he muttered a string of curses.

"Why are you so angry?" she asked. "Wasn't it good for you?" .

"I thought . . . Dammit, I was afraid I'd taken too much."

Carrying her out of the shower, he quickly dried her off, then carried her into the bedroom and placed her gently on the bed.

"Are you sure you're all right?" he asked, drawing the quilt over her.

"I feel wonderful."

"Of course you do," he muttered.

"You're not supposed to growl at me afterward," she complained. "You're supposed to hug me and tell me you love me."

With a shake of his head, he pulled her into his arms, quilt and all. "I do love you. That's the trouble. Next time I promise to take just one taste, don't believe me."

"How much did you take?"

"I don't know. More than I should have." He hadn't meant to, but one taste had only served to whet his appetite for more. He had been hungry for her, and she was so sweet . . . for a moment, he had lost himself in the sheer pleasure of feeding. He swore softly. It couldn't happen again. "Stay here."

"Where are you going?"

"To get you something to eat."

She hadn't realized she was hungry until he mentioned food. "I can do it." She started to get up, only to fall back on the bed when the room began to spin.

"Stay here," he said again, and left the room.

Downstairs, he thawed a steak in the microwave and quickly fried it up, his nose wrinkling at the stink of cooking meat. When it was done, he filled a glass with orange juice, plucked a gold-plated knife and fork from the drawer and carried everything upstairs. On the way back to the bedroom, he made a detour into the bathroom. Using the fork, he scooped up Savanah's crucifix, then went into the bedroom.

Sitting on the edge of the bed, he offered her the cross. "Put it on, and don't take it off again."

With a sigh, she slid the chain over her head. The silver felt cool against her skin.

Rane's expression was grim as he cut the steak and fed it to her.

"It's too rare," she protested. "I like it cooked a little more."

He tried not to notice the juices that oozed from the meat. "It's better for you this way."

He insisted she eat all of it and drink the orange juice, then he tucked her into bed. "Get some sleep."

Hearing the worry in his voice, she said, "I'm all right. Honest."

He nodded, though he wasn't convinced. He had brought her here to protect her but he couldn't help wondering if she wouldn't be safer without him.

He stayed by her side until she fell asleep, then continued to sit there, staring out the window, his thoughts turned toward his brother. Why couldn't he have been more like Rafe? Things had always come easy for his brother. Rafe had been the popular one in school, easygoing, affable, always at home in a crowd, while Rane had always held back a little.

He glanced at Savanah, wondering where their relationship would end. It had been an odd twist of fate that had brought a Vampire and a future Vampire hunter together. No matter which way he looked at it, he couldn't see a happy ending. But even knowing that, he couldn't let her go. As long as those books existed, her life was in danger.

He grunted softly. He could destroy the books, but it wouldn't do much good. He didn't know who wanted them. Even if he put out the word that the books had been destroyed, he had no guarantee that whoever was looking for them would hear of it, or believe it.

Curious, he went downstairs and out to his car where he retrieved both volumes. Carrying them inside, he locked the door, then sat down in the living room, opened the black book, and began to read. It gave him a strange feeling, seeing the long list of names of the Undead. Many of them were familiar to him even though he had never met them.

Putting the black book aside, he picked up the brown one. He wondered how long it had taken Savanah's mother to compile her facts and if she'd had help. There were numerous books about Vampires, but he had never seen one that was so comprehensive or so accurate. She had it all: how to locate Vampires, how to destroy them, the various Supernatural powers they possessed. There was even a short section on Werewolves.

Like Vampires, Werewolves seemed to be immune to aging and disease, but they could be killed by any wound that destroyed the heart or the brain. While there was only one way to become a Vampire, there were numerous ways to become a Werewolf, including being bitten, being cursed, or being born to a Werewolf. A person who was turned against his will wasn't cursed until he tasted human blood, something few Werewolves, or Vampires, for that matter, could resist for long. Most Werewolves were compelled to change at the full moon, though there were some who could change at will.

As dawn approached, Rane went upstairs to check on Savanah, then walked through the house, making sure all the doors and windows were closed and locked and that the protective wards, meant to keep intruders out, were in place. When that was done, he carried the books downstairs to Mara's lair and hid them under the mattress.

Undressing, he stretched out on her bed and closed his eyes. Thinking of Savanah, he cursed his lack of self-control where she was concerned.

Even now, her taste lingered on his tongue.

Even now, filled with guilt and remorse, he wanted her again.

It was early afternoon when Savanah awoke, the nightmare she had just had still vivid in her mind. Rane had been holding her in his arms, his eyes filled with anguish as he told her over and over again how sorry he was for what he had done. At first, she had been confused and then, with crystal clarity, she realized what he had done. He had made her what he was.

Muttering, "It was just a dream," she sat up, stretching her arms over her head. It was then that she saw the dishes on the nightstand. Only then that she remembered what had happened the night before. Rane had taken her blood. He had promised to take just a taste, but he had taken more. How much more? Enough that he had been truly concerned. Had her nightmare been a vision of things to come? If he had taken too much, would he have worked the Dark Trick on her?

The thought sent a shiver of revulsion down her spine. She might be in love with a Vampire, but she had no desire to become one.

Rising, she showered and dressed, then carried the dirty dishes downstairs, rinsed them off, and put them in the dishwasher.

Even though it was well past time for lunch, she was in the mood for bacon, scrambled eggs, and toast.

She was sitting back in her chair, enjoying a cup of coffee, when Rane entered the room, his expression wary as he dropped into the chair across from hers.

His gaze moved over her, long and assessing. "How are you feeling?"

"I'm all right."

"Are you sure?"

"Rane . . ."

He held up his hands in a gesture of surrender. "All right, you're fine, but you could have been dead."

"I know that. Don't you think I know that?"

He dragged a hand through his hair. "Dammit, Savanah, I could have killed you."

"But you didn't. We'll just have to be more careful in

the future." Seeing his expression, she leaned forward and placed her hand on his arm. "I'm a big girl. I know what I'm doing."

He hoped she was right. "I need to rest a while," he said. "I'll see you later."

"All right." She smiled up at him. "Stop worrying about me."

She lifted her face for his kiss, frowned thoughtfully as she watched him leave the room. Did he really need to rest, or was it just his way of avoiding her? If she asked to see where he rested, would he let her? She had never seen a Vampire's lair. Of course, until she met Rane, she had never seen a Vampire, either.

Rising, she rinsed her dishes and put them in the dishwasher, then stood at the window, staring longingly at the pool.

A quick swim was just the ticket. After changing into her suit, she grabbed a book and headed for the door. An odd sensation prickled along her arms and her nape as she stepped over the threshold, almost as if she had passed some kind of invisible barrier.

Shrugging it off, she dropped the book on the table and dove into the deep end of the pool.

The water felt wonderful. She swam for ten minutes or so; then, stretching out on a chaise lounge, she read a book in the shade of an umbrella, rising now and then to dive into the cool water when the sun grew too warm. She dozed for a while, then went into the house to fix a sandwich and a glass of iced tea for an early dinner. She missed cooking for her father. He had always praised her culinary efforts, even when they went wrong. Smiling, she recalled the night she had prepared what she hoped would be an epicurean masterpiece; to her chagrin, it had turned out to be an utter disaster, fit only for the garbage disposal.

Later, sitting in the rec room watching a movie, she found herself continually glancing at the clock, wishing she could make the minutes go faster. The hours passed too slowly, the house seemed too empty, without Rane beside her.

She felt a thrill of excitement as the sun began to set. He would be with her soon.

The thought had no sooner crossed her mind than he was there. Just looking at him filled her with the kind of giddy excitement she hadn't experienced since her first crush on a rock star years ago. Only, what she felt for Rane was far stronger and went far deeper.

"Are you ready?" he asked.

"Ready? For what?"

"Your first shooting lesson."

"Oh." She wrinkled her nose with distaste. "I don't think I could shoot anyone."

"It's less messy than taking a head, or driving a stake through a Vampire heart."

She blew out a sigh. "All right, let's go get it over with."

They went outside, where Rane set up three targets on the east side of the house. He handed her the gloves, loaded the gun while she pulled them on.

"All right," he said, moving to stand behind her. "There's nothing to it." He put the gun in her hand and showed her how to hold it in a two-handed grip. "Don't jerk the trigger. Just squeeze it gently."

Taking a deep breath, Savanah aimed at the first target and squeezed the trigger.

"Not bad," Rane said.

"Not good," she muttered. "I barely hit the thing."

"But you did hit it," he said, giving her shoulder an

encouraging squeeze. "Try again, and this time, keep both eyes open."

To Savanah's amazement, her aim quickly improved. By the time she had moved on to the third target, her shots were hitting the bull's-eye nine times out of ten.

"You're a natural," Rane muttered. "Maybe it's in your blood."

"What's that supposed to mean?"

"You're a born hunter," he said with a shrug.

"Maybe I am," Savanah mused, remembering the letter her father had left her. "Did you know my mother was related to Abraham Van Helsing?"

"No, but it doesn't surprise me."

"What's *that* supposed to mean?"

"Not a thing, except that nothing much surprises me anymore, especially where you're concerned."

For the next thirty minutes, he had her practice shooting while she was kneeling, while she was flat on her back, and then while lying on her stomach. Next, he had her try her hand at shooting while she was walking, and then at a run.

"After all," he explained, "you won't always have the luxury or the time to stand still and take aim."

By the time they quit two and a half hours later, Savanah felt like the revolver had become a part of her.

"Keep it nearby from now on," Rane said, opening the back door for her.

In the kitchen, Savanah put the gun on the table, then went to the sink and washed her hands.

"I went by your house late last night," Rane remarked as she dried her hands.

"Is everything okay?"

"Furniture's a little dusty."

She made a face at him. "Did you see anyone there?"

"No. Whoever was watching the place must have realized you're gone."

"When do you think I can go back home?"

"I don't know. Probably not for a while. I guess you miss it."

She thought about it a minute, then shook her head. "In a way, but it doesn't seem like home anymore."

How could it ever be home again, after what had happened there? She would never be able to walk through the front door without remembering that her father had been killed there, and in that moment, she knew that when this was all over, she would put the house up for sale.

"I need to call Mr. Van Black and see if I still have a job." Not that she needed to work. Her father had left her well-off financially. Still, she needed something to do, something to give her life meaning. Something besides hunting Vampires.

"So, what shall we do this evening?" Rane asked.

"I don't know." Tossing the towel on the counter, she went into the living room and sat down. "Play cards? Watch a movie?"

"Or we could just neck here on the sofa," Rane suggested, dropping down beside her. He took a deep breath, his nostrils filling with the now-familiar fragrance of her hair and skin. He could hear the beat of her heart, steady and strong, could smell the scent of her blood flowing quietly through her veins.

"That sounds nice," Savanah said, snuggling closer. "What will we do if Mara comes home while we're here?"

"Nothing. She won't mind our being here, as long as you don't try to take her head."

Smiling, Savanah kissed his cheek, amused by the bizarre twist her life had taken. Only weeks ago, her days and nights had been boring and predictable. Now, everything had changed. Her father was gone. She had a Vampire for a lover, and she was on the run, hiding out in the home of the world's oldest creature of the night. Yes, indeed, a strange twist of fate, one she might have welcomed if it hadn't cost her father his life.

"You're very quiet," Rane said, lightly stroking her cheek.

"Nothing to say, I guess."

"Don't worry, we'll find the one responsible for your father's death."

Savanah nodded. If it was the last thing she did in this life, she would avenge her father.

And if the Fates were on her side, maybe she could find the monster who had killed her mother, as well.

Chapter Twenty-Eight

Clad in a long white dress reminiscent of the kind Cleopatra had once worn, Mara reclined on a curved settee, her gaze fixed on Kyle. She loved to watch him paint. He wielded his brushes with single-minded concentration. And after each session, he made love to her as gently and sweetly as ever a man had loved a woman.

Only, she wasn't a woman, not in the way he thought she was. Did she dare tell him the truth? She shook the thought away. There would be plenty of time for that, later.

Awareness thrummed through her when he glanced her way. What was there about him that had so quickly and thoroughly captivated her? True, he was handsome, but she had met many handsome men in the course of her existence. Perhaps it was nothing more than the fact that he made her laugh. She refused to entertain the notion that she could be falling in love with him. She had resisted entanglements of any kind for centuries. She had taken lovers, she had created others of her kind, but she had never given her whole heart to any man, living or Undead.

Perhaps it was just being home again that made her vulnerable. It was wonderful to see the Great Sphinx again, to explore the pyramids inside and out. Walking barefooted along the banks of the Nile made her feel young and carefree; breathing the air of her native land, resting in the rich, fertile soil, renewed her in ways nothing else could.

Anticipation curled through her insides when Kyle laid his brush aside and walked toward her.

"It's finished," he said, his tone almost reverent. "It's the best thing I've ever done."

"Finished!" Mara leapt from the settee. Thus far, he had not even let her glance at the canvas.

It was beautiful. Breathtaking. Being somewhat vain, she'd had her portrait painted every twenty-five years or so. The artists changed. The backgrounds changed, fashions changed, but she had always looked the same. Until now. Perhaps it was Kyle's affection for her that made the difference.

"Surely that can't be me," she murmured.

The woman in the painting was exquisite, slender yet curvaceous. Her hair fell over her shoulders in luxurious waves, her eyes were bright with a hint of mischief and mystery, her lips were pink and slightly parted, as if awaiting love's first kiss.

She glanced at Kyle. "Is that how I truly look, or how you see me?"

"It's how you truly look," he said, "but why are you so surprised? It's the same face you see in the mirror every day. You must know how stunning you are."

"Yes, of course." She looked at her image more closely. Of course she looked beautiful. She was a Vampire, with a Vampire's inherent glamour.

"You're displeased?"

"No, of course not." Rising on her tiptoes, she kissed him, and felt again that peculiar tingle.

"Can I keep it for a few days? I'd like to make a copy for myself."

Resting her forehead against his chest, she blew out a sigh. He really was a dear man. How was she ever going to leave him? Would he still love her if he knew what she was? Few mortals who learned her true nature lived to tell the tale. Dare she trust him with the truth?

His hand moved in her hair. His touch sent a shiver of longing coursing through her. Lifting her head, she gazed up at him. Desire lurked in his eyes, the scent of musk rose from his skin.

"Mara, I look at you and I want you with every fiber of my being, every beat of my heart."

She trailed her fingernail down his cheek. "An artist and a poet."

He captured her hand in his and kissed her palm, his tongue like a flame against her cool flesh. "Only a fool in love with a goddess who dares to dream . . ."

"Of what do you dream, Kyle?"

"Of making love to you."

"Come, my love." Taking him by the hand, she led him to the settee and drew him down beside her. "And dream no more."

Chapter Twenty-Nine

Another week went by and Savanah started to get restless. Not that she didn't enjoy being with Rane, but she was beginning to feel like a prisoner. He had gone to her house again last night and when he got back, he had told her he didn't want her going outside unless he was with her, which meant she couldn't go swimming until the sun went down. When she'd started to argue, he'd kissed her until she forgot everything else. Now, she wondered what he knew that he wasn't telling her.

She was anxious to go home, anxious for her life to return to normal, or as normal as it could be without her father, but Rane wouldn't hear of it. He reminded her that Vampires and Werewolves were nothing if not patient creatures, and that just because they hadn't seen or heard anything out of the ordinary in the last week, it didn't mean there was nothing to worry about.

Savanah knew he was probably right, but she still wanted to go home. She missed living in her own house and sleeping in her own bed. She missed going to work. She had called Mr. Van Black and asked for more time off. She had called Jolie a couple of times to see what was happening at the *Chronicle,* she had called the police department to see if they had turned up any leads on who had killed her father even though she knew it was unlikely. As far as she knew, there weren't any Vampire hunters on the force. She grinned inwardly. If she lost her job at the *Chronicle,* maybe she could go to work for the Kelton P.D.

Now, she wandered from room to room on the main floor. The views from the front windows all looked like scenes from picture postcards. Lofty green pines reached upward toward the bright blue sky with the mountains standing like sentinels in the background. Moving toward the back of the house, Savanah gazed longingly at the pool. Sunlight glinted invitingly off the still water, tempting her to go outside and take a quick dip, but Rane's warning echoed in her mind.

Resigned to staying inside until he awoke, she decided to read awhile, only then remembering that she had left her book on the patio table last night. She drummed her fingertips on the window frame. It would only take a moment to run outside and back.

She glanced out the window again. She could see her book lying on the table where she had left it, the pool beyond, and the high wooden fence that surrounded the backyard. There was no one in sight, and no place to hide in the pool area.

Going into the kitchen, Savanah unlocked the door and took a step across the threshold, only to pause when a cold chill skittered down her spine. She was about to dart back inside when a heavy hand clamped over her arm and jerked her out of the kitchen.

A scream erupted from her throat as her attacker dragged her out of the house. Kicking and scratching, she screamed again even though there was no one to hear her.

"Let me go!" She tried to scratch her attacker's eyes, but he held her away with ease. She renewed her struggles as they neared the side gate, but it was no use. The man was close to seven feet tall, as wide as a barn door, and had a grip like iron.

"The books," he said, slamming her up against the house. "Where are the books?"

She stared up at him, her insides suddenly as cold as ice. "I don't know."

"I think you do." Her head slammed against the wall when he shook her. Black spots danced in front of her eyes. "Where are the books?"

"Please, I don't know . . ."

His hand closed around her throat. "Don't make me ask you again."

The strength went out of her legs as her vision blurred. She was going to die, she thought dully, and she hadn't even killed one Vampire. Vampire . . . Rane . . . she would never see him again.

And then, unaccountably, her attacker released her.

Savanah slid to the ground, her hand massaging her throat as she fought to drag air into her lungs. A scuffling sound drew her attention. With an effort, she turned her head, squinting against the bright sunlight.

In the scant shelter of the patio, Rane was fighting her attacker. The scent of blood filled the air as they savaged each other. She could see smoke curling from the back of Rane's T-shirt, smell his burning flesh. How much longer could he endure the sunlight before he went up in flames?

Forcing herself to her feet, she staggered into the house and grabbed her pistol. Standing in the kitchen doorway, she pointed the gun at the intruder's back and then, taking aim the way Rane had taught her, she gently squeezed the trigger.

An inhuman howl filled the air as her attacker grabbed his right shoulder. Bright red blood oozed between his fingers. Whirling around, he started toward her, his lips drawn back in a feral snarl.

Fear coiled in Savanah's stomach as she stared at the inhuman creature striding toward her. Hair sprouted from the backs of his hands; long, curved claws emerged from the ends of his fingers.

She waited until he was several steps away from Rane and then, taking aim at the Werewolf's heart, she fired again, and then again, until the hammer clicked on an empty chamber.

The Werewolf dropped like a felled ox as her last shot pierced his heart, dead before he hit the ground.

Tossing the gun on the kitchen table, Savanah ran out the door. "Rane!"

He had fallen to his hands and knees. Swaying, he looked up at her. The skin on his face was red, blistered where the sun had touched him.

"You're on fire!" Using her hands, she slapped at the flames eating through the back of his T-shirt and searing the skin beneath. "Come on!" she cried, "we've got to get you into the house!"

Grabbing him by one arm, she dragged him inside, then sank down on the floor beside him as all the strength drained from her limbs. For a minute, she just lay there, her body shaking uncontrollably, her nostrils filled with the stink of gunpowder and the awful smell of scorched flesh.

Rane lay facedown on the floor beside her, his eyes

closed, his back muscles twitching. His skin was raw and red in some places, burnt black in others.

She continued to stare at him, afraid he would go up in smoke at any minute even as she wondered how he had survived being outside when the sun was up. Fortunately, he had only been in the sun a short time. The Werewolf's claws had left deep furrows along Rane's arms, down the side of his neck, and across one cheek. Thick, dark red blood oozed from the wounds.

What to do, what to do? Taking a deep breath, Savanah put her face close to his. "Rane? Rane, can you hear me?"

He mumbled something unintelligible.

She started to touch his shoulder, then jerked her hand away. "Rane, what should I do?"

A long shudder wracked his body, and then he opened his eyes. "Are you all right?"

"I'm fine." It was almost the truth. There was an ugly bruise on her forearm where the Werewolf had grabbed her, a lump the size of an ostrich egg on the back of her head, and a horrible sick feeling in the pit of her stomach. She had ignored Rane's warning and almost got both of them killed. How could she have been so stupid?

She looked at him again, the queasy feeling growing stronger. The eyes staring back at her were as red as hellfire.

"Savanah . . . go down to Mara's lair . . . and lock the door."

She didn't have to ask why. He was in pain. He needed blood to heal. And she was the only game in town.

"Savanah, go."

"You need help."

"You can't give me what I need," he said, his eyes blazing. "Get the hell out of here. Now!"

Scrambling to her feet, she ran out of the room and down the stairs to the subbasement as if her life depended on it.

Which she feared it did.

She had never been in Mara's lair before. She closed the steel-reinforced door and slid the heavy bolt home, then stood there, her heart pounding. What was he doing now? How long did she have to stay down here?

She glanced around as she paced the floor. *Staying here wouldn't be much of a hardship,* she thought. She had never seen anything quite like the huge room that surrounded her. Ornate wrought-iron sconces adorned the pale blue walls, along with a number of paintings that looked like originals. Several pieces of artwork she thought might be Egyptian were carelessly scattered around the room. The king-size bed was hung with gauzy white curtains. A thick white carpet covered the floor, muffling her restless footsteps. She paused at an antique dresser to run her fingers over a gold tiara set with what looked like rubies and emeralds. She picked it up and put it on, wishing for a mirror so she could see how she looked, but she wasn't likely to find one in a Vampire's lair. She replaced the tiara, then examined the other pieces of jewelry, one by one, certain that each one was probably worth more than her whole house and everything in it.

Turning away from the dresser, she began to pace again. What was Rane doing up there? She knew he needed blood to heal, but it was hours until sunset. Was he in pain? Did he need to sleep and if so, where would he rest now that she was in the lair? The curtains were open upstairs. What if the sun found him?

Fear shot through her. What if the Werewolf that attacked her hadn't been alone? What if there were more of them, waiting outside? Rane was alone upstairs, wounded and helpless.

Spurred by her concern for his safety, she unlocked the door and bolted up the stairs. "Rane!"

She ran into the kitchen and skidded to a stop. The back door stood open. There was no sign of him.

Surely he hadn't gone outside! Taking a deep breath, she went to the door and took a quick look at the patio and the yard. There was no sign of him out there, either.

Closing the door, Savanah turned the lock, then glanced at the floor. For the first time, she noticed the spatters of blood on the tile, as if he had dragged himself out of the room.

She followed the crimson trail out of the kitchen and down the hall, thinking it was a good thing Mara had chosen tile for the hallway instead of the beige carpet that covered the floor in the living room.

The blood spots ended at a door under the staircase. Savanah stood there a moment, her heart hammering in her chest and then, with a hand that trembled, she opened the door, revealing a combination closet and storage area. A few coats hung on a wooden pole. She couldn't see anything beyond that.

"Rane? Are you in there?"

A low growl rose up from the darkness. And then she saw his eyes, eyes that burned red with need. "I told you . . . to stay . . . away."

"I can't."

He growled at her again, a sound filled with soul-deep pain and need. A sound that tore at her heart even as fear of the unknown rose up within her once again.

She took a step into the darkness, and then another, her love and concern stronger than the fear that screamed in her mind, urging her to turn around and run back down to Mara's lair as fast as her feet could carry her.

She could hear him breathing now, the sound ragged and uneven, loud in the stillness. She shrieked as his hand shot out and closed over her wrist, his grip like iron.

"What do you think you're doing?" he demanded gruffly.

She forced the words through lips gone dry. "You need blood."

"Are you offering?"

She nodded, wishing she could see his face, and then glad that she couldn't. The tone of his voice frightened her anew. He didn't sound like her Rane, but a stranger. A stranger whose eyes burned into hers, threatening to steal her very soul.

"Savanah." Her name was torn from his throat as he dragged her across the floor and into his embrace.

"Rane . . . please . . ." She fought down her terror. "Please don't . . . hurt me."

But he was beyond hearing. With a savage growl, he jerked her off balance. She tumbled into his lap, crying out as his arms imprisoned her. His breath skimmed over her face, her neck, and then she felt his fangs, cold and sharp against her skin, and knew she was going to die.

Trapped in the darkness, unable to move, she closed her eyes and waited for death, only to be jarred to full awareness when, with a vile oath, he pushed her away. Confused, she scuttled out of his reach, her hand lifting to her neck. And then she felt it, the cool touch of the silver chain that had belonged to her mother.

His curses continued to fill the air.

And suddenly, in spite of his earlier warning, she knew what she had to do. Gaining her feet, she backed up until she stood in the hallway. "Come to me, Rane."

Mocking laughter tinged with pain and despair rang out.

"Rane, come and drink."

She jumped when he suddenly loomed over her.

"Are you courting death, Miss Gentry?" he asked, his voice harsh. "Isn't one close call a day enough for you?"

Squaring her shoulders, she met his mocking gaze. His T-shirt was in tatters, there was blood smeared across his mouth and splattered across his chest and arms and down the front of his jeans. His skin was blistered wherever the sun's light had touched him. He looked scary as hell.

She took a deep breath, and then lifted the silver chain over her head and stuffed it into the pocket of her jeans.

Rane stared at her through narrowed eyes as she tucked the cross out of sight. What the hell was she doing? Not long ago, he had told her to put it on and keep it on. She might be dead now if she hadn't followed his advice.

"Savanah, no."

"You need blood." Brushing her hair away from her neck, she turned her head to the side. "Take what you need."

He clenched his hands into tight fists. "Dammit, Savanah, do you know what you're doing?" He closed his eyes, trying to control his hunger, to breathe through the pain that burned through him with every breath.

"I'm not leaving. It's my fault you're hurting. If I'd listened to you . . ."

He stroked her cheek, his gaze moving to the hollow of her throat.

"I'm not leaving," she said again.

"All right." Taking her hand in his, he turned it over,

then stroked the vein in her left wrist with his fingertips. "Don't let me drink for more than a few minutes."

Savanah frowned at him. "But . . ." She lifted a hand to her throat. "I thought . . ."

He shook his head. He could take more, faster, from the vein in her neck, but he didn't trust himself to stop. Drinking from her wrist would take longer and be less satisfying, but it was safer for her.

He could hear the fierce pounding of her heart, smell her fear.

"Tiger heart," he murmured, and lifted her wrist to his lips.

Chapter Thirty

Deep in the fertile earth of the Nile Valley, Mara stirred, then woke, all her senses alert. Werewolf blood had been spilled at her lair in the mountains. Closing her eyes, she reached out into the universe, her preternatural senses narrowing, sharpening, focusing on her mountain retreat. Rane was there. A mortal woman was there. And death was there.

She knew a rarely experienced moment of fear. Had Rane been destroyed? But no, she would have felt an emptiness deep inside if he had ceased to exist.

She concentrated on the blood link that bound them together, let herself experience what he was feeling. He was wounded, in agony from the touch of the sun's light on preternatural flesh. Stubborn, foolish man. Had he not denied the gift she had once offered, the sun would have no effect on him. She wondered what he had been doing outside during the day, wondered if she should go to him.

Intending to rise, she gathered her power around her, only to realize there was no need. He had found nourishment in the woman. And, more than that, he had found love. Perhaps the woman would heal the hurt in Rane's soul and take him home.

Love . . . The word lingered in her mind. She closed her eyes and the image of a man she had known aeons ago rose from the depths of her memory. Hektor. She banished his image and forced herself to think of Kyle instead. Hektor was past history, but Kyle was here, now. He would be waiting for her this evening when the sun set. Perhaps tonight she would discover why her skin tingled whenever they touched. It could be nothing more than physical attraction, she mused, but something told her it was more than that.

Nothing perked up an affair like a hint of mystery.

Smiling faintly, she drifted away into the darkness of oblivion.

Chapter Thirty-One

Pleasure flowed through Savanah as Rane eased his thirst. Odd, that it didn't hurt, that she wasn't more repulsed by what he was doing. She should be shocked, horrified. She should be trying to kill him.

If she didn't stop him soon, he would kill her. "Rane, that's enough."

He looked up at her, his mouth still pressed tightly against her wrist.

"Rane, stop." She pulled the cross from her pocket and lifted it so he could see it.

With a hiss, he released her arm, and then turned his back to her. He took several deep breaths, his shoulders shaking.

Savanah stared at what she could see of his back through his ruined shirt. Blood was supposed to heal the Undead, but as far as she could see, there didn't seem to be any improvement. His skin was still red and puckered in some places, singed and black in others.

Puzzled, she asked, "Why didn't it work?"

"What do you mean?"

"Why aren't you healing?"

"It takes longer to heal the effects of the sun," he replied, still refusing to look at her.

She grunted softly, thinking she still had a lot to learn about the Undead. "Are you all right?"

"I will be."

"Rane?"

"I need to get cleaned up."

She nodded even though he couldn't see her. She wondered if he was angry with her, and then realized that he was ashamed, embarrassed because she had seen him at his worst.

Savanah watched him walk away, noting again that he moved soundlessly across the floor. She stood there long after he was out of sight, wondering what effect this last incident would have on their relationship. After slipping the chain over her head, she rummaged through the linen closet for a sheet. She was about to go outside and cover the body in the patio when her good sense reasserted itself. He could rot out there for all she cared.

Dropping the sheet over the back of a chair, Savanah folded her arms under her breasts. She wasn't going out there alone. The way she felt now, she might never go outside again. Moving to the kitchen window, she stared at the body. It was grotesque. In movies, dead Werewolves always reverted to their human state. But this wasn't a movie. The Werewolf lay sprawled on his back, his face set in a rictus of pain. Hair still sprouted on the backs of his hands, grew thickly on his forearms. His face and clothing were spattered with blood. What if he wasn't really dead, but playing possum? What were they going to do with the body? Should she call the police? Maybe she should discuss it with Rane first.

With a sigh, she grabbed a dish towel, and began scrubbing the blood from the tile.

* * *

Rane stripped off his bloody jeans and ruined T-shirt and stepped under the hard spray of the shower. Closing his eyes, he relived the last hour.

He had been resting in Mara's lair when Savanah's terrified cry had reached his ears. Reacting on instinct, he had flown up the stairs and, following the sound of her heartbeat, he had run out the back door in time to see a giant of a man slam her against the side of the house. Oblivious to the sun's light and his own danger, he had pulled the Werewolf off of Savanah. Had the sun been down, there would have been no contest between them. He would have killed the Werewolf with no more thought or energy than it took to swat a fly. But the sun had been high in the sky, its light burning his flesh, leeching his strength, leaving him weak and vulnerable. He had ignored the pain of his singed flesh, the threat to his own life, his only thought to save the woman he loved.

He laughed humorlessly. In the end, it had been she who had saved his life. Foolish woman, he had almost killed her in return. Had it not been for the heavy silver chain around her neck, there was every chance that she would now be dead, another victim of his insatiable thirst.

He had sworn to protect her. How could he face her again after what he had done? Stepping out of the shower, he reached for a towel and went into the bedroom, only to stop short when he saw Savanah sitting cross-legged in the middle of Mara's bed.

She looked up when he entered the room. He noticed she had changed her clothes. His blood had undoubtedly ruined what she had been wearing earlier.

He had rarely been at a loss for words, but they failed

him now. What could he say to her after what he had done, what she had seen?

"I didn't thank you for saving my life," Savanah said, her gaze not quite meeting his.

"I think you've got that backward."

"Maybe we saved each other."

"Yeah, and then I tried to repay you by ripping your throat out."

"Rane, you're exaggerating."

He shook his head, the pain thrumming through his singed flesh as nothing compared to the self-loathing he felt for what he had tried to do, what he would have done if his fingers hadn't brushed the thick silver chain circling her slender neck.

He stilled when she rose and walked toward him. "Don't."

She stopped, her brow furrowed. "Don't what?"

"Don't come any closer."

"You're still hurting, aren't you? Is there anything else I can do?"

He groaned low in his throat. Was the woman insane? Not thirty minutes ago he had tried to kill her and she had still given him her blood, and now she wanted to do more. There was only one thing that would help. Surely she knew that.

Savanah's heart went out to him. She knew he was hurting, and not just physically. She could see the guilt in his eyes, knew he was berating himself for what he had done. She couldn't deny that he had frightened her badly, that for a moment she had been certain he was going to drain her dry, but even as scared as she had been, she had understood what drove him. He was like an addict, driven by a need he couldn't always control.

Knowing her nearness was making him uncomfortable,

she backed up and sat on the edge of the bed. "What are we going to do about the body?"

"I'll take care of it," he said, his voice terse.

"Should I call the police? I could tell them he attacked me and I shot him in self-defense."

Rane shook his head. "No. I'll take care of it."

She nodded, thinking it was too bad that Werewolves didn't just vanish in a puff of smoke and ash, the way old Vampires did.

"The sun," she said. "You could have died out there." Had the day been brighter, had there been no cover over the patio . . . It sickened her to think about what could have happened to him, and all because she had made one stupid mistake. "Are you sure you'll be all right?"

"Stop worrying." He glanced at the bed. "I need to rest until dark, and then I'll be going out for a while."

His words pierced her heart like a dagger. She knew why he was going out. He needed to feed. She knew it was necessary, knew it was foolish to envy whoever he chose to drink from, but she couldn't help it, and with that jealousy came concern for his prey. Rane needed blood, a lot of blood, and he couldn't take any more from her. Would he take all he needed from one unsuspecting mortal, which would most likely leave his prey dead, or would he drink from many?

With a sigh, she went upstairs, familiar thoughts tugging at her mind. It still amazed her that her life had changed so dramatically, that in only a few short weeks, her world had turned upside down and her once ordinary life was now anything but ordinary. The world as she had known it no longer existed; the cocoon her father had wrapped her in had burst with the knowledge that her mother and father had been Vampire hunters. Even more earth-shattering was the fact that she had fallen head-over-heels in love with a Vampire.

Could her life get any more bizarre?

Clad in black from head to foot, his wounds aching with every move he made, Rane hunted the outskirts of the town for prey. Hunger and pain made him impatient; the fact that the streets were virtually empty increased his anger. He understood why Mara made her lair in this quiet part of the world, but at the moment he wished they were in her home in the Hollywood Hills. There was no end of vagrants and winos on the back streets of Los Angeles. Had he been stronger, he would have transported himself to a city, but the loss of blood, combined with the weakening effects of being out in the sun, had undermined his strength. Hauling the Werewolf's body out of the backyard and carrying it up to the top of the mountains hadn't helped any. He had dumped the Werewolf's remains in a deep ravine where it was unlikely to be found, and if it was discovered at some future time, so be it. There was nothing on the body to connect it to Savanah or himself.

Cursing softly, Rane made his way toward the nightclub on the corner of the town's main street. He had hoped to find a transient, someone who wouldn't be missed should he be unable to stifle the urge to kill, but the streets were empty, and he was tired of looking, tired of hurting.

The club was dark inside. A lone couple danced in a far corner, their bodies pressed so closely together, it was hard to tell where one ended and the other began. Three middle-aged men sat at the end of the bar, bragging about their love lives. Two women shared a table near the front window.

At the bar, Rane ordered a glass of wine, hoping it would help to ease his thirst though he knew it was a vain hope. Only blood, and lots of it, would satisfy his hunger and ease his pain this night.

Turning, with his back resting against the edge of the counter, he eavesdropped on the women's conversation. Both schoolteachers, they appeared to be in their early thirties. They had come to the mountains on vacation. The redhead was single; the brunette recently divorced. Both were childless. Rane grunted softly. That was good. There would be no husbands or children to miss or mourn them.

Opening his senses, he sent his thoughts to the two women, the redhead first and then the brunette. When they looked in his direction, he pushed away from the bar and headed for the door, confident that they would follow.

Outside, he linked his arms with theirs and walked down the street until he came to an alley that dead-ended between two windowless buildings.

Certain that no one would intrude, he admonished the brunette to sit down and close her eyes. After she had complied, he took the redhead in his arms, felt his fangs lengthen in anticipation. He hadn't made a kill in decades; the thought of doing so now filled him with exhilaration. The first taste was like ambrosia on his tongue. This was what he was, what he had always been. Why had he denied himself for so long?

Closing his eyes, he drank, eager to take it all— her hopes, her dreams, her memories. Her heartbeat slowed, and in that instant, he imagined Savanah was there, watching him, her eyes filled with sorrow as he surrendered to the darkness within him.

With a cry of despair, he put the redhead away from

him. After taking several deep breaths, he commanded her to sit down and rest her head on her knees and then, with more force than necessary, he grabbed hold of the brunette and yanked her to her feet.

He drank quickly, his enjoyment gone as guilt rose up in its place. He drank as much as he dared, then escorted both women back into the nightclub. At the bar, he ordered them each a large glass of orange juice and bid them drink it, and then he spoke to their minds, telling them to go home and get something to eat, preferably a steak. When he was certain they understood, he stalked out of the club and into the night.

Outside, his hands clenched against his sides, he drew in a deep breath. Eager for a fight, needing an outlet for his anger, he turned into the wind, hoping to catch the scent of a Werewolf or some other predator, animal or human, even though it was doubtful that, in his current condition, he would survive such an encounter. But the air carried only the smells of earth and pine, and although he knew it was little more than wishful thinking on his part, he imagined he detected the warm womanly fragrance that was Savanah's.

She was sitting in front of the hearth when he returned to Mara's place. She didn't move, didn't say a word, but the question was there, unspoken, in the air between them.

It stoked the fires of his anger.

He held her gaze for several taut moments before he said, "Dammit, stop looking at me like that! I didn't kill anyone."

Her relief was patently obvious and only served to make him angrier. Muttering an oath, he stalked out of the room and took refuge in Mara's lair.

With a sigh, he sank down on the edge of the bed. In

spite of the blood he had taken, he was still weak, his wounds still painful.

Easing down on the mattress, he closed his eyes and in a rare moment of weakness, let himself dream of home.

Chapter Thirty-Two

Clive punched in Roc's cell number for the second time, cursing softly when all he received was a recorded message. Roc had called earlier that afternoon, reporting that he had nothing to report. Clive had instructed him to stay near the house and to call in every hour, sooner if there was any change in the situation. That had been nine hours ago. Since then, nothing.

After throwing the cell phone across the room, he began to pace the floor. Four possibilities occurred to him: Roc had lost contact with the woman and was afraid to report it; he had managed to get into the house, but hadn't been able to find the books; he had found the books and had decided to either keep them or demand some kind of a reward; or he was dead.

For Roc's sake, Clive hoped it was the latter. Those who betrayed him lived to regret it, but not for very long.

Chapter Thirty-Three

Savanah stared out the window, her elbows resting on the sill as she watched the windblown rain slash through the trees. Lightning speared the lowering gray clouds; thunder rumbled in the distance.

She was going stir-crazy. It had taken her hours to fall asleep last night, and when sleep finally came, her dreams had been populated with Vampires and Werewolves that chased her through a long dark tunnel. She ran until she couldn't run anymore and then, suddenly, in the way of dreams, the scene changed and she was alone in a theater, watching a handsome magician clad in a long black cape. She knew a moment of relief and then, with a wave of his hand, the magician disappeared and a huge black wolf stood in his place. With a low growl, the wolf sprang from the stage, landing only inches from her face, so close she could feel its hot breath on her cheeks, see its fangs. Just when she thought it was going to rip her throat out, the wolf changed again, and now it was Rane bending over her, his eyes bloodred, his fangs dripping blood.

She had stared up at him. "You told me you didn't kill anyone," she had said, her voice shaking.

"I haven't," he had replied with a feral grin. "Yet."

Once again, the sound of her own cries had awakened her.

How much longer did he expect her to stay imprisoned in this house? If she didn't get out soon, she would go insane.

She tapped her fingertips on the sill as she considered her options. Her life was in danger, there was no doubt of that. She could either stay here, hiding away like some coward, or she could go home and face her fears. Her mother and father hadn't run away from danger. They had both hunted Vampires.

Yes, a little voice murmured in the back of her mind, *and they had both been killed by Vampires.*

Rane thought she should stay here, but what was the point? The Werewolf's appearance proved that her whereabouts were no longer a secret. What made Rane think that staying here was any safer than going home? Another Werewolf could show up here tomorrow. Mara could return at any time. Just because Rane said it was all right for them to be here didn't make it so. Mara might have other ideas about an uninvited mortal staying in her lair. Savanah knew good and well that she was no match for a Vampire like Mara.

She wanted to go home, and that was what she was going to do. She would fortify her house as best she could and let the chips fall where they may. She had made her first kill, and while it had sickened her, she had proved she could do it. Her parents hadn't shunned the fight, and neither would she.

Her decision brought with it a sense of peace. When she saw Rane, she would tell him what she had decided, the consequences be damned.

Humming softly, she went into the kitchen to make a

sandwich. Carrying it with her, she went down to the rec room in search of something to read. There was no telling when Rane would wake. Until then, she needed something to occupy her time.

The storm didn't sound so loud in the playroom. Standing in front of the bookshelf, she scanned the titles. Mara had a vast library, everything from the works of Shakespeare, Dickens, and Milton to Erma Bombeck and Gary Larsen. It would have taken several lifetimes to collect so many books. Had Mara read them all, Savanah wondered, or did she just like to collect them?

Plucking a copy of *Wuthering Heights* from the shelf, Savanah curled up in one of the chairs and opened the book, only to stare into the distance, thinking about last night. She hadn't said anything to Rane, but he had known what she was thinking. Big surprise. The man could read her mind. He had told her he hadn't killed anyone, but the way he said it . . . Maybe he hadn't taken a life, but she would have bet everything she owned that he had wanted to.

She nibbled on the sandwich while she tried to imagine what it was like to be constantly at the mercy of such an insidious craving. She was addicted to chocolate; there was no doubt about that. What woman wasn't? But she could go without it if she had to. And if she went without it long enough, the craving went away. She had gone a week without any chocolate once, just to see if she could do it, and she had survived with no ill effects. But Rane's insatiable lust for blood never went away. No matter how often he fed, the hunger was still there the next day and the next, and if he didn't feed, the hunger grew a little worse each day until the pain became excruciating.

Shaking off her gruesome thoughts, she looked down

at the book in her lap. Where were her mother's books? What would she do if Rane refused to give them to her?

She had made her first kill. The thought was exciting and repulsive at the same time. But, having done it, she felt the need to record it. If she only knew the Werewolf's name, she could enter it in the book. And her name beside it as the hunter who had destroyed it.

Rane woke late in the afternoon. Staring into the darkness, he assessed his injuries. The bites and scratches inflicted by the Werewolf had healed; the flesh burned by the sun pained him only a little less than it had the day before. It would be days, perhaps weeks, before the worst of his injuries were fully healed. He had forgotten how painful the touch of the sun's light could be, but he would willingly endure that and more to protect Savanah.

A harsh laugh escaped his lips. He hadn't done such a great job of protecting her. Now that whoever was after the books knew where she was, she wouldn't be safe here any longer. She was a smart girl. No doubt that fact had already occurred to her.

He took a deep breath, and Mara's scent filled his nostrils. He had felt the brush of her mind against his briefly last night. No other Vampire he knew of possessed the power to reach across continents and oceans. Truly, Mara was a law unto herself, a creature with Supernatural abilities that bordered on the divine. The inhabitants of the earth could count themselves fortunate that she had no desire to dominate them.

He opened his senses as his thoughts drifted to the other woman in his life. He could hear Savanah moving about in the kitchen upstairs, no doubt preparing something to eat. The thought of food aroused his own hunger.

He needed to feed again. It was the only way to ease the pain that burned through him with every breath.

Sitting up, he swung his legs over the edge of the bed. The movement, slight as it was, made his wounds sing. Hands clenched, he took several slow, deep breaths. Damn, why hadn't he said yes when Mara offered him her blood? Had he done so, he wouldn't be hurting so badly now. One thing was for certain, if she made him the same offer again, he wouldn't refuse.

He grunted softly. Little good that did him now.

Rising, he went into the bathroom and turned on the water in the bathtub. He ran his hands over his face, wincing as his fingers brushed singed flesh. For the first time, he was grateful that he couldn't see his reflection. Imagining how he must look, he found it rather surprising that Savanah hadn't run screaming from the sight.

He undressed while the tub filled, his hands exploring the burned flesh on his arms, neck, and back. Only his legs had escaped the sun's wrath.

With a sigh, he stepped into the tub, sank into the blessedly cool water, and closed his eyes.

Savanah glanced at the clock. It was after four. Rane was usually up by now. Of course, being badly hurt, he probably needed more rest than usual. *And more blood,* she thought with a shudder. She wondered what he would say when she told him she had decided to go home. Would he agree, try to convince her to stay here, or simply refuse to let her go?

She fixed a glass of iced tea, then went down to the rec room, kicked off her shoes, and turned on the satellite screen. Picking up the remote, she flipped through the channels until she found a movie she hadn't seen, then settled back on the sofa. Try as she might, she couldn't concentrate on the screen. Instead, she kept glancing over her shoulder, expecting Rane to appear at any minute. Where was he? She drummed her fingertips on the arm of the sofa. Had he been injured worse than she thought? Maybe he lacked the strength to rise.

She sipped her tea, her anxiety growing with every passing moment. Where the heck was he? A sudden coldness clenched her insides. What if he had died in the night? No! She shook her head. That was impossible.

But what if he had?

She was thinking about going down to the subbasement to see if she could get into Mara's private quarters when Rane walked into the room. She couldn't help staring at him.

"I'd tell you it looks worse than it feels," he said dryly, "but it would be a lie."

"Are you all right, otherwise?"

He shrugged. Because he hadn't trusted himself to be with Savanah until after he'd fed, he had gone hunting earlier, something made possible by the heavy cloud cover that obscured the sun. He had preyed upon four young men he had found camped a few miles farther up the mountain. They had all been strong and healthy, football players by the look of them, and he had fed, and fed well.

Still feeling the need to keep his distance from Savanah, he sat in the chair across from the sofa. He had never been vain about his looks; he knew women found him attractive, but he felt strangely embarrassed by his monstrous appearance. That in itself was odd, he thought, since he was a monster on the inside no matter what his outward appearance might be.

"What did you do with the Werewolf?" Savanah asked.

"I dumped his body in a deep ravine at the top of the mountain."

"Did you know him?"

"No. Why?"

"I just wondered. I've never killed anyone before, you know." She shrugged. "I didn't even know his name."

"His legal name was Samuel Jefferson, according to his driver's license. Does that make you feel any better about it?"

"Of course not!" she retorted. "I killed a man. Taking a life may be old hat to you, but it's a new experience for me."

Rane dragged a hand through his hair. "I'm sorry," he said, his voice gruff. "I didn't mean . . ."

"It's all right. I know you didn't mean it. We've both been under a lot of pressure in the last few weeks."

"That's no excuse. I know how difficult this must be for you."

"Do you?"

"Maybe not. I was no longer mortal when I made my first kill. It came easily to me," he said quietly. "Perhaps too easily."

"I'm not sorry for what I did," she said, a note of defiance creeping into her voice. "He meant to kill us, but . . ."

"But it's an awesome and troubling responsibility, the taking of a life."

"Yes. But given the same circumstances, I'd do it again."

Rane smiled in spite of himself. She had the face of an angel and the courage of a mama bear defending her young.

"I've decided to go home," Savanah said.

"Indeed?"

She squared her shoulders and lifted her chin. "Yes, tomorrow night. I'll be needing my mother's books, so I can pack them."

"I see. And if I think you and the books should stay here?"

"I'm going home, Rane. My whereabouts are no longer a secret."

"I haven't done a very good job of protecting you, have I?"

"I didn't say that."

He regarded her a moment, the tension in the air building until it hummed like a hot wire between them. And then he blew out a sigh. "I'll take you home, if that's what you want."

"Will you stay with me for a while?"

"Stay, as in stay in the city, or . . . ?"

"Stay with me, at my house, only if you want to, of course."

"What do you think?"

A flush rose in her cheeks. "I'm new to all this . . . Vampire hunting," she clarified before he could say anything. "I could use your help."

"Are you sure you want to team up with me?"

"I think we've done all right together so far. That Werewolf would have killed me if it wasn't for you."

He shrugged, reluctant to admit it even though he knew it was true. "He was after the books, wasn't he?"

Savanah nodded. Maybe Rane was right. Maybe she should just burn the damn things. She stared into the distance, remembering the horror of the afternoon, reliving her fear, not only for her own life, but for Rane's as well.

Rane drummed his fingers on the arm of the chair. "I just wish I knew who sent him."

"What makes you think he was working for someone else?" The idea chilled her to the bone. She wanted to believe that, with the Werewolf's death, her worries were over.

"Just a hunch. I keep asking myself why a Werewolf would want the books, and why a Werewolf and a Vampire are working together."

"So he wasn't the Werewolf you smelled at my house?"

"No." Rane ran a hand over his jaw. "I can understand why a Vampire would want the books, but a Werewolf . . . ?" He shook his head. "Unless . . ."

"Unless?"

"I don't know. Vampire hunters have been disappearing, but I haven't heard of any Vampire or Vampires who've suddenly gone on a killing spree. For one thing, Mara wouldn't stand for it. So that leaves the Werewolves and the shape-shifters." He shook his head again. "I'd rule out the shifters, so that leaves the Wolves. Maybe they want to start another war. Maybe . . . hell, I don't know."

"You never answered my question," Savanah reminded him after a moment. "Will you stay with me?"

Savanah felt a flutter of excitement low in her belly when he gained his feet and walked toward her, his movements slow and deliberate as he closed the short distance between them. He loomed over her, tall and dark and dangerous, his eyes glinting with desire. Her body warmed to his gaze.

"What do you think?" he asked again.

There was a lot to be said for being in love with a Vampire, Savanah thought as Rane lifted her into his arms. Cradling her to his chest with one hand, he slipped his other hand under her sweater to caress her belly. It sent shivers of anticipation racing down her spine. A moment later, her sweater was gone and he was kissing her breasts, his breath burning through her bra to warm the skin beneath as he carried her upstairs.

The bedroom was dark, the drapes drawn across the windows.

After setting her on her feet, he quickly divested Savanah of her bra, jeans, and panties; then, sitting on the edge of the bed, he drew her into the vee of his thighs.

"Beautiful," he murmured.

Reaching up, he cupped her face in his hands. Drawing her head down, he kissed her eyelids, her cheeks, the pulse throbbing in her throat, careful to avoid the chain around her neck. No doubt it would burn him when they made love, but he dared not ask her to remove it. His tongue swept over her lips, parting them, then delved inside. The touch of his tongue against her own filled her with a sharp stab of desire.

When she thought she might explode with needing him, he fell back on the bed. Drawing her down on top of him, he kissed her again, long and deep. She groaned softly, certain she would expire on the spot if he didn't make love to her.

He showered her with kisses. His hands moved over her body as if for the first time, fondling, exploring, as if he had never touched her before. He worshiped her with his gaze, with his lips, each touch of his hands stroking skin that yearned for more.

Her own hands were trembling as she pulled his T-shirt over his head. She winced when her fingertips brushed against the ugly burn on his neck. After she dropped his T-shirt on the floor, he obligingly removed his sweatpants and tossed them aside, and then stretched out beside her, his skin cool against her heated flesh.

"Are you sure about this?" she asked. "It won't hurt you to . . ."

"It will hurt more not to."

She ran her hands over his shoulders and down his arms, careful not to touch his singed flesh, fascinated by the rock-hard muscles of his biceps. "It was a brave thing you did, coming outside when the sun was up."

"I'd do it again, for you." And so saying, he covered her mouth with his.

The touch of his lips on hers drove everything from her mind but the need to taste him, caress him. Tears burned her eyes when she thought of how close she had come to losing him forever.

"Hey, what's this?" he asked, capturing one of her tears on the tip of his finger.

"Nothing."

He drew back, his gaze moving over her face. "You're crying. Why?"

"You could have been killed."

"But I wasn't." He drew her into his embrace, his hand lightly stroking her hair. Her concern touched him as nothing else could. Since leaving home, no one had worried about him or cared whether he lived or died. Closing his eyes, he kissed his way along the smooth, warm flesh below her ear, cursed inwardly as his hunger flared to life.

Jackknifing into a sitting position, he turned his back to her. What was he doing? He couldn't hold her, make love to her, and not taste her. And he was sorely afraid a taste wouldn't be enough. Not now, when he hurt like hell. Perhaps never.

He flinched at the touch of her hand on his shoulder.

"Rane? What is it? What's wrong?"

He shook his head. "I can't do this." He shivered as her fingers stroked his nape. Her touch stoked his desire and his hunger. It would be so easy to take her, to sheathe himself in her softness, to bury his fangs in her tender flesh, to drink and drink . . .

Muttering an oath, he gained his feet and stalked

toward the window. His senses told him the storm had passed. Soon, the sun would set. If he drew back the heavy drapes and leaned out the window, how long would it take for the setting sun to turn his body to a pile of smoldering ash?

He took a step forward, watched his hand move toward one of the drapes . . .

"Stop it!" Savanah grabbed his arm and pulled him away from the window. "What are you doing? Have you lost your mind?"

He stared down at her, at the pulse beating rapidly in the hollow of her throat.

"Rane, please . . ." She laid a gentle hand against his singed cheek. "I love you. I can only imagine what you're going through, how painful this must be . . ."

"You can't imagine it! No one can. I can't look at you without wanting you, without wanting to drink and drink until there's nothing left! Why do you stay with me? You should be running for your life. You're in danger, Savanah, more than you know."

His words, the intensity of his gaze, frightened her to the depths of her being and yet she couldn't leave him, couldn't run, not even to save her own life. He was hurting, suffering, and it was all her fault. If she hadn't gone outside, none of this would have happened.

She lifted the silver chain over her head, then brushed the hair from her neck and canted her head to one side.

"Didn't I tell you not to take that off?" He stared at her, his eyes glowing, his hands clenched at his sides. "I'm not sure even that could save you."

"I'm not afraid. Drink, Rane, if that's what you want, what you need."

"Dammit, woman, haven't you heard a word I said?"

"I heard." Cupping his face in her hands, she drew his head down. "Do what you have to."

His hands folded over her shoulders, imprisoning her in his grasp. His tongue brushed his fangs as he inhaled the scent of the crimson river flowing through her veins. She was his for the taking. The thought enflamed him.

He was lowering his head to her neck when she murmured, "I love you."

Rane lifted his head, his gaze meeting hers. And as had happened once before, the trust shining in her beautiful sky-blue eyes, the unconditional love in her voice, calmed the beast within him. He sighed as her arms slid around his waist.

"Savanah." Whispering her name, he rested his forehead against hers. As long as she was his, maybe there was hope for him, after all.

Chapter Thirty-Four

Taking a deep breath, Savanah unlocked the front door of her father's house and stepped into the entryway. She stood there a moment while memories of happier times spent in this house played through her mind—a vague recollection of her mother walking her to kindergarten on the first day of school, the scent of freshly baked cookies that had always lingered in the air on Monday afternoons, the birthday parties and holidays in the backyard, the flowers her father had sent her the day she received her first big assignment at the *Chronicle,* all the nights she and her father had spent talking, laughing, working together.

"Oh, Dad," she murmured, "I miss you so much."

She was about to go into the living room when Rane moved up beside her.

"Wait a minute."

Frowning, she looked up at him. "Is something wrong?"

"I don't think so. Just wait."

Rane moved past her into the living room. Standing in the middle of the floor, he opened his preternatural senses. The air smelled a little stale; other than that, he sensed nothing amiss. After closing and locking the front door, he carried her belongings and one of his suitcases into the living room and dropped them on the sofa.

Following him into the room, Savanah turned on the table lamps. "It's just a house without him," she said quietly. "He's the one who made it a home."

Rane nodded, but said nothing.

Savanah blew out a sigh. She had known it would be hard coming back here, but she hadn't expected it to hurt so much. "Did you bring my mother's books?" she asked.

"No."

"Where are they? Did you leave them at Mara's? I thought . . ."

"I buried them up in the mountains before we left."

Savanah blinked at him. "How can I refer to them if they're not here?" she asked, striving not to lose her temper. "They're my books, Rane. I want them."

"I know you do." He rubbed a hand over his jaw. "But . . ."

"But you don't think I can keep them safe?"

"I don't think you'll be safe as long as they exist."

He was probably right, but right or wrong, she was too tired to argue about it now. Swallowing her anger, she said, "It's late. I'm going upstairs to take a bath." She picked up her suitcase. "Are you staying?"

"If you still want me to."

"I do."

He couldn't help admiring the gentle sway of her hips as she headed for the staircase, or the way the lamplight gilded her hair. He could smell her frustration, knew she was annoyed with him because of the books, but he didn't care. He had to do what he thought was best, and right now, keeping Savanah and those accursed books as far apart as possible seemed like the wisest thing to do.

He glanced up as he heard the water come on in the bathroom. It took damned little effort to imagine her disrobing, her movements graceful and unhurried, her skin smooth and clear, aglow with good health. Warm and alive.

He swore softly as images of Savanah reclining in a tub filled with foamy bubbles sprang full-blown into his mind.

Before he quite realized what he was doing, he was climbing the stairs two at a time. He hesitated only a moment before he opened the door and stepped into the bathroom.

Savanah's eyelids flew open as he entered the room. "Oh! It's you. You scared the heck out of me."

"Sorry." His voice was low, little more than a rasp of sound. The frothy bubbles floating on the surface of the water did little to hide the swell of her breasts or her long, slender legs.

She looked up at him, her head canted to one side, one brow raised in amusement. "Would you care to join me?"

"I can't think of anything I'd rather do."

"Well, come on, then." She sat up to make room for him, watched avidly as he quickly undressed. Her gaze moved over him. The burns on his face looked pretty much the same as they had the day before, but the angry redness on his arms had faded. "Turn around."

He lifted on brow. "Excuse me?"

"I want to look at your back."

The muscles in his jaw tightened as he did as she asked.

"It looks better. I thought you said it would take a long time to heal."

Rane shrugged as he turned to face her. He supposed the blood he had taken from her, along with the blood from the two young women and four men on the mountain, accounted for his healing.

Water sloshed over the edge of the bathtub as he stepped in and sat down, facing her. "You need a bigger tub."

"You think?"

He shrugged. "Maybe not." He spread his legs, then drew her into the vee of his thighs so that her legs rested over his.

"So, here we are, naked in the water again," Savanah said with a grin.

"Indeed."

She touched his cheek. "Does it still hurt terribly?"

"Not as bad as it did." Taking up the soap, he reached around her and began washing her back.

Savanah rested her forehead on his shoulder. "That feels wonderful."

A soft sound of assent rose in Rane's throat as his hands stroked over her soapy flesh. He washed her arms, her neck, her breasts. Leaning forward, he dropped kisses on the crown of her head.

After he had washed her, she took the soap to return the favor, but one touch of her hand on his chest and he was lost. Drawing her into his arms, he rose in one fluid movement and carried her into the bedroom where he lowered her onto the bed and then followed her down, his body covering hers as his mouth claimed her lips in a long searing kiss.

She ran her hands over his body, reveling in the way his skin rippled beneath her fingertips, in the flex and play of his biceps as she kneaded the muscles there. She quivered with anticipation as his hands caressed her, bold hands, strong hands.

Sensations flowed over her and through her—the damp sheets at her back, Rane's heated flesh, the sweep of his tongue across her lips, the brush of his hair against her shoulders as he nuzzled her neck, the rapid beat of her heart, the husky yearning in his voice as he whispered love words in her ear.

Right or wrong, she wanted him, all of him, the good and the bad. Wanted him with a desperation she had never known before. He was the strength to her weakness, a constant in her ever-changing world. The light to her darkness. No doubt he would find that as amusing as she did.

Grinning inwardly, Savanah wrapped her legs around his waist, holding him close, afraid he would change his mind yet again and leave her yearning for more.

But he had no thought to leave her, not now, not ever again.

Closing her eyes, Savanah gave herself into his keeping, body and soul, and as she did so, her thoughts became his, as his became hers. It was amazing, to feel what he felt, to know he experienced her pleasure as she experienced his. There was no shyness between them, no need for words. She satisfied his every desire as he satisfied hers. Truly, they were two halves made whole, two bodies with one heart, one mind.

The touch of his fangs at her throat sent her world spiraling out of control. Sobbing his name, she writhed beneath him, her body quivering with ecstasy until she lay sated and spent beneath him.

Rane's climax came quickly on the heels of her own. With a sigh, he wrapped his arms around her and rolled onto his side so that they lay facing each other, their bodies still intimately joined together.

His gaze searched hers. "Still no regrets?"

"Not one. You?"

He shook his head. He had many regrets in life, but making love to Savanah wasn't one of them. He just wished he was worthy of her love, her trust. He had never intended for their relationship to go this far, never intended to fall in love with her, but now . . . it was beyond his control. He would love her, cherish her, until the end of time.

"And so," he said, "where do we go from here?"

"What do you mean?"

"What do you see yourself doing after we've found the Vampire who killed your father and you and your books are out of danger?"

"I don't know. I haven't thought that far ahead." She worried her lower lip with her teeth. "Do you have plans?"

"None that don't include you. Do you feel the same?"

She glanced down at their bodies, still joined together, then looked at him, one brow raised. "What do you think?"

"I think I want to make love to you again."

"So soon? Can you?"

"I'm not a mortal man, love, have you forgotten?"

"How could I?" She nibbled on his chin, then kissed the tip of his nose. "I'm yours to command."

His gaze moved over her face. Though she didn't know it, she was indeed his to command. He had tasted her blood, made her his as no other woman had ever been his. For better or worse, for the rest of her life, they were bound together. Should she choose to leave him sometime in the future, the blood bond between them would remain. No matter where she went, he would always be able to find her. Whether she wished it or not, she would always be his to command.

Cupping the back of her head in his hand, he claimed her lips with his, hunger and desire rising up like a wildfire in his loins, yet even as he took her, a distant part of his mind hoped she wouldn't be incinerated by the flames.

* * *

Savanah woke with a smile and a groan. Turning onto her side, she glanced at the clock. It was almost four in the afternoon. She supposed it wasn't really so surprising that she had slept so long since Rane had made love to her all night long, each time more wonderful than the last. Sleep had claimed her sometime in the wee small hours of the morning.

Sitting up, she stretched her arms over her head. Where was he? Was he taking his rest somewhere in the house? If not, where would he go? Rising, she put on her robe, then went into the bathroom to wash her face and brush her teeth. She slipped her mother's silver chain over her head, her fingers momentarily stroking the crucifix where it rested between her breasts.

After making her way downstairs, she put the coffee on, and then she wandered through the house, looking for Rane's resting place. She paused a moment outside her father's bedroom, her mind filling with unwanted images of the last time she had seen him, lying on the floor the night he died.

Expelling a deep breath, she opened the door. Rane wasn't in the room. She hadn't really expected to find him sleeping in her father's bed, or in any of the other rooms in the house, since none of them was equipped to completely block the sun's light. On the other hand, she didn't think he would go off and leave her alone, either, so where could he be? One thing was for certain, if he was in the house, she couldn't find him.

Returning to the kitchen, she poured herself a cup of coffee, then popped a couple of slices of bread into the toaster. When the toast was ready, she buttered it, then sat at the table, reliving the night before. She had always heard that men needed a certain amount of time between bouts of lovemaking, but that wasn't true of Rane. She had heard some of her friends complain that their husbands always turned over and fell asleep after making love. Savanah grinned, knowing that was one thing she would never have to worry about.

Sobering, she wondered if she would ever have a husband now.

What if Rane didn't want to get married?

What if he did? It was a topic they had never discussed.

Did she want to marry a Vampire? His parents, his grandparents, his brother and his sister-in-law were all Vampires. What would it be like, to be the only mortal in a family of the Undead? Would they accept her as part of the family, or would they look at her and see only prey?

And why was she even worrying about something that might never happen when her life was still in danger?

Savanah retrieved her other suitcase from the living room and carried it upstairs. She left Rane's on the sofa. She knew he wouldn't mind sharing her bed, but she didn't know if he'd want to share her bedroom, as well. Thus far, he had preferred to take his rest in privacy.

After pulling on a pair of jeans and a sweater, she lifted her mother's Vampire kit from her suitcase and dropped it on the bed. It took only minutes to put her clothes away and when that was done, she sat in the middle of the bed, her fingertips tracing the runes on the top of the metal box before she opened it. She ran her hands over the various instruments of destruction, smiling faintly as she imagined her mother and father doing the same thing in days past. She couldn't think of any two people who had looked less like Vampire hunters, she mused. But then, she had never seen a Vampire hunter, so what did she know?

Her fingertips lingered over one of the smooth wooden stakes. If she had learned anything up at Mara's place, it was that she should always have a bottle of holy water and a stake or two close at hand. With that thought in mind, she wrapped one of the stout wooden stakes in an old scarf and tucked it into the waistband of her jeans, then slipped a bottle of holy water into one of the pockets. She felt a little silly, being armed in her own house, but silly or not, it was the smart thing to do. Her gun was in her handbag. Perhaps it was time to buy a holster and carry the gun on her person, as well. She would have to ask Rane about that later.

She wondered how and where her parents had obtained holy water. Had they gone to the local Catholic church with a jar and asked the priest to fill it up for a good cause? And what about stakes? She seemed to recall that one of the books had mentioned that hawthorn worked the best. Luckily, there were several hawthorn trees growing in the backyard.

Coincidence? She thought not.

She closed the box, then picked up her cell phone, intending to call Mr. Van Black to let him know she was home but would need more time off, only to sit there staring at the screen. Being a reporter didn't seem as important as it once had. It might take years to get the kind of break that would allow her to work in New York City or Los Angeles. In the meantime, she would be stuck here, a small-town reporter covering small-town stories, when she should be devoting all her time and energy to finding and destroying Vampires. Her parents had left her financially well-off. Her father had carried a large insurance policy; her mother had turned Vampire hunting into a lucrative business.

Savanah ran her hand over the top of the box again. To

tell the truth, she didn't know what she wanted to do with the rest of her life. Of course, all things considered, the rest of her life could be days instead of years.

And with that in mind, she punched in Mr. Van Black's number and told him she was quitting.

Rane stirred with the setting of the sun, his senses expanding, his nerves on edge until he detected Savanah's presence inside the house. She was in the kitchen cooking dinner. Something with chicken. Food, he thought. Mortals spent a lot of time thinking about it, preparing it, eating it. He remembered sitting on the kitchen counter helping his mother make Christmas cookies when he was five or six and how he and Rafe had decorated the cookies, the kitchen, and themselves with colored icing. Rafe's favorite dessert had been fudge brownies. He remembered how he and Rafe had argued over who got to lick the spoon and who got the bowl and how once, when their mother's back was turned, Rafe had opened the oven door and the two of them had eaten spoonfuls of warm, uncooked brownie batter.

It seemed like an eternity since he had seen his mother and his brother. And his father. What were they all doing now? Did they think of him often? He had shut them out of his life, blocked the link between himself and Rafe, and yet he couldn't help feeling hurt that they hadn't found him. Had they even tried?

Berating himself for his melancholy thoughts, he burrowed up through the earth alongside the house, then stood there a moment, drinking in the sounds of the night, his senses searching for anything out of the ordinary. When he was convinced that there was no danger lurking in the shadows, he willed himself into the house.

* * *

Savanah opened the oven door to check on the chicken.
Another few minutes and it would be baked to perfection.
She stirred the rice, turned the fire down low under the
corn, and let out a shriek when she turned around and saw
Rane standing in the doorway.

He grinned at her. "Sorry."

She pressed a hand to her heart. "A little warning would
have been nice."

"Next time I'll say, 'Boo.'"

"Very funny. Where have you been?"

"Resting."

"Where? I . . . Well, I looked for you in the house."

"I decided to sleep outside."

"Oh?"

He closed the distance between them and took her in
his arms. "Did you miss me?"

"Maybe."

He grinned at her.

"Okay, maybe a little," she admitted. "Mostly I was just
curious about where you were."

His grin widened. "You're a terrible liar. Did anyone
ever tell you that?"

"Just you." She blew out a sigh. "I quit my job today."
Now that it was done, she was having second thoughts.

"If you're worried about money, don't," Rane said. "I
have more than I need."

"No, it's not that. It's just . . . I don't know. It seemed like
a good idea at the time, but now . . ." She shrugged. "Nothing in my life seems to be going the way I planned."

"I suppose I'm partly to blame for that," Rane remarked.

"Partly." She jumped when the oven timer buzzed.
"My dinner's ready."

Releasing her, Rane watched her take a pan out of the oven and set it on the counter. He wrinkled his nose as the smell of cooked meat permeated the room.

Savanah bustled about the kitchen, setting the table, filling a glass with milk, spooning rice and corn onto a plate, adding a chicken breast.

"Do you want to keep me company while I eat?" she asked, sitting at the table.

He shook his head. "My dinner awaits." Bending, he kissed her cheek. "I won't be gone long," he said, and vanished from her sight.

Rane materialized on the sidewalk. Because he didn't want to leave Savanah alone any longer than necessary, he hypnotized the first mortal who crossed his path, took what he needed, and made his way back to Savanah's.

As soon as he reached the front door, he knew leaving her had been a mistake, perhaps a fatal one. The smell of blood and death hung heavy in the air, and with it, the familiar scent of Vampire.

Chapter Thirty-Five

"Savanah!"

Rane burst into the kitchen prepared for battle, only to find that it was already over. A female Vampire lay in a lifeless sprawl on the floor, a hawthorn stake driven deep into her heart. Savanah stood with her back against the kitchen table, her eyes wide and unfocused.

"Savanah?" Rane stepped over the body. "Are you all right?"

"Is she dead?"

"Pretty much."

"I need to . . ."—the blood drained from Savanah's face—". . . to take her head to make sure."

"What happened?"

Savanah looked up at him, her eyes wide, her face pale. "I was rinsing my dishes in the sink when she came up behind me. She grabbed me and tried to . . . to tie my hands together. She said someone, I can't remember his name, was coming to . . ." She swayed unsteadily. "How could she come into the house? I didn't invite her."

"Your father did." Taking Savanah by the hand, Rane

led her to a chair and urged her to sit down. "Go on. What else did she say?"

"She said he'd kill me if I didn't tell him what he wanted to know. I pushed her away, I don't know how. I had a stake in the waistband of my jeans and I . . . I grabbed it, and when she reached for me again, I . . ."

Savanah swallowed the bitter taste of bile in her throat. If she lived to be a hundred, she would never forget how easily the stake had penetrated the Vampire's flesh, like a knife through butter, nor would she soon forget the horrified look in the Vampire's eyes when she realized what had happened.

"It's all right," Rane said gently. "I think I get the picture." He squeezed her hand. "Savanah, get hold of yourself. Try to remember the name. Who's coming?"

"Cliff? Clayton? No, Clive." She nodded. "Yes, that was it. Clive."

Rane swore softly. Clive. The undisputed leader of the North American Werewolves was as powerful in his own way as Mara was in hers. Rane frowned. It had been Clive and Mara who had ended the old war. What was the Werewolf's interest in Savanah? Rane had never met the man, but he couldn't help wondering if it was Clive's footprint he had seen outside the Gentry home, and if so, why the Werewolf had teamed up with a Vampire.

Rane glanced at the body on the kitchen floor. She had been a pretty woman. Perhaps that was reason enough, but he didn't think so.

"Savanah?"

"I'm all right."

He regarded her through narrowed eyes. Her heartbeat was slower, more regular, the color had returned to her cheeks. "Do you want me to dispose of the body?"

"No. I should do it. I killed her."

He saw the indecision in her eyes, her need to be strong warring with her revulsion at what she had already done, at what still needed to be done.

"I thought she'd disappear or turn to dust."

"Only the very old do that." He placed his hand on her shoulder. "Will it make it easier if I tell you she's the Vampire who killed your father?"

"What? Are you sure?" Savanah looked at the dead woman, the horror at what she had done quickly turning to a sense of victory.

"Yes." He glanced at the body, then back at Savanah. "It's a messy business, taking a head."

"Have you done it before?"

"No."

"I should do it," she said again. "I need to . . ."

"Dammit!" Rane said, pivoting toward the door. "He's here."

He had no sooner spoken the words than the back door slammed open with a bang.

Fear coiled in Savanah's belly as a man stepped into the kitchen. He was as tall as Rane, his body compact and well-muscled. His hooded gaze swept the room in a single glance, his expression hardening when he saw the woman's body.

"Ah, Tasha," Clive muttered, and then his gaze settled on Rane. "I don't want to fight with you over this," he said curtly. "I want the books, that's all."

"Do you always get what you want?"

Clive nodded. "Always."

Rane stepped between Savanah and the Werewolf. "Not this time."

"Want the books for yourself, do you, Vampire?"

"No, I just don't want you to have them."

"It seems there's only one way to settle it, then," Clive

said. "Survivor gets the books." He glanced at Savanah. "And the woman."

"Let's take it outside," Rane said.

Clive jerked his head toward the back door. "After you."

"I don't think so."

Clive winked at Savanah. "I'll be back in a few minutes." He glanced at the dead Vampire, and then back at Savanah. "Be ready to take her place." And so saying, he turned and walked out of the house.

"Rane . . ."

"Get your gun and get the hell out of here." Rane didn't wait for her reply, but turned and followed the Werewolf out the back door.

Savanah stood there a moment, her heart pounding wildly. And then she went upstairs to get her gun.

Chapter Thirty-Six

Clive stood in the middle of the backyard, his hands fisted at his sides, his eyes narrow slits. "To the death?"

"Suits me."

Exhilaration flowed through Rane's body as he summoned his preternatural power. He knew Clive was doing the same. The Werewolf's Supernatural energy danced across Rane's skin like static electricity, alien yet familiar.

They circled each other slowly, their bodies tense and slightly hunched over, their arms loose at their sides.

Rane took a deep calming breath. If he lived, Savanah would live. If he died, she would die. Knowing that, everything else ceased to exist as he focused all his attention on the Werewolf.

Clive darted forward, his hands changing, the nails becoming a wolf's sharp claws as he endeavored to sweep Rane's legs out from under him. Sidestepping to the left, Rane brought his fist down across the Werewolf's back. Clive grunted, then spun away. Wheeling around, he charged again, a yellow-eyed nightmare on two legs. Sharp fangs protruded from his mouth.

Rane blocked the Werewolf's charge again and again,

hardly aware of the bites and scratches he received. His breath came in harsh gasps, his nostrils flaring as the scent of the Werewolf's blood rose in the air. They came together again and yet again, each seeming oblivious to the injuries they sustained, neither inflicting any serious damage to the other.

With a howl of frustration, Clive shifted to wolf form.

An instant later, Rane did likewise.

Again, they were evenly matched in size and strength. Clive's teeth raked the length of Rane's left foreleg, shredding flesh and muscle. With a savage snarl, Rane lowered his head and charged. Clive scrambled backward, his hind legs tangling in his cast-off clothing. With a feral growl, Rane sprang forward, intending to bury his fangs in the Werewolf's throat. He let out a growl as his left leg gave way beneath him and his fangs closed on Clive's shoulder instead of his throat. Blood filled his mouth and he reveled in it. Clive lay still beneath him, his for the taking.

Exhilarated by the thought of destroying his enemy, caught up in the lust for blood, Rane realized a moment too late that Clive was changing again.

Uttering an inhuman cry of triumph, the Werewolf wrenched his shoulder from Rane's jaws. With blood pouring down his arm, Clive pulled a syringe from the pocket of his shredded jacket and jabbed the needle between Rane's shoulder blades.

Rane howled as pain exploded through his back, as hot as the fires of hell. His vision blurred. Shaking his head, he focused on the Werewolf. If he was going to die, he was taking Clive with him. Gathering his rapidly-waning strength, he lunged at the other man, his body shifting in midair. The force of his momentum drove Clive backward to the ground. The Werewolf landed hard, and Rane landed on top of him, his hands circling the Werewolf's neck. Clive bucked and kicked, shrieking and howling in fury as his nails raked Rane's back. It took every ounce of Rane's remaining strength for him to hang on. He didn't know what kind of poison had been in the needle, but it burned through his whole body, leeching his strength, blurring his vision, as he slowly squeezed the life and breath out of the Werewolf.

And then, unable to fight it any longer, Rane tumbled into the blackness that beckoned him.

Savanah ran out of the house crying his name. She spared hardly a glance for the dead Werewolf as she sank to her knees beside Rane.

For a moment, she could only stare at him. He couldn't be dead, she thought. He was already dead, or Undead. He was just unconscious or something. His body was covered with bites and scratches, but none of them looked fatal.

"Rane." She shook his shoulder gently. "Rane, wake up." She shook his shoulder again, harder this time. "Rane, wake up! Dammit, this isn't funny! Wake up! Please!"

He didn't stir, didn't seem to be breathing.

She glanced at the sky, a silent prayer rising in her heart. *Please, please, please, don't let him be dead. Please.*

The night settled around her, deep and dark and quiet. She needed help, but there was no one here, no one for miles. No one who could help her. She rested her forehead on his chest as that painful reality hit home. *There was no one who could help her.*

She glanced back at the house. Somehow, she had to get him inside before morning. But how? She couldn't lift him, not now, when he was deadweight . . . deadweight.

Hysterical laughter bubbled up in her throat, only to emerge in a flood of tears.

She didn't know how long she'd been sitting there, sobbing, when she felt a change in the wind. It raised the hair at her nape and along her arms, made her palms sweat and her mouth go dry.

Scrambling to her feet, with a stake in one hand and her gun in the other, Savanah turned in a slow circle, her gaze seeking to penetrate the darkness in the distant corners of the backyard.

Someone, or something, was out there, hiding in the shadows.

Savanah froze, narrowing her eyes as what looked like a shimmer of silver motes moved toward her through the trees. Certain she was imagining things, she rubbed her eyes and when she opened them again, a man was striding toward her, a tall man dressed all in black.

Lifting her gun hand, she aimed the weapon in his direction. "Don't come any closer."

He didn't stop, or even slow down. "I mean you no harm. I've come to help."

"Are you a doctor?" She knew the question was ludicrous even as it passed her lips. Why would a doctor be lurking outside in the shadows just when she needed one?

Before she could decide whether or not to pull the trigger, the stranger was upon her. Plucking the gun from her hand, he slipped it into his coat pocket.

Savanah stared at the stranger, glanced down at Rane, and then looked at the stranger again. She frowned as realization dawned. The man standing in front of her could be no one but . . . "Rafe?"

He nodded. "At your service."

"What are you doing here? How did you know . . . ?"

"We're twins," Rafe said quietly. "I can feel the pain

burning through him." He glanced at the Werewolf's body. "The bastard injected Rane with holy water."

Fear knotted deep in Savanah's belly. A few drops of holy water on Rane's face and neck had blistered his skin. What would it do to his insides? "Will it kill him?"

"I can't say, but it has rendered him helpless, powerless." He closed his eyes a moment, his jaw clenching. "The pain is excruciating."

"You can really feel what he's feeling?"

"Yes." He let out a long shuddering sigh. "It is beyond description, almost beyond bearing."

Savanah regarded the Vampire. Though he'd said he was feeling his brother's pain, he gave little visible sign of it. She wondered if it was due to some deep inner strength, or if he was making an effort to shield his pain from her eyes. But it didn't matter. Nothing mattered now but Rane. "Can you help him?"

"I hope so." Kneeling, Rafe lifted his brother into his arms, then nodded toward the house. "After you."

Moving quickly, Savanah led the way to the back door. She was halfway across the kitchen when she realized that Rafe wasn't behind her. Of course, he had never been here before. He needed an invitation to enter her home.

Calling, "Come in" over her shoulder, Savanah hurried down the hallway to her father's room. She turned down the covers on the bed, chewed on her thumbnail as she watched Rafe lower his brother gently onto the mattress.

Blood from the numerous bites and scratches that covered Rane's body quickly soaked into the sheets. Vampires were supposed to mend quickly, so why wasn't he? Was it the holy water that kept his wounds from healing, or something else? Something worse?

"You might want to wait outside," Rafe suggested.

"Why?"

"I'm going to give him my blood and hope that it will counteract the effects of the holy water."

"And if it doesn't?"

"Let us hope that it does," Rafe said, his expression grim.

"Get on with it then." Savanah looked at Rane, more worried than she wanted to admit. He looked pale, so pale. She stared at his chest. His breathing seemed shallow and labored. His hands were tightly clenched at his sides; tight lines of pain bracketed his mouth. She yearned to brush the hair from his brow, to wash the blood from his wounds, to kiss his hurts and make them better. "Hurry!"

Rafe glanced at the door and then at Savanah, a silent, none-too-subtle hint that she should take his advice and leave.

Savanah shook her head. "Forget it, I'm staying."

"As you wish." Sitting on the edge of the bed, Rafe removed his jacket and tossed it aside, then rolled up his shirtsleeve. He slid a glance in Savanah's direction and then, turning his back to her, he bit into a vein in his left wrist.

Moving closer to the bed, Savanah saw Rane's nostrils twitch as the coppery scent of blood wafted through the air.

Lifting his brother's head, Rafe held his wrist to Rane's lips. "Drink, Rane."

She watched in horrified fascination as Rane's mouth closed over the bleeding wound.

She didn't know how much time passed. It might have been a minute, it might have been an hour. She couldn't tear her gaze away from the two men on the bed. How had their parents ever told them apart? They appeared to be identical in every way.

After a time, Rafe drew his wrist away.

Savanah watched as he licked the wound, which healed instantly. And then she looked at Rane. As far as she could see, nothing had changed. His wounds, still oozing blood, looked raw and angry.

Moving up beside Rafe, she tapped him on the shoulder. "Did it work?"

"No." Rising, he stared down at his brother. "We need Mara."

"Then get her."

"If I know Mara, she is already on her way."

"But . . . how will she know to come here, that Rane needs her?"

"She's our godmother. When we were born, she took blood from each of us so that she would always know where we were. She'll know what has happened." He looked at Savanah and smiled. "As you surmised, I am Rane's brother, Raphael."

"Savanah Gentry."

"Gentry?" He shook his head. "No, it can't be."

"Excuse me?"

"There was a rather notorious hunter named Barbara Gentry a couple of decades ago."

"She was my mother."

Rafe's gaze moved to his brother before settling on Savanah's face again. "Forgive my impudence, but exactly what is your relationship to my brother?"

Savanah lifted her chin. "I love him."

"I see. And he loves you." It wasn't a question, but a statement of fact.

"Yes."

Rafe nodded, his lips curving in wry amusement. "My folks will never believe this."

Savanah felt suddenly light-headed. "Are they coming,

too?" One Vampire, fine. His brother, okay. Add to that Rane's parents and a Vampire rumored to be thousands of years old, and Savanah thought it might be time to crawl into a hole and pull the hole in after her.

"Rane said he hasn't been in touch with any of you in years. How did you know where to find him?"

"We are more than brothers, more than twins. There is a blood link between us. While Rane was conscious and in control, he blocked it. But tonight . . ." Rafe looked at his brother. "Tonight I felt his pain, and I followed it. Why don't you sit with him while I go dispose of the bodies?"

Relieved to be spared the gruesome task, Savanah sat on the edge of the bed and took Rane's hand in hers. His skin felt cool and dry. What if nothing could be done to save him? What if even the infamous Mara couldn't help?

"Fight, Rane," she murmured. "You've got to be strong." She worried her lower lip between her teeth. Would her blood help?

Savanah was debating whether to suggest it to Rafe when there was a change in the atmosphere. Her skin prickled, the hair raised along the back of her neck. Before she had time to be afraid, a woman appeared beside the bed.

It was Mara. Savanah knew it without being told. And then she frowned. How was it possible for the Vampire to enter the house without an invitation?

The woman didn't spare a glance for Savanah. Sitting on the edge of the bed, she drew Rane into her arms. Lifting her sweater, she made a slit in her left breast with her thumbnail, then pressed Rane's head to her bosom.

She didn't have to tell him to drink.

Savanah stared at the scene before her. It was like something out of a horror movie, one Vampire feeding off another. She couldn't stop watching, couldn't take her eyes from Mara. Clad in a pair of skintight white pants and a black vee-necked sweater, Mara was the most beautiful creature Savanah had ever seen. Her hair fell down her slender back like a fall of black silk, long and thick. Her eyes were green, though green seemed too pale a word to describe them; her skin was pale and flawless; her lips pink and perfectly shaped.

A wave of jealousy rose up in Savanah's heart as she watched Rane suckle at the other woman's breast. It should have been her blood that nourished him, Savanah thought. She was the one who loved him, but apparently her mortal blood wasn't good enough.

After what seemed like forever, Mara drew back. She kissed Rane on the forehead, then eased him down on the bed again and drew the covers over him. Only after rearranging her clothing did she acknowledge that there was anyone else in the room.

Rising, she turned her amazing green eyes on Savanah. "So," she said, "you must be the princess."

"I beg your pardon?"

"'Tis nothing," Mara said with a wave of her hand.

"Is Rane going to be all right?" Savanah asked.

"Of course. He's Nosferatu. He will rise in a few days." Mara laid her hand on Rane's brow, her own brow furrowed. "Holy water is like poison to us, but I had hoped . . ." She gave a toss of her head.

"Hoped what?" Rafe asked, stepping into the bedroom.

"That my blood would speed the healing process."

"But he will get better, won't he?" Savanah asked anxiously. In spite of their assurances, she wasn't reassured at all.

"In time. And now," Mara said, focusing her attention on Savanah once more, "tell me about you. Are you in love with him?"

"Yes."

"And he loves you?"

Savanah frowned, wondering if every Vampire she met was going to ask her the same questions. "Yes."

"And it doesn't matter to you what he is?"

"Of course it matters."

"Yes," Mara said thoughtfully, "I can see where there might be problems, what with Rane being a Vampire and you being a hunter. Have you destroyed any of us yet?"

It was in Savanah's mind to lie, but one look into Mara's eyes and she knew it would be a waste of breath. Lifting her chin, she said, "Yes, I have."

"Clive's whore," Mara said, as if she had known the answer all along. "Good riddance. Had you not destroyed the little traitor, I would have done it myself."

Savanah glanced at Rane. Why were they talking about the dead Vampire when Rane wasn't healing the way he should be?

"And where are the books Clive was searching for?" Mara asked.

"I don't know," Savanah said. "Rane said he buried them somewhere."

"Mara, what the devil is going on?" Rafe asked. "I thought the war was over."

"As did I. Apparently Clive decided to start it again. His wolves have been quietly disposing of Vampires and Vampire hunters, to what end I'm not sure, although I suspect for the same reason they started the last war. He and his kind want to rule the world."

"These books you mentioned," Rafe said. "What have they do to with anything?"

"One of them contains a list of all known Vampires, their countries of origin, and their favorite cities and hangouts. There's also a list of hunters. I imagine being in possession of such a list would have made Clive's task easier."

"What happens now that he's dead?" Savanah wondered aloud.

"I will speak to his lieutenant when I leave here," Mara said. "I will tell him to stop this madness immediately, or I will destroy him and all of his kind."

The expression in Mara's eyes, more than her words, sent a chill down Savanah's spine. She had no doubt that the Vampire could do exactly what she said.

Rafe frowned. "If you can do that, kill all the Werewolves, why didn't you do it when we were at war?"

Mara shrugged. "I had hoped it wouldn't come to that. Killing grows tedious after a while and draws unwanted attention. But I will not hesitate to do it now, if necessary." She glanced at Rane, her brow furrowed. "Come, let us leave him to rest in the dark."

Savanah was reluctant to leave Rane alone but surely Mara knew what was best.

Whispering, "I love you," she pressed a kiss to his cheek, then turned out the light and followed the Vampires out of the room.

Mara and Rafe were sitting side by side on the sofa when Savanah entered the living room a few moments later. She stood in the doorway, never more aware of the beat of her heart, or her own mortality, than at that instant. It was a totally bizarre situation, two Vampires and a fledgling hunter under the same roof.

Striving for an air of confidence, she slid her hand into her pocket, her fingers closing over the bottle of holy water tucked inside. She was pretty sure it would stop Rafe, if necessary. She wondered if anything could thwart Mara. She had been skeptical when Rane told her that Mara was thousands of years old but now, having seen her, after experiencing her overpowering presence, Savanah knew it was true.

Taking a seat on the chair across from the sofa, Savanah clasped her hands in her lap. Had her visitors been mortal, she would have offered them refreshment; in this case, she was the only refreshment in the house, and she wasn't offering. She couldn't help staring at Rafe, amazed by his resemblance to Rane. If she hadn't known better, she would have sworn it was Rane sitting across from her.

Rafe lifted one brow, amused by her scrutiny.

"I'm sorry," Savanah said, "but I've never seen twins who looked so much alike. How did your parents ever tell you apart?"

He chuckled softly. "Sometimes they couldn't. And as teenagers . . ." He shrugged. "We played numerous pranks, not only on our parents, but on our tutors, as well. Mara was the only one we could never fool."

Mara looked at him, an indulgent smile curving her lips. "Where's Kathy? Why didn't she come with you?"

"She went to Italy to attend some rare book auction with my parents."

"Why didn't you go?" Mara asked.

"I felt the need for some solitude."

Mara nodded her understanding. "Have you told them about Rane?"

"Yes."

"I'm surprised they're not here."

"I told them there was no need, at present. If Rane's existence was in danger, they would be here, but since he is likely to recover, they decided not to intrude on his privacy. He's made it clear that he wants no contact with any of us."

"And yet here you are," Mara remarked.

"He is blood of my blood. I came to share his pain."

Sitting there, listening to the two Vampires, Savanah felt as though she had stumbled into an alien world. They spoke of things beyond her comprehension. She glanced from one to the other. They were both beautiful, their skin flawless, their hair thick and lustrous. They looked human and yet, in some subtle way she couldn't quite put her finger on, they didn't. With Rane, she had thought it was because he was extraordinarily handsome, and because she loved him, but now she realized it was more than that.

She yawned behind her hand. Would they think her rude if she excused herself and went to bed? It might be the shank of the evening for Vampires, but it was past her bedtime. Had her guests been mortal, she would have invited them to spend the night. Would they expect her to do so?

"I'm afraid we're keeping our hostess up," Mara said. "Perhaps we should go so she can get some sleep."

With a nod, Rafe gained his feet. "It was a pleasure to meet you, Miss Gentry."

"Savanah, please."

He smiled at her, his expression so like Rane's it made her heart ache. What if they were wrong? What if Rane didn't recover? What if he remained unconscious forever?

Mara bid Savanah good night, assuring her again that Rane would be his old self in a few days.

Savanah nodded, felt her heart skip a beat when Mara and Rafe held hands and disappeared from her sight.

Chapter Thirty-Seven

He couldn't open his eyes, couldn't move, couldn't speak. Blackness thicker than anything he had ever known engulfed him. He fought against it, struggled to make his way to the surface, but to no avail. It surrounded him, smothered him. This was death, he thought. Clive had destroyed him and now he was in hell. He could feel the flames eating through his flesh, burning through his veins. The agony was excruciating.

Now and then he thought he heard Savanah's voice. Was she here, too? He tried to call for her, but no sound emerged from his lips. And then he heard Rafe's voice. *Ah, Rafe,* he thought, *how I've missed you.*

"Drink, Rane." Rafe's voice, filled with urgency, and with it the scent of blood. It dripped past his lips and he swallowed convulsively. For a blessed moment, it eased the pain. For a blessed moment, the darkness seemed to recede, but then it returned and with it, the same excruciating pain he had known before.

A cruel joke, to offer him a moment's respite. He wanted to scream his agony, but again, no sound rose in his throat.

Time passed; how much, he didn't know. Time had ceased to exist in the thick darkness that held him fast. It was unlike anything he had ever known, this blackness. It oppressed him in ways that the Dark Sleep did not. It weighed him down, smothering him. Perhaps he really was dead, caught in some hellish limbo from which there was no return.

And then he heard Mara's voice, felt her presence there, beside him. Hope fought its way through the darkness. Mara. The queen of their kind. Surely her ancient blood would revive him. He drank greedily, and like Rafe's blood, it eased the pain for the moment, but it didn't draw him out of the darkness. Only Savanah could do that.

Ah, Savanah, with hair like spun moonlight and eyes as blue as the sky. Savanah, who should have taken his head and had given him her love instead. It was her blood he craved, her voice he longed to hear, her touch he ached for.

Savanah. Only her blood, thick and warm and filled with life, could rescue him from the darkness.

Savanah stared at the place where the two Vampires had stood, thinking there were some things she would never get used to, like Vampires who could appear and disappear in the blink of an eye. But at the moment, she was only interested in the Vampire resting in her father's bed.

Going into the kitchen, she filled a pan with warm water and then, with some trepidation, she went into her father's room, put the pan on the bedside table, and turned on the light. Rane lay as before, eyes closed, barely breathing, unmoving. He was a big man; undressing him was no easy task. When it was done, she could only stare at him. His wounds still hadn't healed, but at least they didn't look any worse.

Expelling a sigh, she went into the bathroom for a washcloth, a towel, and a bar of soap. Returning to Rane's side, she washed him from head to foot, wondering, as she did so, why neither Rafe nor Mara had suggested it. Of course, they'd both had other things on their minds, or maybe they had just assumed that Savanah would do it.

When she finished washing Rane, she changed the sheets. Again, no easy task, rolling an inert body from one side of the bed to the other. She was sweating and breathing heavily by the time she finished, but he looked more comfortable, and she felt better because of it.

After pulling the covers up over his chest, she smoothed a lock of hair from his brow, then bent and kissed his cheek.

"If this was a fairy tale and I was a princess, maybe you'd wake up," she murmured.

But it wasn't a fairy tale, she wasn't a princess, and he didn't wake up.

With a sigh, she dumped the pan of bloody water down the toilet, then turned out the lights and closed the door behind her. She carried the pan into the kitchen and rinsed it out, then went upstairs where she took a quick shower, slipped into her nightgown, and brushed her teeth. She stood there a minute, staring at herself in the mirror over the sink as the night's events replayed in her mind. If she called Jolie and told her what had happened, Jolie would never believe it in a million years. If Mr. Van Black printed the story in the paper, people would assume it was fiction.

Staring at her reflection in the mirror, she, too, found it hard to believe.

With a sigh, she went to bed and pulled the covers up

to her chin, only to lie there, staring up at the ceiling, while the house settled around her. She heard the wind rustling the leaves of the tree outside her window, the tick-tick of the clock on the nightstand, a distant siren, the howling of a dog.

But it was thoughts of Rane that kept her awake as one hour slipped into the next. Rafe and Mara had assured her that Rane would recover, but what if they were wrong?

Rising, Savanah pulled on her robe, then padded barefooted down the stairs. She paused at the foot of the banister, wondering if Rafe and Mara had returned, but she had no sense of their presence as she moved quickly down the hallway to her father's room and opened the door.

Rane lay on the bed as before, unmoving.

Savanah stood in the doorway for a moment, watching him, wondering if she was doing the right thing. Rafe and Mara had both given Rane their blood and it hadn't wrought any visible change in his condition. What made her think that her blood, her weak, mortal blood, would make a difference when the blood of the Queen of the Vampires had failed to heal him?

And yet she had to try.

Moving into the room, she sat on the edge of the bed. Murmuring Rane's name, she stroked his brow, and then lifted his head into her lap. Too late, she realized she should have stopped in the kitchen for a knife with which to make an incision in her flesh since she was pretty sure she couldn't do it with her thumbnail.

She started to get up, then remembered that her father had always kept a pocketknife in his nightstand, a keepsake from his childhood scouting days. Opening the drawer, she picked up the knife. The blade was small and very sharp.

Taking a deep breath, she made a shallow cut in her left wrist.

Recalling what Rafe had done, she held her wrist to Rane's lips and murmured, "Drink, Rane."

The scent of her blood cut through the pain as cleanly as a surgeon's scalpel. Like a blind pup, he followed the smell, then latched on to the source. The warmth slid down his throat—living blood, pure and fresh, as rich and smooth as the finest wine. The beat of her heart was like music to his ears. This was what he needed, what he had yearned for. The pain fled, leaving him weak. And grateful.

He murmured her name, then sank down into blessed, healing, oblivion.

Chapter Thirty-Eight

Savanah woke late the following afternoon. She had spent the night at Rane's side, wanting to be there if he regained consciousness. It was a strange experience, sleeping beside a Vampire, wondering if he knew she was there. Wondering what her parents would think if they knew she was in love with one of the Undead. Of course, she knew what they would think. They would be appalled.

Vampires had killed her parents; she had sworn to follow in her mother's footsteps and yet, instead of taking Rane's head, she had given him her blood, and would do so again and as often as needed to prolong his existence.

After she showered and dressed, she went into the kitchen to fix a late breakfast, surprised at how hungry and thirsty she was. No doubt her increased appetite was due to the fact that she had given Rane her blood the night before. She didn't know how much he had taken, but she had been light-headed and unsteady on her feet when it was over, and terribly thirsty, so much so that she had downed almost a quart of orange juice.

She had just finished putting her dishes into the dishwasher when the doorbell rang.

Savanah couldn't hide her surprise at seeing Mara and Rafe standing in the sunlight on her front porch.

Stepping back, she invited them in. She was glad to see Rafe, less so to see Mara. Preternatural power radiated from the other woman. It was disconcerting, and frightening. Mara carried herself with the air of a queen granting favors.

Taking her courage in hand, Savanah followed the two Vampires into the living room.

Mara took a seat on the sofa and Rafe sat beside her.

"How is Rane?" Rafe asked. "Is there any change?"

"I think he's better." Savanah perched on the edge of the chair. "I gave him some of my blood last night."

Mara and Rafe exchanged glances.

Savanah lifted her chin defiantly. "You got a problem with that?"

Mara looked at Rafe and smiled, revealing strong, even white teeth. "Oh, I like her."

Rafe grinned. "Me, too."

Feeling as though she had just passed some kind of test, Savanah glanced from one to the other.

"I'm going in to see Rane," Rafe said, "and leave you two to get acquainted."

Savanah felt a moment of anxiety at the thought of being alone in the room with the most powerful Vampire in the world, but she quickly shook it off. She was tired of being afraid, refused to be intimidated in her own home.

"You must have questions you'd like to ask," Mara said, "if not about me, then about Vampires in general, or perhaps about Rane, in particular."

"How did you get into my house last night without an invitation?"

"All those silly rules no longer have any effect on me," Mara said. "I come and go as I please, when I please, where I please."

"Rane said you were truly immortal."

"As close as you can get," Mara said with a faint grin.

"So, you can't be destroyed?"

"Are you planning to try?"

Mara's tone was mild, but Savanah heard the steel underneath.

"No, I'm just curious. If you're immortal, then I guess that means that holy water doesn't have any effect on you the way it does on Rane, and that a stake through your heart is just a minor injury."

"Something like that," Mara allowed, her grin widening.

"Rane said you were born in the time of Cleopatra."

"Actually, I was made the same year she became Egypt's queen. I spent my early years as a slave in the house of Chuma, one of the King's advisors, until he gave me to one of his trusted allies. Shortly thereafter, a Vampire brought me across against my will. I killed him for it and gained my freedom. As for Cleopatra, I admired her greatly, and so I arranged to meet her. She was a beautiful, intelligent woman only a few years younger than I when she became the ruler of Egypt. To adhere to the law of the time, she was forced to have a consort while she reigned, either a son or a brother, and so it was that she married her brother Ptolemy when he was twelve. Of course, everyone knows the story, how she refused to share her throne, how she captivated Caesar and bore him a son, how she seduced Mark Antony after Caesar was killed."

Mara paused a moment, her thoughts obviously turned inward. "It was a sad day when Antony was defeated. Soon after, Cleopatra was taken to Octavian. He informed her that he had no interest in any relationship with her, personal or otherwise. He intended to place her in chains and display her in all the cities she had once ruled over. I offered to bring her across, but the heart had gone out of her. Caesar was dead and Antony was dead and her son, Caesarion, had been killed. And so it was that she chose to die by the bite of an asp, believing, as the Egyptians did, that those who died by snakebite would never be forgotten." Mara sighed. "In that, at least, she succeeded."

Savanah stared at the Vampire. If what Mara said was true, she was over two thousand years old. It was inconceivable.

Savanah was about to ask Mara about Rane's parents when Rafe entered the room.

"He looks much better," Rafe said, taking a seat beside Mara. "The pain is gone. I think Savanah's blood was just what he needed."

Mara nodded. "Amazing, what love can do," she remarked, her words tinged with a hint of wonder. "I've never really understood it."

"Haven't you ever been in love?" Savanah asked in amazement. Surely, in two thousand years, Mara must have been in love at least once.

"Mara?" Rafe looked at her, one brow arched, as he waited for her answer.

"There was a man, a long time ago . . ." She shook her head, as if to dispel the memory. "I've never let myself care too much for any of the mortal lovers that I've taken in the past. I've never trusted those of my own kind. . . ."

"Not even me?" Rafe asked with a teasing grin.

Mara ignored him. "I'm not sure I'm capable of love, not in the way you love Kathy, or the way Savanah seems to care for Rane, but now . . ."

Rafe glanced at Savanah and winked before nudging Mara in the side. "Go on."

"I met a man in Egypt," she said with a wistful smile. "Perhaps he's the one I've been waiting for. Now, if you'll excuse me, I'm going to go check on Rane."

Before either of them could ask her more questions, Mara flowed out of the room. There really was no other word for the way she moved, Savanah thought. It was as if her feet didn't touch the floor.

"She's quite remarkable," Savanah mused.

"Do you think she's finally fallen in love?"

"You know her better than I do. What do you think?"

"He would have to be quite a guy. So, are you going to marry my brother?"

"I don't know. He hasn't asked me."

"And if he did?"

"I don't know. I don't want to be what he is, and as much as I love him, I'm not sure we'd ever be truly happy together. We've only known each other a short time."

And for most of that time, her life had been in danger. They had been on the run, hiding from those who had killed her father. It had added a touch of danger to their lovemaking, made everything seem more urgent. Now that Clive was dead and the books were safe, she couldn't help wondering what effect it would have on her relationship with Rane. Was it really love she felt for him, or just a lingering crush on the magician who had so fascinated her when she'd been a little girl? Or maybe gratitude because he had been there when she needed someone to lean on, someone to dry her tears and help her find her way in a world that had turned upside down?

"I don't know," she said again. "How did your wife cope with having a Vampire husband?"

"You would have to ask her," Rafe said, chuckling. "We had some pretty hairy times, ourselves."

"Of course, the war was going on then."

Rafe nodded. "We had some close calls with a couple of grandmothers."

"Grandmothers!" Savanah exclaimed. "You're kidding, right?"

"Not at all," Rafe said, grinning. "They were Vampire hunters who were also involved in some pretty wild experiments. They invented a drug they hoped would destroy the Undead and cure the Werewolves."

"What were they planning to do, go from house to house and inoculate the Supernatural community?"

"No, they were going to add it to the water supply. I can tell you from personal experience that it didn't work."

"What happened to the grandmothers?"

"I brought them across."

Savanah blinked at him. "You turned them? Against their will?"

He nodded. "And I would do it again."

"But . . ."

"Would you rather I had killed them?"

"No, but . . ."

"If I had let them go, they would have continued their experiments. As it was, they had already killed several innocent people. They had to be stopped. I did it the best way I knew how, short of taking their lives."

"But you've killed people?"

"A time or two, in self-defense."

Savanah took a deep breath. "And Rane? Has he taken many lives?"

Rafe regarded her for a long moment, then said, "I think that is a question you should ask him yourself." He lifted one brow. "I find it curious that you haven't asked him already."

"I don't think I wanted to know the answer."

"And now?"

"I need to know. If we're to have any kind of lasting relationship, I need to know everything."

Rafe nodded. "I only know of one life that he's taken. It happened the night we became Vampires. He thinks no one in the family knows what he did, but I know, just as I know that it preys on his mind. I believe it's his guilt over that death that drove him away from us."

"Why would he feel guilty? It's what Vampires do, isn't it? I'm sorry, I . . ." She stared at Rafe. She hadn't meant to speak the words aloud, was surprised by the barely suppressed accusation in her voice.

"Yes," Rafe said, his own voice tight. "It is."

"I'm sorry," she said again. "Please forgive me. It's just that Vampires killed both of my parents and I . . . I'm supposed to be a hunter, like my mother. It's supposed to be in my blood, and . . ." She closed her eyes and took a deep breath before looking at Rafe again. "I'm rambling, forgive me."

"There's nothing to forgive. It can't be easy, loving a Vampire. There are many adjustments that must be made on both sides. Not every mortal can accept us for who and what we are."

"Nor can every Vampire accept what he or she becomes," Mara said, entering the room. "Many destroy themselves." She paused beside Savanah. "Rane will most likely awaken when the sun goes down. He'll need to feed, and he'll need more than you can offer. If you're smart, you won't offer him anything."

"Because he might not be able to stop?" Savanah asked.

"Exactly. And now I must take my leave."

"Going back to Egypt?" Rafe asked with a knowing grin.

"Perhaps. It was interesting meeting you, Savanah Gentry. I wish you well, but leave you with this warning: if you hurt Rane, I'll come after you. His family is my family. Do you understand?"

Savanah nodded, unable to speak past the icy lump in her throat. She understood Mara perfectly.

Rafe stood and gave his godmother a hug. "Keep in touch."

"Of course. Give Kathy and your parents my love when you see them again."

"I will."

A wave of her hand, and the Vampire queen was gone.

"I suppose I should also be going," Rafe said. "Tell Rane if he wants to see me, I'll be close by."

"All right. Thank you for everything."

"I hope we will meet again."

"Me, too," Savanah said, and then sighed as Rafe vanished from her sight. She would never get used to that, she thought, and went into the kitchen to pour herself a cup of coffee.

It was like rising from the depths of hell a layer at a time, Rane thought as he fought his way out of the smothering darkness. He didn't know how much time had passed, how many days and nights he had been trapped in his deathlike sleep, unable to move, unable to speak.

Sitting up, he glanced around. Though the room was dark, he could see clearly, knew he was in Savanah's house, in her father's bed. He took a deep breath, his senses expanding, searching. Mara and his brother were gone; Savanah was in the house alone.

Savanah, with the smile of a heavenly angel and a body to drive him mad. Savanah, whose blood had put out the unbearable fire in his veins. The thought of her blood aroused his hellish thirst. His tongue brushed his fangs. He needed nourishment and it waited for him in the living room.

Hunger drove him from the bed; consideration for Savanah sent him to her father's closet in hopes she had not yet disposed of her father's clothes. He pulled a pair of black sweatpants from a hanger, found a T-shirt in a dresser drawer. The pants were a trifle short, the T-shirt a little snug, but they would do for now. He didn't know what she had done with the clothes he'd been wearing, but wouldn't be surprised if she had disposed of them.

Barefooted, he padded down the hallway into the living room.

Savanah was sitting on the sofa with her back toward him. Lamplight shimmered in her hair, turning the silver to gold, bathing her skin with a soft rosy glow. She was beautiful, desirable in every way, and she was his. All his. For the taking.

She gasped, startled when he appeared on the sofa beside her. "Rane!" She pressed her hand over her heart. "I'm so glad to see you. How are you feeling?"

He didn't answer, merely continued to watch her.

Like a cat at a mouse hole, she thought. A very big, very hungry cat. And she was the mouse. Small and helpless. Prey for the cat.

Fear made her heart beat faster. She knew by the sudden glow in Rane's eyes that he was aware of what she was feeling. He had told her once that he could smell fear; no doubt she reeked of it.

"Mara said you would need to feed," Savanah said, her words tripping over themselves. "Maybe you should go out for a while." What was she saying? Sending Rane out now was like signing someone else's death warrant.

Rane's lips peeled back, revealing his fangs. "No need to go out."

Savanah's heart skipped a beat. "Rane . . ."

Lifting one hand, he stroked her cheek. "You saved me," he said. "It wasn't Rafe's blood, or Mara's, but yours." His eyes, red as flames, burned into hers.

"Rane, please . . . don't."

He ran his knuckles along her neck, up and down, slowly, up and down.

"Rane . . ."

He recoiled from the stark fear in her eyes, fear that he had put there. Filled with self-loathing, he lurched to his feet.

"Tell me to get out," he said, his voice gruff. "Now, before it's too late, rescind your invitation."

"I do," she said. "I rescind it now."

And just like that, he was gone, and she was alone.

Chapter Thirty-Nine

Rane stalked the dark streets, his anger and self-loathing growing with his hunger. He had been a fool, a fool to think he could stay with her, near her, and never hurt her. A fool to think he could continue to deny what he was. He was a hunter, a predator, meant to roam the world alone. Forever alone. He had managed to keep the monster inside him under control for the last few months, but now . . . He slammed his fist into the side of a building, leaving a hole six inches deep in the stucco. Pain splintered through his hand. It hurt, but not enough.

He left Kelton behind and headed for the city, his destination the slums where the dregs of society gathered. He took the first mortal who crossed his path, bent over her neck, and drank. He drank enough to satisfy his hunger, then released the woman from his thrall and sent her on her way. He watched her stagger down the street. He was no better than the drug dealers and pimps who frequented this part of the city, he thought glumly. Driven by an insatiable need, he, too, preyed on the weak and the helpless.

The thought brought him up short. That might have

been true once, but no more. He had not taken a human life since he met Savanah, nor had he been tempted to drain his last victim dry. In Savanah's house, it hadn't been the uncontrollable monster he feared rising up in him again, but simply a need for nourishment.

He swore softly. He had frightened Savanah away for nothing.

Savanah slept in her father's room that night. It seemed fitting somehow. The only two men she had ever loved had stayed in this room, slept in this bed. She had lost them both, but, somehow, sleeping where they had slept gave her a small measure of comfort. Her father was dead, and she would never see him again. In his own way, Rane was also lost to her.

"Rane," she murmured, "where are you now?"

She had been afraid of him earlier, even though, in her heart of hearts, she had been certain he would never hurt her; yet, at his bidding, she had sent him away. She wished now that she had refused. She should have made him stay so they could face their fears together because she knew, as surely as the sun would rise in the morning, that it had been Rane's fear for her life that had driven him away.

Turning onto her side, she closed her eyes, wondering how long it would take him to realize the truth, and what she would do if he didn't.

Rane stood in the late-afternoon shadows across the street from Savanah's house, his thoughts in turmoil. It had been three weeks since he had walked out on her. Three weeks that seemed like three years. He hadn't killed any of the women he had preyed upon in all that time, nor had he taken the life of the mortal male he had preyed upon less than an hour ago. The knowledge replayed itself in his mind over and over again. He hadn't killed any of them, nor did he have any inclination to do so. Why? That was the question that plagued him. Why?

Only one answer came to mind. Savanah had given him her blood when he needed it most, given it to him of her own free will because she loved him. He had tasted her blood before, but he had never taken as much as he had when he lay trapped in the darkness with holy water sizzling through his veins like liquid fire. He didn't know if it was her blood that had healed him, or the fact that she loved him, but it didn't matter. She had saved his life and in so doing, she had somehow tamed the beast he had been fighting for the last ninety years. His only fear now was that he had frightened her so badly, she would never trust him again.

He was trying to summon his courage to knock on the front door when Rafe appeared beside him.

"What the hell are you doing here?" Rane asked.

"I'm happy to see you, too," Rafe said dryly.

"You didn't answer my question."

"I wanted to make sure you had healed. Now that I see you have, I'll say good-bye."

"Don't go. I appreciate what you did for me, you and Mara."

"You owe us nothing," Rafe said. "It was the woman who saved you."

"But you came." Rane frowned at his brother. "How did you know where I was?"

"When you were ill, I felt your pain, and I followed it."

"Some good came out of it, then," Rane muttered.

Rafe nodded. "I tried to sense your presence before, but there was only emptiness where our bond used to be."

Rane flinched at the unspoken accusation in his brother's voice. "I'm sorry. I didn't mean to hurt you, but . . ."

"Why, Rane, why did you block the bond between us? Why did you cut me out of your life?"

Rane took a deep breath, then loosed it in a long, slow sigh. "I was afraid if I stayed, the old man would find out what I'd done. That Mom would find out." He met his brother's gaze. "That you'd find out."

"Find out what?" Rafe asked, frowning.

"That I wasn't like you! That first night when the old man took us hunting, I went out later, alone, and . . ." Even now, all these years later, he couldn't say it, couldn't tell his brother what he had done.

"Is this about the woman you killed the night we were turned?" Rafe asked.

"How do you know about that?"

"How could you think I wouldn't know?"

Rane stared at his brother in disbelief. "You've known about her all this time?"

"Of course."

Rane searched his brother's mind, looking for some sign of disgust or disappointment. He found neither. "What about Mom and Dad? Did you tell them?"

"No, although I think Dad knew, or at least suspected."

Rane grunted softly. "We never could put anything over on the old man," he muttered ruefully.

Rafe laughed softly. "I missed you."

"No more than I missed you." With tears stinging his eyes, Rane embraced his brother, thinking that he had stayed away from his family all these years for nothing. "They're all okay? Mom and the old man? The grandparents?"

Rafe nodded.

"And Kathy? You're still happy with her?"

"Yes. So," Rafe said, his voice gruff, "what are you going to do about your woman?"

Rane looked at the house across the street. Through the open window, he could see Savanah sitting at the desk in the living room, her back toward him. Sunlight shimmered in her hair. "I don't know. I'm afraid . . ."

"She loves you, brother. Any fool can see that."

"Yeah, but is love enough? She wants to be a Vampire hunter, like her mother before her. I can't help thinking that if she pursues that line of work, it's going to drive us apart, sooner or later. I've never had any feelings of loyalty to others of our kind. Hell, I've killed a few of them myself, but . . ." He shook his head. "I don't know, Rafe. I just don't know."

"There's only one way to find out," Rafe said, shrugging. "You love her. She loves you. Can you picture living the rest of your life without her?"

"No."

"I think that's your answer."

Rane clapped his brother on the shoulder. "I think you're right. If she says yes, I'll want you to be my best man."

"I have always been the best man," Rafe said, grinning. "Now, go see your woman."

Savanah closed the old photograph album and dropped it back into the bottom desk drawer. Hardly anyone printed pictures these days, preferring to look at them on their computers or satellite screens. One of these days, she intended to electronically convert the photos in her grandmother's album so she could view them on the computer. Still, there was something very satisfying about being able to hold the album in her hands, to run her fingertips over pictures taken of her mother when she was a little girl.

Pushing away from the desk, Savanah gained her feet, then stood there, at a loss for something to do. She really needed to get those books from Rane, she thought, though she had no idea how she would accomplish that now. Still, she couldn't very well hunt Vampires if she didn't know who they were, or where they might be found.

She glanced out the window. There were still a few hours of daylight left. Maybe she'd go out in the back and do a little weeding. She hadn't gone out there since the night Rane had fought Clive.

After pulling on a pair of old jeans and a short-sleeved sweatshirt, she shoved a stake in her waistband, slid a bottle of holy water into her pocket and then, grabbing her mPod, she marched out the back door, studiously avoiding the far side of the yard where torn-up grass and dark brown stains bore mute evidence of a deadly battle.

With the latest hits playing in the background, she lost herself in the simple task of pulling weeds. The air was warm; perspiration trickled down her back as she moved from one flower bed to another. There was something enormously satisfying in getting her hands dirty.

After an hour, she stood and wiped her hands on her jeans, intending to go inside and make some lemonade.

She had only taken a few steps toward the back door when she realized she wasn't alone.

Stake in hand, she whirled around, and came face-to-face with Rane. Excitement sprang up within her and with it, the urge to run into his arms and tell him how much she had missed him. And then, as a drop of sweat trickled down her neck, her initial excitement quickly turned to panic. It was broad daylight.

"What are you doing out here?" She looked up at the clear blue sky and then back at Rane, expecting him to go up in flames at any moment. "Are you crazy? Get inside, quick!"

"I'm all right, Savanah."

"But . . ." She glanced at the sky again. The last time he had ventured out in the daylight, his clothing had caught fire. "How? I don't understand."

"I owe it to Mara. Her ancient blood . . ." He shrugged. "I can endure the sun's light for short periods of time now. Within a year or so, it won't bother me at all."

"Well, that's . . . amazing. Come on in. I'd feel better if we were inside."

"As you wish."

He followed her into the kitchen, waited while she dropped the stake on the table and then went to the sink to wash the dirt from her hands.

"Let's go into the living room, shall we?" Savanah asked, pleased that her voice sounded so calm when she was anything but calm on the inside.

She sat down on the sofa. Rane settled into the chair across from her. She could tell nothing from his expression. Why had he come here?

His gaze moved over her, long and slow, as if to memorize every line and curve. Had he come to tell her good-bye forever? It wouldn't surprise her, not after the way they had parted the last time. She folded her arms over her breasts, her heart pounding with dread.

"How have you been, Savanah?" he asked quietly.

"I'm okay." She didn't have to ask how he was. Judging from the way he looked, and the fact that he could now move about in the sun's light, he was better than okay. It had been three weeks since she had seen him last, she thought, blinking back her tears, yet it seemed like forever.

"Savanah, I . . ."

Feeling suddenly cold, she ran her hands up and down her arms. "Just say it and be done with it."

"Will you marry me?"

"What?"

"Will you marry me?"

She stared at him, speechless. She loved him. She ached for him in all the lost, lonely regions of her heart and soul. But . . . marriage? She had considered it, of course, wondered what it would be like to be the only mortal in a family of Vampires, but she had never dreamed it was a possibility. She came from a long line of Vampire hunters. He was a Vampire.

"Savanah?"

"I don't know . . . I never expected . . . I thought you came here to tell me good-bye."

He slid from the chair to kneel before her. "I know it won't be easy for you," he said, taking her hand in his. "I'm not the easiest guy in the world to live with. I have a lot of baggage, but I don't think I can go on without you." His thumb stroked the back of her hand. "I haven't taken a life in a long time, although the temptation has always been there, until you gave me your blood. I don't know what happened. I can't explain it, but for the first time since I became a Vampire, I feel like I'm really in control. You did that."

"You don't have to marry me because you're grateful, or because you want a lifetime supply of my blood."

"Savanah, if all I wanted was your blood, I could take it any time I wished." Lifting her hand to his lips, he kissed her palm. "I love you. I think I've loved you for years."

"Oh, Rane . . ." She slid off the sofa into his lap, her arms twining around his neck. "I love you, too!"

"Then you'll marry me?"

"Yes, oh, yes!"

"Do you think you'd like to be a magician's assistant? It might be good for my act to have a pretty woman on stage."

"I'll be whatever you want me to be."

Murmuring her name, he buried his face in the wealth of her hair, his arms holding her close, his throat tight with unshed tears. "I'll do my best to make you happy."

"You already make me happy."

Looking up, he brushed a lock of hair from her face. "So, what do you say we go see my folks?"

"So soon?" she exclaimed.

"There's nothing to be afraid of."

Nothing? A lone mortal, who was supposed to be a hunter, in a den of Vampires?

"You've already met Rafe. That wasn't so bad, was it?"

"No, but . . ."

"Remember when you said my being a Vampire was just a quirk? Well, think of it as a hereditary quirk. My family all suffer from it, but they're good people."

Savanah settled in his lap. "So, tell me about them."

"Well, my grandfather Roshan is somewhere around four hundred years old."

"Just a baby when compared to Mara," Savanah muttered.

"I guess you could say that. My grandmother Brenna is a witch."

"I thought she was a Vampire?"

"She is."

A witch *and* a Vampire. Now there was a combination to be reckoned with, Savanah mused.

"You'll like her," Rane said. "Grandfather went back in time and saved her from being burned at the stake."

"You're kidding? People can't go back in time."

Rane shrugged. "Maybe not, but my grandfather did. You'll have to get one of them to tell you the whole story. My father is a mechanic, or at least he used to be. I don't know if he's still working or not. I haven't seen any of them in years." Mara had told him that they had all moved to some little town in Oregon about five years ago, and that Kathy's friend, Susie, and her Were-tiger husband, Cagin, had followed a year later.

"What about your mother?" Savanah asked.

Rane shrugged. "She's just Mom."

"And they all like being Vampires?"

"So far." He brushed a kiss across her lips. "No one will pressure you to accept the Dark Gift, love. That decision will be yours."

"But you'd like me to?" Her joy at his proposal ebbed as reality again crept in.

"Very much." He kissed the length of her neck, his mouth warm against her skin.

"Rane, be honest. Do you really think we can make a life together?"

"Don't you?"

"Maybe for a while, but what happens when I'm old? I don't mean forty or fifty, but what if, God willing, I live to be a hundred and ten? You'll still look the way you do now. You'll want a woman who can keep up with you, one who can make love all night long, and . . ."

Rane put his hand over her mouth, silencing her. "Stop that."

She kissed his palm, then drew his hand away. "It's something we need to think about, no matter how painful it might be."

"Savanah . . ."

"Most couples grow old together. We won't."

Rane swore softly. "Have you changed your mind about us?"

"No, but . . ."

"I'm going to Oregon to see my folks. I want you to come with me."

"We haven't settled anything."

"I love you," Rane said. "You love me. Everything else can be worked out, in time."

She looked into his eyes, his beautiful dark eyes, and wanted more than anything else in the world to believe him.

"Come home with me," Rane coaxed softly, "meet my family. We won't say anything about getting married."

"All right."

Drawing her close, he kissed her, long and hard and deep. "We'll leave tomorrow."

Chapter Forty

They left at sunset. Savanah stared out the window. The ocean was beautiful in the waning light of the setting sun. Once she thought she saw a whale break the surface. Gradually, the sky grew darker, until it was hard to tell where the sea ended and the horizon began.

With a sigh, she glanced at Rane. He drove with his left arm resting on the open window, his right hand lightly gripping the steering wheel. A breeze ruffled his hair. Just looking at him made her stomach curl with pleasure. They had made love last night. She smiled inwardly, remembering the wonder of it. She didn't know if it was because they were now unofficially engaged, or because they had been apart for so long, but she had wanted him desperately and she hadn't been afraid to show it. She didn't remember ever being so uninhibited, or so vocal. Thinking of it now brought a rush of heat to her cheeks.

Feeling the weight of her gaze, Rane looked over at her and smiled. "You okay?"

"Definitely okay," she said, recalling how she had insisted on being the aggressor in their lovemaking. She had batted his hands away when he tried to undress her.

Determined to have her own way, she had undressed him, slowly and deliberately, then pushed him down on the bed. He had laughed, amused by her provocative behavior, but the laughter had died in his throat when she began a slow striptease. Neither had been laughing when she slithered into bed beside him.

She lifted a hand to her neck, her fingertips exploring the place where he had bitten her. He had taken only a little, but it had enhanced their lovemaking, heightening the pleasure of every kiss, every stroke of his hand.

Rane pulled over about an hour later so Savanah could get a quick bite to eat. She ordered a cup of coffee and a doughnut to go and they were back on the road.

It was a little after ten when they drove over the cattle guard at the town's entrance. A sign proclaimed that Porterville had been incorporated in 1911 and had a population of five hundred people.

Since neither of them had ever been there before, Rane decided to have a look around. As he drove slowly through the town, Savanah counted two museums, a library, a historical society building, a couple of nice-looking restaurants, a gas station, and an old-fashioned general store. Thick stands of timber grew along the roadside and lined the distant fields.

"It's a beautiful place," Savanah remarked.

Rane pulled up in front of a motel, then turned to look at her. "Do you want to spend the night here, or go find my folks' place?"

"Let's stay here tonight."

"Still nervous about meeting them?"

"A little. What if they don't like me?"

"Savanah . . ."

"What if they look at me and all they see is dinner, or dessert? Stop that, it's not funny!"

He tried to say he was sorry, but he couldn't stop laughing.

Savanah punched him in the arm, realizing, too late, that it was going to hurt her fist more than his arm. The man had muscles of steel.

Rane took a deep breath, glanced at Savanah, and burst out laughing again.

"Anytime you're through, I'd like to check into the motel and take a bath."

"Sor—sorry." He switched off the engine and got out of the car.

She didn't wait for him to open her door. Grabbing her handbag, she swept into the office.

With a shake of his head, Rane grabbed her overnight bag and followed her inside. She was really something, he thought, and wondered how he had ever survived without her.

Rane squeezed Savanah's hand. "Just relax. They're going to love you."

"Right." Savanah took a deep breath as they walked up the pathway to his parents' house. It was a pretty place, white with dark green trim. Tall trees rose behind the house; a riot of colorful flowers surrounded a small fountain. It didn't look the least bit the way she had expected a Vampire's home to look. It was like expecting Dracula and finding Mary Poppins.

Savanah looked up at Rane as he knocked on the door. There was a faint tremor in the hand she was holding, and she realized he was just as nervous as she was.

The man who opened the door looked enough like Rane to be his brother. He had the same chiseled features, strong jaw, and thick black hair. The only difference she could see was in their eyes—Rane's were black, his father's were dark brown.

Vince Cordova took one look at his son and drew him into his arms. "Welcome home, son."

All Savanah's fears melted as she watched the two men embrace; the love and affection between them was almost palpable.

Clearing his throat, Vince held his son at arm's length. "I can't believe you're here. Let me have a look at you. Why didn't you tell us you were coming?" Vince glanced at Savanah. "This pretty lady must be Savanah." Releasing his son, Vince held out his hand. "I'm Rane's father."

"I'm pleased to meet you, Mr. Cordova."

"Just Vince. Come on inside. I can't wait to see Cara's face when she sees the two of you."

The inside of the house was lovely, all done in shades of green and mauve. A pretty woman with long blond hair sat in a chair beside the fireplace. She looked up from the book she was reading when they entered the room, her blue eyes widening when she saw her son.

"Rane!" The book fell to the floor as she jumped to her feet.

"Hi, Mom."

She hugged him fiercely, her eyes filling with tears. Tears that Savanah noticed were tinged with red.

"I can't believe you're home," Cara said, wiping her tears with one hand. "Why didn't you tell us you were coming? Oh, it doesn't matter, I'm so glad you're here." Still hugging her son, she looked at Savanah. "Thank you for bringing him home."

"I didn't . . ."

"Oh, yes, you did," his mother insisted. Releasing Rane, she offered Savanah her hand. "I'm so happy to meet you."

"Thank you, Mrs. Cordova."

"Cara," she said, squeezing her hand. "Well, come in and sit down. I want to hear everything."

The next hour passed quickly as Rane brought his parents up-to-date on what he'd been doing since he left home. Savanah was completely charmed by his parents, both of whom were sympathetic when they learned of her father's death.

To Savanah's surprise, Rane's mother offered her a glass of iced tea and a slice of chocolate cake, neither of which Savanah had expected to find in a Vampire's house.

"We keep food on hand for the neighbor kids," Cara explained. "They love to come over after school. Especially the teenage boys. They're always coming around, asking Vince to fix their cars, or make them go faster."

Vince grinned at Savanah and shrugged. "They're good kids."

Rising, Cara said, "I should call Rafe and tell him you're home."

"Don't forget to call your folks," Vince reminded her with a smile. "We'll never hear the end of it if you don't."

"You're right about that," Cara said, and went in to the other room to make her calls.

Rafe and his pretty blond wife, Kathy, showed up a short time later, and Cara's parents arrived some twenty minutes after that. Kathy and Rane's grandparents greeted Savanah with welcoming smiles as they introduced themselves. Cara's father, Roshan, was tall and lean with powerful shoulders and long limbs. His hair was black, his eyes a bold midnight blue set beneath straight black brows, but it was Cara's mother who held Savanah's attention.

Brenna DeLongpre seemed too pretty to be a witch. Fiery red hair fell to her waist, her eyes were almost as green as Mara's. She wore a white peasant blouse over a colorful, ankle-length skirt; a necklace of amber and jet circled her throat.

Vince brought out a bottle of vintage wine. After filling everyone's glass, he lifted his own, and said, "A toast to the prodigal, who, though away from us, was never out of our hearts or our thoughts."

"Here, here," Rafe said.

"And to the woman in his life," Cara added. "May she always feel welcome in our presence and in our home."

Rane slid his arm around Savanah's shoulders. Drawing her close, he whispered, "See? I knew they'd love you. So, will you marry me?"

Chapter Forty-One

Savanah glanced around the room. No one would ever think any of the occupants were Vampires. She was finding it a little hard to believe herself.

Rane poked her in the ribs. "You didn't answer me."

"They really are wonderful people, aren't they?"

"I think so." He looked at her, his dark eyes intense. "You still haven't answered my question."

"Yes, Rane, I'll marry you whenever and wherever you want."

"She said yes!"

Savanah glanced over her shoulder, startled, as Brenna announced her decision to the room.

"I'm sorry," Brenna said, hurrying over to give Savanah a hug. "I didn't mean to eavesdrop, really, but . . . welcome to the family!"

"This calls for another toast!" Vince said.

The next few minutes were hectic as everyone came over to wish Rane and Savanah well. Amid bear hugs and smiles, Savanah found herself wondering who would perform the ceremony, since it was illegal for Vampires and mortals to intermarry.

Rane must have been reading her mind because a moment later, he put the question to his father.

"There's only one place to hold the wedding," Vince said, smiling at Cara. "Right?"

"Yes, of course," Cara replied.

"And only one priest to join the two of you together," Brenna declared.

"Father Lanzoni," Rafe and Kathy said in unison.

"Who's Father Lanzoni?" Savanah asked.

"He's the priest who married us," Vince said, giving his wife's hand a squeeze.

"And us," Roshan said, smiling at Brenna.

"And us," Kathy added, linking her arm with Rafe's.

Rane kissed Savanah on the cheek. "We can't break a tradition like that, can we?"

"No, indeed," she agreed.

"So, when's the big day?" Kathy asked.

"Whenever Savanah wants," Rane said. "We haven't really had time to discuss it."

"We'll have to let Mara know," Vince said.

"Speaking of Mara," Roshan said, "I hear she's taken a mortal lover. Is that true?"

"I don't know for a fact," Rafe said, "but I'd say it's a safe bet."

"I wonder if she'll bring him to the ceremony," Brenna remarked.

"I wonder if he knows what she is," Cara mused.

"Well, one thing is certain," Vince said, refilling his wineglass, "we know she'll come."

The next week was filled with excitement and anticipation the likes of which Savanah had never known. Once she made the decision to marry Rane, there seemed little reason to wait. The women in Rane's family were more than supportive, and they were all eager to help with the planning, although there was little to plan. There was only one choice for a church, and no need for a caterer.

The one thing Savanah did need was a dress. To that end, the females in the family whisked her into Portland to go shopping. White dresses were no longer in vogue for brides, and Savanah tried on dresses in every color of the rainbow.

Though she had always envisioned herself walking down the aisle in a long white gown, the one she fell in love with was a pale, pale blue. The lines of the gown were simple yet elegant, modest yet sexy.

When Savanah stepped out of the dressing room to show Kathy, Brenna, and Cara, the looks on their faces told her she had made the right choice.

"Perfect!" Kathy and Brenna exclaimed.

"Rane's going to love it," Cara said, giving Savanah a hug. "You'll be a beautiful bride."

Savanah picked out a shoulder-length veil to match the dress, as well as a pair of heels. Leaving the bridal shop, they went to a store that specialized in lingerie. Savanah's initial embarrassment at picking out such personal items in the company of Rane's mother and grandmother soon gave way to laughter as they examined a variety of undergarments, including edible underwear and crotchless panties, which brought a rush of heat to Savanah's cheeks as she imagined wearing them for Rane.

She picked out a long, black nightgown and matching peignoir, several pairs of bikini panties, bras, a robe and slippers. Cara insisted on buying her a different-colored teddy for every day of the week. Brenna gifted her with a shimmery silver nightgown that looked like it had been made from stardust and moonbeams.

Kathy chose a flowered nightgown, a matching velour robe, and fluffy pink slippers. "For *after* the honeymoon," she explained with a shrug. "Or for those mornings when you don't feel like getting dressed. After all," she said, gesturing at the pile of gossamer gowns, "you can't answer the door in any of those."

The only time Savanah felt the slightest bit ill at ease was at mealtimes. Rane's parents assured her that she was welcome to cook in the house, but she politely declined, preferring to eat at one of the restaurants in town. Rane always accompanied her in the evening, lingering over a glass of wine while she ate dinner.

Mara showed up the night before the wedding with a handsome young man in tow. As Mara introduced Kyle to Rane's family, Savanah couldn't help wondering if Kyle Bowden knew that, except for the two of them, everyone else in the room was a Vampire.

She was glad when Mara and Kyle took their leave and Vince and Cara went to bed, giving Rane and Savanah some time alone in the living room. Though they had shared a bed in the past, Savanah had told Rane she wouldn't feel comfortable doing so in his parents' house, and he had acceded to her wishes.

Now, sitting on the sofa, Rane pulled Savanah closer to his side. "Nervous about tomorrow?" he asked, one hand lightly massaging her nape.

"A little." She snuggled against him. "We haven't talked about it much lately, but I'm still hoping to find the Vampire who killed my mother. Do you think I ever will?"

"I don't know, but you've got a lot more help now."

"What do you mean?"

"My family. Mara. They'll all help." Frowning, he ran his hand over his jaw. "You know, it occurred to me before that Mara might know who the killer is."

"How could she possibly know that?"

"You always ask the tough questions," Rane said, blowing out a sigh. "It has to do with her power. She's lived a long time. I'm not sure how she does it, but she seems to be able to tap into whatever affects the Vampire community. It wouldn't surprise me if she knows who killed your mother."

Savanah bolted upright. "When can we ask her? Do you know where she's staying? Can we call her tonight?"

Rane slipped his arm around her shoulders and drew her back down beside him. "I don't know where she's staying, and even if I did, I doubt if she wants to be disturbed."

He was right, of course. Savanah had seen the way Kyle Bowden had looked at Mara. No doubt the two of them were curled up in a bed somewhere. Savanah let out a sigh. She had waited this long for information about her mother's killer; she could wait one more night.

Kyle came awake abruptly, not knowing what had roused him. Sitting up, he switched on the bedside lamp, then turned to see if Mara was asleep, only to find her side of the bed was empty.

"Mara?"

Gaining his feet, he prowled through the hotel suite, turning on the lights as he went. There was no sign of her. Frowning, he returned to the living room and sank down on the sofa. Where would she have gone at this time of the night?

Mara. She was a mystery wrapped in an enigma. True,

he had only known her a short time, but she surprised him on a daily basis. She looked to be about twenty years old, but there were times when he would have sworn she was older. Much older. He sometimes found himself studying her, looking for some sign that she'd had a face-lift or other cosmetic surgery, but her body was toned and taut, her skin flawless.

And then there were the people he had met earlier that night. It had been all he could do to hide his astonishment when he overheard one of the Cordova brothers call Vince Cordova "Dad." Until then, Kyle had assumed that Vince was another brother. Impossible as it seemed, all of them—men and women alike—appeared to be in their late twenties or early thirties.

His thoughts turned to Mara again. Since the day he met her, he had thought of little else. She was like an addiction he couldn't shake, a thirst he couldn't quench. A riddle he couldn't solve.

He remembered a conversation they'd had while still in Egypt. They had been in his hotel room, watching an old movie about Antony and Cleopatra. They had discussed the movie when it was over. Kyle had made a comment about Cleopatra. He couldn't remember now what he'd said, but Mara had corrected him and then, her expression wistful, she had told him about Egypt's most famous queen. Kyle was no expert on the subject. He'd had no way of knowing if what Mara had told him was historically correct or not, yet everything she had said carried the ring of truth. It was almost as if she had known the Egyptian queen personally. It reminded him of an old *Twilight Zone* episode in which a beautiful woman mesmerized men, then, with the help of a beetle, took their life force, thereby keeping herself forever young.

Chiding himself for his fanciful thoughts, he turned off the lights and went back to bed. If there was one thing he did know about Mara, it was that she loved the night. No doubt she had just gone out for a walk in the moonlight.

Chapter Forty-Two

It was late afternoon when Savanah awoke. Sitting up, she glanced around the guest room. Rane's mother had quite a knack for decorating; the room, done in shades of gray and blue with red accents, looked like it had been taken from the pages of *House and Home* magazine.

Savanah glanced at her watch. Since staying here with Rane's parents, she found herself waking later and later each day. She supposed she would have to adjust her hours to Rane's, though now that he could come and go as he pleased during the day, finding time to be together was no longer a problem.

She wondered if he was awake yet, and if he was as nervous as she was.

Today was their wedding day. She had always dreamed of a big wedding, always imagined herself walking down a flower-strewn aisle on her father's arm, but that wasn't possible now.

"Oh, Daddy," she murmured, "I wish you were here."

Rising, she ran her hand over the gown hanging on the back of the closet door. The dress made her feel beautiful. Would Rane think the same when he saw her?

After showering, she pulled on a pair of shorts and a shirt and went into the kitchen. The house was quiet, leading her to believe that everyone else was still asleep. She poured herself a glass of orange juice, then stood at the sink, staring out the window. She had avenged her father's death. Tonight, she would ask Mara if she knew the name of the Vampire who had destroyed her mother. Strange thoughts for a bride-to-be, she mused, yet these days her life was nothing if not strange.

Rane and his parents rose just before sunset. Since Savanah had decided to get dressed at the house, Cara shooed the men away, insisting it was bad luck for the groom to see the bride in her gown before the wedding. That simple little superstition somehow set Savanah's mind at ease. Rane's family might be Vampires, but they had managed to retain their humanity.

It wasn't until she was dressed and realized there were no mirrors in the house that Savanah regretted her decision to get dressed at home instead of at the church.

"You look lovely," Cara said, arranging the folds of Savanah's veil. "Rane is a lucky man."

Clad in a tea-length dress of mauve silk with her hair piled artfully atop her head, Rane's mother looked pretty enough to be a bride herself.

"You've been so good for him," Cara said, taking Savanah's hands in hers. "You do love him, don't you?" she asked, her gaze searching Savanah's. "If you're not sure, if you're having any doubts, tell him now, before it's too late."

"I love him more than anything. I've had my doubts," Savanah admitted, "but I can't imagine my life without him."

"What about children? You do know that Rane can't give you any?"

"Yes, of course."

"Adoption is always an alternative," Cara said with a wink. "I don't know if Rane told you, but I was adopted."

Savanah nodded. She and Rane had talked about it one night. She was tempted to ask his mother what it had been like, having Vampires for parents, but she didn't quite have the nerve. Perhaps another time, when she knew Rane's mother better.

Cara squeezed her hand. "Welcome to the family, daughter. I hope you and Rane will be as happy as his father and I have been."

"Thank you." Savanah accepted her mother-in-law's embrace.

"Do you have everything?" Cara asked. "Something old?"

"My future husband?" Savanah said, grinning.

Cara laughed. "Something new?"

"Everything I have on."

"Something borrowed?"

"You've got me there."

"Here." Removing her pearl necklace, Cara fastened it around Savanah's neck. "Something blue?"

"My garter."

"Perfect!" Cara exclaimed.

"Thank you for everything."

"You're more than welcome. Shall we go? Our chariot awaits."

The chariot turned out to be a white stretch limo. Feeling like Cinderella going to the ball, Savanah gathered her skirts around her and ducked inside.

"Well, isn't this nice?" Cara asked, sitting across from Savanah.

"Very. Thank you."

"It was Rane's idea," Cara said, her expression softening.

"You must have missed him very much."

"You can't imagine! It's wonderful to have them both home again. Sometimes I can't help wishing they were still my little boys. They grow up so fast," she said with a wistful smile. "Too fast."

Not knowing what to say, Savanah stared out the window. Not for the first time, she wished her father was there beside her.

It was late when the limo turned down a long, winding road lined by ancient oaks and pines. Savanah hadn't known quite what to expect from a church frequented by Vampires. Something dark and gloomy, decorated with leering gargoyles and fallen angels. Her expectations couldn't have been farther from the truth. Tall trees and lush greenery surrounded the old church, which looked almost ghostly in the light of the full moon. The air was filled with the fragrant scent of evergreens and dew-dampened earth. The sweet song of a night bird blended with the cheerful chirp of crickets and the croaking bass of a bullfrog, their evening songs combining in a moonlight serenade.

"It's lovely," Savanah murmured as she followed Cara up the walkway to the entrance.

"It is, isn't it? It's pretty during the day, but it's even more beautiful in the moonlight."

Savanah clutched her bouquet, her heart skipping a beat when Rafe opened the door leading into the vestibule. Once again, Savanah was taken aback by how much Rane and his brother looked alike. She wasn't sure how she knew it was Rafe. She would have to ask Rane about that later. Maybe it had something to do with the fact that not only did she love Rane, but she had shared her blood with him.

After telling his mother how nice she looked, Rafe took her by the hand and escorted her down the aisle to her seat, and then came back for Savanah.

With a wink and a smile, he placed her hand on his forearm. "Ready?"

Savanah nodded. She had a brief glimpse of the chapel as Rafe walked her down the aisle. The altar and the pews were carved from burnished oak. Moonlight streamed through the red, blue, and gold stained-glass window above the altar. The carpet was a deep blue. A sad-faced Madonna stood in one corner, her arm outstretched.

Rane's parents and grandparents sat in the first pew on one side of the aisle; Kathy sat behind Rane's parents, along with a man and a woman Savanah didn't recognize. Mara and Kyle sat holding hands in the front row on the other side of the aisle. Mara looked resplendent in a silver gown that shimmered in the candlelight. Her hair, as black as ink, stood out in sharp contrast to her gown.

And then Savanah saw Rane waiting for her at the altar, and everything else faded into the background. He had always been the most handsome of men, but now, dressed in a black tux, his hair shining like ebony, he fairly took her breath away.

Rafe gave his brother a wink, then placed Savanah's hand in Rane's, and took his seat. Turning, Rane and Savanah faced the priest.

Father Lanzoni was of medium height. His hair was black and wavy, laced with silver at his temples. He smiled down at the two of them, his hazel eyes filled with warmth. "Welcome, my children." His gaze moved over Rane's family. "It gives me great pleasure to see you all again, and to share this sacred moment with your family."

The priest focused his attention on Rane and Savanah. "Marriage is a holy institution ordained by God for the blessing of His children. If you wish to have a happy marriage, one that will last, you have only to put the happiness and welfare of your spouse above your own. It is something easily said and yet not always easy to do. As you look into each other's eyes, as you repeat your vows, I urge you to remember how you feel this night, and to hold the memory close in times of struggle and sacrifice.

"I will say the words that bind the two of you together, but it takes more than words to bind one soul to another. The true marriage between you must take place within each of your hearts.

"Savanah Gentry, do you promise to love and cherish Rane Cordova, here present, for as long as you shall live?"

Savanah squeezed Rane's hand. "I do."

"Rane, do you promise to love and cherish Savanah Gentry, here present, for as long as you both shall live?"

Rane gazed deep into Savanah's eyes. "I do."

"Then, by the power vested in me, I now pronounce you husband and wife." He smiled at Rane. "You may kiss your bride."

Rane gazed at Savanah for stretched seconds, wanting to imprint the beauty of this moment in his mind and heart, to always remember the radiance of her smile, the love and trust shining like a bright blue flame in her eyes.

Drawing her into his arms, he murmured, "I will love you forever," and then he kissed her.

Savanah leaned into him, her eyelids fluttering down as he deepened the kiss. Heat flowed through her, threatening to melt her very bones, and she clung to him, afraid her legs might give way beneath her. He had kissed her before, and often, but never like this. It was a kiss of love, of possession, branding her heart and mind and soul. She was his now, forever his.

When he took his lips from hers, it took her a moment to regain her equilibrium.

And then the priest was saying, "I give you Mr. and Mrs. Rane Cordova," and Rane's family was crowding around them.

Later, back at the house, Rane introduced Savanah to Susie and Cagin, who were close friends of the family, and who were also a Vampire and a Were-tiger, respectively.

It was a gathering unlike anything Savanah had ever attended. She could only wonder what Kyle Bowden thought of it, since as far as she knew, he was still unaware of the fact that he and Savanah were the only two mortals in the house.

Several bottles of vintage red wine stood on a cloth-covered table, alongside a platter of tiny sandwiches and a small cake. Savanah eyed the cake curiously. She had just decided it was simply for decoration, since the majority of the people present couldn't eat it, when Rane's mother gathered everyone together to watch the bride and groom cut the cake.

Savanah looked at Rane, a silent question in her eyes.

"As most of you know, Rane is allergic to sugar and flour," Cara said, a mischievous twinkle in her eye, "so he won't be eating any cake. But we didn't want Savanah to miss out on such a delightful tradition. So . . ." She handed a knife to Rane with a smile. "You're on."

Rane cut a narrow slice of cake, speared a piece with a fork, and offered it to Savanah.

Feeling a little self-conscious, she accepted his offering.

"And now, please join me in a toast," Vince said. "Rafe, if you please."

Rafe opened a bottle of wine and after everyone had been given a glass, Vince lifted his. "To Rane and Savanah. May they enjoy a long and healthy life together."

Rane grinned at his father as echoes of "Here, here" rose in the air. "Thanks, Dad."

Vince set his glass aside and slipped his arm around his son's shoulders. "Take good care of her, son."

Rane winked at Savanah. "That's my plan."

Vince wrapped his other arm around Savanah. "If he doesn't treat you right, daughter, you come to me, and I'll set him straight."

"I'll do that," Savanah said with a smile.

Later, when the initial excitement had worn off and Rane's family sat in the living room, reminiscing about other weddings, Savanah managed to get Mara alone.

"I've been wanting to ask you something," Savanah said, keeping her voice low. "I was wondering . . . that is, Rane said you might know the name of the Vampire who killed my mother."

"What makes you think she was killed by one of us?" Mara asked with some asperity.

"My father told me," Savanah replied, somewhat taken aback by Mara's sharp tone.

"A young Vampire named Tarkan brought your mother across, but he's not the one who destroyed her."

Savanah stared at Mara. "If he didn't do it, then who did?"

"Are you sure you want to know?"

"Of course," Savanah said, frowning. "Why wouldn't I?"

"Sometimes ignorance is, indeed, bliss."

Savanah glanced at Rane, who was standing across the room, talking to his brother, and felt a sudden iciness creep into her heart. What if Rane had lied to her? What if he had killed her mother? She told herself it was impossible, but what if it was true? She could forgive him a lot of things, but not that. Never that.

"Yes," she said, her voice little more than a whisper. "I want to know."

"It was your father who destroyed your mother."

The words pierced Savanah's heart like shards of glass. "No." She shook her head. "No! I don't believe you."

"It's true, nonetheless," Mara said.

"How could you even think such a thing?"

"I know everything that happens in my world," Mara said. "Your father destroyed your mother at her request. She begged him to do it, and he could not refuse her."

"But he said a Vampire killed her."

Mara lifted one shoulder in an elegant shrug. "In his mind, that was true. He believed that the Vampire who turned her was responsible for her death, and in a way, I suppose he was right. But it was your father who . . ."

"Mara, spare her the gory details," Rane said, coming to stand beside Savanah. "She's heard enough."

"Thank you for telling me," Savanah said.

With a nod, Mara excused herself.

Savanah blinked back her tears. Now that the first shock was over, it seemed right that her father had taken her mother's life. Better to die by the hand of one who loved you, she thought, than by the cruel hand of an enemy.

"Oh, Daddy," she murmured, and felt her heart break for the terrible secret her father had carried for so many years. Knowing what he had done explained the sadness that she had often seen in his eyes, the melancholy moods that had sometimes overwhelmed him, the nights he had sat in the backyard, a bottle of whiskey his only companion.

Rane squeezed her hand. "Are you all right?"

"Yes." It was over. The Vampire who had killed her father was dead, destroyed by her own hand; and now that she knew who had destroyed her mother, she could finally put her mother's memory to rest, as well, and with it, any thought of following in her mother's footsteps. Her family had been touched by enough killing.

"What do you say we go find a place where we can be alone?" Rane suggested.

"I'd say, 'Let's go.'"

They bid farewell to Mara and Kyle, who were returning to Egypt in the morning.

"Do you think they'll last?" Savanah asked, watching them walk away.

Rane shrugged. "I don't know. I hope so. She's been alone a long time."

Savanah nodded, wishing that everyone could be as happy as she was at that moment.

Savanah and Rane bid his grandparents farewell, told Rafe and his wife to stay in touch, thanked his mother and father for their hospitality, and left the house.

A full moon lit their way to Rane's car. Savanah had packed her things earlier in the day; her suitcases were in the trunk.

She glanced at Rane as he started the car and pulled onto the road. Feeling her gaze, he looked over at her and smiled, then took her hand in his. "Happy?"

"Very."

"Did I tell you how beautiful you are?"

"No."

"Remind me later."

She winked at him. "Oh, I will." She rested her hand on his knee and then, slowly and suggestively, stroked her way along his inner thigh.

Grabbing her hand, he raised it to his lips and turned it over, his tongue lightly stroking the sensitive skin of her palm.

The touch of his lips sent frissons of heat stealing through every part of her body. Just like that, she wanted him, needed him. "Can't you drive any faster?"

Chuckling softly, he goosed it up to seventy. Ten minutes later, they pulled into the hotel parking lot. Rane grabbed Savanah's overnight bag, swung her into his arms, and strode into the lobby. Holding her close with one hand, he signed the register, then carried her swiftly up the stairs and into their room.

"We could have taken the elevator," Savanah said, linking her arms around his neck.

"Too slow." He kissed her then, a long lingering kiss, and then carried her into the bedroom. A look turned the lights on low as he gently lowered her on to the bed. "You're beautiful," he murmured. "The most beautiful woman I've ever known."

"It's just the dress," she said. "It makes me feel beautiful."

"No," he said, "it's you who make the dress beautiful."

At his words, warmth swelled within her heart. "I love you, Rane. No matter what the future holds for us, I'll always love you."

He kissed the curve of her throat as his hands finessed the gown from her body until she wore only her lacy bra, panties, and high heels. "That's a good look for you," he said, a wicked gleam in his eyes.

"Well, you look a little overdressed for my taste." Kneeling on the bed, she removed his jacket, tie, and shirt, then skimmed her hands over his shoulders and down his chest, loving the feel of his cool flesh beneath her hands, the way his muscles quivered at her touch.

His belt came next, then his shoes, socks, and trousers.

Rane slid his finger under the edge of her bra and suddenly it was gone.

"I see you haven't lost your touch for magic," Savanah remarked with a smile.

"Watch this," he said, and an instant later her shoes and panties were on the floor.

Laughter bubbled up inside her as she tugged his briefs off and tossed them on top of her cast-off clothing.

"My way's faster," Rane said, tucking her beneath him.

"Maybe so." She licked his chin. "But fast isn't always best. Sometimes slow and easy is the way to go."

"Is that how you want it?" he asked, nipping at her earlobe. "Slow and easy?"

"Yes," she said. "This time."

"Your way this time." His hands moved over her, butterfly soft. "Next time, my way."

Savanah snuggled against her husband, her fingertips playing in the hair at his nape. "I like your way best."

His way, she thought, had been amazing. It had been like flying through rainbows, drifting through stardust, racing with the moon. She had never known such pleasure. She had often heard the term "two halves made whole" but never, until this night, had she truly known what it meant. There had been moments when she had been Rane, when she had known what he was thinking, feeling, desiring, and she had done her best to please him, and in so doing, found pleasure beyond anything she could have imagined.

Rane nuzzled the side of her neck. "Happy?"

"Oh, yes." She smiled at him, and then her expression turned serious. "Can I ask you something?"

"Sure."

"I probably should have asked you about this sooner, or maybe later, but . . . well, I know this probably isn't the right time, our being on our honeymoon and all . . ."

"Just ask me, sweetheart."

"Okay." She took a deep breath. "If I decide I'd like to have a baby in a year or two, would you mind?"

"Are you talking about adoption?" he asked, thinking about how his grandparents had adopted his mother. She hadn't found out they were Vampires until she was a woman grown.

"No, I was thinking of artificial insemination."

Rane pondered that possibility for a moment. His first reaction was that he didn't like the idea of Savanah carrying another man's seed, but when he thought it out, he realized he was being foolish.

"I think it's a wonderful idea," he said, thinking it would be easier to love a child that was a part of Savanah than a child conceived by strangers. "Now that we've got that settled, would you think about doing something for me?"

"Something like becoming a Vampire?" she asked.

"Something exactly like that."

"Yes," she said, "I'll think about it." In fact, in spare moments, she had been thinking of it quite a lot. If she decided to accept the Dark Gift, she wouldn't want to wait until whatever children she had were grown, the way Rane's mother had. Savanah blew out a sigh. Rane looked thirty and he would always look thirty; she was twenty-five. If she waited until her children were grown to become a Vampire, she would be forty-five or fifty. No doubt people would think she was Rane's mother instead of his wife. But it was a decision she didn't have to make now.

Drawing Rane's head closer, she brushed a kiss across his lips. "Let's do it again," she whispered. "Your way."

Epilogue

Three years later

"Breathe, Savanah. That's right, love. Slow, deep breaths."

She glared up at Rane as another contraction threatened to split her in half. Why had she ever thought natural childbirth was the way to go?

Rane brushed a lock of hair from her brow, then took her hand in his. "Savanah, look at me."

"I am looking at you."

His gaze locked with hers, his mind melding with hers, blocking the worst of the pain. "Just keep looking at me," he said, his voice low and hypnotic. "It'll be over soon and you'll be holding our daughter in your arms."

Rane glanced at the doctor, who nodded at him. "Keep talking to her. The head's crowning, we're almost home."

Rane rubbed his thumb over the back of Savanah's hand. "You're doing fine, sweetheart. Just another few minutes . . ." He continued to murmur to her, telling her that he loved her, until the doctor asked him if he'd like to cut the cord.

Feeling like he was in a dream, Rane looked at his daughter for the first time. She had pale skin, dark blue eyes, and a thatch of thick brown hair.

He cut the cord, which was thicker than he would have thought, hovered over the nurse while she checked the baby's vital signs. When the nurse took the baby out of the room to clean her up, Rane returned to Savanah's side. Bending down, he kissed her on the cheek. "She's beautiful, just like her mother."

Savanah smiled a sleepy smile.

"Thank you, love." Never in all his life had Rane expected to be a father. It didn't matter that the child wasn't biologically his. From this day forward, he would be her father in every way that counted.

Murmuring, "I love you," he kissed Savanah's cheek again, only to realize that she had fallen asleep. He couldn't blame her for being exhausted. Watching Savanah labor to bring their daughter into the world had given him a new respect for the strength and courage of females everywhere.

Moments later, the nurse returned and placed his daughter in his arms. "She's adorable," the nurse said, smiling. "Just ring if you need anything. I'll be right down the hall."

Rane stared at the tiny scrap of humanity cradled in his arms. She was small and perfect, from the top of her fuzzy little head to the soles of her adorable little feet.

"Hello, darlin'," he murmured, and would have sworn that she smiled as she curled one of her fingers around his much-larger one.

Rane glanced at Savanah. She had given him more than she would ever know. She had restored his faith in himself, given him her love and her trust, literally saved his life. And in addition to all that, she had given him a daughter.

He was marveling at his daughter's tiny perfect toes when Mara materialized beside him. She looked radiant, as always.

"I've been expecting you," Rane said.

"Oh?"

"Sure. When Rafe and I were old enough to understand, our father told us that you named me and Rafe, and how you took our blood so you'd always know where we were."

Mara lifted her brows. "Do you have a problem with that?"

"No," Rane said, grinning. "I warned Savanah you might show up."

"Should I leave?" she asked imperiously.

"Of course not. Don't you want to hold your new godchild?"

Mara smiled brightly as she took the baby from Rane's arms. "Have you given her a name yet?"

"No. Savanah wants to name her Barbara Lynn after her mother."

"And you don't?"

He shrugged. "She doesn't look like a Barbara to me."

"No, she doesn't." Mara gazed into the baby's eyes. "Her name will be Abbey. Abbey Marie."

Rane repeated the name, and then he nodded. "It fits."

With a nod, Mara used her thumbnail to make a shallow cut in the pad of the baby's thumb, and then she licked the single drop of blood that oozed from the tiny cut. "There," she murmured, licking the wound to seal it. "She's beautiful, Rane. Cherish her." Mara glanced at Savanah. "Cherish them both."

Rane nodded. "Are you okay?"

"Of course. Why wouldn't I be?" Mara placed the baby in Rane's arms and then, with a wave of her hand, she was gone.

Rane frowned as she vanished from his sight. There was something Mara wasn't telling him, but he had no idea what it might be.

With a sigh, Rane pressed a kiss to his daughter's silky-soft cheek. In a little while, he would take the baby out to show his family, but for now, for these few precious moments, his daughter was his and his alone.

And his life was again filled with magic.

Dear Reader,

I hope you enjoyed Rane's story. I really love this family! I recently finished Mara's story, which will be published sometime in the future, and will be the last book in my Night series . . . I think.

Here's wishing you a Happy Valentine's Day, filled with chocolate Vampires and marshmallow Werewolves ☺.

Best,
Madeline
www.amandaashley.net

If you liked this Amanda Ashley book,
check out her other titles—
available now from Zebra!

AFTER SUNDOWN

He Has Become What He Once Destroyed

Edward Ramsey has spent his life hunting Vampires. Now he is one of them. Yet Edward's human conscience—and his heart—compel him to save beautiful Kelly Anderson, and soon their growing love is his reason for living. And as the ancient, stunning, and merciless Vampire Khira seeks supremacy among Los Angeles' undead, Edward and his former nemesis Grigori Chiavari, once Khira's lover, must unite to stop her—before the city, and everything they cherish, is in her power . . . After Sundown.

A WHISPER OF ETERNITY

In Amanda Ashley's compelling, lushly sensual novels, Vampires exist alongside humans—but their desires are not relegated to the shadows. Now, a timeless passion is shattered by dangerous immortal ambition—unless an eternal kiss can hold back the darkness of true death . . .

He Will Not Lose Her Again

When artist Tracy Warner purchases the rambling seaside house built above Dominic St. John's hidden lair, he recognizes in her spirit the woman he has loved countless times over the centuries. Drawing her into the fascinating, seductive world of the Vampire, he aches to believe that this time she will not refuse his Dark Gift. But when Dominic's ancient rival appears in Sea Cliff, hungry for territory and power, Tracy becomes a pawn in a deadly game. To save her—and the passion that burns between them—Dominic must offer . . . A Whisper Of Eternity.

NIGHT'S KISS

He Has Found His Soul's Desire . . .

The Dark Gift has brought Roshan DeLongpre a lifetime of bitter loneliness—until, by chance, he comes across a picture of Brenna Flanagan. There is something hauntingly familiar in Brenna's fiery red hair and sensual body, something that compels him to travel into the past, save the beautiful witch from the stake, and bring her safely to his own time. Now, in the modern world, Brenna's seductive innocence and sense of wonder are utterly bewitching the once-weary Vampire, blinding him to a growing danger. For there is one whose dark magick is strong . . . one who knows who they both are and won't stop till their powers are his . . . and they are nothing more than shadows through time . . .

DESIRE AFTER DARK

Sexy Vampires, dangerous devotion, unparalleled romance—no one does desire after dark like bestselling author Amanda Ashley. Now, in her enthralling new novel, she explores a passion as smoldering as it is risky . . .

Vicki Cavendish knows she should be careful. After all, there's a killer loose in town—one who drains women of blood, women with red hair and green eyes just like her. She knows she should tell police about the dark, gorgeous man who comes into the diner every night, the one who makes her feel a longing she's never felt before. The last thing she should do is invite the beautiful stranger into the house . . .

Cursed to an eternity of darkness, Antonio Battista has wandered the earth, satisfying his hunger with countless women, letting none find a place in his heart. But Victoria Cavendish is different. Finally, he has found a woman to love, a woman who accepts him for what he is— a woman who wants him as much as he wants her . . . which is why he should leave. But Antonio is a Vampire, not a saint. What is his, he'll fight to keep and protect. And Victoria Cavendish needs protecting . . . from the remorseless enemy who would make her his prey . . . and from Antonio's own uncontrollable hunger . . .

DEAD SEXY

In the Still of the Night

The city is in a panic. In the still of the night, a vicious killer is leaving a trail of mutilated bodies drained of blood. A chilling M.O. that puts ex-Vampire hunter Regan Delaney on the case, her gun clip packed with silver bullets, her instincts edgy. But the victims are both human and Undead, and the clues are as confusing as the Vampire who may be her best ally—she hopes . . .

Master of the City, Joaquin Santiago radiates Supernatural power like heat from a blast furnace, but he's never met a creature like Regan Delaney. She intrigues him, fires his hunger, and unleashes his desire, but before he can enter her world, or she his, they must confront a vicious, elusive killer who is an enemy even to his own . . .

NIGHT'S TOUCH

One Kiss Can Seal Your Fate . . .

Cara DeLongpre wandered into the mysterious Nocturne club looking for a fleeting diversion from her sheltered life. Instead she found a dark, seductive stranger whose touch entices her beyond the safety she's always known and into a heady carnal bliss . . .

A year ago, Vincent Cordova believed that Vampires existed only in bad movies and bogeyman stories. That was before a chance encounter left him with unimaginable powers, a hellish thirst, and an aching loneliness he's sure will never end . . . until the night he meets Cara De-Longpre. Cara's beauty and bewitching innocence call to his mind, his heart . . . his blood. For Vincent senses the Dark Gift shared by Cara's parents, and the lurking threat from an ancient and powerful foe. And he knows that the only thing more dangerous than the enemy waiting to seek its vengeance is the secret carried by those Cara trusts the most . . .

DEAD PERFECT

Be Careful What You Wish For . . .

Only a woman with nothing left to lose knocks on a Vampire's door and asks for help. Shannah Davis is convinced that the mysterious dark-haired man she's followed for months can save her life—if he doesn't kill her first. But though Ronan insists he can't give her what she needs, his kiss unleashes a primal hunger that makes her feel truly alive for the first time.

After centuries of existence, Ronan has done the unthinkable. He has fallen in love with a mortal—and one with only weeks to live. Sensing the fear and reluctance beneath Shannah's request, he offers her a different bargain that will keep her near him during the time she has left. Every hour spent together leaves him craving her touch, her scent, her life's essence. Soon, only Shannah can satisfy his thirst. But if he saves her from death, will she love him for it—or spend eternity regretting what she has become?

NIGHT'S MASTER

Passion Has a Darker Side . . .

Kathy McKenna was sure that the little Midwestern town of Oak Hollow would be isolated enough for safety, but the moment the black-clad stranger walked into her bookstore, she knew she was wrong. Raphael Cordova exudes smoldering power, and his sensual touch draws Kathy into a world of limitless pleasure and unimaginable dangers.

Oak Hollow was supposed to be neutral territory for Supernatural beings. Instead it has become home to an evil force determined to destroy them—and kill any mortal who gets in the way. As leader of the North American Vampires, Raphael has always put duty first, but then, no woman ever enthralled him the way Kathy does. And as the enemy's terrifying plan is revealed, Raphael's desire could be a fatal distraction for all his kind, and for the woman he has sworn to love forever . . .

And keep an eye out for Amanda's next book,
coming in October 2009.
Turn the page for a sneak peek!

There was nothing the least bit remarkable about the old Underwood Art Gallery located on the corner of Third Street and Pine. And nothing particularly remarkable about the paintings displayed inside. For the most part, the works of art were uninspired scenes of landscapes and seascapes and an occasional still life, except for one rather large painting in the back of the gallery. It depicted a tall, fair-haired man wandering in the moonlight through a heavily wooded forest that bordered a calm blue lake.

The painting was by an artist named Josef Vilnius, and was aptly titled "Man Walking in the Moonlight." Karinna Adams had never heard of Vilnius, but it was an interesting piece in that the colors seemed to change depending on the time of day—the blues and greens and golds bright and cheerful when she observed the painting during the afternoon, the hues more somber and subdued when she arrived at the gallery in the evening. The changes in hue were especially puzzling since they had nothing to do with the gallery's interior lighting and seemed to be some anomaly inherent in the painting itself. It was most peculiar, and it had drawn Kari back to Underwood's time and time again.

Tonight was no different. Kari stood in front of the mysterious painting, her gaze moving from the old rowboat tied up alongside the narrow wooden dock to the gray stone castle perched high atop a grassy hill. A shaggy black and white dog slept in the shade on the north side of the castle, a gray kitten frolicked in a bed of flowers. A lamp burned in an upstairs window. Swirls of blue-gray smoke curled up from one of the castle's many chimneys. A white horse grazed in a large grassy field, its coat shining like silver in the moonlight. The horse looked so real, she wouldn't have been surprised to see it galloping across the greensward.

Kari had visited the Underwood gallery every night after work for the last two weeks. And every night, the man in the painting had either been in a different pose or in a different location, first walking in the moon-shadowed woods, now fishing from the boat under a starry sky, now looking out at the night from one of the castle's second-story windows, now resting on a large rock near the water, now sitting on the edge of the dock.

Tonight, he was astride the horse, his head turned to look back at the castle on the hill. Moonlight shimmered in his hair, which fell past his shoulders. He wore a loose-fitting white shirt, snug brown breeches, brown boots, and a long black cloak that fell in graceful folds over the horse's hindquarters. His hair was dark blond, as were his brows above deep brown eyes. He had a sharp nose, a sensual mouth, a strong, square jawline. He was a remarkably handsome creature, and she often wondered if the artist had used a live model, or if the figure had been drawn from the artist's imagination.

Kari moved closer to the painting, trying to determine

how the figure of the man moved from place to place. So far, she hadn't been able to determine how the artist had managed such a remarkable feat. At first, she had thought the man might not be a part of the painting itself, but perhaps a cut-out figure that could be moved and posed at will. But she had quickly dismissed that idea. He had to be a part of the painting, just like the boat, the dog, the kitten, the horse, and the castle. She wondered if the artist had painted several versions of the same scene and the gallery owner changed them from time to time, just to mystify the public, but that hardly seemed likely. Perhaps Vilnius had just used the same technique that made it seem as if the eyes of a painting were following you, like the ones in Disneyland's Haunted Mansion.

With a shake of her head, Karinna glanced at her watch. The gallery would be closing in a few minutes. She could scarcely believe she had been standing in front of the painting for almost an hour!

When she looked back at the canvas, the man was staring at her.

Startled, Kari took a step backward, then leaned forward, her eyes narrowing as she studied the figure. His lips seemed to be moving, forming the words, "help me."

Contemporary Romance by

Kasey Michaels

More by Bestselling Author

Lori Foster